HEMINGWAY

and His Conspirators

HOLLYWOOD, SCRIBNERS,
AND THE MAKING OF
AMERICAN CELEBRITY CULTURE

LEONARD J. LEFF

ROWMAN & LITTLEFIELD PUBLISHERS, INC.
Lanham • Boulder • New York • Oxford

ROWMAN & LITTLEFIELD PUBLISHERS, INC.

Published in the United States of America
by Rowman & Littlefield Publishers, Inc.
4720 Boston Way, Lanham, Maryland 20706

12 Hid's Copse Road
Cummor Hill, Oxford OX2 9JJ, England

Copyright © 1997, 1999 by Rowman & Littlefield Publishers, Inc.
First paperback printing 1999

British Library Cataloguing in Publication Information Available

Library of Congress Cataloging-in-Publication Data
Leff, Leonard J.
    Hemingway and his conspirators : Hollywood, Scribners, and the
making of American celebrity culture / Leonard J. Leff
        p.   cm.
    Includes bibliographical references and index.
    1. Hemingway, Ernest, 1899–1961—Appreciation—United States.
2. Authorship—Economic aspects—United States—History—20th
century.   3. Authors and publishers—United States—History—20th
century.   4. Literature publishing—United States—History—20th
century.   5. Authors and readers—United States—History—20th
century.   6. Hemingway, Ernest, 1899–1961—Film and video
adaptations.   7. Hemingway, Ernest, 1899–1961—Publishers.
8. Charles Scribner's Sons—History.   9. Authorship—Marketing.
I. Title
PS3515.E37Z68935   1997
813'.52—dc21
    [B]   97-11766
                                                              CIP

ISBN 0-8476-8545-4 (alk. paper)

Printed in the United States of America

∞ ™ The paper used in this publication meets the minimum requirements of
American National Standard for Information Sciences—Permanence of Paper for
Printed Library Materials, ANSI Z39.48—1984.

The background reveals the true being of the man or thing.

If I do not possess the background, I make the man transparent,

the thing transparent.

–Juan Jiménez, *Selected Writings*–

There was a great shouting going on in the grandstand overhead.

Maera wanted to say something and found he could not talk.

Maera felt everything getting larger and larger and then smaller and smaller.

Then everything commenced to run faster and faster as

when they speed up a cinematograph film.

Then he was dead.

–Ernest Hemingway, *In Our Time*–

for

Mary Lou Mortlock

CONTENTS

PREFACE

Not long before Black Tuesday 1929, the owners of the Ad-Tissue Corporation announced in the press that they had remodeled their factory and would soon start printing advertisements on rolls of toilet paper. Anyone whose business was the written word could not resist a wisecrack, or a prank, like marking through the two Ad-Tissue owners' names and penning in two new ones, say, "Fitzgerald" and "Hemmingway." The humor—and spelling—belonged to Scott Fitzgerald, whose best audience for such japes was his friend Ernest Hemingway. For the creator of *The Sun Also Rises* and *A Farewell to Arms*, though, the profession of authorship was no laughing matter.

Authors were under pressure from editors and spouses and mortgage bankers to produce the disposable and the saleable on demand, or so Hemingway believed in October 1929, less than one month after *A Farewell to Arms* appeared. He had concluded in haste and anger that the shelf life of any one book was brief, and that authors could not live on "good books." Publishing, he told Max Perkins, his editor and advocate, was no more than a racket. His assault on books and the trade spared only one target, the public, perhaps because it aroused both fear and desire, like a lover he dare not cross.

What Hemingway suppressed in correspondence he confronted in fiction, as early as 1923.

The first matador got the horn through his sword hand and the crowd hooted him out. The second matador slipped and the bull

caught him through the belly. . . . The kid came out and had to kill
five bulls because you can't have more than three matadors, and the
last bull he was so tired he couldn't get the sword in. He couldn't
hardly lift his arm. He tried five times and the crowd was quiet because it was a good bull and it looked like him or the bull and then
he finally made it. He sat down in the sand and puked and they held
a cape over him while the crowd hollered and threw things down into
the bull ring.

Hemingway would return again and again to the theme of the test, the
soldier or matador versus the hostile forces of nature or humanity. He
would also return to a complementary theme, less obvious though no less
true: the test *as observed*, the test as performed before and for the recognition of the crowd.

According to a nineteenth-century issue of the *Atlantic Monthly*, the great
writers wrote "for the relief of their own mind and without thought of
publication." Perkins believed in 1926 that he had signed such an author;
as he told Fitzgerald, Hemingway was "one of those whose interest is much
more in producing than in publishing." But though Hemingway endeavored to shun the spotlight and allow Perkins and Charles Scribner's Sons
to sell his books and foster his reputation, he needed the approbation of
the crowd. Inside the serious writer of the 1920s was the notorious personality and durable exhibitionist of the 1940s and beyond. Early on, the conduct of his career was the mirror of his every contrary impulse.

The 1920s, the decade of the ascent of Ernest Hemingway, the decade
of *In Our Time*, *The Sun Also Rises*, and *A Farewell to Arms*, was also the era of
modern advertising—bold, and noisy, and professionalized. Anything
could be sold, even books, if only they were marketed well. The nonfiction
sales leader of 1925 *and* 1926 was Bruce Barton's *The Man Nobody Knows*, a
portrait of Christ as "go-getter, a man with a talent for business." He was
Babbitt without tears, and the astounding reception accorded the book
showed that, whatever else, America rewarded those who knew how to
package goods.

"Did you see that one of Bruce Barton's 'The Man Nobody Knows'
headed 'Christ the Executive' illustrated with two pictures, in juxtaposition,
of groups of men around a table?" Perkins asked Scott Fitzgerald in 1926.
"One showed Christ and the twelve apostles; the other a twentieth century
'Chairman of the Board' and the directors of a corporation. I'd meant to
send you that and lost it as a genuine whiff of the U.S.A." Perkins had
turned down *The Man Nobody Knows*. "Of course it might sell," he report-

edly warned the Scribners board, and months later Charles Scribner II groused, "But you didn't tell me, Mr. Perkins, that it would sell four hundred thousand copies."

Bruce Barton had found the pulse of the 1920s. He had grown up in Oak Park, Illinois, the nephew of Clara Barton, the doyenne of the Red Cross, and the son of William E. Barton, the local Congregationalist minister. Reverend Barton crusaded for "clean money" and, additionally, lauded the enterprising work that produced it. Clean money served as currency and metaphor for the pastor and his flock. "Get acquainted with as many nice people as you can," parishoner Clarence Hemingway counseled his son Ernest in 1920, for they are "a real asset in life's bank as the years go on." America had once been about self-reliance and character, or as Ralph Waldo Emerson wrote in *Essays: Second Series*, the "moral order seen through the medium of an individual nature." The twentieth century was about nice people and the twisted version of another Emerson saying, "Hitch your wagon to a star."

Advances in photojournalism in the second and third decades of the new century conspired with the movies and the accent Hollywood placed on renown and success not only to produce one famous person after another, on the screen and off, but—more important—to equate celebrity and success. Many of the fresh names and fresh faces deserved acknowledgment, for their talent was bounteous—Charlie Chaplin on screen, Bessie Smith on the phonograph, even Ty Cobb on the diamond. Many others deserved less, like Floyd Gibbons, who turned heads because he could speak almost three hundred words per minute. The Cyclopean broadcaster (during the war he had lost one eye) would once have been a filler, if that. In the 1920s he was hot news, for stardom, which had once accreted slowly, like moss on a rock, could now, like gas engines or soda crackers or other consumer goods, be mass manufactured.

The Hollywood producer was a first- or second-generation immigrant who, lacking history or shame, turned out a product for a general audience and sold it with razzmatazz. The modern publisher was likewise someone who "announces, proclaims, or advertises something; one who makes a thing widely known." Publishers turned out sausage, of course, as *The Man Nobody Knows* proved. As cultural institutions, though, often run by their founders' sons or grandsons, the older or "better" American publishers hoped that a large audience would buy the occasional book, but they would not grub for cash or customers: they dealt in substance, not surface; in authors, not stars. They were adherents of literature, conservators whose status hinged on an association with great, rather than go-getting, authors. In the 1920s Edward H. Dodd, whose house dated back to the nineteenth century, purchased the American branch of John Lane, an English house known for publishing more new poetry than any of its peers. Hollywood ballyhoo for Lane or even Dodd authors was almost inconceivable.

Almost inconceivable, for in the 1920s, even as one trade journal sneered at "publicity hypnosis," another started a roster of "Recent Motion Pictures Based on Published Book and Play." Horace Liveright rode the trend: he published books and produced plays, and understood the synergy between the two even when, poorly capitalized, he could not manage to profit from it. Other publishing houses—and authors—had begun to sense the advantage that the sale of theatrical and screen rights could confer on books and authors, and the ways that Broadway and Hollywood could be swayed to pursue such rights. By the 1920s Doubleday was running full-page advertisements for single books in the *New York Times*, while Harper & Brothers started advertising in the rotogravure sections of other newspapers. Their audience was the lay reader and the theatrical and screen producer. Alfred Harcourt meanwhile took *Elmer Gantry* on the road; in Kansas City, Missouri, where Methodists gathered for their General Conference in mid-decade, the publisher covered the town with forty-nine *Elmer Gantry* billboards, thirteen of them illuminated.

Max Perkins could appear rather ill at ease with the carnival side of modern publishing, the fanfare needed to assure authors and publishers their fair share of an enlarged book market and the publicity and notice that attended it. Any reserve may have been congenital. He had been born in 1884, the grandson of Charles Callahan Perkins, an independently wealthy Harvard graduate who could have entered business but chose to go abroad and study art, eventually becoming a critic; according to his biographer, Max Perkins had his grandfather's artistic flair and well-bred manner. Perkins's reserve may also have been in deference to his employer. Scribners was more the house of announcements than billboards, the publisher of United States Presidents Coolidge, Harrison, Roosevelt, Taft, and Wilson. When a Scribners book sold tens of thousands—a *Roosevelt's Letters to His Children* (1920) or an *Americanization of Edward Bok* (a Pulitzer Prize winner in 1923)—it was usually because of who Roosevelt and Bok were before they were authors, one the Rough Rider, the other the beloved editor of the *Ladies' Home Journal*. Scribners was pleased to have "best-sellers" (a recent American invention) but preferred to rely on the character of the work, rather than mass distribution or mass publicity, to sell it.

Charles Scribner's Sons had only one fiction best-seller in the early 1920s, Arthur Train's *His Children's Children*, and the author's modus operandi fascinated Perkins. "He calls conferences of his magazine editor, his movie producer, and of me as representing his publisher," Perkins told one associate in 1925. "There his manuscript is discussed scene by scene. It's a strange way to write a book." Arthur Train also understood the synergy. He understood that publishing and a literary career were now about texts and pictures, delivered to millions by wire and wireless and celluloid.

Though Scribners was slow to harness the media engines of the century, Perkins was no naif. He had started in advertising, and as editor he applied the lessons he learned. Accepting *This Side of Paradise* in 1919, he had thanked Fitzgerald for waiting for "us conservatives" to come around. He had also asked the author for "any publicity matter" and photographs he could send. Nothing was spelled out, or needed to be: authors and authors' photographs could sell books and spur fame. Concerned that the public would judge the book and the author by the cover, Fitzgerald answered with a query. Could the wrap be "something that could be[come] a set— look cheerful and important like a Shaw Book"? Perkins had other ideas. "We want it to look popular," he responded, not "too essay like, too eso- teric." The author's photograph, which Perkins circulated, traded on Fitz- gerald's glamor and good looks; wisely, too, for in the movie-mad 1920s the "popular" was boosted by the "handsome." As Perkins understood, wider and sped-up news coverage of books in a booming national press, along with the potential windfall that Broadway and Hollywood could grant to books and authors, meant that vetting a manuscript was only the begin- ning of an editor's job. More than ever, the real work was taking author and book to market.

Perkins looked closely at magazine serialization, book club editions, and advertising (never his preference) as roads to revenue and exposure. He may not have been aggressive enough for Arthur Train, but he was far from averse to promotion or publicity. He could read authors—their manu- scripts and their psyches—and he could act on the intensity of their desire for literary celebrity. His task was relatively easy with Fitzgerald: as the au- thor and Princeton graduate once wrote his editor, he hoped "to be en- dorsed by the intellectually élite & thus be *forced* on to people." But Perkins's task was more complicated with another young American writer who appeared to regard the machinery of publishing as a conspiracy against art.

Born in Oak Park, Illinois, one generation later than his editor, Ernest Hemingway was wounded by a trench mortar shell during the Great War, won honor in the American press as a war hero, and by 1919 had returned home and started writing. His best early fiction, composed under the tute- lage of Ezra Pound and Gertrude Stein in Paris, was about character, not personality. It was about duty and honor, and morals and manners and manhood. It was for an intelligent reader, too, one who could infer the sinew beneath the skin—the graphic diction, the clarity of the incidents, the narrative compressed beneath the tip of the iceberg, which, the author later said, was all he wished to show. Hemingway wrote because he had to, and because he was an artist. As he often told himself and others, he wanted fame only as the product of achievement, and then only as the Renaissance understood fame, as reputation.

More than most other serious authors of his time, though, Hemingway was acutely aware of audience. He may even have gone to Paris in 1921 not because he had rejected Main Street but because he wanted its notice, because in France, where expatriates were the rage, he could both write (or learn to write) and be counted among the important American writers. In spring 1923, keeping one eye on the prose, another on the crowd, the apprentice author told one correspondent, "I want, like hell, to get published."

Hemingway signed with Liveright, and then, when the publisher declined *The Torrents of Spring*, with Charles Scribner's Sons. Scribners thought of its house as more literary than entrepreneurial; it wanted "to put [Hemingway] to the front, and hold him there." The front connoted solid notices, decent sales, and a reputation constructed on the bedrock of lasting artistic achievement, and to that end Charles Scribner pledged, in early correspondence with the author, "to act for you and advise you in order that you may get the best return from your work without jeopardizing your future by turning out books and stories 'written to order.' " Like Scribner, Perkins also strove for balance. He believed that quality and endurance, rather than exposure and public relations, were the cornerstones of an author's career; accordingly, as editor he enhanced the reception of Hemingway's short-story collections by arranging the contents for commercial effect, and, arguably, controversially, he broadened the audience for the novels by toning down the coarse language of *The Sun Also Rises* and *A Farewell to Arms*. As Scribners executive, though, he used the rapidly evolving Hemingway persona—occasionally with Hemingway's implied or expressed consent—to market the books and promote the name of the author.

For *A Farewell to Arms*, the story of an American lieutenant and the English nurse he loved and lost, the reviews were superb, the early sales extraordinary, and the publicity intense. Hemingway was good looking and photogenic; he was no Paris phony but a virile storyteller with the masculine grace of a model. The press readily published the photographs that Scribners circulated and that the author had furnished, from the retouched studio portraits shot by Helen Breaker to the Kodaks taken on the ski slopes of Europe and on the docks beside a prize tarpon he had landed. And gradually, like reviewers and reporters, the general public embraced novel and author.

Again and again Hemingway professed that he hated the traffic in photographs, Book of the Month Club editions, and stage or movie adaptations that could bring an author fame and fortune; he wrote, in other words, "for the relief of [his] own mind and without thought of publication." Certainly he wanted an audience to hear what he had to say about valor or love or the anatomy of fiction. And certainly he needed money to sustain the grand life he led after 1929. Beyond that, however, he radiated personality, and he cultivated publicity even as he pretended to scorn it. In his first letter to Perkins, he mentioned—and not wholly facetiously—that it would be "worthwhile to get into Who's Who." In short, he wanted fame in both the Renaissance and the contemporary sense.

The mass media of the late 1920s transformed the relationship between Americans and their public figures. Capitalizing on professional sports, network radio, and Hollywood motion pictures, the press and its syndicated gossip columns produced a desire to know the renowned—who they were, how they lived, and what they thought. Athletes appeared as "themselves" in newspaper feature stories and in advertisements for beverage and tobacco products. Political satirists like Will Rogers appeared as "themselves" on radio and on tour throughout the country. And movie stars appeared as "themselves" to tell all (more or less) in ghost-written articles for *Screen Book* or *Photoplay*. By 1931, with *A Farewell to Arms* having won a large audience, Ernest Hemingway was also composing a so-called celebrity text, *Death in the Afternoon*. In that nonfiction manuscript about bullfighting, he took as his subject—overtly—the self.

The narrator of *Death in the Afternoon* lectured, postured, joked, educated, preached, and entertained. Closing the distance between narrator and reader, he showcased the matador and, worse, the aficionado, *the* aficionado—the "glamorous personality" of the author. Hemingway so appeared to control the orbit of his career by then that Perkins only minimally edited the manuscript. *Death in the Afternoon* was taut and vivid but also self-conscious and condescending. On its publication in October 1932, neither reviewers nor book buyers much liked it. The press coverage was nonetheless plentiful.

If sales of *Death in the Afternoon* disappointed author and publisher, Hollywood's adaptation of *A Farewell to Arms* surpassed everyone's expectations. The picture, released in December 1932 by Paramount, was hugely successful. Helen Hayes and Gary Cooper were the nurse and the lieutenant, but Hemingway was more, an Author God who, according to studio publicity, had created one of the outstanding autobiographical novels of the century. Hemingway had often chided Scribners for the very publicity he had aroused or generated. Not unexpectedly, then, he denounced Hollywood—publicly—for the press releases that told entertaining stories about him. But the rebuke was too little, too late. He now had the international fame that he had long abhorred, and wanted, and feared, the personal rather than literary fame that would so wound him and his work. He was now and forever a star.

Between 1923 and 1933, Hemingway rose from obscurity to prominence not only because he had talent and personality but because he was adopted and championed by publishers as well as reprint houses, reporters, photographers, and especially movie companies. He knew that the literary marketplace of the 1920s could be both rewarding and dangerous. He also knew what the magnifying glass of the new media could do to and for his reputation. He was nonetheless interested in the sale and promotion of his books and—more important—the accoutrements of a literary career and the blandishments of a culture of celebrity.

Hemingway may have been deeply ambivalent about the merchandising of authors as images and icons. He may also have been helpless before the prospect of stardom. As one character tells another in *Across the River and Into the Trees*, one of the later and weaker novels, " 'I love to have people see us.' " *Hemingway and His Conspirators* chronicles the signs of that love and the ways that, early on, an author as well as a publisher and an American press and cinema helped create the popular literary phenomenon we call "Ernest Hemingway."

Chapter One

THE
BATTLER

In the parlor of the Hemingway home in Oak Park, Ernest chattered by the hour "without stopping—perfectly unconscious of audience." Grace Hemingway was the observer and recorder, and she adored her son, then less than four years old and more conscious of audience than she thought. He was so docile, she also wrote in his baby book, that he "asks constantly whether he can do this or that, rather than to make a mistake and displease us." He recited Tennyson and acted out *Hiawatha*, and loved "to be invited to sing for company," performing *John Brown's Body* with "great unction, in his deep voice." Grace had been trained as a singer, and her children knew her as mother, artist, and judge, not always in that order. On *John Brown's Body*, she noted that young Ernest was "somewhat indifferent as to time." He was not only conscious of audience, then, but conscious of criticism.

Grace Hall Hemingway could be moody and autocratic. She had wed Clarence Edmonds Hemingway, a family doctor, in 1896. Marcelline was born in 1898, Ernest in 1899. By 1904 she had two other daughters and could not concentrate attention or affection on her son. Her husband taught Ernest about the outdoors but suffered from bouts of depression that caused physical and emotional separations from Grace and the children. No longer content to sing for company, Ernest gravitated to fiction. It hardly mattered that the oral adventure yarns he spun for pals had been pinched from Richard Harding Davis or Rudyard Kipling. He made the telling as audacious as the tales, the narrator the equal of the swashbuckling hero, as though the *I* of the stories could hide the sources and spellbind the listener.

At Oak Park High, Ernest Miller Hemingway appeared as Richard Brinsley Sheridan in the school play, *Beau Brummell,* a comedy about a man who fashioned himself into a celebrity. Though the part was colorful and the curtain calls rousing, Ernest was essentially a solo performer who needed a vast but invisible audience. Thus literature. In 1916 he wrote at least two stories for the high-school literary magazine, one all blood and guts, the other knockabout humor. Both were plotted to make the school notice Hemingstein (Hemmingway's alias).

Ernest used the alias, which he had coined, as advertising for the persona of the young writer—part outsider, part social lion. When he was chosen Senior Class Prophet, the local newspaper forecast "something exceptional from Hemingway." The prediction was sound. In October 1917, as a cub reporter on the *Kansas City Star,* he learned to tell a story with clarity and directness. He savored "the romance of newspaper work" and the notion of an audience reading accounts of the murders and robberies he covered. But journalism was too easy and too passive for a boy who worshipped Teddy Roosevelt (the author and subject of books) and who in late 1917 read other reporters' dispatches from abroad.

Myopic and thus barred from the Army, Hemingway joined the Missouri Home Guard, then in spring 1918 enlisted in the Red Cross as an ambulance driver. He later recalled that when he shipped out for Italy, he saw the war as a contest between the American home team and the Austrian visitors. Nearer the front he revised that impression.

He had served less than six weeks when, thirteen days before his nineteenth birthday, in July 1918 by a river near Fossalta, Italy, he was gravely wounded by Austrian mortar fire.

Convalescing at the Red Cross hospital in Milan, Ernest met Agnes Von Kurowsky. She was graduated from Bellevue Nurses Training School in summer 1917 and, she later recalled, "was always looking for adventure." Ernest provided it. He was "impulsive, very rude, 'smarty,' and uncooperative," another nurse said. "He gave the impression of having been badly spoiled. He always seemed to have plenty of money which he spent freely for Italian wine and tips to the porter who brought it." The *enfant gâté* was serious about Agnes. Though almost eight years her junior, he romanced her from his hospital bed and called her "the missus" in letters to school chums. He also showed her the press accounts of Ernest Hemingway, late of Oak Park and casualty of the Great War.

The coverage in the *Chicago Tribune,* the *Oak Park Oak Leaves,* and other newspapers had thrilled the former *Kansas City Star* reporter. "Gee, Family, but there certainly has been a lot of burbles about my getting shot up!" he wrote from the hospital in August 1918. "It's the next best thing to getting killed and reading your own obituary." The echoes of Tom Sawyer were patent, not only because Twain's boy had once witnessed his own funeral but because he was so breathless for attention.

"If you do not grow about a cubit on acct of your popularity and miraculous escape, you will be unusual," Doctor Hemingway wrote his son. Popularity had become an article of faith—and trade—in the ripening consumer culture back home. Between 1909 and 1929, as Americans tripled the dollars they spent on clothes and autos and leisure, and as the press turned entertainers into newsmakers and vice versa, ordinary folks could read more and more about their extraordinary counterparts. During the war, stories of grace under fire were part propaganda and part publicity, grist for the new "show" business. "Your letter telling about your wounding in detail, ending with 'Leave us keep the home fires burning' was printed in last night's Chicago 'Herald,' " Marcelline wrote Ernest in October 1918, unsure of where the accent should fall, on the wounding, or on the occasion it offered for wide coverage of her brother's nascent celebrity.

"Heroes Back Loaded Down with Medals," the *New York American* shouted. Preceded by this and other press clippings about the "Italian Cross of War" he had earned, Hemingway returned home in January 1919. Agnes Von Kurowsky had promised they would wed when he could support her, so he spent the winter writing sketches and tales à la Ring Lardner and O. Henry for the *Saturday Evening Post* and *Red Book*. The money was potentially great. An increase in Americans' disposable income had turned the weekly or monthly magazine into an avenue of display windows for consumer goods, and as advertising revenues and circulation figures rose, so did the fees that editors offered authors. *Red Book* and *Woman's Home Companion* paid well into three figures for stories, and almost six for serialization of novels. Motion picture companies pushed rates even higher. In 1900 *New York World* reporter Roy McCardell sold ten scenarios to American Mutoscope and Biograph Pictures for $150. In 1912 Hollywood offered him $30,000 for one serial. So great was the demand for stories that in 1915, when Hemingway spent fifty cents for a baseball ticket and another fifty cents for a copy of Caesar's *Gallic Wars*, major urban newspapers were running the movie studios' calls for scenarios.

World Film Corporation, Fort Lee, New Jersey, is in the market for five-reel subjects running to not less than two hundred scenes. Stories must have original plots—not necessarily with what is known as "punch," but depicting a young innocent girl in country life. No costume plays considered, nor those dealing with crime or crooks. American stories preferable.

In the second decade of the century, a good published story could sell for $1,000, and by 1919, having produced most of the royalty-free classics, Hollywood was paying much more for an original or previously adapted property. As the *New York Times* would report on 27 June 1920, "Apparently a season's run in New York automatically makes a play worth about $100,000 to the film producers."

Though money may not have sparked Hemingway's ambitions, it could not have been absent from his thoughts. The fat purses of the writing contests, the public hunger of the movie companies for story ideas, the numerous magazines and the abundance of fiction they published—these and more showed that writing was a profession that could pay. "I've written some darn good things," Ernest told one friend in March 1919. "And am starting a campaign against your Philadelphia Journal the Sat. Eve. Post. I sent them the first story Monday last. And havent heard any thing yet of course. Tomorrow another one starts toward them. I'm going to send 'em so many and such good ones . . . that they're going to have to buy them in self defence." What Henry James had resisted (what he called friction with the market), young Hemingway embraced.

The content of that early work was derivative, and the voice inauthentic. Consequently, the manuscripts were returned. In March 1919 Agnes broke off the engagement. Ernest was inconsolable. "I set out to cauterize out her memory," he wrote, awkwardly, to one friend in June 1919, "and I burnt it out with a course of booze and other women and now it's gone."

On Kenilworth Avenue in Oak Park, with *her* music room on one side of the house and *his* clinic on the other, Grace and Ed wondered where Ernest was headed. He should go "down Traverse City way and work at good wages," his father had urged. Grace also believed that Ernest could not succeed as a writer, but her opinion only hardened his resolve and the tension between mother and son. Occasionally they quarreled. When she built her lake cottage, despite her husband's "strong opposition and much abusive language," Ernest accused her of paying for the cabin with college money that belonged to her children. He had her sharp tongue, that was obvious. He also had her stubborn independence.

Until December 1919 Ernest shoveled gravel for the county in upper Michigan. He also continued to produce short fiction. "I doubt if worse stories were ever written," he later recalled. "I was always known in Petoskey [Michigan] as Ernie Hemingway who wrote for the Saturday Evening

Post." The point was, he was known. Was the desire for notice also genetic? In July 1920, when mother and son fought, Grace pleaded for more gratitude and more interest in her "ideas and affairs."

> Little comforts provided for the home; a desire to favor any of Mother's peculiar prejudices, on no account to outrage her ideals— Flowers, fruit, candy, or something pretty to wear, brought home to mother, with a kiss and a squeeze—The unfailing desire to make much of her feeble efforts, to praise her cooking, back up her little schemes; a real interest in hearing her sing, or play the piano, or tell the stories that she loves to tell . . .

Beyond her weak eyes, Ernest had inherited her searching glance. The audience was out there, and he would claim it.

In 1920 Hemingway freelanced for the *Toronto Star* and later, reluctantly, took an editing job in Chicago on an agricultural magazine, the *Cooperative Commonwealth*. Evenings and weekends he was once more writing sketches and tales on spec for the popular magazines. He had the bones of one story he especially wanted to tell, no fake blood and guts but the real McCoy, the night of the Austrian mortar fire. Since July 1918 he had returned constantly to Fossalta, telling one version of the story to reporters, another to high-school students, another to local civic clubs. He told one pal he " 'had been badly wounded leading Arditi storm troops on Monte Grappa' " when in truth he had been on canteen duty handing out cigarettes and chocolate. The callow author had the gift of invention and persistence. By September 1921 he was writing a novel about the war, and at least one other person believed it would be great.

Hadley Richardson and Ernest Hemingway had been introduced in October 1920. She was tall and hardy, with red hair and freckles. She was also eight years his senior. He had an open face, not subtle enough, she thought, but he had poise and wore the cape of an Italian officer without affectation. He told her he was a writer, and the fact that he was unpublished scarcely counted. She wanted direction in her life just as he wanted absolute approval. They courted in short visits and long letters. In December a wealthy acquaintance from Fossalta days invited Ernest to Italy for six months. It was "the biggest chance of my career," Ernest told Hadley. "Career hell—I haven't one," he added, "but I'm liable to with this Rome thing." Though he declined the opportunity, the capital *C* on "Career" had shown Hadley how matters stood on work, and on wives. "Don't think I am ambitious except to be [a] balanced happy intelligent lady, making the man happy," Hadley wrote from St. Louis in April 1921. "Am ambitious to understand and stimulate the said [man] in his artoostic kereer." They wed on 3 September 1921. In their tiny flat Ernest had all the room he needed.

As Hadley understood, Ernest was dead serious about becoming known and talked about. "No, really, did they have me married in France?" he wrote one friend only weeks before the wedding. "Gaw. Tell me all about it. Did I desert her, or what? D'ya think I'll be a bigamist? Tell me all about it. I'm frightfully interested." The tone was playful, the urgency real.

What Hemingway would be known for (beyond such personal details as his wedding) was another question. Here, Sherwood Anderson was instructive. Anderson had met Hemingway in October 1920, and the author of *Winesburg, Ohio*, published in 1919 to fine reviews, had become tutor and supporter. Fiction was about more than plot and character, Anderson told Hemingway. It was about truth and pitch and control. Hemingway should read contemporary fiction and literary history, Anderson advised, and start distinguishing between serious and popular writing. Anderson had not belittled the popular and may even have given Hemingway a copy of Ben Hecht's *Erik Dorn* (1921); he nonetheless coaxed the young author to broaden his tastes and his definition of literature, to read not O. Henry and Kipling (whom Anderson spotted in the Hemingway fiction he read) but the Russians and the authors who appeared in *Poetry* and the *Dial*, the latter especially, since it paid its contributors. Anderson had other practical tips. He talked about how to navigate the world of editors and publishers, and when to demand a good price for the work. Finally, he talked about Paris, about the cafés and inexpensive apartments, the cathedrals and public gardens, the culture and the freedom. A grateful Hemingway absorbed it all, and one additional lesson. He apparently interested Anderson less because of what he wrote—it was apprentice work, and poor—than because of what he promised and how he acted. Personality could smooth the road to fame and success.

Hemingway may have turned away from popular fiction but not popular culture. He lacked "seeds" (slang for money) and yet occasionally attended a farce or melodrama in Chicago, where he saw William Collier once and Lenore Ulric ("the magic mistress of a thousand emotions") twice on stage. He had gone on dates to movies in Kansas City and probably Chicago too. He rarely reported on what he saw, though, perhaps because the features were uninteresting, perhaps because, particularly in the second decade of the century, he thought they were beneath him. But rationalization of the movie industry and the so-called studio system was gradually changing biases like those, even among authors. In 1919 Samuel Goldwyn hired "Eminent Authors" to insure that "all Goldwyn pictures are built upon a strong foundation of intelligence and refinement" and to reassure an anxious, increasingly middle-class audience about the caliber of its screen entertainment. On another such errand, Goldwyn imported *The Cabinet of Dr. Caligari* (1919) for American exhibition. "It is a healthy thing for Hollywood, Culver City, Universal City, and all other places where movie film is being produced, that this photoplay has come along at this time," Carl Sandburg told Chicagoans in May 1921. "It is sure to have healthy hunches and show new possibilities in style and method to our American Producers." For every German tale of madness Hollywood imported, however, it released a hundred reels of the Keystone Kops. When Ernest and Hadley, encouraged by Sherwood Anderson, planned their trip abroad in 1921, they had no reason to think the movies would figure in Ernest's future.

Preceded by Anderson's letters of introduction, the Hemingways arrived in France in December 1921. Ernest was "a very delightful man" and "a young fellow of extraordinary talent," Anderson had written Lewis Galantière, the Paris secretary of the International Chamber of Commerce. The Hemingways would be "great playmates." Galantière at once contacted Hemingway, who was not hard to find. "Well here we are," Hemingway wrote Anderson from the cultural center of Paris. He was seated "outside the Dome Cafe, opposite the Rotunde that's being redecorated," and feeling grateful for Anderson's letters to Galantière as well as to Sylvia Beach, Ezra Pound, and Gertrude Stein. He had been in Paris less than three days and was already known. And on every count—literary and social—he was determined to exceed expectations.

Hadley would tap her trust fund and her inheritance to pay for travel and books and other necessities for more than two years, but the Hemingways would live on the cheap in literary Paris, where one poet friend was assumed to be rich because his children had bicycles. Ernest wore his poverty as the cape of virtue. Sheridan of *Beau Brummell* had become Marcello of *La Bohème*, and his baritone voice carried well beyond the Quarter. " 'It was an event when this towering figure passed the sidewalk tables at the Dôme. Arms waved in greeting and friends ran out to urge him to sit down with them,' " Nathan Asch later told Malcolm Cowley. Ernest " 'wouldn't quite recognize whoever greeted him. Then suddenly his beautiful smile appeared that made those watching him also smile.' " He was a notable character, even among expatriates, where nonconformity was the rule. He could be mercurial and abrasive. When he faulted at tennis, he "sizzled." His racquet "would slash to the ground and everyone would simply stand still and cower." When he sparred, he could turn a Sunday afternoon practice round into a title bout. He could also drink liter upon liter of wine, and outrage—or charm—the sidewalk tables. Tall and strong and hand-some, he played against his looks. He was casual about grooming and ap-pearance, theatrically so, and may have understood the peculiar attraction of unbarbered hair or custom tweeds "so homespun that you smell the genuwind peat smoke in the wool." He was the real thing costumed as the real thing. He was the performer par excellence, most content when active and, above all, when watched, whether the role was amateur boxer or bon vivant or journalist.

News writing was not a career but a provisional job until he could sup-port Hadley with his serious writing. In 1922 he was reporting current events freelance for the *Toronto Star* and the International News Service, occasionally taking fees and expenses from both companies for identical work. In April he covered the Genoa Economic Conference. He was no ideologue; though he read the international papers and traveled with vet-eran reporters, he was unsophisticated about politics and the havoc of Eu-ropean fiscal policy. Worse, the proceedings of the conference were conducted in secret. So he turned the problems of news gathering into the story. He reported on the conference with the sharp *I* that had arrested interest in the schoolyard a half dozen years before, the *I* whose logarith-mic function was *you*, the audience he never forgot. He was the performer as reporter. He was of and at the event, observer and observed.

"You can write," the talent scout for *Cosmopolitan* declared in 1922. Though the scout bought nothing from Hemingway, he passed along the advice that what "they can't buy in the States at this time is enough nice love stories with youth and beauty and spring and all that stuff—and humor stories. . . . if you do some more stories and if you can just as easily do a bright and 'sweet' yarn as you can a tragic one, you will find your market will be 50% easier to make." Both Ed and Grace had used the language of money in their letters, a point not lost on their son, for whom "seeds" was one index of fame. Moreover, *Cosmopolitan* had been a beacon for the young author. The yarn was not literature, though, and the zeitgeist of literary Paris only intensified his commitment to serious writing and his fear and distrust of anything else.

Cosmopolitan nonetheless hinted at what lay ahead for one who sought an international reputation or the fees it could bring. Once a muckraker, *Cosmopolitan* had been recast as a women's magazine and built a circulation of about one million. Since William Randolph Hearst owned both *Cosmopol-itan* magazine and Cosmopolitan Pictures, the latter a shell corporation that produced films starring Hearst's mistress, Marion Davies, he had in hand the protocols that would define the entertainment industry for the rest of the century. Hearst's corporations could plant and harvest a property wholly in house: the magazine ran an author's story, the movie picture company adapted and produced it for the screen, and the newspapers advertised and wrote about it from coast to coast. According to the *Authors' League Bulletin*, however, a publisher should be a publisher "and not a dealer in serial, dramatic, motion picture, and other rights." Hemingway would later add that serialization could injure a literary work, though the Ernie Hemingway who wrote for the *Saturday Evening Post* might have wanted to contest the point.

Sherwood Anderson's letters had gradually opened doors. Ezra Pound was "cantankerous in temperament," Hadley thought, and as outré in dress and manner as any poseur at the Café Rotonde. He was also a constant friend and powerful agent. He taught Hemingway how to anchor the abstract in the concrete, and routed him toward Homer, Donne, Stendhal, Eliot, and others who would influence him; he also promoted Hemingway's work among the editors of the little magazines. He was even courageous enough to take boxing lessons from Hemingway, for whom the physical was the test of character. When Hemingway wrote Anderson that Pound had risked "his dignity and his critical reputation" in the ring, Anderson could only have wondered what "critical reputation" had to do with it. Anderson would soon learn that Hemingway saw authorship as blood sport, and occasionally repaid favors with a punch in the nose. For the moment, Hemingway genuinely appreciated Pound's businesslike literary counsel.

In February 1922 Ernest had met Alice Toklas and Gertrude Stein, "the Italian peasant" whose breasts, he told Hadley, must weigh ten pounds each. Gertrude Stein was mother and mentor. She not only used her Picassos and Cézannes to teach the young writer about structure and composition, she proselytized for the clean, spare prose that would "rebuild" the language. "Gertrude Stein and me are just like brothers," Hemingway wrote in March 1922. In the boxing ring he was the equal of Ezra Pound; in the salon, the equal of Gertrude Stein, or so he wished. He was ardent for literary reputation, and would take from his professors what he needed to achieve it.

Gertrude Stein saw literature as the mastery of rhythm and refrain. In 1922 her shadow fell across "Up in Michigan," the Hemingway story of a chaste young woman's secret crush on a blacksmith. Ernest had begun the story in Chicago the year before, when he still pursued the popular audience. The manuscript opens:

> Wesley Dilworth got the dimple in his chin from his mother. Her name had been Liz Buell. Jim Dilworth married her when he came to Horton's Bay from Canada and bought the mill with A. J. Stroud.

Hemingway had borrowed manner (and more) from E. W. Howe, whose sketches of small-town America had appeared in the *Saturday Evening Post.* Howe's characterization of James Hadley Searles was representative:

> Jim put in his letter at the Presbyterian church; he said that was the thing to do in getting acquainted in a little town, but a good many knew he was not strict. Indeed, he hinted that if he cared to he could controvert a good deal the minister said, and one time, when some of the young men sent to the city for a bottle of whisky, he gave them to understand it was no new thing to him. But otherwise he was guilty of no particular devilment and was well behaved, though his talk always had the sarcastic tinge common with highly educated men who do not succeed very well.

Even in the 1921 version of "Up in Michigan," though, Hemingway had been "harder" than Howe.

> Liz was frightened and sick when she got up to her room. She put on one of her unwell pads because she was afraid of ~~the~~ blood getting on the sheets ~~and~~. She felt ashamed and sick and ~~spent~~ cried and prayed until she fell asleep. She woke up frightened and stiff and aching. It was still dark. "What if I have a baby?" she thought. It was the first time she had thought about it. It really was. She was so frightened the sweat ran down under her armpits ~~and~~ she [was too frighted to] ~~couldn't~~ cry. She thought about having a baby until it was morning.

One part of the story, revised in Paris under Stein's eye, had her pulse.

> Liz liked Jim very much. She liked it the way he walked over from the shop and often went to the kitchen door to watch for him to start down the road. She liked it about his mustache. She liked it about how white his teeth were when he smiled. . . . One day she found that she liked it the way the hair was black on his arms and how white they were above the tanned line when he washed up in the washbasin outside the house.

What follows could have happened in Winesburg, Ohio. Flushed with whiskey, Jim goes into the kitchen one night and invites Liz out. On the hard boards of the dock he roughly takes her, then falls asleep or passes out, she cannot tell. She covers him with her coat and walks home as the bay sends a cold mist through the woods.

No matter the version, in "Up in Michigan" romance and sex collide. Seeing Jim, Liz grows "weak" inside. Jim is the stronger character, the character who goes hunting and returns with "a big buck . . . stiff and hard." The deer augurs the action on the boards of the dock. " 'Oh, it isn't right,' " Liz says as Jim tries to enter her, "but she wanted it. She had to have it. . . ." Was it seduction or rape?

Sitting in "the kitchen next to the stove pretending to read a book," Liz watches Jim as he reads the *Toledo Blade*, hauls a deer to the smokehouse, or drinks whiskey with his pals. He never returns her look. He "never thought about her." Do appearances lie? " 'He's come to me finally,' " Liz thinks as he touches her. " 'He's really come.' " Perhaps *she* has seduced *him*. Perhaps he has gone to her because he has sensed her adoration and cannot stay away, and perhaps he hurts her because, as would become a touchstone in Hemingway, she has exposed his weakness. The story was about the consequences of passion and desire. It was also about authorship, a cautionary tale for the Ernest Hemingway who wanted to be published in the slick magazines. The cornerstone of a serious literary career was not only disregard of the gaze but scorn for the saleable. "Up in Michigan" is "a very good story and has been re-written by Morley Callaghan many times in saleable terms," the author would later note, as though he understood that the audience, like Liz Coates, was as dangerous as a cocked gun.

En route to Lausanne in December 1922, Hadley lost a pack of her husband's manuscripts and carbons. Ernest was apparently devastated but agreed with Pound that a good story was locked in memory while a bad one lacked "proper construction, and never *wd.* have been *right.*" Soon he was "constipated up with stuff to write," and between excursions to the race tracks, the ski resorts, or the Fiesta of San Fermin in Pamplona, he was "working 14 to 18 hrs a day" to hone his craft. Sherwood Anderson had told him that popular fiction was a "perversion of life." Accordingly, he now wrote stories less for *Red Book* or the *Saturday Evening Post* than for the *Little Review* and *Double Dealer*. The unadorned prose was plain enough for the masses, though, since the author was a double dealer: his short sentences were not only the bedrock of innovation but also entrée to editors and readers beyond the little magazines.

Hemingway was merry when he won attention. He spent part of Christmas 1922 with his war buddy "Chink" Dorman-Smith in Les Avants.

The hotel gave a concert party at which Hem agreed to perform [Chink later recalled]. He sang a bawdy song in some sort of German about a particularly unfortunate family with unlimited domestic troubles. This was ill-received by a stodgy Anglo-American audience. When the curtain fell and there was no applause except from Hadley and myself, Hem reappeared before the curtain to say 'I seem to have displeased the more respectable members of the audience.' Thereafter we patronised the less hostile Bains d'Alliez and the Montreau beer-hall. Nevertheless it was a good song.

As author, Hemingway would like to have appeared in *Cosmopolitan* but not at the cost of losing the "respectable" coterie that applauded the diction and compression of his stories and sketches.

"Soldier's Home," composed in April 1924, was representative of the Hemingway style. Harold Krebs returns from war long after the parades have ended. Distanced from family and friends and the middle-class role that awaits him, he looks at the young women of the town but shuns contact. He spends hours reading history or shooting pool to fend off thoughts of the atrocity of battle. "He did not want any consequences. He did not want any consequences ever again. He wanted to live along without consequences." When Mrs. Krebs speaks of the Lord, he knows he can no longer lie. He decides to leave home.

The narration was taut and oblique. On hearing that his mother prays daily for him, Harold falls silent. The narrator conveys what Harold thinks in one sentence, as candid as a snapshot, as eternal as a still life. "Krebs looked at the bacon fat hardening on his plate." Krebs sees piety as the grease of small-town life, and the fixed stare he focuses on the fixed plate conveys the desolation he feels. Throughout the story the cadenced prose boxes in the character. "He thought about France and then he began to think about Germany. On the whole he had liked Germany better. He did not want to leave Germany. He did not want to come home. Still, he had come home. He sat on the front porch." The story does not say what Krebs thought or why he returned home late. But the last sentence of the paragraph rubs like flint against the sentences that precede it, as in D. W. Griffith, where juxtaposition mattered even more than image. Krebs seated on the porch was both the mark of American small-town life and the essence of the hollow man.

"Soldier's Home" was potent writing; as such, it made Hemingway melancholy about the years it took to become known. "Nonsense," Ford Madox Ford said at tea that April, "you will have a great name in no time at all!" Though Hemingway was no sycophant, he knew that Ford and others had influence and hoped that their friendship would lead to publication and promotion. "I am fond of Ford," he wrote to Ezra Pound in May 1924. "This ain't personal. It's literary." The despair continued. He now had a son, John Hadley Nicanor, born in Toronto in October 1923, when Ernest worked briefly for the *Star*. "Now we haven't got any money anymore," he wrote Pound in July 1924, "I am going to have to quit writing and I never will have a book published." Had he forgotten that Hadley's more than forty thousand dollars' worth of investments produced income, or that *Three Stories and Ten Poems* (1923) and *in our time* (1924) had recently appeared? Since *Three Stories* and *in our time* were small press books, printed in limited editions, they were not real books, at least not to the author. Hemingway was like the fallen soldier in one war sketch from *in our time*, talking to another fallen soldier, apparently dead. That soldier, the narrator says, sardonically, "was a disappointing audience." To an audience that counted, however, *in our time* was quite real, and the author quite alive.

In April 1924 Three Mountains Press had published *in our time*, 170 perfect copies for sale, thirty pages long, thirty francs per book. The volume contained miniatures and sketches. Generally less than three hundred words long, each "chapter" focused on the corrida, the confusion the war had caused, or the initiation of a young man, later called Nick Adams, the alter ego of the author. Though Hemingway disliked the lowercase letters used in the book ("very silly and affected to me," he told Edmund Wilson), Sylvia Beach may have found them, along with the woodcut of the comely author in the frontispiece, appealing enough to put *in our time* alongside *Antic Hay* and *Swann's Way* in the window of her bookstore, Shakespeare and Company. Aldous Huxley and Marcel Proust outsold Ernest Hemingway, though, not only because they were known but because they had written novels. The price of *in our time* may also have blocked sales: thirty francs would have been a luxury for anyone as poor as the Hemingways appeared to be.

Hemingway had not expected to profit from *in our time*. Authors saw such volumes as debuts, formal balls that heralded talent and achievement. Publishers saw them as literary teas, perhaps even teas for two, where critics could meet (and later publicize) authors. In one sense *in our time* brought Hemingway more notice than publication of a magazine short story would have; in the *Chicago Tribune*, for instance, the gossip column about literary Paris called the author one of the "epic talents . . . destined to create a new literature on the American continent." New York publishers not only clipped such notes but scoured Europe for undiscovered talent. Frequently the young authors they signed could produce only another slim volume of short stories, but publishers ground them out to form "relationships" and to secure by contract the author's next book, which the publishers always hoped would be the more marketable product, the novel. If everyone was lucky, negotiations for dramatic or motion picture rights followed.

Boni & Liveright was one publisher among many with eyes and ears abroad. Albert Boni was a former Greenwich Village radical, and Horace

Liveright a colorful speculator and former stockbroker. Liveright was publishing moneymakers, like Gertrude Atherton's *Black Oxen* (1923) and Anita Loos's *Gentlemen Prefer Blondes* (1925), the sorts of books that earned authors huge returns and Hollywood offers. He was also publishing Eugene O'Neill, Hart Crane, Ezra Pound, Conrad Aiken, e. e. cummings, and in the Modern Library series, international authors who tended toward the subversive or avant-garde. Liveright relished sensation and scandal. In 1925, under investigation by the Federal Trade Commission for representing as leather the bindings of his reprint series, he not only took on the long-suppressed Dreiser novel *The "Genius"* but motored to Albany to oppose the so-called clean books bill. When the New York grand jury charged that he had brought out a salacious book, he hired state senator James J. Walker, better known as Beau James, to defend him, then pleaded—loudly—not guilty. Boni & Liveright was a pioneering yet "never an entirely 'respectable' publishing house."

Leon Fleischman, the well-to-do Liveright scout, met Hemingway in Europe, when another house author, Harold Loeb, introduced them. The visit went well. Leaving the apartment, though, Hemingway had turned red. "Double god damned kikes!" he roared, reportedly, annoyed apparently by Fleischman's lack of instant approval or his condescension. Since Hemingway and Gertrude Stein had agreed (so they told one another) that worldly success meant nothing, the rage may have been only a show for his friends Loeb and Kitty Cannell. On balance he was excited by the interest of an American publisher.

Hemingway was meanwhile awaiting word on other work then in circulation. "I'm sending you The Big Two Hearted River," he told Ernest Walsh and Ethel Moorhead in winter 1925, "as it is the best thing I have done by a long shot." In the story as finally published, Nick Adams walks alone into the woods, the seeker of its true pleasures. He pitches a tent, cooks buckwheat cakes, and fishes for trout. Like Krebs, he wants no consequences. As darkness falls, he chokes back thought. Hemingway later said that the "story was about coming back from the war but there was no mention of the war in it." Through ritual and ceremony, and the friction beneath, the author made the reader feel the unexpressed.

By February 1925, thanks to its scout, F. Scott Fitzgerald, Charles Scribner's Sons had heard of Hemingway and *in our time*. Scribners was an utterly respectable house, which Max Perkins continued to lead into the twentieth century. Harvard class of 1907, Perkins had graduated in 1914 from advertising to editorial, where, to succeed, he knew he had to sign and hold new talent. It was not easy, since the literary lions of the era dined on "strong meat." In *Winesburg, Ohio*, published by Ben Huebsch, who cofounded the

American Civil Liberties Union, Sherwood Anderson had exposed the despair and alienation of Main Street; he portrayed drunks, religious fanatics, homosexuals, and misogynists. One woman wrote to the author: "I do not believe that, having been that close to you [at dinner one evening], I shall ever again feel clean." Perkins had no stomach for the vulgar or indecent; he nonetheless understood that he had to broaden Scribners' long-entrenched Standards of Propriety.

By September 1919 Perkins had charted a course. He brought to the board a young Princeton graduate's second novel, *This Side of Paradise*. Opinion went against the manuscript, for under Scribners' colophon of the lamp was a business operated as a cultural institution. One editor called the novel trivial. Charles Scribner II said it had no literary value. Let others publish contemporary literature, the more robust the better, from Eugene O'Neill and Theodore Dreiser to the exponents of the *expérimental*. Scribners was beyond reproach, and would stand with the president of the American Library Association against books of an "immoral tendency." Perkins won out, though, and the long relationship between editor and author began. As Scott Fitzgerald later confessed, there was a "curious advantage to a rather radical writer in being published by what is now an ultra-conservative house."

Like Horace Liveright, Perkins read *in our time* and marveled at its scrupulous technique. The echoes of Gertrude Stein and Sherwood Anderson aside, the contents were original—and difficult. They were not stories per se but "chapters" that rewrote the hierarchy of fiction, and made action and character—the essence of the *Cosmopolitan*, *Saturday Evening Post*, and even *Scribner's Magazine* story—the servant of mood and voice. Moreover, the words and sentences were so chiseled and the narratives so concentrated that the book read more like poetry than prose.

Perkins scanned *in our time* ruefully. He knew that his colleagues would find it as unpleasant ("Christ please please please christ . . . Please please dear jesus," a wounded soldier chanted in one passage that appeared in the slender volume) and explicit as he himself almost found it. An author who wrote about "wops" and venereal disease and the roaring blood of the bull belonged not with Charles Scribner's Sons but with Horace Liveright or Thomas Seltzer, the American publisher of *Casanova's Homecoming* and *Women in Love*. *in our time* was nonetheless an astounding calling card, and because of its sensuality and modern character, the author was, in theory, one who could attract the general public. Perkins wrote to congratulate Hemingway and to ask whether he had anything that would interest "the trade." The letter never arrived.

Walsh and Moorhead accepted "Big Two-Hearted River" for *This Quar-*

ter, and gradually the author started not only producing pieces for the new magazine but serving as an assistant editor—proofreading, taking galleys to the printer, collecting pictures. It was not personal; it was literary. He was also collecting rejection notices from American magazines like *Harper's, Vanity Fair,* and, hardly forgotten, the *Saturday Evening Post.* He had sent George Lorimer "a real bull fight story, one written without bunk." In the cover letter he said that he had tried to do for the corrida what Charles E. Van Loan had done for the boxing ring. It was flattery, since Van Loan was a former *Post* editor whose sports stories Lorimer revered. "The Undefeated" was about the last fight of the seasoned torero Manuel Garcia. The heat in the *plaza de toros* was oppressive. The odds were unfavorable.

> In the front row of seats the substitute bull-fight critic of *El Heraldo* took a long drink of the warm champagne. He had decided it was not worth while to write a running story and would write up the *corrida* back in the office. What the hell was it anyway? Only a nocturnal. If he missed anything he would get it out of the morning papers. He took another drink of the champagne. He had a date at Maxim's at twelve. Who were these bull-fighters anyway? Kids and bums. A bunch of bums. He put his pad of paper in his pocket and looked over toward Manuel, standing very much alone in the ring, gesturing with his hat in a salute toward a box he could not see high up in the dark plaza. Out in the ring the bull stood quiet, looking at nothing.

The press was detached, the president unseen, the bull looking at nothing. Manuel was unappreciated and unacknowledged but not defeated, even when he tripped on one of the cushions tossed from the stands. "Oh, the dirty bastards! Dirty bastards! Oh, the lousy, dirty bastards!" he says of the crowd. Hemingway had found the story "easy" to write, perhaps because he understood its embattled hero. He was not alone, though, for friends like John Dos Passos and Harold Loeb were arguing his case in New York, and soon they would prevail.

In March 1925 Boni & Liveright offered to publish a collection of stories to be called *In Our Time.* Three months before, less despondent about the course of his career, Hemingway might have declined. He had been "all for keeping out of the manuals of the Semites as long as possible," and the Liveright house was a Jewish house. Leon Fleischman scouted writers, Isidore Schneider handled public relations, Edith Stern managed the office, and Richard Simon sold the books. Liveright was a Jewish firebrand, not proper enough for Oak Park. An offer was an offer, though. "Delighted. Accept," Hemingway responded. "Dat should mean fall publication," he told one boyhood friend, "from 2 to 500 seeds immediate advance on royalties—and the enditer [sic] launched in N. Y. makes a male feel good." The five hundred dollars was an exaggeration; still, as he understood, he would now be known beyond the Left Bank salons and cafés. He would also have a publisher whose logo was "thrusting and emphatic" and whose print advertisements were done in "very bold type and heavy black borders," a design that matched the content of stories about war and blood and sex.

"Up in Michigan" was part of the manuscript, but Hemingway may not have been surprised that Liveright asked to exclude it from the book. According to recollections in *A Moveable Feast*, Gertrude Stein had called the story *inaccrochable*, or "dirty," and even its author had wondered, anxiously, whether the whole collection would be burned on the steps of the Oak Park library. Grace and Ed Hemingway had shown the way the wind blew. They had ordered ten copies of the Three Mountains Press limited edition of *in our time*, then reportedly mailed the "filth" back to the publisher. Hemingway wanted the public to see *In Our Time* as literature rather than cause célèbre, so he replaced "Up in Michigan" with "The Battler." The new story was about Nick Adams's meeting a fallen boxer and the devoted man who cares for him. The undercurrents of incest and homosexuality were neither gratuitous nor prurient; they were nonetheless one more "sales angle" for the book.

Homosexuality—when muted—had occurred in fiction at least since the second decade of the century. In "The Cat and the King," for instance, published in *Ladies' Home Journal* (October 1919), a young female college student's "crush" on an older female student leads to a prank and a bed in the infirmary. " 'I feel better,' " the coed tells the woman physician who attends her. "She said it neatly and glibly and lay with closed eyes, waiting for what might happen." The doctor takes her pulse. "She held the wrist a minute and dropped it slowly, her eyes on the face. 'I shall look in again before I go to bed. She may need a quieting draft to make her sleep.' " Though "The Battler" was no "Cat and the King," the boxer does ask Nick to take his pulse. Hesitantly, Nick does, and as he notes the thick wrist and bulging muscles, he feels "the slow pumping under his fingers." Nick drops the wrist, then, taking it up again, feels "the slow hard throb under his fingers." The contact, the anxiety, and the throb lend the scene a sensual charge. Like Jennette Lee, the author of the *LHJ* story, Hemingway may have understood both the narrative and the commercial power of homoeroticism. He certainly understood the spell that eros more generally exerts over an audience. "Tell us about the French women, Hank. What are they like?" read the hook on the title page of *In Our Time*. The book promised the shocking and the pathological. As Hemingway told Liveright, it had "a good gambling chance to sell."

In spring 1925 Hemingway banked the two-hundred-dollar advance from Liveright and corrected the galleys of the forthcoming book. He was finally an author of real books, as Scott Fitzgerald could see, as Pauline Pfeiffer could see. Pauline was an assistant at Paris *Vogue*. She was very clever and very shrewd, especially about money, Hadley later remarked. Money. Harold Loeb and Kitty Cannell had introduced Pauline and her sister Jinny to Ernest, who preferred Jinny. "I'd like," he said, "to take her out in her sister's coat." Pauline later visited Hadley at her apartment. Ernest looked every inch the artoost, unshaven, reading in bed, dressed for tramping the Michigan woods. Not much, she thought.

Fitzgerald had another response. Loyal to Scribners and fond of Perkins, he had read Hemingway and recommended him to the firm in 1924. Months later (the story went) the two authors bumped elbows at the Dingo Bar in the rue Delambre and introduced themselves. Fitzgerald had very light wavy hair, Hemingway later noted in *A Moveable Feast*, "a high forehead, excited and friendly eyes, and a delicate long-lipped Irish mouth that, on a girl, would have been the mouth of a beauty. . . . The mouth worried you until you knew him and then it worried you more." That night Fitzgerald passed out standing up. Another night he showed Ernest his books, not *This Side of Paradise* or *The Beautiful and Damned*, but the ledger accounts of money earned. Money. Money, authorship, and drink would become the vectors of the relationship.

"Didn't miss one vintage from Montrachet to Chambertin," Hemingway later wrote Pound about travel with the Fitzgeralds. "Elaborate trip." The rub was Zelda. She was a young southerner with hard eyes, a coquette who was jealous of her husband's work. Ernest disliked her—but not enough to scuttle the friendship with Scott. As Hemingway later observed, without charity, Scott tended toward hero worship. Fitzgerald indeed respected the "little Paris books" of Ernest and wished as well for an intellectual following. But he was no lapdog. Though Hemingway had appeared in *Der Querschnitt* and the *transatlantic review*, and was the darling of such literary elite as Ford Madox Ford, Ezra Pound, and Gertrude Stein, Scott Fitzgerald was the premier author of the Jazz Age. He had an American reputation, especially in the slick magazines, and the money to prove it. Moreover, he wrote well. He could teach Ernest many things.

Fitzgerald talked to Hemingway about Scribners and Max Perkins, dear, generous, responsive, and discerning Max. The "personality of you," Scott once told the editor, compensates for the retrograde "publishing ideas" of the house, which "evolved under the pre-movie, pre-high-literacy-rate conditions of twenty to forty years ago." Perkins belonged to the "pre-movie" generation. As late as 1936, when he went to see *The Charge of the Light Brigade,*

> Max made his middle daughter, Peggy, accompany him to the theater. He stationed her so that she could watch both the screen and her father, who stood in the lobby. They waited an hour and a half for the climactic moment. When she saw that Errol Flynn was about to lead the charge, Peggy signaled, Perkins advanced through the lobby, stood in the aisle, and observed the Brigade's routing. Then Max and his daughter promptly retreated.

In the spirited 1920s, Scribners (like Perkins) had an air of "ultra-conservative" eccentricity about it. In 1919 one veteran employee had been embarrassed to find the word "bitch" in *This Side of Paradise.* Another was later fired for an indiscretion after twenty-four years' service to the firm. "[Y]our conduct has been unworthy of a gentleman," Charles Scribner II answered the employee's appeal, "and, as you must realize, our House measures the value of our representatives by the highest standards."

If Scribners was more conservative than what it published, Hemingway was less modern than what he wrote. He valued tradition and name. He had deep roots in Oak Park, where villagers voted Republican, supported progress, and read *Scribner's Magazine.* Hadley need not have apologized (as she had) for her narrow lip; he liked what she called her "Puritan upper" and her long, unbobbed hair and her reserve. He had frowned on her posing nude for her sculptress friend Marguerite Schullyer, and he had chided his own friend Y. K. Smith for having an open marriage. That was before Paris. In France he had grown tolerant. Slowly. Gertrude Stein may have been his "brother," but she too was in an open marriage he could not countenance. And though he treated homosexuals and homosexuality in prose, his narrators could be hard on both: "Once I remember [the Fairies] were all gone to Brussels for a week and were back before I noticed they were gone away and a week's enjoyment of their absence was lost." Perhaps he belonged not with Horace Liveright or Thomas Seltzer but with Charles Scribner's Sons.

Hemingway was naive about publishing, Fitzgerald told Perkins. He learned fast, though, due in part to the contact with Perkins. In February 1925 the editor had offered the author a frank discussion of why Scribners could not have published the Three Mountains Press book:

> [*in our time* is] so small that it would give the booksellers no opportunity for substantial profit if issued at a price which custom would dic-

tate. The trade would therefore not be interested in it. This is a pity because your method is obviously one which enables you to express what you have to say in very small compass, but a commercial publisher cannot disregard these factors.

When Perkins wrote again to the author in spring 1925, the industry was in a slump. Fiction sales since February "had been between fifty and sixty per cent of normal," Alfred Harcourt had told one author. "Perhaps the public is pausing for breath before they decide to go off on another reading bust—maybe in a new direction. We will know more about that in the autumn." Hemingway was part of the new wave, yet Perkins moved toward Hemingway by indirection: as he hinted via references to profit and commerce in letters of early 1925, the industry accommodated authors who tried to accommodate the industry.

Hemingway responded to the second Perkins letter on 15 April 1925, only weeks after he signed with Liveright. The text was euphoric. "I was very excited at getting your letter. . . ." And "I cannot tell you how pleased I was by your letter. . . ." And "I do want you to know how much I appreciated your letter. . . ." Publishers were gentlemen; according to Henry Holt, none "would go for another's author any more than for his watch." Charles Scribner II agreed—"unless the author had first decided to make a break." Hemingway had contracted for three books with Liveright and told the publisher he had "great admiration and confidence in you as a property builder." Mere flattery, of course, since Max Perkins had already alienated what little affection the author had for Horace Liveright.

Words and phrases like "custom" and "the trade" were not lost on Hemingway. He itched to "bring out a good fat book in N. Y. with some good publisher," a good book so that he could earn the reputation he wanted, a fat book so that he would draw the audience he needed. He was essentially a miniaturist, though, and wondered whether he could meet the demands of Scribners and the booksellers. When he was not delirious in that April 1925 letter to Perkins, he was defensive:

> Somehow I don't care about writing a novel and I like to write short stories. . . . Somehow the novel seems to me to be an awfully artificial and worked out form but as some of the short stories now are stretching out to 8,000 to 12,000 words maybe Ill get there yet.

He had of course promised the next book—the novel he would write, the novel he had contracted to write, the novel he was not sure he could write—to another publisher. He had written twenty-seven pages of it and stalled; the short stories may have stretched to twelve thousand words, but the novels petered out at half that. Searching for what he later called "one true sentence," he produced only false starts. Perhaps he needed a holiday.

On June 25 Ernest and Hadley took the train from Paris to Pamplona for the fiesta. Duff Twysden would be there, one of the boys, Hadley said, tall and slender and good company. She had divorced one husband and was divorcing another as she gadded about with her fiancé, Pat Guthrie. Robert McAlmon, who had published *Three Stories and Ten Poems*, had introduced Ernest to Lady Twysden. "The title seemed to electrify him," McAlmon recalled. Soon Hemingway was smitten. Duff was not particularly attractive, and though she could play the piano and paint, her real talent was seduction. She had no inhibitions. She also had a wonderful deep laugh and the capacity to have men pay her bar bills, which were legendary. Many had intercourse with her, or said they had, or wanted to, or said they wanted to. When she preferred the bistro to the bed, she surrounded herself with homosexuals. She was Musetta of *La Bohème*, and Hemingway may have had an affair with her. Certainly (as Michael Reynolds has shown) he was close enough to record her parlance: "We can't do it. You can't hurt people. It's what we believe in place of God." "I have never been able to have anything I ever wanted." "And I looked at you and I thought I wouldn't be able to stand it." Good raw material for fiction.

"Seems he was ready to try anything once," a friend from Toronto recalled of "Hemmy." "If he heard of anything new that anybody was eating anywhere in the world he would swallow it himself to discover what it tasted like. He claimed to have masticated slugs, earthworms, snails, ants, and all sorts of other Epicurean delicacies." In Pamploma, he and everyone else had indigestion. Trout fishing was not possible because the loggers had fouled the water at Burguete. Pat Guthrie was drunk and nasty, and Harold Loeb was mooning around Duff, for whom he had fallen. Concerned about the reception of *In Our Time*, apprehensive about the novel that would not come, Hemingway was bluff and authoritarian. "You were not to disagree with the Master in any way," Donald Ogden Stewart recalled. The sexual tension between Hemingway and Harold over Duff almost produced a fistfight. "I don't want to hit you," said Harold when they were outside. "Me, either," said Ernest. Good raw material for fiction.

The seed had been planted, and the sprouts included the adventures of a band of Americans en route to Pamplona. "The story is fairly funny," Hemingway wrote one friend in late July. "Have Ford in it as Braddocks. The master goes well as Braddocks." Days later he wrote Sylvia Beach that he had fifteen thousand words. Weeks later, having averaged two thousand words per day, he had fifty thousand words. He counted words. He always

counted words, especially when words counted, especially when he needed lots of words for the booksellers. It was "going to be a swell novel," he claimed to one correspondent, "with no autobiography and no complaints."

In August Boni & Liveright sent along the modish dust jacket for *In Our Time*. It featured endorsements from Sherwood Anderson, Ford Madox Ford, Gilbert Seldes, John Dos Passos, Donald Ogden Stewart, and others. Hemingway lacked their reputations but not their notoriety. H. L. Mencken had called *in our time* the "sort of brave, bold stuff that all atheistic young newspaper reporters write," and to the American press the author was as brave and bold as his stuff. A news story datelined 28 July 1924 and syndicated by the *Chicago Tribune* had identified Stewart, Dos Passos, and Hemingway as "American writers resident of Paris" who had gone to Pamplona for the running of the bulls. Darting into the ring to protect Stewart, Hemingway had been "saved from death only because the bull's horns were bandaged." The hometown edition of the *Tribune* headlined the account "Bull Gores 2 Yanks Acting as Toreadores" and even featured a photograph of the solemn local hero. Though Pamplona 1925 would be covered as fiction rather than news story, Hemingway was using the spice of autobiography to season the novel. The tang would draw the public to the Master.

Liveright printed just under fourteen hundred copies of *In Our Time*, a generous run for a first book of short stories. He also sent review copies to newspapers and magazines across the country and, perhaps more important, made good on the ballyhooing he had promised on the author's behalf. "I'm sure that you will become a property and if I say it myself, as who should, you'll find that we're pretty good builders," he had told Hemingway in May 1925, and part of the "construction" involved the courtship of the press. He routinely dined with the eleven literary opinion makers of New York. He entertained them, he touted his list, and he dared to tell them which of his books belonged on page one of their review sections. He also circulated vignettes about his authors. One blurb said that having completed seventy-five thousand words on his next book, Hemingway found he "had to work nights because the stuff was so strong I could not sleep. So sometime next year there will be a novel." That sort of publicity was one cut above the "Bull Gores" account: at least the derring-do here was literary, and won Hemingway notice within the industry. Moreover, because some of the stories of *In Our Time* had originally been published in the *Little Review* and the *transatlantic review*—the "cucoo magazines" whose contents were in legal oblivion and perhaps public domain—Boni & Liveright had helped secure American copyright for the author.

Hoping for some perspective, Hemingway stored the draft of the fiesta novel and, fueled by the appearance of *In Our Time*, turned his attention to short fiction. "Fifty Grand" was "not the thing I'm shooting for," he told Fitzgerald; it belonged (like "The Undefeated") to the category of stories "that are easy for me to write." Based on several disputed boxing matches in the early 1920s, "Fifty Grand" was notable for its final twist. Prizefighter Jack Brennan, convinced he cannot win, bets fifty thousand dollars on his opponent. But when Jimmy Walcott fouls him, he knows he's been set up. Walcott will take the loss; Brennan will lose the bet. Heroically Brennan stands up until he can foul Walcott back, hand him the decision, and claim the "fifty grand." The double-cross thus becomes the counter-double-cross.

In "Fifty Grand" Hemingway tried to balance the literary and the popular. The strategy was transparent but not unsuccessful. The scenes at the training camp, the scale room of the Garden, and the hotel room where Brennan and the narrator play cribbage are understated and controlled; the scene in the ring is overt and almost melodramatic. Perhaps the story was "easy" because it played to the crowd, because Jack Brennan *and* Hemingway gave the audience a show. That last section was the money section; it was the part of the story that would boost the chances of a magazine sale. Before the final bell, however, Brennan and Hemingway struggled to redeem themselves. In the eleventh round, Hemingway wrote, Brennan's "money was all right and now he wanted to finish it off right to please himself." However derivative the action, which echoed not only O. Henry but Kipling and Lardner, the mode was all Hemingway.

> [Walcott] backed Jack up against the ropes, measured him and then hooked the left very light to the side of Jack's head and socked the right into the body as hard as he could sock, just as low as he could get it. He must have hit him five inches below the belt. I thought the eyes would come out of Jack's head. They stuck way out. His mouth come open. The referee grabbed Walcott. Jack stepped forward. If he went down there went fifty thousand bucks. He walked as though all his insides were going to fall out.

"Fifty Grand" closed on an ironic note. " 'It's funny how fast you can think when it means that much money,' " Brennan says. Hemingway had written that easy story to earn some money and some exposure, and in the end it was another story about authorship, and yet another cautionary tale for an ambitious author about to be launched in New York.

"We've been seeing a lot of Pauline Pfeiffer," Hemingway told Harold Loeb as *In Our Time* appeared. Pauline was bright and fresh, just what the author needed in the wake of his first trade book. Liveright had published the collection on October 5. Less than one month later, Hemingway wrote Loeb:

> So far I tell everybody I am very satisfied with Boni and Liveright, that they have treated me very decently, that I am very pleased, etc. It's up to them to keep me happy though and that means they've got to give In Our Time a good ride and that I must have a good advance on the novel. I'm not sore but I'm annoyed that they have done nothing in Chicago where hells own amount of books are sold and which is my home town and where I would have a certain amount of sale anyway.
>
> They are certainly putting Sherwood over big and will evidently make the boy a lot of money. I suppose it all takes time and they know what they are doing. They are evidently playing the book of stories as a sort of classic and then planning to splurge on the novel. I think they're damn good publishers.

Since advertisements for a "classic" would have been gauche, Liveright had counted on reviews to sell *In Our Time*. Hemingway was miffed, and restive, for critics could be harsh. In the May issue of the *transatlantic review*, one critic had pronounced Dada dead "although [Tristan] Tzara still cuddles its emaciated little corpse to his breast and croons a Rumanian folksong . . . while he tries to get the dead little lips to take sustenance from his monocle." The critic was Ernest Hemingway, who called other critics the "eunuchs of literature." Just the same, he subscribed to a clippings service (an indulgence for anyone but an author interested in audience), and what he paid for, he read.

In Our Time contained "Soldier's Home," "The Doctor and the Doctor's Wife," "Indian Camp," "My Old Man," "Cat in the Rain," "Big Two-Hearted River," and other stories. Astonishing for their spareness, they were linked by the vignettes of *in our time*. One such interchapter opens:

> They shot the six cabinet ministers at half-past six in the morning against the wall of a hospital. There were pools of water in the courtyard. There were wet dead leaves on the paving of the courtyard. It rained hard. All the shutters of the hospital were nailed shut.

The cabinet ministers were faceless, and the hard rain premonitory. Despite the assonance of "wet dead leaves" and the terse rhythm of shutters "nailed shut," the mood was austere and the theme elusive. So much was left out. So much was implied.

The press hailed the strong prose of *In Our Time*, and remarked—usually unfavorably—on the candor, what the St. Louis *Globe Democrat* called the profound lack of taste. As a syndicated story in the conservative *Daily Oklahoman* explained, the content of the collection was "terrible and beautiful." But the kudos from Sherwood Anderson (among others) pasted across the dust jacket boomeranged. The *New Republic* found "something of Sherwood Anderson, of his fine bare effects and values coined from simplest words, in Hemingway's clear medium." The *Saturday Review of Literature* noted the "obvious traces of Sherwood Anderson," and the laudatory notice in the *New York Herald Tribune* reported that Hemingway was "very strongly under the influence of Sherwood Anderson." Hemingway had been launched in New York, yet appeared to be in dry dock.

It was "enough to turn your stomach to have to read that sort of crap," Hemingway told one friend. Before the appearance of the fiesta novel, he would have to silence the comparisons to Anderson. The answer was a parody; it was a stencil job where Anderson would furnish the form and content, Hemingway the irony and exaggeration. Nothing could be simpler for an author whose humor had always been praised and who had recently been told by *Cosmopolitan* that humor was in demand in the United States. That Liveright now published Anderson only enhanced the pleasure.

Set around Petoskey, Michigan, *The Torrents of Spring* focuses on the knockabout characters Scripps O'Neil and Yogi Johnson. One plot strand concerns Scripps's marriage to an older woman, Diana, while another concerns Yogi's visit to a drinking club for educated Indians. Diana adores Scripps, an author, and she strives, like the beanery she works for, to be "Best By Test." Terrified that Scripps may leave her for another woman, she subscribes to the *Dial*, the *Bookman*, and the *American Mercury*. Finally, though, Scripps tells her: " 'I don't give a damn about Mencken any more.' " At the drinking club, Yogi and two "woods Indians" carouse until the "town Indians" discover that Yogi's "tribe" comes from Scandinavia. With "black negro laughter," the bartender boots out the trio. On a wintry Michigan night, with an Indian woman and her papoose behind him, the stark naked Yogi walks down the railroad tracks, and the short novel ends.

A carbonate of barbs and literary small talk, *The Torrents of Spring* ribbed Gertrude Stein but jabbed Sherwood Anderson. It was *Oedipus Rex* as ha'penny farce: the narrator had assumed the voice of Anderson, the older author, and not only exposed his weaknesses but violated his property. In *Dark Laughter* (1925), a novel about race in America, Anderson had used the repetitions, amateur psychologizing, and simple, introspective characters that had distinguished *Winesburg, Ohio*. Hemingway lacked the humor of Fielding and the cleverness of Lardner, but he captured the technique of Anderson, and skewered his idiosyncrasies. Dashed off at Thanksgiving, the parody was good enough to make Anderson and his publisher squirm.

Liveright had promised Anderson one hundred dollars per week against royalties, one hundred percent of the foreign rights reserved to the author, and, eventually, a uniform edition of the works. That alone might have been enough to inspire Hemingway to take Anderson down a peg, and yet he had not written *The Torrents of Spring* solely to irk Anderson or (as often assumed) to break with Liveright and go with Scribners. (He could probably have abrogated his contract by fussing about the advance or royalty schedule Liveright offered for the fiesta novel.) He had also written *The Torrents of Spring* to sell. As he understood, the 1920s savored parody. Donald Ogden Stewart's *Parody Outline of History* had been a best-seller, and the decade rewarded those who, like Alexander Woolcott or Sinclair Lewis, could put on and send up. Between the wit of the manuscript and the publicity that surrounded Anderson, Hemingway thought that *The Torrents of Spring* was marketable. Accordingly, when he sent it off on December 7, he asked Liveright for a prominent illustrator and a fat advertising budget. Despite the rarefied humor of the novel, he obviously hoped to reach beyond the literary clique to the general reader.

"Pauline Pfeiffer gets here tomorrow to stay for Xmas and New Years," Hemingway wrote Fitzgerald from Schruns on Christmas Eve. That was the whole paragraph, one sentence, as keen and straight as a needle. Ernest was attracted to Pauline—her dark bobbed hair, her reedy figure, her pert sexuality. Since adultery was another Oak Park taboo he respected, he may have "wanted" but not "had" her. They walked together, though, laughing, talking, perhaps touching. Hadley pretended not to notice, while Pauline pretended not to foresee the consequences. The rain that season forced skiers from the slopes. Inside the cabin, Pauline, Hadley, and Ernest dealt three-handed bridge or played horsey to John Hadley and his new Christmas whip. It was so wholesome and innocent, and so inevitable.

"That you should criticize our exploiting of *In Our Time* is ridiculous," Liveright wrote Hemingway that January. "*In Our Time* will sell some day—after your first successful novel." Liveright may also have been right about *The Torrents of Spring*, a "cerebral" parody and a "vicious caricature" of Anderson. In chapter 11, for example, the author had put down the sword and picked up the blunderbuss. Yogi recalls Fred, "the chap in the book by Anderson." On patrol in no-man's-land, Fred saw another soldier and shot him, the only time he had "consciously killed a man. You don't kill men in war much, the book said. The hell you don't, Yogi thought, if you're two years in the infantry at the front." Later the dead soldier haunted Fred. "It's got to be sweet and true. That was the way the soldiers thought, Anderson said. The hell it was. This Fred was supposed to have been two years in an infantry regiment at the front." The sermon on the literature of war bordered on diatribe:

Nobody had any damn business to write about it, though, that didn't at least know about it from hearsay. Literature has too strong an effect on people's minds. Like this American writer Willa Cather, who wrote a book about the war where all the last part of it was taken from the action in the "Birth of a Nation," and ex-servicemen wrote to her from all over America to tell her how much they liked it.

For Hemingway, cinema represented the "fake" and literature the "real," and, worse yet, Cather's movie-house research had been rewarded with fan mail.

Liveright rejected *The Torrents of Spring*. Hadley also found the novel "detestable" and, with John Dos Passos, thought that her husband should not publish it. Pauline disagreed. She not only liked the manuscript but wanted to tell the publisher so; she had become outspoken at *Vogue*, she noted, and would be happy to be outspoken with Liveright. Hemingway saw *Torrents* as a jeu d'esprit for the literati, the critics, and (he was naively convinced) the general reader. It was the declaration of independence from Anderson and the literary tradition. It was the punch that set up the knockout blow for the fiesta novel. He would not shelve the manuscript.

Liveright wanted *The Sun Also Rises*, née *The Lost Generation*, but its author acted as though the publisher "had broken up his home and robbed him of millions." Hemingway was revising *The Sun Also Rises*, which was "damned good," he told Fitzgerald, who was contacting New York publishers about both *The Torrents of Spring* and *The Sun Also Rises*. The suitors were responsive, in part because a lackluster spring season had been followed by a robust autumn. "Business is good," Alfred Harcourt told one author, and, indeed, Harcourt had read *In Our Time* and offered to publish— unread—both *The Torrents of Spring* and *The Sun Also Rises*; he said they could " 'rock the country.' " Max Perkins stood behind Liveright in the queue but had not promised to publish either *The Torrents of Spring* or *The Sun Also Rises*. Horace Liveright held as hostage the plates of *In Our Time* (which would "sell some day") and thought his contract valid for *The Sun Also Rises*. The author was on tenterhooks.

"Perhaps if Mr. and Mrs. Hemingway should go to America, or just Mr. Hemingway should go to America," Pauline wrote Ernest in January 1926, "I might go with them or just him and tell [Horace Liveright] a few things." Perhaps Pauline was right, Hemingway thought: rather than depend on transatlantic mail, three weeks over, three weeks back, he should go to New York. Europe was stuffy, too, since he was wed to Hadley and in love with Pauline.

Leaving Hadley behind in Schruns, he traveled to Paris, then to Cherbourg. Pauline wrote Hadley that she and Ernest had seen one another in Paris as much as possible—it was so wholesome, so innocent. She had a trust fund as well, and cited it to show her affection for the Hemingways, Ernest, Hadley, and John Hadley, nicknamed "Bumby." On February 4 she wrote Hadley: "Ernest said he wrote you that Bumbi is to be one of my heirs, that is, of course, if I die before he becomes a financial maggot thru his own efforts." Now it was Pauline and Ernest who joked about artoostic kereers.

Hemingway may have worked on the *transatlantic review* and produced serious and innovative work, but he was also serious about sales and exposure. The trip to the States was, as his biographer Carlos Baker says, a "business trip." It was also an education. As Ben Hecht wrote, the real strangeness of New York

> lay in things you could not see—the fact that there were theatrical seasons and music seasons, and that the skyscrapers were full of magazine offices and publishing houses. There had been only one Covici in Chicago. New York seemed to swarm with Covicis—all clamoring for works of art to launch. At times I felt like I had come to no city at all but to a bazaar in which I and a few thousand like me were for sale under the loose stock label of artists.

Hemingway had never spent much time in New York; moreover, except for very short trips to the East Coast and Oak Park, he had spent almost no time in America since winter 1921. Much had changed, especially about authors and publishers and markets.

In the years 1910–1920, according to agent Ann Watkins, a book inched along a straightforward assembly line: the trade edition, the illustrated or gala edition, and the reprint by Grosset and Dunlap, "who leased the plates and paid the publisher ten cents a copy." In the 1920s, though, a book attracted buyers interested in theatrical and (especially) motion picture rights. The industry that had produced *The Birth of a Nation* (which Hemingway may or may not have seen) had come of age. From 1924 to 1926, it sold $47 million in real estate bonds, $54 million in other bonds, and $81 million in stocks. Theater construction exploded. In 1925, the year before Hemingway came home, America had twenty thousand movie houses, eighteen million seats, and $750 million in box-office sales. Production costs rose proportionally. Films that cost $10,000 to $30,000 before the war now cost $50,000 to $100,000 and more, the greater expense incurred in part by the cost of the fiction and dramas on which the pictures were based. Studios were now vertically integrated, too, capable of producing, distributing, and exhibiting product. In short, motion pictures were a major American industry that aggressive publishers could use to their and their authors' advantage.

If Scribners was wary of the new markets, other publishers—and authors—were not. In the early 1920s Alfred Knopf sold *A Lost Lady* (1923) so skillfully that Warner Bros. reportedly paid Willa Cather $10,000 for the screen rights. Edith Wharton turned from Scribners, her former publisher, to Appleton, and saw her prospects and income rise. Appleton understood the value of exposure. The author earned $18,000 for serialization of one of her most famous novels in *Pictorial Review*, $15,000 as an advance against royalties, and $15,000 (again Warner Bros.) for the screen rights. "And to an appreciable extent," R. W. B. Lewis notes, "*The Age of Innocence* (as the book [1920] was shortly renamed) came into being as the result of a shrewd estimate of the literary market by both the editor of a slick picture magazine and the representative of an up-and-coming firm of publishers." Wharton was distressed to learn that the *Review* had pared the story to create more space for the illustrations; "I cannot consent to have my work treated as prose by the yard," she told her editor, and yet she allowed the same magazine to serialize *The Glimpses of the Moon* (1922) for $17,000 and Hollywood to secure the screen rights for $13,500.

As Ann Watkins said, the studios could be coy. They would tell an agent or publisher that they were uninterested in such-and-such property and might venture " 'a coupla thousand berries' " on it. But authors could also play the game. Wilbur Daniel Steele was a "crossover" writer who sold one sort of story to the literary magazines like *Harper's* for $300, and another to the slicks like *Pictorial Review* for $2,000. The *Pictorial Review* was buying the name "Steele" as well as the fiction the author wrote; in fact, as Watkins noted, the *Pictorial Review* charged part of the $2,000 fee to the promotion department. Steele and the *Pictorial Review* were beneficiaries in common, for despite its desire to sell Sani-Flush (one of its many advertisers) rather than further the course of literature, the *Pictorial Review* boosted the visibility and value of the authors it published, especially with the one audience that (literally) counted—Hollywood.

The success of the screen version of *The Glimpses of the Moon*, which opened in April 1923 with dialogue by Scott Fitzgerald, helped Wharton become known well beyond the book trade and the *Pictorial Review*. She was perhaps never a celebrity, but, increasingly, many other authors were. *Time* was instrumental. By April 1925, hardly less than one year old, with a circulation of one hundred thousand, the magazine had perfected a nascent form of journalism. The *New Republic* and the *Literary Digest* reported the news as issues, *Time* as personalities. The week it began publishing, *Time* reviewed Gertrude Atherton's *Black Oxen*. The two-column notice had four sections: "The Story," "The Significance," "The Critics," and "The Author." The first two sections made the review look rather like the reports that Hollywood scenario departments routinely prepared for studio executives. True to the early mission of *Time*, the third section condensed the critics' reception of the book. The brief last section offered biographical tidbits. A photograph of the author appeared in the center of the page, however, and the caption spoke not of *Black Oxen* but Atherton, "[w]ho has coined a word—'Sophisticates'—for the intellectual aristocracy of New York." In other words, the author was the "newsmaker."

Though *Time* had not yet run a portrait of Hemingway, its review of *In Our Time* had commended the author as a personality. "He appears to have lived considerably himself, in unusual ways and places. He knows how trout-fishing in Michigan feels; how Yankee jockeys, straight and crooked, ride on European tracks. . . . He knows what it is like to pot German soldiers scaling a garden wall; to ski in the Tyrol; to bum on Canadian freight trains; to be in love, just at first and then really." He "appears" in one short sentence, then "knows" and then "really" knows in the long ones that follow. A writer had been born, and so had a persona.

Time, one of the megaphones of the culture of celebrity, had sensed and influenced changes in the American zeitgeist. As Richard Schickel has noted, in the 1920s the country and the personal concerns of its people were not so altered that the "public life" of the community could no longer flourish. "But there was this trouble with it: it seemed to be very small potatoes. Its rewards and recognitions seemed paltry compared to what was going on elsewhere, where the images were made, where the truly glamorous made work seem like play and fame was the spur." The elsewhere was chiefly Hollywood, where, in the 1920s, another Liveright author resided. One entry in the diary of Theodore Dreiser read: "Am wishing for money & success in my work." For at least one such reason, writ large, Ernest Hemingway had boarded the *Roosevelt* in France and set sail for the bazaar that was New York.

In Oak Park the Hemingway children had been taught to keep diaries of their expenditures, and Ernest could be as precise about money as he was about language. When Hadley was owed $7,400.57 on a bond sale in 1924, her husband expected her to receive $7,400.57, not $7,400.00. The trip to America was in part about dollars and cents. Having rejected *The*

Torrents of Spring, Liveright wanted to "cash in on" *The Sun Also Rises*, probably because, as Hemingway reasoned, the publisher was "supposed to have dropped $50,000 in last theatrical venture." That was Christmas 1925, before Ernest and Horace met. Nothing in New York would change the author's mind.

Scribners was the "ultra conservatives." Dodd, Mead was the "pious Presbys." And the "Boni and Liveright office was the Jazz Age in microcosm, with all its extremes of hysteria and of cynicism, of Carpe Diem, of decadent thriftlessness," one happy associate recalled. "To recapture its atmosphere one would not, like Proust, dip a madeleine into a cup of tea, but a canapé into bathtub gin." Hemingway arrived at the brownstone on West 48th on February 10. The operation looked like that of the *transatlantic review* or *This Quarter*—creative and chaotic. Liveright could rob an author of tens of thousands not through cunning but through honest error or poor business sense. Hemingway wanted out. Graciously, Liveright opened the door.

Like Scribners, Knopf and Harcourt were interested in Hemingway less as author of *The Torrents of Spring* (the parody rivaled the short-story collection as a market risk) than as author of *The Sun Also Rises*. Another of the "Semites," Alfred Knopf called Horace Liveright "cheap and flamboyant" for publishing sexy books like *Black Oxen* (about monkey gland injections) and *Flaming Youth* (about flappers), while he (Knopf) " 'had the honor to announce the publication of the Such-and-Such Sage.' " (Knopf was in fact not bashful about publicizing books.) Alfred Harcourt, formerly an editor at Henry Holt, now published the Bloomsbury group—Strachey, Woolf, Forster—and Hemingway thought he "might be less conservative [than Scribners] in regard to certain somewhat broad scenes." Hemingway liked what he knew about Perkins, though, and the name Charles Scribner's Sons.

On February 11 Hemingway browsed the Scribners bookshop on Fifth Avenue, no doubt looking for copies of *In Our Time*, then boarded the elevator at the rear of the store. The third floor was accounts, the fourth advertising, and the fifth editorial, and all of them, including the bookshop, hinted of must. Charles Scribner's Sons was the publisher of Henry James and (off and on) Edith Wharton, less the crossroads of American literature than the museum. Accordingly, the mood on five was Dickensian. The office furniture belonged in an old country doctor's waiting room, and the divans were as comfortable for reading manuscripts as for the editors' afternoon naps. Scribners acquired manuscripts based on its venerable reputation, not its advances, which in the 1920s ranged from the low four figures to the high three. There were compensations. Unlike, say,

Houghton Mifflin, Scribners rarely touched the author's text until it returned in galley or page proof, and even then only barely. The editorial benevolence helped some books, hindered others.

The poses, the opinions, the bonhomie: Hemingway would not ordinarily have been to Perkins's taste. The editor was married and the father of five daughters, but, as he told his colleague John Hall Wheelock, he preferred sedate bachelor associates; they worked harder and accomplished more. When later Wheelock himself wed and called on the Perkinses one Sunday afternoon, Max "stayed upstairs reading manuscripts all the time we were there." The bride was hurt, but the groom knew that Max was just being Max. He could use that passive aggression at work. He averred in correspondence and conversation that the manuscript belonged to the author, not to the editor or publisher. He was less tender than his predecessors, though, and on contested passages in manuscripts he expected to be heeded and sustained. When authors demurred, he could become abject or terse. Authors who feared they had hurt or offended him made the concessions he wanted.

Unlike Liveright, the voluptuary and dandy, Perkins was the burgher and college professor. He dressed in a custom-made suit worn thin at the elbows and stood at a custom-made oak desk; it was raised like a lectern so that he could work standing up, a technique Hemingway later adopted. Hard of hearing, Perkins listened closely to Hemingway. One topic may have been the stories of *In Our Time* and the sales of the book. Authors typically needed consolation, and editors could tender it. A writer could not expect to make much money from the publication of books of short fiction, Scribners editor Roger Burlingame had told John P. Marquand, as Perkins could have told Hemingway, but "the author gets his work before the critics, gets a recognition, a permanency of name, in short a *succès d'estime.*" Though this was publishers' boilerplate, it was true for beginning authors and it no doubt appealed to Hemingway.

What Perkins found in Hemingway, Hemingway found in Perkins, not only the cool surface and strong undertow but the traces of misogyny and fatalism. Perkins had a "Rough Rider" ashtray on the corner of the desk, for Scribners was the publishing house of the former president, an author whose hunger for attention was notable and whose books were part of the construction and display of his persona. Hemingway, who revered Teddy Roosevelt, needed an audience. He wanted respectability, and he liked Max Perkins. He was home.

Perkins thought *The Torrents of Spring* "grand." Scribners would publish it just as Hemingway wanted it—with no endorsements on the dust jacket, though later several would appear in the advertisements. Almost overnight, the Scribners art department would dope out an illustration à la Ralph Barton and *Vanity Fair* for the dust jacket, so recent a phenomenon that Perkins still called it the wrap, short for wrapper, originally a blank sheet to protect the more durable bindings that publishers had started using around 1900. Hemingway was meanwhile on the loose in New York. He drank with the American painter Mike Strater, traded gossip with Dorothy Parker and Robert Benchley, and cultivated the influential critic and editor Paul Rosenfeld. Then, on February 15, he returned to Perkins's office and looked at the sketch of Scripps and Diana planned for *The Torrents of Spring* dust jacket. Perfect. On February 17 he signed with Charles Scribner's Sons. Busy promoting the sale of theatrical and screen rights to *An American Tragedy,* Liveright may not have noted the defection.

Hemingway stayed in America for less than two weeks. He could have gone to Oak Park, less than two days by train, but chose not to risk sermons from his mother and father about the content of his work. En route to Schruns he stopped in Paris, where the *Chicago Tribune* would report that he had "just concluded a most advantageous contract with Scribner's for the publishing of his books." Hadley would soon detect that his interest was not in publishing alone. The attraction to Pauline was not hard to fathom. She was the daughter of rich Arkansas cotton farmers. Though Ernest had not wanted a college education, he had wanted to attend college, and Pauline had her degree in journalism from the University of Missouri. She was a playful kitten with an assurance born of knowledge and privilege. " 'The very rich are different from you and me,' " Julian (of "The Snows of Kilimanjaro") would note. And the response was, "Yes, they have more money." Hemingway was interested in who had money and how they used it. He loved Pauline because he loved Pauline, but she had worked for the house organs of the leisure class, *Vogue* and *Vanity Fair,* and her confidence and smart-set connections may have been part of what he loved.

In late March Hemingway finished revisions on *The Sun Also Rises* and had them typed. In early April he corrected proof on *The Torrents of Spring.* His career was finally moving. Despite the unspoken stress in his marriage, he was also writing both long fiction and short. *Collier's* was reading "Fifty Grand," the boxing story; he was revising "The Killers" and several others; and English publishers, cued by Liveright, were at last scanning *In Our Time.* Though Chatto & Windus, Fisher Unwin, John Lane, and others passed, Edward O'Brien (who had read Hemingway in 1923) persuaded Jonathan Cape to offer a contract and twenty-five-pound advance for the collection. Hemingway was sanguine about the future, at least the future of Ernest Hemingway the professional.

The short stories written that season, as he awaited the appearance of *The Torrents of Spring,* nonetheless bore traces of apprehension. "An Alpine Idyll," for example, was written in April 1926. The macabre story-within-a-story occurs at an inn near the Silvretta, where the narrator and his friend have been skiing. There the narrator, a forerunner of Nick Adams, hears the sexton tell the tale of a mountain-bound peasant whose wife died during the winter. Until spring the husband stood her in a shed. " 'Her mouth was open,' " the husband says, " 'and when I came into the shed at night to cut up the big wood, I hung the lantern from it.' " Her disfigured face shocks the local priest but not the narrator and his friend: at the end of the story, appetite intact, they order dinner.

A Poe sketch lengthened into a story, "An Alpine Idyll" was about the need to face death—the death of the spouse, the death of the marriage—and move on. It was also about bridging the distance between author and audience. The gruesome story of the peasant finally matters less than the characters around it, the storytellers and the auditors—the sexton who relates the tale in a German dialect, the innkeeper who suspects the narrator has not understood, and the narrator who, when the sexton finishes, asks the innkeeper: " 'Do you think it's true?' " The story was about the author reaching beyond the narrative to gauge its reception.

Hemingway sent "An Alpine Idyll" to *Scribner's Magazine* in May 1926, and the limbo that followed was so uncomfortable that he wrote Perkins four weeks later to ask whether the manuscript had ever arrived. As he told Perkins, he had three other stories in manuscript but hadn't "had them re-typed and sent on as [he] was waiting word about The Alpine Idyll." Hemingway had chosen Scribners over Knopf and Harcourt and others because he yearned to appear in *Scribner's Magazine.* Fitzgerald had counseled him that once the magazine ran his stories, the publisher could issue them in a collection, a family arrangement that would "reward" author and publisher. Yet money alone was not the reason Hemingway was so eager.

Throughout each issue, unlike *Pictorial Review, Scribner's* appealed to its patrons' wealth or good taste. There can be "no finer, more correct way to Europe than by *White Star, Red Star* or *Atlantic Transport Lines,*" read one steamship company's advertisements. *Scribner's Magazine* did not sell ocean voyages; it sold the prestige that certain readers—and certain authors—coveted. As one Scribners editor later recalled, *Scribner's* readers "treasured their copies, filed them, often bound them and ranged them on shelves along with their most precious books." Schools and colleges made the magazine required reading, and families used the copy on the drawing-room or library table as "a mark of distinction." Writing to *Scribner's* editor Robert

Bridges, the "crossover" author Don Marquis reported that he had sent a story to *Collier's*:

> [They] usually pay me 30¢ a word and grab up anything that I send them, but they sent it back with the notice that while they liked it themselves they thought it was over the heads of their readers—in which I entirely agree with them. I am not going to send it anywhere else, but am going to take the $750. which you offered for it, as after all I really do want it to get to a public which has some brains in its skull.

Scribner's maintained the "higher, purer" literary standards of other "quality" magazines. It had an audience smaller than that of the literary retailers *Cosmopolitan* or *Collier's*, but its audience was the only one worth addressing, for it contained "the thinking people," what Perkins called "the real book reading public."

Though *Scribner's Magazine* published not only American writers but work that was "American in scene and substance and feeling," Bridges may have been more conservative than anyone else at Charles Scribner's Sons. In 1920 Bridges had asked John Galsworthy to delete the phrase "unappeased sexual instincts" from the magazine's serialization of his forthcoming novel. Galsworthy acceded, grudgingly, since he remained convinced "that starved sexual instinct *is* responsible for very much emotional vagary in many directions." Bridges had equally conservative taste in narrative technique, and rejected "An Alpine Idyll" as too grim. It was "for people interested in reality which most want to cover up." Hemingway was testy: Bridges sounded like an editor of one of "the big money advertizing magazines." More concerned than ever about the reception of *The Sun Also Rises* in the hands of readers and, perhaps, an editor, Hemingway sent Perkins the typescript of the novel in late April. Then, with Hadley in Antibes on holiday with Bumby, the author went to Spain for the corrida.

Chapter Two

THE SUN ALSO RISES

"You've got to stand up and fight for it," Louise Perkins told her husband in 1926. He had read *The Sun Also Rises* and wondered whether he could—or should—defend it before the board. It was an "extraordinary performance," he wrote Hemingway. "No one could conceive a book with more life in it." Or, for Charles Scribner's Sons, more candor. The novel follows Jake Barnes, Bill Gorton, Brett Ashley, Mike Campbell, and Robert Cohn across the Pyrénées to see the running of the bulls in Pamplona. Along the way, Lady Ashley has affairs with Mike, Robert, and the bull-fighter Pedro Romero—but not with Jake, whose war wound has crippled him sexually. Brett's no sadist, the drunken Mike says, just a normal, healthy woman. She's also the saddest and cruelest character in the novel. When she renounces Pedro to wed Mike, she tells Jake that they could have been good together. And Jake responds, " 'Isn't it pretty to think so?' "

The Sun Also Rises was short on plot but not on sensation or, as any book publisher or film producer would have noted, sensationalism. Lady Ashley was, more or less, Lady Twysden; Mike Campbell was Pat Guthrie; Robert Cohn was Harold Loeb; and the bullfighter Pedro Romero was Niño de La Palma. The Champs-Élysées regulars would know the originals, and see the correspondence between Hemingway and Barnes, the narrator of the story. Barnes was a reporter and sportsman who could be tough, sardonic, and honest, sensationally honest. Undressing for bed, he looked in the mirror. "Of all the ways to be wounded. I suppose it was funny," he thought, funny having the desire but not the ability or, perhaps, the apparatus. Away from the mirror, Jake had "a rotten habit of picturing the bedroom scenes of [his] friends," and while as narrator he stopped short of describing the scenes, he showed his friends' drunkenness, whoring, and debauchery. They were the *génération perdue*.

The lost generation was in revolt against the complacent generation, the America that had descended from Jonathan Edwards and Anthony Comstock, the America that in 1924 had rallied round the campaign slogans "Don't Rock the Boat" and "Keep Cool with Coolidge." Still, the provocative aspects of *The Sun Also Rises* could also be found in the popular music, fiction, melodrama, and movies of the era, and while Hemingway and Scribners had no use for such genres, they had at least some interest in their wide audiences. From Port Arthur, Texas, to New York, New York, the true confession and sex magazines sold thousands of copies, to men as well as women. In 1925 one magazine editor advised prospective contributors: "Here's a man, see? And his wife, see? And another man. Write about that. And let the shadow of a bed be on every page but never let the bed appear." Another editor announced:

> I am particularly partial to the story attacking conventional morals, exposing their hypocrisy and pointing to a higher standard. And the moral of a story need not be the conventional one: it can be personal, original, even weird, if it can be put over as superior to existent morality.

The demand for racy material was so heavy that one editor told prospective contributors he would pay for "sex stories" on acceptance, other stories on their appearance in print.

Book publishers were no less ready to merchandise sex, especially when the work could pass as literary. Alfred Knopf had only recently published Willa Cather's *Youth and the Bright Medusa*, a story collection that opened with "Coming, Aphrodite!" Cleaning out his closet one day, a painter finds a knothole, peeks through, and sees his neighbor exercising, naked, before her mirror. "He had never seen a woman's body so beautiful as this one—positively glorious in action." He begins to imagine painting her, and the language the author uses, the "explosions" and "discharges" as the painter traces "the up-thrust chin or the lifted breasts," turns voyeurism into masturbatory fantasy. If, according to the *Nation*, *Youth and the Bright Medusa* was "the triumph of mind over Nebraska," then *The Sun Also Rises* was the triumph of mind over Oak Park. And if (as Louise Perkins had foretold) Max Perkins would have to fight for the Hemingway novel, the question would center on why Scribners, rather than Knopf or Liveright or another upstart house, should publish it.

In late May the Scribner editorial board convened. A vigorous discussion ensued, and when the vote went for *The Sun Also Rises*, Perkins may have swallowed hard. An uneasy champion of the novel, he had told Fitzgerald that it was "almost unpublishable." Hemingway, on the other hand, was ecstatic. For an author accustomed to payment in copies, the fifteen-hundred-dollar advance looked enormous.

Less than three days after that board meeting, Scribners published Hemingway's *The Torrents of Spring*. The novel was twice a stunt: it was a parody and (knocked out in a fortnight) the work of a prodigy. Though the latter was enough to earn the book attention, the print run was 1,250 copies, fewer than Liveright had ordered for *In Our Time*. No one had counted on large sales. Three advertisements appeared in the *New York Times* (two of them omnibus advertisements for Scribners books) and none in *Publishers' Weekly*, for Scribners had taken on *The Torrents of Spring* chiefly to establish a relationship with the author. Whatever publicity the novel generated was rather like a movie trailer for Hemingway's next work.

The presentation of *The Torrents of Spring* was nonetheless handsome. The paper was heavy, the margins and spacing wide, and the book fatter than the word count justified. "The publishers have given the book a dress fit for a masterpiece," the *Outlook and Independent* wrote. "If the book proves to be the 'Don Quixote' of the Chicago School it will be labor well spent on their part." Reviews that appeared in the *Springfield* (Massachusetts) *Evening Union*, the *Columbus* (Ohio) *Dispatch*, the *Louisville* (Kentucky) *Herald Post*, the *Portland Oregonian*, and other such papers concluded that Hemingway was no Cervantes. Many reviewers made a fetish of the author, though, less because the novel was literary "news" than because Hemingway was good copy.

According to Margery Latimer in the *New York Herald Tribune Books*, "Mr. Hemingway's name, which one hears everywhere now, [may be] more familiar than his prose, which is narrow, robust and excellent in its limited area." While the *New York World* ended its review of *The Torrents of Spring* with a paragraph about Hemingway (a northern Illinois native who "had an interesting youth with his father, a physician"), the *Nation*, the *Kansas City Star*, and *Time* magazine opened on—and personalized—the author. "Ernest Hemingway says he wrote this novel in ten days," Allen Tate announced in the *Nation*, "and there is no reason for believing that Mr. Hemingway, besides being the best contemporary writer of eighteenth-century prose, is also a liar. The novel is short." Driven by the five *W*s, the *Kansas City Star* stressed *who* over *what* in lauding its adopted native son and his new book. "This young Ernest Hemingway, who left the staff of The Star in the early days of the World War, volunteered in the Italian army and got himself gloriously shot up, has, in spite of it all, not lost his love for shooting. That is proved by his audacious little volume, 'The Torrents of Spring.' " And, finally, *Time*: "It seems that young Mr. Hemingway, who works like a nailer over his own writing, with extraordinarily promising results, was going about his business in Paris, lunching frequently with Scott Fitzgerald, Ford Madox Ford, John Dos Passos and even H. G. Wells, when a copy of *Black* [*sic*] *Laughter* by Sherwood Anderson reached him and caused him a bit of a pain." Though Hemingway taunted his mother about reading "the *Atlantic Monthly* just so some one would see [her] doing it," he must have been happy to have had an association with Wells (whom he would not meet until 1940) mentioned in *Time*'s review.

Hemingway had come from nowhere to nascent prominence in a period defined not only by the sort of American journalism that *Time* advocated but also by the final stage of the conversion of "readers" into "markets." Like cosmetics, automobiles, or motion pictures, publishing was an industry whose future depended on turning out a product for a mass audience. The author was part of that product, the more promotable the better. And though an "ultra conservative" like Charles Scribner may have thought that trading on an author as liar or veteran or nailer was vulgar, other publishers thought it merely good business. The movie industry, for instance, saw movies as packages and used such names as "Fannie Hurst" or "Anita Loos" as colorful lures on the posters outside the local theater. In addition, the movie industry had urged the book industry to follow suit. In 1919 the advertising and publicity director for Vitagraph Motion Picture Company had four recommendations for readers of *Publishers' Weekly*. One, publishers should produce rather than overproduce. Two, bookstores should be less "points of exchange" (dollars for books) than cultural and recreational trade marts. Three, publishers and bookstores should cultivate a reading public that buys books. And four, the industry should lay aside its "dignity" and stress the human interest that books and their authors generate.

The *Authors' League Bulletin* had noted as early as 1919 that "to the author with a living, moving story, which is capable of visualization, [the screen] offers a field as wide or wider than the printed page." For Ernest Hemingway, for the moment, the point was moot: *The Torrents of Springs* was not a story for the screen. Finally, though, as a parody of Sherwood Anderson, it was not only a literary jeu d'esprit but the sort of personality contest (Anderson vs. Hemingway) that was catnip to the American book press of the 1920s. And the reviews that brought Hemingway such vast notice were truly a fine set of coming attractions for *The Sun Also Rises*.

In spring 1926 Scott Fitzgerald read *The Sun Also Rises* in manuscript and recommended that Hemingway cut the first fifteen or so pages, essentially the backstory of Cohn and Lady Ashley. Loosely written, Fitzgerald noted, the pages tended "to envelope [sic] or (and as it usually turns out) to *embalm* in mere wordiness an anecdote thats casually appealed to you." In manuscript *The Sun Also Rises* was not a conventional narrative that, conventionally, began on a strong note. Hollywood had accustomed movie audiences to strong hooks, though, and the ambitious novelist could not squander the opening of a work. Fitzgerald did not refer to motion pictures in his critique of *The Sun Also Rises*; still, he mirrored their ethos. "When so many people can write well & the competition is so heavy," he told Hemingway, "I can't imagine how you could have done these first 20 pages so ~~carelessly~~ casually. You can't *play* with peoples attention. . . . I can't tell you the sense of disappointment that beginning with [Jake's] elephantine facetiousness XXXXXXXXXX gave me. Please do what you can about it in proof." In one sense, the motion picture was the real competition. And, in another, the movies' sine qua non was people's attention.

Hemingway reread the pages. Popular success was important, but popular success alone would align him with Michael Arlen or Sinclair Lewis. Fitzgerald had noted that the "false start" on the manuscript of *The Sun Also Rises* reminded him of Michael Arlen, a comparison sure to nettle Hemingway. And Sinclair Lewis (then, as later, to Hemingway) was "that freckled prick" whose sales, productivity, and sloppy prose were all of a piece. Hemingway nonetheless heeded Fitzgerald's advice and lopped off the opening pages, including a passage that sounded autobiographical. "Like all newspaper men," Jake Barnes confessed, "I have always wanted to write a novel, and I suppose, now that I am doing it, the novel will have that awful taking-the-pen-in-hand quality that afflicts newspaper men when they start to write their own book." Perkins could understand why the whole section had been cut, he told the author, but he also thought that, recast, a sort of prologue could help "a reader to whom your way of writing will be new and in many cases strange." The author would not bend and later explained why.

> I would like very much to do it for you but I think we'll find maybe, in the end, that what I lose by not compromising now we may all cash in on later. . . . You see I would like, if you wanted, to write books for Scribner's to publish, for many years and would like them to be good books . . . with luck learning to write better all the time—and learning how things work and what the whole thing is about. . . . I'm very sure one will [sell] if they really are good—and if I learn to make them a

lot better—but I'll never be able to do that and will just get caught in the machine if I start worrying about that—or considering it the selling.

Like Fitzgerald, Perkins advocated clarity and concessions to the audience; he said nothing more about a foreword, though, since on other points he could not afford to be silent. Editors were educators, Kenneth McCormick observed; they taught authors the publishing process. Perkins would start with names and "words."

Perkins was uncomfortable with the nasty fun that Hemingway poked at Joe Hergesheimer, Glenway Wescott, and Henry James. " 'What was the matter with James?' " a beanery customer had asked in *The Torrents of Spring*. When Perkins asked the same question apropos *The Sun Also Rises*, about a reference to an accident that reportedly wounded James sexually, Hemingway said that James was "simply an historical example" in the dialogue. Like Sherwood Anderson in *The Torrents of Spring*, James and others in *The Sun Also Rises* were targets for literary and oedipal potshots; they allowed Hemingway to claim an association with the literary establishment even as he scorned the pleasure of their company. But Perkins was resolute. "Henry James's bicycle" became "Henry's bicycle."

"The bulls have no balls," Mike Campbell said. Because Hemingway lived abroad, Perkins wrote the author in July 1926, he was probably unaware of the "moronic yappers" who attacked publishers "not only on grounds of eroticism which could not hold here, but upon that of 'decency', which means *words*." An item on the New York state legislative agenda of 1923, the clean books bill opposed "indecency" and "words" in novels. Horace Liveright and a host of authors had crusaded against the bill in Albany. Meanwhile, Arthur Scribner (Charles's brother) had served on a publishers committee with Alfred Harcourt and George Palmer Putnam to study the issue, and when Scribner urged inaction as their strategy towards the bill, Harcourt and Putnam resigned. In the event, though revived in 1924 and 1925, the bill was never passed, so Scribner was, for three years running, proved right. His unwillingness to take on the solons, though, underscores the contrast between the publisher Hemingway had left and the new one he had taken on.

The clean books bill returned in 1926, and, as Perkins knew, was not the only problem. With *The Sun Also Rises*, as written, the press or pulpit could use "words" as calls to arms. The New York Society for the Suppression of Vice (whose sway ranged beyond New York) could be especially dangerous; it could discard the seriousness of purpose of *The Sun Also Rises*, harvest it as one more dirty book, and halt sales. The stink would fast reach Hollywood, where, under the *Formula*, a self-censorship policy adopted in 1924, producers had agreed

> to prevent the prevalent type of book and play from becoming the prevalent type of picture; to exercise every possible care that only books or plays which are of the right type are used for screen presentation; to avoid the picturization of books or plays which can be produced after such changes as to leave the producer subject to a charge of deception; to avoid using titles which are indicative of a kind of picture which should not be produced, or by their suggestiveness seek to obtain attendance by deception, a thing equally reprehensible. . . .

Enforcement of the *Formula* was willy-nilly; by 1926, though, Motion Picture Association President Will Hays had established a Studio Relations Office in Hollywood, and if Scribners had published *The Sun Also Rises* as written and incurred legal action, the brouhaha that followed would have handed the office the machinery needed to hold back a screen adaptation of the novel.

Though Hemingway would not have compromised for a Hollywood sale, he was nonetheless curious about movies. What Liveright was then doing for *An American Tragedy*—producing reams of publicity to sell the Dreiser novel *and* the theatrical and screen rights—showed what an aggressive publisher could do for an author, especially when, like *An American Tragedy* or *The Sun Also Rises*, the work had a blush about it. A scandalous *Sun Also Rises* could of course cut both ways. A cause célèbre could raise the novel's visibility yet lower its value as a property, especially on the West Coast. So Hemingway would cooperate, within reason, on "words," not only because he too feared legal repercussions but because he wanted to do what was needed, according to Perkins, to expand rather than erode the audience. He changed "balls" to "horns," and in a ditty about "pity" supplied blanks for an offensive rhyme word. He wrote Perkins that he would cut whatever he could in proofs but that certain words "used in conversation in The Sun etc. are justified by the tragedy of the story."

Perkins understood that, and more. Gossip about a neutered text could scare off the contemporary authors Perkins needed to sign and thus adversely affect business. Moreover, a bowdlerized *Sun Also Rises* would appear tame. In the best-selling *Green Hat*, published in 1924 by Doran & Company, whose colophon was the tree of knowledge, Michael Arlen had depicted a nymphomaniac (one review called her "a declassée and wanton breaker of hearts") and opened a door for the "bitch" Lady Ashley; he had also, not incidentally, drawn more Hollywood bids than he could field.

The young readers Hemingway and Scribners wanted to attract were not naifs. According to Percy Marks's nonfiction *Plastic Age* (also 1924), college students cursed like soldiers, freely surrendered to sexual drives, and (like Hemingway) read and adored Havelock Ellis. *The Sun Also Rises* was another hot book. Perhaps its literary value would muzzle the yappers while its shock value would increase sales and entice Hollywood.

In March 1925, goosing Liveright and his sales department, Hemingway had predicted that *In Our Time* "will be praised by highbrows and can be read by lowbrows. There is no writing in it that anybody with a high-school education cannot read." *The Sun Also Rises* was also market wise. Though the prose was notable for its concreteness and hardness, and for the scent of the moderns, Pound and Stein and Joyce, its author was no zealot. He had not severed words from their denotations, as Stein had done in *Tender Buttons* (1914), or associated parts of the novel with hours of the day or organs of the body, as Joyce had done in *Ulysses* (1922), or spun webs of archaic and esoteric allusions, as Pound had done in the early *Cantos* (1925). In part he had shaped *The Sun Also Rises* to appeal to readers who found his method too elliptical or (Perkins's word) too "strange." He had understood what was wanted. The plot of *The Sun Also Rises* was coherent, the action causal, and the characters fashionably indecent. George Doran had turned down *In Our Time* but urged the author to write a novel with a "series of shocks," while in late 1924 a Paris literary agent had asked Hemingway for " 'stories told by real American flappers with all the utterest insolence of this kind of animals.' " Brett was a fallen flapper whose creation may have shown what the author had learned from the rejection slips—and limited sale—of *In Our Time*: *The Sun Also Rises* was not twelve pages old before the *poules* appeared, and then Brett.

When published, *The Sun Also Rises* would have what Hollywood called production values, from Brett and the Spanish fiesta and bullfights to the three *F*'s, movie lingo for feuding, fussing, and fornication. Charles Scribner II may have found it a rude cousin to the novels he usually published, but under Jake Barnes's tough talk were the scandal and sentiment that appealed to general readers. Moreover, the characters and moral stance of the novel were at heart conventional, for though the author had portrayed fornication and infidelity, he had not condoned them.

Pursuing the audience, lowbrow and high, Hemingway wanted to serialize *The Sun Also Rises* in *Scribner's Magazine*. The robust content of the story might have benefited the magazine—whose prim stance toward "unappeased sexual instincts" had probably hurt circulation—but editor Robert Bridges declined the novel. He would not build sales on seaminess. Perkins understood; no magazine "with an eye to their heterogeneous public" could serialize a work of debased sexuality.

The new mail-order publishers to whom Perkins sent *The Sun Also Rises* also had misgivings. When Perkins submitted *The Sun Also Rises* to the Book of the Month Club in summer 1926 (apparently without consulting the author), the club was only several months old. The staff had liked the Hemingway novel and thought it would appeal to subscribers. "They really want books they can bite into and which they feel have been worth spending time upon," club cofounder Harry Scherman said of his readers. *The Sun Also Rises*, though, had more bite than other Books of the Month. Henry Seidel Canby, Dorothy Canfield Fisher, Heywood Broun, Christopher Morley, and William Allen White were on the board of the club, and though one had praised the genius of the author's method and another his technical excellence, they cited the "somewhat disagreeable" content of the fiesta novel when they declined it as their featured attraction. The loss was palpable. The book clubs were a vital point in the expanded literary circuit of the 1920s; more specifically, between 1920 and 1925, as the number of titles published increased twofold, club adoption not only spawned monumental publicity for a featured book but, finally, often produced a quick and lucrative Hollywood sale for the author.

In early August Perkins sent Hemingway the proofs of *The Sun Also Rises*. "I've tried to reduce profanity but I reduced so much profanity when writing the book that I'm afraid not much could come out," Hemingway responded. He changed some names, and, moreover, the "bulls [were] now without appendages." If earlier he had catered to Scribners' apprehensions about Comstockery in order to expand rather than erode the audience, he had strong new reasons to keep doing so. "In today's mail," he told Perkins, "there is an invitation to broadcast Torrents of Spring from the Sears Roebuck radio station W L S accompanied by a short talk and the information that 'it gives common people a real thrill, to be remembered always, to hear the voice of a well known, admired author.' (And who do you think that would be?)" Trying hard to keep both ego and humor within the bounds of the parentheses, he closed the letter by asking Perkins to pay the money owed "Mr. the original Romeike" clippings service so that news of the author would continue to arrive.

"Mr. the original Romeike" ran an office just south of the fur district on Manhattan's lower West Side. Each morning the newspapers poured into Henry Romeike's Original Press Clipping Bureau, and each evening, thanks to the battery of clerks who scanned and snipped all day, the papers were nothing but shreds. Tagged with the date, the name of the newspaper, and the Romeike logo that stressed the word "Original," the clippings were then mailed to Romeike subscribers—actors, authors, publishers, trade groups, and motion picture and theatrical production companies; political, civic, and religious leaders; and any and all others who, like Ernest Hemingway, courted or monitored public opinion. A celebrity culture was spawning a celebrity industry (or vice versa), and further south, near city hall, papers also poured into the Reliable Press Clipping Bureau. Albert Romeike owned the Reliable, and because there was money in the celebrity culture, the war between the Romeikes was heating up. For *The Sun Also Rises*, Scribners would use one Romeike, Hemingway the other.

Over the years, the Hemingway clippings were pasted into scrapbooks that followed the author to France, Key West, Cuba, and Sun Valley. In summer 1926, though, Hemingway had been far removed from the literary markets of New York. He had been at the Fiesta of San Fermin, with Hadley, Pauline, and Gerald and Sara Murphy, generous good friends. Later that season Hadley had confronted her husband directly about Pauline. He lashed out, then confessed that he was in love with Pauline. That was the pattern, with his wife, his friends, and his editor. Strike, then repent. Just before Scribners published *The Torrents of Spring*, Hemingway had written Sherwood Anderson to say that *Dark Laughter* was "rotten." He had hoped, though, that his "lousy snooty" parody would not hurt Anderson, for, as he noted three times, "you are my friend." In August, Ernest and Hadley separated, and in September, she proposed that Ernest and Pauline not see one another for one hundred days, after which he could have a divorce. Pauline went home to Arkansas. Ernest stayed abroad, and the tenderness of the dedication of *The Sun Also Rises*, the last sentence that he wrote for the novel, recorded the pain. "This book is for Hadley and for John Hadley Nicanor."

In New York meanwhile, Scribners sent *The Sun Also Rises* into production. "In those days," Charles Scribner IV later recalled, "there was no systematic copy-editing done on trade books before the typescript was sent to our own Scribner Press for composition." A contemporary survey of American books published in early 1923 had shown the result: industry wide, there were misprintings and repeated lines as well as errors in orthography and typography, spelling and punctuation, and diction, syllabification, and spacing. The rise of the copyeditor would occur later in the decade; meanwhile, according to Charles Scribner IV, *The Sun Also Rises* appeared to go "straight into galleys without preliminary work." For better or worse, sans copyediting, sans book club adoption, sans magazine serialization, sans "words," the novel was all but ready for the public.

In early fall Hemingway sent "An Alpine Idyll" to *New Masses*, "the most peurile and shitty house organ I've ever seen." As he wrote Perkins, selling one story "would increase my chances of selling others—other magazine editors must think if Scribners Magazine wont publish his stories— (granted that the stories arent exactly what they're used to or expect) why should we take a chance?" He had mailed *Scribner's* "The Killers" "just to see what the alibi would be." There was none: Bridges accepted "The Killers" in September 1926 and, two months later, two more stories. "The Killers," "A Canary for One," and "In Another Country" were written as *The Sun Also Rises* approached publication. They were complementary and would make a commendable group, Hemingway told Perkins. They were alike. They were about stasis, paralysis, and the author who wrote them. "The Killers" was the most accessible.

Hemingway had again begun the story in the shadow of *Saturday Evening Post* writer E. W. Howe, with an ordinary character poised to confront an extraordinary occurrence. Though finally far more complex than Howe in both structure and technique, the finished manuscript bore traces of the desire for a popular audience. Two gangsters enter Henry's Lunch-Room one evening. They are dressed like twins, in gloves and overcoats they never remove. " 'We're going to kill a Swede,' " they announce, and hold captive the diner staff—Nick Adams, George the counterman, Sam the cook—as they wait for the victim. Ole Andreson never appears. After the gangsters leave, Nick decides to warn the Swede. On his bed at Mrs. Hirsch's boardinghouse, Andreson lies fully clothed; he refuses to look at Nick or even, despite what Nick tells him, to move. Back at the diner, Nick tells George: " 'I can't stand to think about him waiting in the room and knowing he's going to get it. It's too damned awful.' " George has the last word, the useless advice that Nick "better not think about it."

"The Killers" was a story of fragile appearances and hard truths. The setting was a diner that had once been a saloon. The gangsters looked like a "vaudeville team" and joked about " 'kosher convents' " but loaded real bullets in their prop, a sawed-off shotgun. Like other Nick Adams stories, "The Killers" centered on innocence lost. Nick "had never had a towel in his mouth before," the narrator says, and that towel—another of the gangsters' gags—leaves a taste as bitter as the vision of the Swede on the edge of the abyss. " 'What do you think it's all about?' " one of the gangsters asks George. The counterman will not answer. " 'Talk to me, bright boy,' Max said. 'What do you think's going to happen.' " Max could have been named for Max Perkins, in whose hands Hemingway had placed his fiesta novel and thus his reputation. More than innocence lost, "The Killers" was about arrested time, from the diner clock that runs twenty minutes fast (so does not tell time) to Ole Andreson who refuses to run at all. More than arrested time, "The Killers" was about waiting—the gangsters waiting for the Swede, Ole Andreson waiting for doom, and, perhaps, Hemingway waiting out the years it took to become known.

In "A Canary for One," an American couple on a *rapide* train to Paris meet a "quite deaf" American woman traveling with a caged canary. Two years before, the woman confides, she broke off the romance of her daughter and a Swiss student. " 'American men are the only men in the world to marry,' " she says. Ironically, the husband notes, he and his wife "were returning to Paris to set up separate residences."

The O. Henry twist made "Canary for One" transparently autobiographical, for its revision occurred as the breakup with Hadley ensued. It was another story about arrested time. The American woman longs for control, caging her canary and her daughter. Yet the world defies her. Looking at three smashed-up train cars littering a nearby track, she says, " 'I was afraid of just that all night.' " She has " 'terrific presentiments about things sometimes.' " The story is about fear of the unknown, especially the dread of waiting: the canary waits for morning, the American woman for the crash, the American couple for the divorce. And in another separate residence, an actual one, not far from the Gare de Lyon in Paris, the creator of "Canary for One" also waited. Pauline was coming, and so was the reaction to *The Sun Also Rises* from critics, booksellers, and readers.

Begun after Hemingway returned Scribners' corrected proof of *The Sun Also Rises*, "In Another Country" would open with an evocative still life.

> In the fall the war was always there, but we did not go to it any more. It was cold in the fall in Milan and the dark came very early. Then the electric lights came on, and it was pleasant along the streets looking in the windows. There was much game hanging outside the shops, and the snow powdered in the fur of the foxes and the wind blew their tails. The deer hung stiff and heavy and empty, and small birds blew in the wind and the wind turned their feathers. It was a cold fall and the wind came down from the mountains.

"In Another Country" focuses on the relationship of the narrator (the forerunner of the hero of *A Farewell to Arms*) and an Italian major. Both characters undergo physical rehabilitation at a Milan hospital, uncertain of the efficacy of the machines. " 'You have confidence?' " the doctor asks. " 'No,' said the major." The story has little action and only one incident, told in retrospect, the illness and death of the major's wife, which has turned the major even more bitter.

"In Another Country" has slivers of the autobiographical. Like the author, the major prizes language; as the narrator says, the major "spent much time while we sat in the machines correcting my grammar." Like the author, the major has also been wounded in an accident rather than combat, and lies awake nights because he misses his absent spouse. " 'A man must not marry,' " the major tells the narrator; " 'he should not place himself in a position to lose. He should find things he cannot lose.' " As servant of the machine and the leather straps that corset his withered hand, the major stares past framed photographs of restored hands and, "looking at nothing," allows despair and paralysis to overtake him.

It was not despair or paralysis but doubt that overtook Hemingway. *The Sun Also Rises* was "Christ's own distance from the kind of novel I want to write and hope I'll learn how to write," he told Sherwood Anderson and intimated to Scott Fitzgerald and Max Perkins. That ideal novel would favor Literature over Licherchure. "An Alpine Idyll" had been "a leetle literary," Ezra Pound thought. "ANYTHING put on top of the subject is BAD," he preached. "Licherchure is mostly blanketing up a subject. Too much MAKINGS. The subject is always interesting enough without the blankets." According to one review of *In Our Time*, Hemingway was "oblique, inferential, suggestive rather than overt, explicit, explanatory." He would have to be all of them to please highbrows and low.

Was an artistic career an oxymoron? Could an artist have integrity and acceptance? a great name and a great audience? "I hardly think [Ernest] could come into a large public immediately," Perkins had told Fitzgerald in early 1926. Hemingway wanted that large public, though, and reputation to boot. *The Sun Also Rises* raised the stakes. The week he started "In Another Country," he heard that Ernest Walsh planned to publish a broadside against him. The editor of *This Quarter* would contend that Hemingway had "sold out to the vested interests." Hemingway was steamed. As he told Fitzgerald, "Now it seems from a flawless knight of LITERATURE I have become a hack writer in the pay of SCRIBNERS earning these vast sums." Plainly, Walsh had struck a nerve.

In the 1920s, when books lay at the center of American culture, when authors (rather like movie stars) were "celebrity items" in the syndicated literary columns of the New York press, when serialization and other ancillary sales could reach beyond five figures—authors could indeed "sell out." But "selling out" (an expression that had entered the language only a generation before) was at best an elastic concept. "I hope they do award me the Pulitzer prize on *Arrowsmith*," Sinclair Lewis told Alfred Harcourt in confidence in spring 1926. The author planned—publicly—to refuse the award and thus "make it impossible for any one ever to accept the novel prize (not the play or history prize) thereafter without acknowledging themselves as willing to sell out." Lewis was miffed because the 1921 Pulitzer committee had chosen *Main Street* for the novel prize only to have the Pulitzer board veto the decision because the book failed to portray " 'the highest standard of American morals and manners.' " In a colorful advertisement for *Main Street*, though, an advertisement that Lewis called "a corker," Harcourt had brandished committee member Robert Morss Lovett's irate denunciation of the board as a weapon to spur sales of the novel. Surely the conversion of high dudgeon into carnival barking stretched the border between "selling" and "selling out."

Publishers' advertisements had once featured a grouped selection of books from their lists or a socially conscious theme, for instance "the joy of reading." Starting in the 1920s, the advertisements featured individual books or authors. Brentano's had bus posters for Ernest Pascal's *Dark Swan*, Knopf had men wearing sandwich boards for Floyd Dell's *Moon Calf*, and several publishers were considering the exhibition of pictures and text on electric signs in Times Square. But not all publishers were so conscientious, especially when a book was not expected to sell. One notable author learned that her publisher, Houghton Mifflin, had never forwarded a copy of her new novel to the *New Republic* or the *New York Globe*; she repeatedly asked the house to contact the *Globe*, and when the review copy never arrived, she took the paper one of her own. Perkins, however, had mailed out review copies of *The Sun Also Rises* with photographs and a John Blomshield drawing of the author. Though apparently lackadaisical about contacting the movie companies, he had also reserved display space for the novel in newspapers and magazines, which the movie companies closely read, seeking new properties. In addition, Scribners' advertising staff liked *The Sun Also Rises*. They were supposed to show no favoritism, Perkins told Hemingway, but "they of course do, for they cannot help it. The quality of their work is inevitably affected;—and in this case it would be affected in the most favorable way." Then again, the one-column notice set for the *New Yorker* was dominated by a sketch of Hemingway, "whom Ford Medox Ford called 'the best writer in America of the moment.' "

The misspelling of Ford Madox Ford was portentous. The print run of *The Sun Also Rises* would be just over five thousand, each copy sporting dozens of gremlins, from "Muy buenos" for "Muy buenas" to "Lyons" for "Lyon." While common in the industry—Harcourt's *Babbitt* (1922) had 104 editorial lapses, Knopf's *Things Near and Far* (1923) had 107, Boni & Liveright's *Hairy Ape* (1922) had 29—such errors may have been more common at Scribners than elsewhere. Edith Wharton had found *Ethan Frome* (1911) "*very* badly printed. . . . I have never seen so many defective letters and various typographical untidiness in any book you have published for me, and I think a protest ought to be made." A decade later, *This Side of Paradise* was so full of typos that many reviewers saw Fitzgerald henceforth as "a muddleheaded pseudointellectual, a glib illiterate who could not spell Samuel Johnson's name correctly." On *The Sun Also Rises* even the dust jacket was ill proofed, and listed Hemingway as author of "*In Our Times*." Fortunately, reviewers as a rule chose not to notice or comment.

On the back cover of the illustrated dust jacket of *The Sun Also Rises* was a sketch—a cost saver—rather than a photograph of the author, below which appeared a facsimile of his signature. Though Hemingway thought the drawing looked more like Jake Barnes, "a writer who had been saddened by the loss or atrophy of certain non replaceable parts," he was nonetheless happy "to have at last succeeded in looking like a writer." On the flap, where Scribners sold the novel (and the author) to readers, Perkins informed highbrows that *The Sun Also Rises* "was written in a spirit of literary revolt" with "a deep sense of underlying tragedy." He reassured middlebrows, however, that "humor pervades, sometimes pure fun, but often of a satirical sort."

Perkins understood the value of an arresting cover, and on *The Sun Also Rises* he reached out to "the feminine readers who control the destinies of so many novels." On the face of the jacket was a Hellenic figure seated beneath a desiccated bush. Her head was bent to her shoulder, one hand draped over her knee, another holding an apple. Her robe billowed round her exposed thigh. Two apples dressed the title of the book. What Cecil B. de Mille's "studies in diminishing draperies" had done for Hollywood, the artist Cleonike Damianakes had done for Scribners: "Cleon" had made sex respectable. The design—the languor, the apple, the thigh—breathed sex yet also evoked classical Greece. Not too much Literature, not too much Makings, and by early October, well before the official publication date, the novel was in the stores.

"This novel is unquestionably one of the events of an unusually rich year in literature," the *New York Times Book Review* noted and the other New York papers echoed. Beyond Manhattan, though, Hemingway was still an acquired taste. *The Sun Also Rises* "begins nowhere and ends in nothing," wrote the *Cincinnati Enquirer.* The *Springfield* (Illinois) *Republican* added that "after a few chapters, one wearies of the absence of plot or character development." Provincial book reviews once touched neither sales nor reputation. But geographically, thanks to the advent of the book-by-mail clubs, the market for books was expanding. Consumers spent more on books, and publishers published more of them. As such, the trade could not overlook reviews (however scarce) in the newspapers of Bellevue, Nebraska; or Ashland, Oregon; or Oak Park, Illinois.

"What have your family written to you about it if anything?" Hemingway had asked an old high-school friend in December 1925, referring to *In Our Time*. "Oak Park re-actions are swell." One year later Grace Hemingway rendered her opinion on *The Sun Also Rises*. She reportedly found it one of the "filthiest books of the year." The Chicago journalist Fanny Butcher also had reservations about the candor of the novel, and though Ernest could discount her opinion—she was "*not* an intelligent reviewer," he argued—he could not ignore her tending to side with his mother, in print, in his hometown.

Reviews could wound and maim. "The heroine of 'The Sun Also Rises' is another lady of 'The Green Hat,' except that she is a little more outspoken and a little heavier drinker," noted the *Chicago Tribune*. The yoking of *The Green Hat* and *The Sun Also Rises* once more annoyed Hemingway, not least because, as he had told Perkins in November 1926, perhaps misspelling the name on purpose, "I have never read a word of [Michael] Arland." The Bulgarian émigré had become an American arrivé. "He is mostly in moving picture circles," Carl Van Vechten had told Hugh Walpole in spring 1925. "His play, The Green Hat, with Katharine Cornell, is playing in Chicago to about $19,000 a week and he is making lots of money. Also I hear that he is being paid $25,000 to write a scenario for Pola Negri." Hemingway soon wondered what made one sensational book a modest literary success, another a major cultural phenomenon, and by Thanksgiving he had read or at least scanned the Arlen novel. *The Sun Also Rises* was no "cheap book" like *The Green Hat*, he told Perkins. The editor quickly agreed; Arlen's Iris March was nothing more than a "saccharine lady . . . all smeared over with fake 'glamour.' " Hemingway wisecracked that Arlen could rewrite *The Sun Also Rises* and "sell millions," but of course Michael Arlen fans were not the audience Ernest Hemingway wanted to reach.

Authors generally wore the carping of Middletown reviewers as a badge of honor. The authors insisted they wrote books for neither critics nor readers but, as William Faulkner said, "for the sake of writing the books." More conscious of audience than his peers, though, Hemingway regarded books as public performances, and he pored over the reviews, even (or especially) the sour ones. "If you enjoy the stench of garbage; if you can slack your thirst from a bucket of bilge water and be contented; in short, if your thoughts hover around that region of the human anatomy bounded by the knees and the belt," wrote the *Miami News*, "you will be thrilled by Ernest Hemingway's new novel."

The bilge splashed Hemingway and Scribners. *The Sun Also Rises* was "coarse and uncouth as it can be," one reader scolded the publisher. "It is nothing but twaddle and drink." A New Hampshire public library trustee went further. The novel was "worse than worthless," he wrote the publisher, and the library copy "will therefore be destroyed." Countless libraries never bought the novel at all, denying it, for the moment, what Perkins called "a permanence and finality." As late as 1933 the St. Louis Public Library had 472 volumes of Sinclair Lewis and 30 of Hemingway; Boston had 290 of Lewis and 3 of Hemingway. Max Perkins could have cited the novel's epigraph from Ecclesiastes ("One generation passeth away . . . The sun also ariseth") or its characters' spiritual hunger, and defended the book on moral grounds. Instead, he told his correspondents that professional critics had found the book beyond reproach, and, as proof, he quoted from some of them. Charles Scribner was still leery of *The Sun Also Rises*; like the reviews good and bad, though, the letters of protest demonstrated that Ernest Hemingway was no longer an obscure American author.

For the American press that covered it, *The Sun Also Rises* was no less engaging than its author. "It is rumored, with what accuracy I do not know, that Mr. Hemingway has at one time and another fought bulls in Spain as a mode of making a livelihood," the *New York Herald Tribune Books* notice opened. "Whether or not that is true, he writes of bull-fighting with extraordinary insight; he is clearly an expert." In *Time*, once more, he was the observant son of Doctor Hemingway and the cocky American expatriate. Marking his rise in station, many other reviews featured the photographs of the author that would enhance his popularity and develop his persona.

In 1859 Oliver Wendell Holmes had anticipated that photography would divorce form and matter. Thereafter, "every conceivable object of Nature and Art will soon scale off its surface for us. Men will hunt all curious, beautiful, grand objects, as they hunt the cattle in South America, for their *skins*, and leave the carcasses as of little worth." The Scribners publicity staff had energetically proven Holme's point. They had liked *The Sun Also Rises* as much as the advertising staff had, and had in part been responsible for the photographs and personal items that appeared in and alongside the reviews. Perkins wrote Hemingway:

> We have three publicity men in the house and all of them were particularly wild over your book, and have been ravenous for any kind of advertising materials, and anxious to go the limit on any hint. This is as it should be, but it makes it hard to hold them down, and you feel as if you were restraining a naturally good impulse when you do it.

Perkins, formerly in advertising, had furnished the trio "one or two notes" about Hemingway as high-school football hero, valiant soldier, and bullfight aficionado. Less restrained than the editors, the publicity men had in turn scattered about photographs and thumbnail biographies of the author, including facetiae and anecdotes about his personal life and whereabouts. According to the *Dayton News,* the *Johnstown* (Pennsylvania) *Democrat,* the *Haverhill* (Massachusetts) *Gazette,* and other newspapers in Ohio and Montana and California, Hemingway "listed bull fights near the top for recreation" and had "gone to Pamplona, Navarra, Spain, to see the season's bull fights."

Hemingway was queasy about the press releases. Neither he nor Fitzgerald cared for Whitney Darrow, Scribners' publicity head, who had tabbed *The Great Gatsby* a novel for the carriage trade. Darrow has "the wrong psychology," Fitzgerald wrote Perkins in 1925, "about what class constitute the bookbuying public now that the lowbrows go to the movies." Darrow *and* Perkins had sold *The Sun Also Rises* across class lines, and Hemingway understood that squibs and feature stories about him had helped promote the book. Scorn for the marketplace was a cornerstone of the American literary tradition, though, and Hemingway wanted Perkins and others to know that he was not an entrepreneurial author. The mask was convincing but not always intact: in 1925 and 1926, he canceled, then resubscribed to the clipping service that sent him articles and reviews that mentioned his name or published his photograph. "Of course the whole thing that is wrong is this damned clipping system," he later wrote Perkins. "No living person should read as much stuff about themselves as they get through those cursed clippings." He could not stop them, though, because abroad, or so he said, lamely, they were practically the only mail. " 'I know you have to read them,' " the heroine of the posthumous Hemingway novel *The Garden of Eden* would tell her husband, an author who fetishizes his reviews. " 'But even in an envelope it's awful to have them with us. It's like bringing along somebody's ashes in a jar.' "

"Robust, hulking, handsome, vivid, [Hemingway] is probably the slouchiest figure in Montmartre," wrote one reporter who had known him since 1924. "Throughout the seasons he wears canvas shoes; in summer, tennis trousers and sport shirts; in winter, tweeds and brown, flannel blouses; almost always, a Basque beret. This fashion of dress is not an affectation; it is a naturalism." A writer skilled at making fiction look like fact could also, if he chose, turn affectation into naturalism. But Hemingway had changed. In late 1926, no longer second string in the window of Shakespeare and Company, he had replaced his full beard with an elegant mustache. He was prep-school attractive in his tailored pants and white sweater, and, in love with another woman, Pauline, four years his senior, he had lost what he called that "fat, married look."

At last he was becoming known, and (at least in part) for professional reasons. In England, William Heinemann's interest in *The Sun Also Rises* had moved Jonathan Cape to offer a fifty-pound advance on the novel, and though Hemingway would long resent the niggardly advance, the British editions would become pillars of his international reputation. In America, the response to Scribners' *The Sun Also Rises* was strong enough for a second printing of two thousand one month after publication, then a third printing of two thousand one month later. It was selling, and Hemingway was especially pleased when he recalled how Boni & Liveright had treated *In Our Time*.

> Sylvia Beach orders 12, they send her 6. Sells them in one day and has to cable for more. It has been six weeks since Brentano's ordered theirs and they haven't come. Various people write me that they have read reviews and had to order the book. It not being on sale. Evidently they made up their minds in advance that it was not worth trying to sell a book of short stories.

The Sun Also Rises was on sale, but not continuously. Scribners used short print runs; accordingly, rather than order one large fourth printing of the novel, the publisher would order four small ones, so that throughout January, February, and March 1927, copies of the novel would appear, then disappear, then reappear, convulsively, in the marketplace. For holding down inventory and protecting an author from the shame of the "remaindered" book, the practice was sound. For increasing sales, it was questionable, but Scribners' philosophy on most books was a negative one—to avoid losing money. The policy could have comic overtones when the company doused its own publicity fires. In 1924, for instance, John C. Van Dyke's scholarly *Rembrandt and His School* claimed that only thirty-five of eight hundred paintings attributed to the Dutch artist were decidedly his. On publication day, when Scribners' publicity staff released the author's hitherto undisclosed conclusions to the press, the "news" not only made the front page of many papers but lingered on as art experts debated the statement. Having published a limited edition of twelve hundred copies of the book, though, Scribners had assured only a tiny sale. The publisher had greater expectations for Hemingway, but as Fitzgerald could have told him, *This Side of Paradise* and apparently *The Great Gatsby* had (like *The Sun Also Rises*) gone through a number of low-volume reprintings and suffered the consequences. A less frugal house would have sold more copies of Fitzgerald and Hemingway.

Professionally, Hemingway had been "sucked in by ambition to do some very good work now." He had long wanted to serve Mammon and God, ambition and good work. But five thousand people had bought *The Sun Also Rises*, then two thousand more, then two thousand more. The author could sense the audience. "Papa" he now called himself, and around town he was showing off the persona of the sage. "I remembered all your advice about contract-making," Thornton Wilder wrote Ernest, "but I couldn't be as dirty as I resolved to be." Writers needed resolve and honesty, said Hemingway. At the Closerie des Lilas he confided to Herschell Brickell that one writer they both knew was a fine storyteller. "But did you ever notice that when he writes he always takes his pen in hand?" Brickell dished up the pronouncement (originally Jake Barnes's in the manuscript of *The Sun Also Rises*) in his *New York Evening Post* book column, then noted that Hemingway never takes "pen in hand." It was a nice compliment for the author, and for the performer who had begun to portray him so well.

Playing to the audience was of course pathetic and offensive, as *The Sun Also Rises* had shown. The praise of author Robert Cohn's "fairly good publisher . . . rather went to his head," Jake Barnes says. Cohn even plans to return to America when his book appears so he can savor the applause of " 'a lot of little chickens.' " The spurned Frances Clyne mocks Cohn but apparently understands his need; she " 'likes a lot of people around,' " and when she dresses down Cohn, she loves "to have an audience." The despicable Cohn and Clyne are performers, especially Cohn, " 'a great little confider' " who gloats over his affair with Brett Ashley, then, when she abandons him, snivels over it, all in public. Lady Ashley is no less base. She enters the novel as a goddess among mincing homosexual men, and later at Pamplona becomes "an image to dance around." As Jake says, " 'she can't go anywhere alone.' " As Brett herself admits, she wants " 'staring at.' "

Money could buy an audience. Robert Cohn belonged to "one of the richest Jewish families in New York." He had been the husband of "a rich wife," and had funded and operated a quarterly magazine to serve his vanity. "It was his money and he discovered he liked the authority of editing," Jake Barnes sneers. Money could also show that an author, no longer "unconscious of audience," had worked the crowd or concentrated more on the business than the art of literature. When Jake objects to the sheer number of artists and writers on the Left Bank, the *poule* Georgette Leblanc responds that " 'some of them make money.' " Jake knows that an author may earn money and respect. The plain-dealing Bill Gorton "made a lot of money on his last book, and was going to make a lot more," but was untouched by his public. Even as he stored away experience for his next book, he fished and caroused and taught Jake about "irony and pity." Where does Jake stand? In the morning hours that follow the restless nights, he finishes his prayers, then adds an intentionally humorous coda, a plea for what he disparages yet values. "I prayed," Jake says, "that I would make a lot of money."

Art and audience and authorship. " 'We all ought to make sacrifices for literature,' " one character in *The Sun Also Rises* jeers. Another more admirable character does choose art over audience. The connoisseur Count Mippipopolous, a fat man with an elk's tooth on his watch-chain, declines to write a book about wine for one reason: " 'all I want out of wines is to enjoy them.' " And the purest and most admirable character in the novel chooses neither art nor audience but both. In the corrida Pedro Romero attends to the bull and Lady Ashley:

> Everything of which he could control the locality he did in front of her all that afternoon. Never once did he look up. He made it stronger that way, and did it for himself, too, as well as for her. Because he did not look up to ask if it pleased he did it all for himself inside, and it strengthened him, and yet he did it for her, too. But he did not do it for her at any loss to himself. He gained by it all through the afternoon.

Brett represents the threat that audience poses for art. Romero represents the antidote. The bullfighter has "the old thing, the holding of his purity of line through the maximum of exposure." Though Hemingway may have been close to Jake, who shows grace under pressure, who searches for faith, he yearned to emulate Romero. He wanted to write prose "pure" enough to renovate the conventions of fiction even if he had to suffer the pain and loss that "exposure" could always bring. As he would learn, however, "exposure" could have an even more dangerous meaning—and price—in the new century.

Editors could be blunt with authors who were unashamed of publicity (the bigger the better) and who agreed that regular literary production moved a career forward. Within months of the appearance of *Elmer Gantry*, Alfred Harcourt wrote Sinclair Lewis to request a new novel "for next fall. After all we have done with *Gantry* this year [1927], the lack of a novel from you would be sorely felt in our sales next year." Perkins could not be as blunt with Hemingway, and it was his reserve that, over the years, so enhanced their association. As early as December 1926, less than two months after Scribners published *The Sun Also Rises*, Perkins had suggested, as casually as possible, that Hemingway "round up" a short-story collection for spring 1927. "We begin to prepare for the fall in May," Perkins had said, "and a finished book is a much better thing to send a salesman out with than a dummy."

The haste was bad, the salesman worse. "In Our Time came out last November—Torrents in the early summer—The Sun in Oct.," Hemingway had told Perkins. "Don't you think we might give them a rest? Or isn't that how it's done?" Though *Harper's* had already asked to serialize his next novel, he would write another one only "when things get straightened out and my head gets tranquil." He meanwhile assured Perkins that he was working on stories as well as a nonfiction "bull fight book." He could not be rushed, because if *The Sun Also Rises* experienced prolonged sales, "there will be a lot of people with the knife out very eager to see me slipping—and the best way to handle that is not to slip." Two days after he sent that paranoid note, he filed divorce papers. The law and the banns would help straighten out the failed marriage to Hadley and the romance with Pauline; they were soluble problems compared with the relationship of author and audience.

Sales were integers of "exposure," as Hemingway, who requested and pondered sales reports, understood. He was a counter, and an amasser. A visitor to the Red Cross hospital in 1918 "sat at his bedside watching him pry out a piece of steel that had wiggled its way to the surface of his skin. When he picked the steel loose he dropped it into a pillbox and tabulated the number recovered on a pad. Eventually, the total count was over two hundred." He counted trout caught, he counted miles traveled, and he counted money, money spent and money earned. "What are the sales of The Sun—if it isn't too much trouble," he wrote Perkins when the novel had been out for several months. The question appeared in a postscript, the tone nonchalant, the placement conspicuous. Though Perkins had urged Hemingway not "to be discouraged, except financially," by the commercial failure of *The Torrents of Spring*, sales were an index of audience and the proof that Grace Hemingway had been wrong about her son's goals and profession. For *The Sun Also Rises*, sales continued slow but steady.

Fitzgerald understood what drove Hemingway, and on occasion teased him. "The [*Saturday Evening*] *Post* now pays me $3500," he wrote Ernest some months after *The Sun Also Rises* appeared, "this detail so you'll be sure who's writing this letter." The note further explains why *Scribner's* so attracted Hemingway. Notorious for the small fees it offered even big writers (Don Marquis was one, Fitzgerald another), the magazine had paid Henry James one hundred fifty dollars for short fiction in the late 1800s, and paid Hemingway only fifty dollars more for "The Killers" in 1926. The low rate proved to Fitzgerald and others that Ernest Hemingway was writing fiction "all for himself inside." By December 1926 he had assigned Hadley all royalties from *The Sun Also Rises*, an asset that for years and years would pay dividends as reprints of the novel—taught in college courses across

America—raised the share price of "Hemingway" stock. He had been moved by generosity and guilt. Having witnessed in others the consequences of success, he had also been moved by self-interest. Money corrupts, or so, on Mondays, he thought. On Wednesdays he prayed he would make a lot of money. On Fridays he found he could not joke about what he called the "liturary careeah."

Christmas 1926 Hemingway had skied with Archie and Ada MacLeish. They were new friends to replace old ones killed off by *The Torrents of Spring* and *The Sun Also Rises*. Duff Twysden had been incensed on reading the roman à clef. Hemingway had erred, she later told him: she had *not* slept with "Pedro Romero." Don Stewart laughed off his double, Bill Gorton, but Kitty Cannell was hurt by Frances Clyne, and Harold Loeb was furious about Robert Cohn. "Gahd though," one old pal wrote Hemingway, "aint you afraid Cohn [Loeb] will slip tri-calcium ferro-aganic gas into your aperatif some day? You doan leave the cad precisely untouched." With Hemingway, friendships blazed, then flickered out. *The Sun Also Rises* was the price of acquaintanceship with the Master.

Once Ernest collected Pauline at the dock in Cherbourg in early January, they departed for Gstaad. On January 27 Hadley won her divorce, but it would not be final for months. Evenings that winter, Hemingway answered his mail. "It will be a great pleasure to see you again in Paris," he wrote Chard Powers Smith, who had taken offense at his portrayal in a Hemingway story, "and somewhat of a pleasure to knock you down a few times, or perhaps once, depending on your talent for getting up." Two weeks later, he took almost the same tone with his mother. He wanted to assure her that he was no sensationalist and *The Sun Also Rises* no filth. Though the book was popular and the royalties were already "running into several thousand dollars," he was uninterested in audience reaction. He thought it more important, he told her, "to write as well as I can, with no eye on any market, nor any thought of what the stuff will bring, or even if it can ever be published—than to fall into the money making trap which handles American writers like the corn-husking machine handled my noted relative's thumb." The anger that lined his correspondence betrayed more than the loss of Hadley: in the blackest corner of his mind, he could hear the noise of the crowd and the sharp sound of drawn knives.

Sporting epigrams from Gertrude Stein and the Bible, however, *The Sun Also Rises* was finally a *literary* best-seller about libidinous Brett Ashley and, according to the *Chicago Tribune*, "utter trivialities." For the popular audience, Spain and the fiesta could not fully compensate for the undernourished plot, the static and generally unappealing characters, and (per the Hollywood three *F*'s) the fourth *F*, Jake Barnes's sexual frustration. The author himself later admitted that the novel was not beyond criticism. As he reasoned, impotence was "a pretty dull subject compared with war or love or the old lucha por la vida [struggle for life]." Reviewers alone had not brought Hemingway to accept the fact that *The Sun Also Rises* had sold thousands rather than tens of thousands. A publisher—and not Charles Scribner's Sons—had helped.

Visiting Boni & Liveright in February 1926, Hemingway had met the head of advertising, Isidore Schneider. Hemingway may have encouraged an acquaintanceship on behalf of the promotion of *In Our Time*, but even after he went to Scribners, he and Schneider corresponded. Himself a writer—books as well as advertisements and jacket copy—Schneider had a literary sensibility. He had bought a copy of *The Torrents of Spring* (one of the eleven hundred or so sold), and told Hemingway in June 1926 that he found parts "actually as dull as Anderson." His shrewd comments on *The Sun Also Rises* cut deeper. He disliked "the trick of the plot," the complementary unsexed man and oversexed woman. Worse, he said, he saw through Jake Barnes, who had played to the audience, and gotten caught.

He became fused with you and by the end of the story you didn't do any better than the writers of most autobiographical novels. You gave a goody picture of yourself, as a generous, forgiving, suffering kind of man without any definite character—the blank of goodness that one nearly always puts down when he is writing about himself.

Still worse, "I couldn't like, or dislike the people in the book. I just didn't care about them, except the bull fighter." While Hemingway probably ranted about Schneider's assessment, he could not pass over it, for too many reviewers had also found the characters cold. "The chief criticism seems to be that the people are so unattractive," the author wrote Perkins, "which seems very funny as criticism when you consider the attractiveness of the people in, say, Ulysses, the Old Testament, Judge [Henry] Fielding and other people some of the critics like."

The Sun Also Rises was a crossroads. Unconcerned with professional advancement, Hemingway could have proceeded with only "literary" short stories—which had been a shining critical success. Unconcerned with popular reputation, he could have followed *The Sun Also Rises* with a "bull fight book" or another novel of "dislikable" characters. He wondered whether he could write for himself and a large audience, and have the literary career he wanted. Here, Charles Scribner's Sons could help.

Scribners authors Waldo Frank and Scott Fitzgerald trod roads opened to Hemingway. They wrote, respectively, for the elite and the larger audience, and each author envied the literary reputation of the other. Hemingway saw Frank as one of those "New York Jews" who wrote "a lot of Blah Blah" for the intellectual weeklies or quarterlies. Frank had founded *Seven Arts* magazine in New York in 1916, and thereafter was instrumental in bringing continental culture to the United States and, for that matter, vice versa. He was also a devotee of South American literature. His essays and fiction borrowed from but also criticized Freud and Jung; they also inveighed against American materialism, which he compared to barrels of withered California fruit. Like Hemingway in the early 1920s, he was esteemed by his peers.

Frank denounced middlebrow American taste, loathed the book clubs, and proudly and defiantly wrote for an intelligent elite. Reviews were often laudatory but sales slack. When sales of *The Torrents of Spring* had flagged, Perkins had assured Hemingway that he was highly regarded "by those whose opinion as a rule prevails in the end." Frank had written more books than Hemingway, though, and never won an audience beyond the critics. Sagging under the weight of his literary reputation, he vowed to write a novel that would win both public recognition and—the token of his desperation—Book of the Month Club acceptance.

Perkins submitted the manuscript of the resultant novel to the Book of the Month Club, whose endorsement, Frank hoped, would "help to break the psychological attitude in which American readers have been trained that I am difficult, unpopular, not-to-be-read. (Only to be talked about)." Dorothy Canfield Fisher, an older member of the BOMC board, had told Perkins that she admired Frank's "gifts and sincerity" but could not understand his work. She was "quite deaf," she added, and Frank's book came across like certain conversations—"blurred." Frank would not acquiesce. It was essential, he wrote Perkins two weeks later, to "break the legend of difficult reading, of inaccessibility, which has been built around me." Promotion alone could do only so much. Frank had once more written a book for the discriminating, and eventually the hapless author would leave Scribners for various small publishers.

Though Scott Fitzgerald was also a literary writer, he had an audience. *This Side of Paradise* had been published in 1920, and within seven months, despite the erratic reprinting schedule, had sold thirty-five thousand copies. Short stories in popular magazines, along with *The Beautiful and Damned*, had consolidated Fitzgerald's reputation.

Hemingway saw Fitzgerald as mentor; following his tips, he had reworked the openings of both *The Sun Also Rises* and "Fifty Grand," the boxing story that the *Saturday Evening Post, Liberty,* and *Collier's* had praised and rejected. The longer he knew Scott, though, the more Hemingway doubted and, finally, mistrusted him. His European travels and free spending on cars and liquor suggested a bottomless wealth that, Hemingway later discovered, Scott did not have. Fitzgerald was self-destructive even in his work: he wrote good fiction, then added the bumps and twists that made it saleable. It was whoring, Hemingway later wrote in *A Moveable Feast.* Unintentionally, Perkins had countenanced it.

Though Perkins respected Fitzgerald and Hemingway equally, he handled them differently. In 1921 Perkins had welcomed personal letters from Fitzgerald about life abroad not only because the news interested him but because he could convert it into "discreet but effective publicity." Almost immediately, the promotion of Fitzgerald's work in newspaper features and advertising linked the author with what Perkins called "the flapper idea." That merger of author and fictional world would not die—nor would Scribners let it. On the wrap of *The Beautiful and Damned* was an illustration of a woman who resembled Zelda, almost as much a character in the public prints as her husband, and a man who resembled (as Fitzgerald said) "a sort of debauched edition of me." The book had sold reasonably well in stores, then gone to literary hell.

Like motion pictures consigned to the ten-cent houses, popular novels also had "second runs." In 1923 the *New York Daily News* serialized both *The Beautiful and Damned* and *This Side of Paradise,* condensed and, as necessary, censored. Fitzgerald wrote "talky" books, the editor of the *Daily News* told Perkins, so it had been necessary to cut *Paradise* "to speed up the action" and "get the chapter climaxes necessary for a successful newspaper serial." While other writers appeared in *Smart Set* or *Scribner's Magazine,* Fitzgerald appeared in the *Daily News* or the *Atlanta Georgian* along with "The Gumps" and "Doris Blake's Answers to Problems of Love." The audience was enormous; the pay was trivial, though, usually around one hundred dollars, and the cost in literary reputation incalculable.

Hemingway charted a perilous course, on one side the lack of exposure that confounded Frank, on the other the blaze of exposure that burned Fitzgerald. By 1925 even Perkins had conceded that Scott Fitzgerald's "personal reputation [had] injured his books" and given him "an altogether frivolous look in the eyes of the trade and the public." Too many books and too much publicity could do the same for Ernest Hemingway. "Don't you think we might give them a rest? Or isn't that how it's done?"

On publication of *The Sun Also Rises,* two young women had written Hemingway to say how fascinated they had been by his description of "real places" and by what they assumed was his "vivid and interesting life." Would he please send them a picture of himself? Planning to respond à la John Greenleaf Whittier, the amused author asked Scribners to unearth pictures of aged New England gentlemen that he could autograph and send his fans. It was not time to give them a rest.

"I don't mind reading about Hemingway the writer, or Hemingway the expatriot," Pauline wrote Ernest as *The Sun Also Rises* entered its third printing, "or Hemingway the bull-fighter, or Hemingway the satirist, or Hemingway the punctured balloon, or Hemingway the man, or even Hemingway the artist. But I WONT read—cant read—about Hemingway the legendary character. At least not unless he is in the same room." By 1927, though, the plastic age had adopted *The Sun Also Rises* as ready reference. "All the Yale undergraduates impressed as hell that I know you," Thornton Wilder wrote from New Haven, and at Smith College, according to Malcolm Cowley, women were "modeling themselves after Lady Brett." (" 'Her name's Lady Ashley,' " Jake Barnes told Robert Cohn, but Hemingway would not correct Cowley.) "Hundreds of bright young men from the Middle West were trying to be Hemingway heroes," Cowley added, "talking in tough understatements from the sides of their mouths." Hemingway had become a minor American phenomenon; even his divorce was news in papers from Detroit to Chicago. It was not time to give them a rest. It was not how it was done.

"As for movie rights [to *The Sun Also Rises*] please get the best you can i.e. the most money," Hemingway had told Scribners in December 1926. But money, as important as it was, may have been no less important than the popular audience the author had been wooing since he had performed *John Brown's Body* for company, appeared as Sheridan in *Beau Brummell* in the high-school play, and spun sketches and tales on spec for the *Saturday Evening Post* and *Red Book*.

Though taught in Paris that audience was secondary to craft, Hemingway continued to hunger (and to suppress or scorn the hunger) for the sort of renown the movies could confer, or, probably second best, the sort of recognition and prestige the theater could confer. Novels like *The Sun Also Rises* were routinely optioned and occasionally adapted for the stage. In 1919 Broadway had hosted 140 plays, a record high for the decade. In the 1920s Broadway *averaged* 225 plays each season. The rewards for authors were rich. According to Fitzgerald, a 1926 stage version of *The Great Gatsby* was "something of a *succès d'estime* and put in my pocket seventeen or eighteen thousand without a stroke of work on my part." The popular author George Ade told one film producer that "real winners such as 'The College Widow,' 'The County Chairman' and 'Father and the Boys' [netted Ade] as high as a hundred thousand dollars for a single play before the piece was finally sent to the stock companies." Like the book clubs, the theater was yet another point—and an exceptionally lucrative one—on that new literary circuit of the 1920s. In addition, as Ade well understood, having sold story ideas to the movies for as much as fifteen thousand each, Broadway was entrée to more bounteous Hollywood bids for an author's work.

Early on, two producers William Brad Jr. and Dwight Deere Wiman had expressed interest in a stage version of *The Sun Also Rises*. There were certainly stage and movie possibilities in the fiesta novel, Perkins wrote Hemingway. Like Broadway, though, which would use the novel more as blueprint than bible, Hollywood "would require, I should think, such a revision to make a movie story, that you might hesitate."

In an *Atlantic Monthly* essay in 1915, "Class-Consciousness and the 'Movies,' " Walter Prichard Eaton had argued that in towns where movies and theater coexisted, "the line of cleavage [was] sharply drawn in the character of the audience, and this line [was] the same line which marks the proletariat from the *bourgeoisie* and capitalist class." Hemingway agreed: the movies were prosaic. He was now more than just curious about Hollywood offers and terms, though, for, as he reasoned, authors who surrendered the screen rights of their work were not "selling out" but merely "cashing in." The movies could change what they wished, Hemingway had told Perkins. But Scribners should ask thirty thousand dollars for the novel "*as a minimum*—and take whatever you can get in *cash.*" He apparently concluded that the cash would belong to Hadley (per her generous divorce settlement) and that, furthermore, the movies could not affect what he wrote or how the literary world ranked his work.

"If one feature of 'The Sun Also Rises' demands separate discussion," Conrad Aiken had stressed in his review of the novel, "it is Mr. Hemingway's use of dialogue. The dialogue is brilliant. If there is better dialogue being written today I do not know where to find it." Appearing in 1928 or 1929, as sound movies bloomed, *The Sun Also Rises* might have skipped Broadway and reached Hollywood solely on the punch of the characters' speech. In the silent picture days of 1926 and 1927, though, when the studios could buy Olive Higgins Prouty's runaway best-seller *Stella Dallas* for a bargain-basement fifteen thousand dollars (granted, an aberration), no studio would pay thirty thousand dollars for a "literary" novel that had won only a relatively small reading audience.

Months passed as Broadway considered *The Sun Also Rises*. Perkins was consoling. "These people are the most eccentric and vacillating in the world next to the movie people," he said of the New York producers Brady and Wiman. "You can never count on anything until you have a signed contract,—I must almost say, a check." Both Broadway and Hollywood had

talked of options rather than purchases, perhaps because the lost generation had less marquee value than the Jazz Age, perhaps because Scribners,
unlike Liveright, had not known when to pitch, when to play coy.
Deals for *The Sun Also Rises* might have evolved with Liveright. By 1927,
though the publisher had fallen out with Dreiser over the sorts of Broadway
and Hollywood sales that interested Hemingway, Eugene O'Neill had continued to champion Liveright for spurring on the Book of the Month Club
to consider *Strange Interlude* and for encouraging collectors like A. S. W.
Rosenbach to bid on the playwright's manuscripts. "It is no question of an
immediate sale," O'Neill told Agnes Boulton in autumn 1927, "but given
the time, [Liveright] thinks he can work them up to a big price." *The Sun
Also Rises* meanwhile had only "piddling stinking" nibbles of between one
hundred fifty and five hundred dollars, Hemingway later said, and that too
perhaps an exaggeration. No movie in *The Sun Also Rises* unless it caught
on as success or scandal, Scott Fitzgerald had said early on. And no movie
meant no exposure—no reprints or movie editions, no drugstore sales or
department store gondolas, no features in the popular press or free publicity for the Hemingway short-story collection soon forthcoming.

   Hemingway "wanted staring at." And (among others) Burton Rascoe
was happy to oblige. In early 1927, Rascoe devoted part of his syndicated
column "Sketches of 'Little Old New York' " to an account of an amateur
boxing match between Hemingway and Charles MacArthur. The two had
agreed to pull punches, Rascoe said, but Hemingway was a professional
prizefighter who had boxed his way through college. When the blows
hissed too close, Hemingway decked MacArthur. Rascoe would not vouch
for the accuracy of the tale; nonetheless, "such is the story that is going
around New York." The clipping service sent the article to Hemingway. "As
I never went to college and have never told a living person that I went to
college that just was amusing as fantasy rascoe," the author wrote Perkins.
"But if Scribner's repeated it, people would think I had put it out and
those that knew me would think I was mad." In the next breath he wrote a
parody for the *New Yorker*, with one section, "The True Story of My Break
with Gertrude Stein," starring "Ernest Hemingway—the writer." And he
not only offered Perkins "all the pictures you want" but again acknowledged the obvious, that he could not stop reading the clippings he was
sent.
   Just after the Rascoe story broke, Fitzgerald wrote Hemingway on stationery of the Hotel Roosevelt, "formerly the warehouse where Theodore
Roosevelt kept his jock straps—you remember, of course, how balls kept
growing on him after the Spanish-American war until—poor wounded

heart—he scarcely knew where to turn." Fitzgerald continued to serve Hemingway as agent and mentor; he solicited offers from the *American Mercury* ("Got [Mencken] to say he'd pay you $250 for anything of yours he could use") and *Vanity Fair.* Invoking the Rough Rider, he also showed Hemingway how masculine excess could be turned to ridicule. Hemingway had already asked Perkins to "lay off the Biography," but the steady post-Christmas sale of *The Sun Also Rises* had occasioned a small Scribners publicity campaign. In January Perkins had written Hemingway to request photographs, whether formal portraits or even snapshots, anything that would reproduce. Two days later he had written to request short biographical sketches. "Papers are glad to print almost anything we send about you, and we are very hard put to it. I even took one or two incidents out of your letters."

As the Rascoe story once more shows, contemporary journalism was personality journalism even on the literary pages of newspapers. Careful readers of *The Sun Also Rises* could see that Hemingway was conservative in many ways. Since he had based the novel on real people and real events, though, reporters assumed that he was as loose as his characters. Scribners encouraged the human interest stories about the author, and, despite promises of "discreet but effective publicity," helped manufacture news about him and the book whose sales had reached almost eleven thousand. Sales sparked news stories, which sparked sales, which sparked news stories. "Ernest Hemingway" (whoever *that* was) was good copy.

Absent the personal publicity that the author disliked, the key to the advancement of the author was the short-story collection that had been suggested in December 1926. Hemingway had reconciled himself to the book his publisher wanted, and in fact had thrown himself into its assembly. He spent much of the winter writing, revising, or selecting the stories and sketches, among them "An Alpine Idyll," "The Undefeated," "The Killers," "A Canary for One," and "In Another Country." "Up in Michigan I'm anxious to print," he wrote Perkins in February 1927; "it is a good story and Liveright cut it out of In Our Time. That was the reason I did not want to stay there." Though the "reason" may have been a sly threat to Perkins, who had cut "words" from *The Sun Also Rises,* Hemingway had other concerns about the collection. He fretted over the title of the book (he had chosen *Men Without Women*) and the order of the stories; he was also uneasy about the theme, what he called the absence of "the softening feminine influence." He was aware that the stories alone would not sell the book, and in early February he went to the local photographer in Gstaad to have a picture made for Scribners' avid publicity men. Not yet divorced, not yet remarried, the author may have looked like one of the men without women.

"I want the book to be full 2.00 size but there is no use sending stories that would just be filler," Hemingway wrote. Perkins agreed. *Men Without Women* must not shortchange readers or reviewers. The title would of course attract both. "I don't know anything about titles here in Gstaad," the author confessed in February 1927, and though he had ransacked Ecclesiastes for a better one, he had settled on "Men Without Women hoping it would have a large sale among the fairies and old Vassar Girls."

The "Girls" were key. Fitzgerald had been convinced that the reputation of *The Great Gatsby* as "*a man's book*" had hurt sales, since, according to the mythology of publishing, women bought more fiction than men and preferred books about male-female relationships. *Cosmopolitan* had rejected "Fifty Grand" because it had insufficient "popular" interest, which Hemingway translated into "had no woman interest." The characters in *Men Without Women* were indeed bullfighters, boxers, and tramps. For instance, "Banal Story" was part tribute to the torero Maera, part parody of *The Forum.* Hemingway had included it, he told Perkins, because the prominent critic Edmund Wilson "liked it very much." Other stories also tended toward the literary, but women were present or felt, and often integrally, in such stories as "A Canary for One," "Up in Michigan," and "In Another Country." Stories like "The Killers" or "Up in Michigan" were for general readers, male or female.

As Hemingway worked to finish and arrange the contents of *Men Without Women,* Perkins concentrated on design and packaging. What "the flapper idea" had done for Fitzgerald, "the masculine idea" could do for Hemingway: the *Nation* had called *The Sun Also Rises* "Hard-Boiled," and though the title *Men Without Women* could offer book review editors another catchy headline, the democratic notion of "Men" and "Women" could also rally curious readers of both sexes.

One problem, though, was the scene on the dock in "Up in Michigan." Fitzgerald suggested that Perkins explain to Hemingway "that while such an incident might be lost in a book, a story centering around it *points* it. In other words the material raison d'être as opposed to the artistic raison d'être of the story is, in part, to show the physiological details of a seduction. If that were possible in America 20 publishers would be scrambling for James Joyce tomorrow." Calling on Max as she passed through New York en route to Oak Park, where the elder Hemingways would meet Bumby, their first grandchild, Hadley suggested that "Up in Michigan" needed only careful pruning. If only that were possible: the passage in question was the obligatory scene, and Perkins most likely expected to battle Hemingway over it.

The dust jacket of *Men Without Women* would feature a small bull silhouetted against black. It would recall the Spain of *The Sun Also Rises* and associations with ritual, courage, and maleness. It would recall as well the persona of Hemingway, who, according to gossip still circulating through the press, had once been a bullfighter. The dust jacket was Perkins's domain, Hemingway said. Had the author wanted another subject for the illustration, though, he would have spoken up, as he had on *The Sun Also Rises*. In truth, he wanted a bull but not that bull. The artist had drawn a long-legged bull thin through the withers, with "a faintly lesbian look which might be very attractive in a cow but would never get a bull anywhere." Scribners "defeminized the bull," which Hemingway then found masculine but tame. Perkins thought the sketch "a valuable little mark for the book, useful in advertising."

Throughout spring 1927, Hemingway avoided the novel that, again, he needed to write. The paperwork on the divorce from Hadley dragged through the French courts for almost three months, while her husband traveled to Switzerland with Pauline and later tramped through Italy with reporter Guy Hickok. On May 10, divorced for three weeks, Ernest wed Pauline in a Catholic ceremony. Under the guidance of the bride, and for the occasion, the groom was better dressed than usual.

The parents of the couple were absent from the Catholic ceremony and the civil one the following day. The Pfeiffers were probably invited, and, unlike Ed and Grace Hemingway, they could have afforded the transatlantic tickets. Since 1920 Paul and Mary Pfeiffer had "owned" Piggott, Arkansas—the bank, the cotton gin, the land and the tenant farms on it. Moreover, each of the four children had trust funds that produced as much as thirty-six hundred dollars per year. Ernest and Pauline had apparently not informed his parents of the wedding. Dr. Hemingway suffered from depression and paranoia. He nursed the prophetic fantasy that he would lose all his financial assets, and when he traveled, he traveled alone, for his mental health. Carving out an independence beyond her own solo trips to the East or West Coasts, Grace was pursuing a career in painting. Ernest knew they frowned on divorce, so he planned to convey the news of the marriage later.

Max Perkins, also absent from the wedding, blessed it with sales reports on *The Sun Also Rises*. "We get small orders from points all over," he wrote several weeks before, noting that the novel was at nineteen thousand copies. The reports were a subtle reminder, as Hemingway collected stories for

Men Without Women, that a novel was necessary for the advancement of his career. Hemingway shrugged off the hint. It was "better to write about what you can write about and try and make it come off than have epoch making canvasses," he told Perkins. The declaration may have persuaded author more than editor.

On honeymoon near Avignon, with an heiress associated with *Vogue,* Hemingway was on the threshold of becoming far bigger news than his books. And "news" was on his mind. "I guess you will agree we got Lindberg a nice lot of publicity," he wrote Scott. Hemingway probably thought that he could separate the public from the private self; but like Charles Lindbergh, then en route to Paris aboard the Spirit of St. Louis, he would learn fast and hard that he could not.

By early summer *Scribner's Magazine* had published "The Killers," "A Canary for One," and "In Another Country." Working throughout the honeymoon Hemingway had also completed two more short stories, "Ten Indians" and "Hills Like White Elephants." In July the *Atlantic Monthly* would publish "Fifty Grand." "I think it reflects the greatest credit on you," an old Paris friend wrote Ernest, "that you have been making all the high brow magazines, when most of them wouldn't consider this type of realistic work unless it was of the very highest merit, on account of the fact that most of them number a great many old ladies among their readers." (Magazine editors were very cautious; when *Smart Set* published Cather's "Coming, Aphrodite!" it not only dressed the naked young woman "in a pink chiffon cloud of some sort" but deleted the references to thighs and breasts.) The acceptance note on "Fifty Grand" was a surprise, and a pleasant one, though Hemingway predicted that the story would be run on "special easily inflammable paper with punctures along the edge so it will detach so that subscribers can detach it and hurl it into the fire without marring their files of the Atlantic." He was nonetheless pleased to appear there. "They were too gentlemanly to mention money," he told Fitzgerald. "Do the Atlantic pay?" The money was good—three hundred fifty dollars, or almost double *Scribner's* fee for "The Killers." Money plus status was a windfall.

In July 1927, the news of their marriage having been reported in the American and international press, Ernest and Pauline attended the Fiesta of San Fermin at Pamplona. They traveled that summer—Valencia, Madrid, La Coruña, Santiago de Compostela, Hendaye Plage—and stayed for days here, weeks there. Though he proofed the galleys for *Men Without Women* in mid-August, he wrote nothing more substantial than personal letters. None was more charged than the one to Doctor Hemingway on September 14, a skein of facts, omissions, and lies.

In that six-page apologia, Hemingway wrote that he was now a "public performer" who occasioned "a great deal of talk. I pay no attention to any of it and neither must you." He protested that he had been faithful to Hadley, and loved his son, Bumby. He also added that Pauline was not what his father had called her, a "Love Pirate." He then addressed his parents' embarrassment about his work. Though he posed as disdainful of Oak Park, he rued the fact that he had offended the family, and asked his parents to take pride in what he wrote, including the forthcoming short story collection.

"Now I Lay Me" was another Nick Adams story. In manuscript, the author had called the *I* narrator "Ernie." One part of the finished story read:

> About the new house I remember how my mother was always cleaning things out and making a good clearance. One time when my father was away on a hunting trip she made a good thorough cleaning out in the basement and burned everything that should not have been there.

She had destroyed what her husband prized, the arrowheads and stone axes and stone skinning knives that, hard and durable, avouched his manhood. Her announcement of her handiwork was borne on an arctic breeze. " 'I've been cleaning out the basement, dear,' my mother said from the porch. She was standing there smiling, to meet him." She was standing there, over him, meeting and not greeting him, her power in her smile. "I'll write often if we can lay off of literary criticism and personalities," Hemingway told his father, but in neither correspondence nor fiction would the author keep his end of the bargain.

Hemingway put continents and oceans between himself and Oak Park but not between his career and an advocacy of the American work ethic that Oak Park had fostered. He closed that letter home with a resolution straight out of Horatio Alger or Bruce Barton, the author of *The Man Nobody Knows*. "We are going to Paris next week and I am starting a novel and will work very hard until Christmas vacation," he wrote. He could no more distance himself from Oak Park than he could from the audience. The latter including the critics and the distinction they could confer. "What about all these prizes?" he asked Perkins in the joking letter he wrote the next day. The punch line, though, was at least half serious: "I am now writing a novel myself so I'm very interested."

Other publishers moved at once on such requests. "I have looked into the Nobel prize procedure," Harcourt told Sinclair Lewis, admittedly a best-selling author by 1925.

> Their prize is awarded by a close corporation of professors consisting of 18 members. The procedure seems to be foggy. I have made a delicate suggestion to Stuart Sherman that he take some steps to that end from America. I have written to Cape to see what he can get done in England, and I have asked him to have your Swedish publishers see if they can start something in the Scandinavian countries, and I am sure [German publisher] Kurt Wolff would help.

What Harcourt found good business, Scribners found vaguely crass. Perkins and Scribners had much to offer an author, and though they would watch for prize contests, they would not engage so openly in boosterism.

In Paris that fall, Hemingway had energy to spare. He was "going to write a swell novel," he told Fitzgerald in September 1927, but would "not talk about it on acct. the greater ease of talking about it than writing it and consequent danger of doing same." He bragged to Archie MacLeish less than one month later that "Papa has been working like a son of a bitch and has nine—count them but don't read them—chapters done." The book had started as an account of Red Ryder, the fugitive he had covered for the *Toronto Star.* In a notebook entry for March 1926 he had outlined the saga.

> The flight—the hiding in the woods—the bank robbery in Toronto— the double crossing by his girl in Minneapolis—the arrest—the double crossing newspaper men in Minneapolis—the trip back to Toronto and Kingston—or it will be a story of all the tough guys. The jockeys, the bartenders—the Italian crooks—the pugs—Kid Howards—all the places. It will not be the story of a weak disappointed youth caught and sucked up by fate. It will be the story of a tough kid lucky for a long time and finally smashed by fate.

Months later the story detoured, as Michael Reynolds has shown. *A New Slain Knight* was no longer about Red Ryder but about Crane, a soldier of fortune so dangerous that the American government has denied him a passport. Crane buys a phony one for one hundred dollars, and receives some free advice from the *capo* who pockets the money: " 'I hope you have a long life, settle down and stop all this nonsense.' " The novel was less about adventure, though, than about life lessons. Crane travels to New York with his son. En route he teaches the boy how to deal with *capos*, police collars, and homosexual advances. Hemingway dramatized none of the twelve revolutions Crane had been in, and had Crane talk less about sedition than about crime and literature. "If he ever got started on writers and books he was liable to go on forever and I could never change him," says Jimmy Crane, the narrator and the son. "He was interesting about wars or hunting or fishing or fairies or people or places but he was never interesting about writers or books."

A soldier of fortune with criminal connections could be a strong locomotive for a book. Popular culture was rife with guns and gangsters. Elmer Rice's *The Adding Machine* (1923) and Theodore Dreiser's *An American Tragedy* (1925) had also explored lower-middle-class crime and criminals, while *The Great Gatsby* had portrayed a bootlegger with underworld associations and American dreams. Hemingway had learned what happened when crime, literature, and current affairs crossed paths. "Everybody is talking about 'Fifty Grand,' " Perkins wrote the author in July 1927, not only because it "appeared neatly at the moment of the Dempsey-Sharkey fight" but because it complemented news stories about mob connections to the sport. No wonder Hemingway was stoked: topical and literary, *A New Slain Knight* could be epoch making, his first book for the new American mass market.

The more Perkins heard about *A New Slain Knight*, the more excited he became. In July he had urged Hemingway to concentrate on the novel, not its serialization, but by October he wanted to discuss a magazine sale. *A New Slain Knight* could be the breakthrough, the book that could make Hemingway as famous as Sinclair Lewis. Serialization in *Scribner's* would promote author, novel, and magazine, whose new format (larger type, fewer pictures) would be unveiled in January 1928 in another attempt to rescue the monthly. Parts of *A New Slain Knight* would no doubt be hard boiled, since Hemingway planned to continue to write about what he understood best—"one form and another of killing." Violence could nonetheless finally prove a "valuable little mark for the book."

By November *A New Slain Knight* had reached a reported fifty thousand words; then, for reasons never explained, it stalled. That autumn Hemingway had suffered from hemorrhoids, a lingering viral infection, and an eye injury that Bumby had accidentally caused when they were going to the toilet one dark night. "Figured I could probably write by touch on the typewriter," he told Perkins, "but stuff written on the [typewriter] is not much good—and nothing I write is any good until it's rewritten several times and how would you re-write if you couldn't see?" In one letter after another he wrote about the wounds and ills that had blocked *A New Slain Knight*; as he told Perkins, he had nothing else to write about.

The Hemingways' German holiday may also have affected the novel. In late 1927 Ernest and Pauline went to Berlin for the bicycle races, and there met Sinclair Lewis, whose works were indeed epoch making. *The Sun Also Rises* had been published before *Elmer Gantry*, but when the two authors met, *The Sun Also Rises* had sold about twenty thousand copies, *Elmer Gantry* more than ten times that. Hemingway scoffed at Lewis for his hail-fellow dialogue but envied his success: *Elmer Gantry* had been a Book of the Month Club selection that drew protests, threats of cancellation, and—thanks to both—enormous numbers of readers.

Lewis and Hemingway shared common ground, for Gopher Prairie (*Main Street*) was the brother of Oak Park, and Zenith (*Babbitt*) the brother of Chicago. The author of *In Our Time*, *The Torrents of Spring*, and *The Sun Also Rises* had written no more than a short story about urban America, though, and even an idle conversation with Lewis may have helped convince him that he could not portray in a novel a revolutionist and soldier of fortune rooted in American soil.

One problem was voice. Hemingway had started narrating *A New Slain Knight* in first person, then changed, not because (as he told Perkins) first person was too easy but because it was too restrictive. In fact, he probably could not "hear" Jimmy Crane as he had heard first-person narrators Jake Barnes and Nick Adams. "I should have gone to America two years ago when I planned," he confessed as he calculated the future of the novel. "I was through with Europe and needed to go to America before I could write the book that happened there." Dorothy Parker, who had crossed the Atlantic with Hemingway in February 1926, contended in print that he could not "write of any event at which he has not been present." Perhaps she was right, or perhaps the chances for commercial success that such a novel offered were too daunting.

Men Without Women was published in October 1927, minus "Up in Michigan," which Hemingway had apparently, and not wholly successfully, tried to revise. The book sold for two dollars, the same price as *The Sun Also Rises*, and had a first printing of 7,650 copies, 50 percent more than *The Sun Also Rises*. Gremlins and omissions were minor, though Perkins's flap copy on the jacket noted that the volume contained thirteen stories (it contained fourteen), and that six were previously unpublished (four were).

Hemingway was as apprehensive as ever about the reception of *Men Without Women*. Pauline's uncle, Gus Pfeiffer, ordered multiple copies of the book for friends and relations, assuring his beloved nephew that practically no one in the family was unacquainted with the content of modern literature. Beyond the Pfeiffers, opinions differed. Edmund Wilson called the stories art, Dorothy Parker called them reportage, and dozens of other reviewers continued the debate as notices appeared in the *New York Evening Post,* the *Boston Transcript,* the *Springfield* (Illinois) *Republican,* the *New Yorker, Time,* and the intellectual serials. For a short-story collection, the press coverage was enormous. Once more, though, it verged on the personal. In the *New York Herald Tribune Books* Virginia Woolf portrayed Hemingway as an author who "lets his dexterity, like the bullfighter's cloak, get between him and the fact." The true writer, she concluded, "stands close up to the bull and lets the horns—call them life, truth, reality, whatever you like,—pass him close each time."

Hemingway said that he and Pauline hung reviews "on a hook in the bathroom—as reading matter they run to just about the right length and they're not too much honored by the occasion." He was even less subtle in the poem he wrote that winter, later published in the *Little Review.*

> Sing a song of critics
> pockets full of lye
> four and twenty critics
> hope that you will die
> hope that you will peter out
> hope that you will fail. . . .

In the bathroom or elsewhere, Hemingway read the critics. Max Perkins's associate Wallace Meyer visited Paris in 1927. Drinking vermouth with the author at his flat, Meyer sensed that "he isn't at all displeased by an occasional puff—although he's quite unaware of that fact." On the other hand, "adverse criticism . . . does nothing but unsettle him a little bit." The Virginia Woolf review infuriated him. Yet the sheer number of reviews and the heat they generated not only made him the most talked-about of younger writers but, as Perkins expected, fanned sales of *The Sun Also Rises,* which nearly every review of *Men Without Women* mentioned. It was fashionable to read Hemingway. Since public libraries barred him, it was also necessary to buy Hemingway in order to read him.

The *New York Times* advertisement for *Men Without Women* featured the bull and what Perkins called "the curious incandescence of his most bullish feature." About the highlighted genitals (which were later effaced in advertisements) Perkins had "mixed emotions." They embarrassed him yet underscored what reviewers said about Hemingway, that he described life "openly, frankly, and without prudery." On 26 November 1927 Scribners' full-page notice in *Publishers' Weekly* told the trade that the reviews and "wide-spread word-of-mouth comment make this a book on which you may safely reorder in quantity." Store owners had been stung by "literature" before, thus the word "safely," thus the full, rather than half or quarter page, *PW* advertisement.

The first printing of *Men Without Women* sold out at once, the second almost as quickly. Though the conservative print runs probably hurt short-term sales, they also occasioned notices that touted the success of the collection. *Men Without Women* was less than six weeks old when Scribners announced the "Third Large Printing." By January 1928 the publisher had ordered a fifth printing of *Men Without Women* and an eighth of *The Sun Also Rises*; by April the short-story collection had sold more than nineteen thousand copies, while the novel edged toward twenty-five thousand. In addition, Liveright planned to order a third printing of *In Our Time*, and among book collectors *in our time* (print run: 170 copies) had become a grail.

The book that follows *Men Without Women* "*has* to be good," Hemingway told Perkins, thinking of "the old thing, the holding of his purity of line through the maximum of exposure." He was not the only author caught between art and audience, invention and convention, but he articulated the conflict more directly—and more frequently—than others. The day he finished *The Torrents of Spring* he wrote to Archie MacLeish:

> I think that would be the awful thing about a success because if you made money on a book or in some way got so that each fall or spring or whenever it was you had to have a book ready then you would be a proffessional writer. It might look just as good. Nobody might know the difference. But there would be a hell of a lot of difference. That's why you ought to have about six years work ahead before you get published. Because they might like the first one.

Though the quality of the book that followed *Men Without Women* mattered to Scribners, the accounting and sales departments also believed that a professional writer whose short-story collection had sold twenty thousand copies should be strongly encouraged to produce a novel. "They want to turn everything into a novel," Perkins sighed. "They would have turned the New Testament into one, if it had come to us for publication." The days of discreet publicity were over. Scribners was ready to advertise whatever Hemingway wrote as the work of genius—reason enough that the author found it hard to confront *A New Slain Knight* or anything else.

Hemingway was known. "Author Hemingway was a football star and boxer at school. In the War he was severely wounded serving with the Italian Arditi, of whom he was almost the youngest member," *Time* reported, though only the "severely wounded" was accurate. Conducting a mock interview with the "legendary hero of the bull-ring," John Riddell told *Van-*

ity Fair readers what he saw when the author of *Men Without Women* stepped into the arena: "As he flung open his dialogue with both hands, the bull charged, tail up. Hemingway swung his plot clear and, as the bull re-charged, brought around his dialogue in a half-circle that pulled the bull to his knees. We all applauded." Even Grace Hemingway acknowledged the fame of her son. "Have you any friends or pull in the Art World?" she wrote the week that early reviews of *Men Without Women* appeared. "It would give me standing [as a painter], to exhibit in the Paris Salon or even at a less important show. I'll risk passing the juries if you could negotiate the chance for me to exhibit." Hemingway laughed off the request, not only because he referred to her as the sum of her press releases ("my mother 'Mother of Four Takes Up Painting at 52' ") but because her publicity could spill over and render him more celebrity than author.

"Your name is very much in the public prints hereabouts," Perkins wrote Hemingway, whose style had been parodied in *Vanity Fair* and by James Thurber in the Christmas number of the *New Yorker*. Editors of college textbooks (overseen by Perkins) also recognized Hemingway. In 1927 Harper & Brothers published a selection from *in our time* in *Contemporary Types of the Short Story*, while D. C. Heath included part of "Big Two-Hearted River" in *Prose Models: For Use with Classes in English Composition*. Hemingway also graced other anthologies. And he was required reading in several University of Chicago writing courses. Notorious for pirating *Ulysses*, Samuel Roth printed several Hemingway stories without permission or fees, a corrupt business that, Hemingway told Perkins, cooled one's fondness for the Jews. The reprints were nonetheless an index of market demand, and, fortunately, other collections paid the author. Certain that *Best Short Stories* turned stories into "classics," Hemingway approved the inclusion of "The Killers" in the 1927 volume, then in the 1928 *O. Henry Memorial Prize Stories*. The *O. Henry* was fairly lousy, Hemingway told Perkins. Like *Best Short Stories*, though, the *O. Henry* wanted Hemingway for the prestige and commercial edge he lent the series, and in turn the book conferred on the story the status of a property suitable for Hollywood.

Negotiating the sales and collecting the permissions fees, Perkins talked "business" with other editors and "reputation" with the author. In summer 1927 he had submitted one story to the *New Yorker* rather than the *New Republic* because, he told Hemingway, the former "would give you much more of a public, and a better one too." By fall 1927 the author of *The Sun Also Rises* and *Men Without Women* could reach well beyond the readership of both magazines. *Harper's Bazaar* wanted a story, and *Vanity Fair* a piece on Spaniards; even *Cosmopolitan* wanted the American and British serial rights to Hemingway's next novel and the movie options that would follow.

In February 1927, hearing the siren song of the market, Hemingway had vowed "not to sell or send out anything for a year—unless I have to sell a story to eat." In February 1928 he resolved to have an agent work more actively to peddle "the stuff."

Perkins—and Scribners—must have been delighted. "I mean, good Lord," editor John Hall Wheelock later recalled, "how [Max] worked with Hemingway . . . when he had tons of [other] work to do here at Scribners." Unlike Perkins, who took no commission on fees collected for the author, an agent would charge for services rendered. In return, an agent would know what popular magazine would consider an oblique story because the editor wanted "Hemingway" on its cover. Or what popular magazine would pay high dollar for a boxing story because the editor needed to attract more male readers. Or what popular magazine would take any story because its new young editor wanted to publish new young authors. An agent could market "Hemingway" because he knew its value—in rank, in newsworthiness, in literature. That Hemingway had an agent would subtly enhance his commercial reputation, too, and his appeal and access to Hollywood. It would suggest that the market was coming round to "Hemingway" rather than vice versa. Most important for Scribners, the author's magazine appearances would constitute substantial free advertising for his books.

Perkins had recommended Paul Reynolds to Hemingway as "the best agent for you." Reynolds, who had tried to place a Hemingway manuscript as early as November 1926, was aces in New York, with outstanding contacts in film, theater, and publishing. He had been Willa Cather's agent since *My Antonia* (1918), and as she had predicted, he had increased both her wealth and her fame, selling *The Professor's House* (1925) to *Collier's* for ten thousand dollars. Fitzgerald had endorsed the selection of Reynolds, and then, placing his finger on Hemingway's ambivalence about money, added that the agent would "get you good prices." Naturally Fitzgerald touched a nerve.

In early 1928, concurrent with renewing his contact with Reynolds, Hemingway considered leaving Scribners for another house. "Max Ravage who writes for money only," Guy Hickok wrote Hemingway in January 1928, "tells me that he wonders how so dead a house as Scribners comes to be your gold mine. He thinks they know nothing about 'selling' books, and that you get your 'phenomenal sales' in spite of them." Doubleday had contacted Hemingway, and so had Liveright.

Frank Doubleday had created an enormous distribution network in the early 1900s, then, in 1920, had founded the Literary Guild of America and acquired the Heinemann firm in England. In short, no publisher then in business had a longer reach. And yet Doubleday had the aura of a "money only" company. A cofounder of the Book of the Month Club said that his organization attracted readers, while the Literary Guild attracted consumers who were lured "on price appeal, so that [the Literary Guild] got a reader with somewhat different expectations." Frank Doubleday's son was flinty about such criticism, especially from authors. "I know I do a lot of things that seem to you cheap," Nelson Doubleday would tell Ellen Glasgow, "but I don't do them from choice, I have to make that plant pay its expenses. My father invested nine million dollars in it in all, and it employs eleven hundred people." Doubleday was clearly the wrong publisher for the author of *Men Without Women*. On the other hand, a representative of Horace Liveright had shown up in Paris offering Hemingway an advance of three thousand dollars on novels and one thousand dollars on short-story collections, with 15 percent royalties and—the spark—100 percent authorial control over reprint and ancillary rights. But Liveright was no more responsible then than he had been several years before. Charles Scribner said that it was "not good manners, to say the least, for publishers who have always enjoyed the pleasantest relations to approach one another's authors." Hemingway concurred, since anyone "who would steal a writer from another firm might be expected to steal from the writer too." Strictly speaking, of course, Hemingway had abandoned—not been stolen from—Liveright.

Established publishers like Scribners stole nothing from authors, who nonetheless hardly needed reasons to decamp. Sherwood Anderson went through at least three publishers in the 1920s. At a dinner to launch *A Story Teller's Story* (1927), he rose and said: "Sorry, Ben, you've been very nice to me, but my next book is going to be published by Horace Liveright." Ben Huebsch's staff and friends were in attendance, and, as one guest recalled, it was "a horrible blow" to the Viking balance sheet and ego. In 1928 Hemingway was still chasing Anderson's shadow. *Scribner's Magazine* had paid the author of *Winesburg, Ohio* more for one Christmas story than it had Hemingway—in toto—for "The Killers," "A Canary for One," and "In Another Country." For Hemingway, the issue was not money, he hinted, but fairness. He also objected to Scribners' royalty schedule and (a common complaint among authors, no matter the publisher) what he thought was the slack promotion of his books.

What Scribners doled out in promotion, other publishers lathered on. By November 1927, for instance, Hemingway may have learned from Sinclair Lewis that Harcourt had saturated Kansas City and other towns with banner advertisements for *Elmer Gantry*. When stores were flooded with "gift books" and "holiday books" at Christmas 1927, though, Scribners had eased off "on advertising 'The Sun Also Rises' until the rush [was] over." In fact, the *New York Times Book Review* had carried advertisements for *The Sun Also Rises* throughout fall 1926 and would carry advertisements for *Men Without Women* well into spring 1928. If no holiday advertisements for the fiesta novel had appeared after December 12, Hemingway was told, it was not personal; it was policy. Unconvinced, the author turned to Gus Pfeiffer for counsel. Publishers "can make books sell. Through reviews— arousing interest—courosity. Propaganda etc.," Uncle Gus wrote Ernest in prose no secretary ever touched. Pfeiffer had amassed a fortune in cosmetics and pharmaceuticals and, like Hemingway, valued reputation at least as much as money. Scribners was "perhaps too conservate." It was nonetheless honest, and lent authors status. "You have however no good reason to change publishers and it seems wise to keep them." Perhaps the worth of the publisher *was* its conservatism: as Hemingway had told Perkins in fall 1927, an association with a household name like Scribners could make his work seem "classic and unsuppressable." Paul Reynolds could generate the money, and Scribners the prestige.

Hemingway's mood soured late that winter. "Wrote a story a few days ago to warm up to get back into stride before re-starting the book," he told Perkins in February 1928, "and thought it might do for the Magazine but it is no bloody good." He was the professional writer who could not write, who understood too well the darkness of the Andrew Marvell lines he probably knew by heart, the allusion in "To His Coy Mistress" to the winged chariot of time and death.

Death had pursued Hemingway at least since Fossalta. It ordered his thoughts, shaped his dreams, and followed him to the ski slopes and the corrida. It affected not only the content of his work but the very fact that he was an author, since, finally, he wrote to deny the void. He was haunted by fear and death, as he showed in a pithy anatomy of fear and death that he composed in 1928. As adolescents we see death as what happens to others, he wrote. As adults we learn that we are not immune from death yet still think that fear originates with the presence of danger, that it is physical and transitory. As mature adults, we accept fear as possessive and constant. Fear approaches in the night. "Fear grows through recognition." He later discarded the fragmentary passage but not the convictions behind it. The divorce, the remarriage, and an accident that for weeks left him blind and unable to read or write had been lessons in fear and the limits of control. So had *A New Slain Knight.* He had raced through twenty-two chapters of the novel, then told Perkins that "there is a *very very* good chance" that it must be laid aside until later. He could "fix" the problems, he intimated, and mentioned in several letters that he intended to return to the manuscript. To suggest otherwise would mean that the danger was neither physical nor transitory, that the fear had now spread, which in fact it had. Throughout that winter, it had been "difficult to work." That he was a professional writer may have added to the pressure.

"I work *all* the time," Hemingway told Perkins in early spring 1928. Though not prolific, he earned more and more from magazine sales and royalties, and Uncle Gus's rent checks on the Hemingways' flat at 6, rue Férou (along with three hundred dollars per month from the trust fund for Pauline) freed the budget for travel and clothes, including the maternity wear that Pauline would soon need. The marriage seemed blissful and, for Hemingway, salutary. Wallace Meyer found Pauline "small, not good looking, intelligent, friendly, simple, and quiet." She seemed "a little bit older than he," and was an "excellent wife for him." Pauline was the ballast, the temperate influence on the roaring boy who, when he read Virginia Woolf's review of *Men Without Women*, ranted that he "would have enjoyed taking the clothes off Virginia Woolf this noon and permitting her to walk down the Avenue de l'Opera letting every one, truth, reality, whatever she liked—pass her close each time."

The winged chariot picked up speed. When a bathroom skylight fell on Hemingway one night in March, the horseshoe gash on his forehead was large enough to require nine stitches and catch the eye of the press. The accident caused an outpouring of concern. Hadley wrote to commiserate, Perkins asked Guy Hickok for an on-site status report, and Ezra Pound queried from Rapallo: "Haow the hellsufferin tomcats did you git drunk enough to fall upwards thru the blithering skylight!!!!!!!!"

The accident had been reported in a wire service story that lacked only an attendant halftone to make it and the author (virtually as famous as his work) front-page news. Perkins understood the worth of a good photograph. "Pictures we do want very badly," he had told Hemingway in November 1927. "We have tried to have drawings made from photographs, but they are no good, and all the photographs have been used many times. If you have anything, send it soon." Only hours after the accident, smirking at a camera outside Shakespeare and Company, Hemingway stood with crooked smile and one leg cocked while Sylvia Beach looked up at his bandaged forehead. That snapshot was hardly what Perkins wanted. And so, coaxed perhaps by Pauline, who also understood the power of images, Hemingway honored an appointment to sit for a professional photographer.

Helen Breaker had photographed Hemingway in St. Louis in summer 1921. "You are magnificent in almost every one," Hadley had written Ernest. "Even in the ones that aren't so good of you, there is something of your aroma that feeds my starved soul." Hadley and Ernest later chose George Breaker to manage her trust fund—unaware that he was an embezzler. Helen won a divorce and moved to Paris. Ernest appeared in her studio to rally her and, possibly, to seek forgiveness for what he had done to Hadley, her close friend.

He wore a coat, sweater, and tie to the sitting. He was clean shaven except for his broad mustache. When Helen saw the horseshoe gash, she must have flinched: the prominent wound was so dark and thick that it would wreck the composition of the portrait. Ernest wore his wounds as medals, though, and in one shot tucked cheek in shoulder and pointed his grazed forehead toward the camera. The author as drover, or roustabout, or bullfighter. In other shots he removed his tie and opened his collar; he also wore a cap either pulled down low or tilted to obscure the gash. The key light was neither intense nor, for that matter, spread across the frame. The fill light was equally soft. In one shot Hemingway looked thoughtful, in another sardonic, in another anxious to be done. "I think she is probably a very good photographer," he wrote Perkins, "and that you will like the pictures." The ones that captured the sensuality of the author were indeed stunning. Touring America in 1927, Hadley had found that Perkins was right, "Hemingway" was known. The Breaker photographs would add a striking face to the colorful name.

In between accidents and studio sittings, Hemingway was once more hard and (finally) productively at work. In a new story that resembled "In Another Country," he was writing about what had happened in the summer of 1918—the incidents, the characters, the emotions. The more he wrote, the more it "goes on and goes *wonderfully*," he told Perkins. He was writing what he knew about, again in first person. The finished text would open with a simple and majestic description:

> In the late summer of that year we lived in a house in a village that
> looked across the river and the plain to the mountains. In the bed of
> the river there were pebbles and boulders, dry and white in the sun,
> and the water was clear and swiftly moving and blue in the channels.

Hemingway looked hale in the photographs he posed for in March 1928, in part because the embryonic story was clear and swiftly moving. Pauline wanted to have their baby in America, however, so they were closing the Paris flat and booking passage home. Ernest was agreeable; he had heard about a sunny place off the Florida coast, and reckoned that, like Pauline and her baby, he and his novel could also prosper there.

Chapter Three

A FAREWELL TO ARMS

"WE ARE FIVE OR TEN DAYS OUT ON OUR TRIP OR TRIPE TO CUBA WHICH promises to extend indefinitely into the future. I have often wondered what I should do with the rest of my life and now I know—I shall try and reach Cuba. It is certainly hell to try and write." "Papa" was corresponding with his cabinmate on the RMS *Orita*, "Miss Pfeiffer or may I call you 'Mrs. Hemingway'?" In late March 1928 they were en route to Florida, to Key West, notable for its exotic flora and its gumbo of Yankee, Hispanic, and southern accents. On arrival, despite a parade of visitors, the author continued work on the untitled story about the war.

As usual Hemingway wrote in pencil, on letter-sized unlined paper. Each day he reviewed the previous day's pages, then used the margins or spaces between the lines to add, amend, or revise. Apparently he or Pauline recopied the heavily marked sheets. The manuscript was "going finely," he wrote Max Perkins in late spring 1928. He also expounded on the secret of writing well. An author writes—just writes. He then tosses away the bad, publishes the good, and never thinks "that he must have a GREAT novel to live up to the critics." Brave words, which, decoded, bore witness to the speed—and high quality—of his own work in progress.

The novel that had germinated for a decade had its roots in sketches the author had been writing since 1918. One began "Nick lay in bed . . ." and centered on a nurse and her soldier patient. Another also concerned a nurse and soldier, and though one version of it may have been among the manuscripts that Hadley lost at a Paris train station in December 1922, another appeared in both *in our time* and *In Our Time*. "A Very Short Story" opened like a Brothers Grimm: "One hot evening in Milan. . . ." What followed was no fairy tale. Cool and fresh in the hot night, a nurse named Ag tends an unnamed soldier. The two are intimate, even bawdy, sharing "a joke about friend or enema." They plan to wed, but he returns to the States and she has an affair with an Italian officer that, she assumes, will end in marriage. The letter she writes her soldier boy says that they had been children in love, and that their separation was for the best. According to the ironic final paragraph, Ag does not wed her Italian officer; moreover, the soldier "contracted gonorrhea from a sales girl in a loop department store while riding in a taxicab through Lincoln Park."

In June 1925, two years after he had begun "A Very Short Story," Hemingway had turned once more to war and romance in "Along with Youth a Novel," but the tale of Nick Adams and the Ospedale Croce Rossa Americana had waned after twenty-seven pages. In November 1926 he had written "In Another Country," the story of the wounded soldier "afraid to die and wondering how [he] would be when [he] went back to the front again." Then, in March 1928, just before he sailed for the States, Hemingway found the door to the novel. A wounded lieutenant is carried, painfully, into a hospital and settled, painfully, in bed. More sketch than story, the piece ended with the soldier "happy on the smooth firm bed," where "he lay without moving, hardly breathing, enjoying the lessening pain and the coming of sleep." That image of supineness and arrested motion was the foundation for the manuscript that went on so wonderfully, the work that would eventually become *A Farewell to Arms*.

Though Hemingway developed the narrative without an outline, its long gestation, from the Nick Adams stories he wrote for *In Our Time* to the military books he read, such as Thomas Page's *Italy and the Great War* (Scribners, 1920), contributed to the steady rush of chapters. He completed the opening section of the novel in Key West in late spring 1928. Lieutenant Henry has been wounded at Plava, and is en route to the Milan hospital, the section of the novel that wanted no research. Hemingway planned to finish the book before midsummer, which shows that he projected a shorter work than evolved and, more important, that he was attuned to the market. He hoped for publication in fall, "the only decent time to bring out a book," he wrote Perkins. But since he also hoped to have the manuscript "cool off" for two or three months before he returned to it, he alluded to spring or fall 1929 as alternative dates.

Though buoyant, the letter to Perkins had several curious fissures. Hemingway used "but" four times in the paragraph about the novel, twice at the beginning of sentences. He wanted to finish the novel—but could not be rushed. He wanted to serve art—but could not snub the trade. The concern was audience. Though the *Oak Parker* had called him "one of the acknowledged leaders in contemporary literature," he was peeved that no one in Key West knew him as the author of *The Sun Also Rises* and *Men Without Women*. He bared his ambition when he wrote Perkins that once "I get the novel done—if it is too late for this fall—I could do quite a lot of stories and that would keep the stuff going until the next fall and then the novel would come out and we would have stories enough for a book of them to follow it."

Hemingway had completed more than two hundred pages of the novel when he and Gus Pfeiffer drove to Arkansas, where Pauline was visiting her family. Piggott was "a christ offal place," Hemingway said, but neither the town, the heat, nor the in-laws could wholly stop the novel. By early June the author had completed 279 pages. By midmonth, having driven Pauline to Kansas City to await the birth of his second child, he had structured the rest of the narrative and knew that he would carry it through Frederic's desertion and Catherine's pregnancy. For an author whose metier was the short story, the outline inspired confidence. Meanwhile, after an eighteen-hour labor and cesarean section, Pauline gave birth to Patrick Hemingway. The doctor had opened her like a picador's horse, Hemingway wrote to one friend. "It is a different feeling seeing tripas [insides] of a friend rather than those of a horse to whom you have never been introduced." It was a bluff account. The emotion was between the lines, though, where it would also appear in an account of labor and delivery in the novel.

Throughout summer 1928 Hemingway became increasingly sanguine about the future of the manuscript. Nurse Barkley and Lieutenant Henry were tragic lovers caught up in the sweep and horror of the Great War. The Caporetto retreat was intense, the conflict affecting, the characters sympathetic.

Hemingway sensed the commercial potential. Straining for humor and stumbling over the words, he wrote Perkins that "I think I will have to get a large advance on my next book to insure . . . it being advertized in florid and gigantic manner in order that Scribners must sell a large number of copies to get the advance back." In truth, Hemingway feared the shadow of a large advance: an author at work should not have to contend with the publisher and the trade looking over his shoulder.

"The photograph by Miss Breaker is being used everywhere," Perkins had written Hemingway in spring 1928. "So is a photograph Waldo [Peirce] brought from Pamplona of you and a steer." Perkins had loved the Helen Breaker portraits, but the horseshoe gash on the author's forehead had been distracting. Had Hemingway been gored or shot, the torn flesh would have played as tragedy. He had gone to the toilet and pulled down the skylight, though, and that bit of comic business would play as farce, no matter how much Ernest thought the cut made him resemble the agent of "Big Northern Bootleggers or Dope Peddlers." Perkins had chosen the photograph with the wound obscured by the cap.

As Perkins understood, the Breaker and Peirce photographs would boost sales of *Men Without Women* and even the clothbound edition of *The Sun Also Rises*. "This Breaker woman makes very good looking portraits," Guy Hickok wrote Hemingway. The retouched photograph was "so Rudolph Shiekish that I almost expected to see under it,—'Ernest Hemingway, in Men Without Women, by Metro-Paramount-Famous-Lasky,—Now at Roxies.' " In one sense, that was the point. Celebrity conflated distance and nearness, the extraordinary and the ordinary, and had done so for a half century. The portrait of Walt Whitman in the frontispiece of *Leaves of Grass*, for instance, had shown the writer as an exponent of literature who had the common touch. And Perkins, again moving by indirection, may have counted on the photos of Hemingway, both personality and writer, as fresh bait for the ancillary markets—not only the book clubs, newspaper syndicates, and reprint houses but Broadway and Hollywood.

Only the rare short-story collection sold well, so Hollywood and even the reprint houses were not much interested in *Men Without Women*. "The fate of my stuff has been to always be turned down as too something or other," Hemingway told Perkins, and then later everyone says "that of course they could have published it." Now that the author had been widely publicized, though, an assembly-line edition of *The Sun Also Rises* was feasible. The reprint publishers Grosset and Dunlap wanted the book for the Novels of Distinction series. It was ideal for the series: having stirred controversy yet not been suppressed, it could travel uncensored through Grosset's broad distribution network. The sale would "not bring much money," Perkins wrote Hemingway, for the terms were "fixed, and invariable." There were nonetheless other advantages.

The Novels of Distinction appeared "in all sorts of places that are beyond the reach of the regular audience," Perkins noted, and added as inducement that reprints also "tend to enlarge an author's audience." But Perkins may have confused Grosset's Dollar Library (the Novels of Distinction) with its seventy-five-cent series, which reprinted almost everything that would sell, and sold it almost everywhere. The latter was retailed in stationery shops, drugstores, train depots, and newsstands like the one in Oxford, Mississippi, which, according to William Faulkner, "carries nothing that has not either a woman in her underclothes or someone shooting someone else with a pistol on the cover." Sinclair Lewis was uneasy enough about the series that, despite brisk sales, he complained to his publisher that he was being mass merchandised. Oddly, however, while the cheap editions were not advertised, the Novels of Distinction (stocked by bookstores, large department stores, and a few large newsstands) were, and thus had an even better chance of reminding film companies that an author was ripe for screen treatment. In 1926 the studios had read *The Sun Also Rises* and taken no action. In 1927 they had read "The Killers" and taken no action. The promotion of *Men Without Women* had sparked interest, and by autumn 1928 the Fox Film Corporation was contemplating a twenty-five-hundred-dollar offer for the screen rights to "The Killers." The Grosset edition of *The Sun Also Rises* would raise author and novel higher on the Hollywood agenda.

By late July 1928 Ernest had returned to Arkansas with Patrick and Pauline, who (her husband wrote) had a scar that made her forehead "look like nose picking (a terrible simile)." The story of Frederic Henry and Catherine Barkley continued without major complications, and in early August Hemingway drove west to find a place where he could "fish and work and finish the bloody book." In and around Wyoming, he completed another 139 pages of manuscript. Sentences were his forte, sentences and paragraphs, the "very small compass" that had so astounded Perkins in 1925. The spare diction and impersonal tone were hard to sustain beyond the length of a short story, yet he pushed himself to write long fiction because he wanted a reputation as a major author, perhaps only because he wanted a reputation as a major author. "To hell with novels," he told Waldo Peirce as the summer wore on. "I could write a short story of 12 pages and feel fine and probably it would be better stuff. As it is have been in a state of suspended something or other for 3 or 4 months."

Writing the first draft of *A Farewell to Arms* was leaving Hemingway "mentally pooped." In letters to Fitzgerald and MacLeish as well as Hickok, he called the novel that "bloody book," apparently because what had exited the body had entered the book—the author, the experience, the life's blood. Reading through the entire manuscript in late summer, though, he banished doubts about its worth. The novel was "Swell—cockeyed wonderful," he wrote to an old friend, and he celebrated with a gallon of wine and half gallon of beer. Another writer would have succumbed to the hangover that followed. Not Hemingway, who concluded the letter with a word picture that he immediately retouched: ". . . have gastric remorse today and cant work at all—but will in a little while anyway." No less than the characters, the author would exhibit grace under pressure.

Pauline arrived in Wyoming as Hemingway sent Catherine into labor. The pain and fear that Pauline and Ernest had experienced in Kansas City were present in the novel, from Catherine's moans in the delivery room to Frederic's vain search for religious consolation. "Wait until Pauline and I tell the inside story of our lives," Hemingway wrote Hickok that August, having just read a personal essay ("Becoming a Father at 60 is a Liberal Education") by Lincoln Steffens in the September *American Magazine*. Though Hemingway sneered at public confessions and exhorted Scribners to keep his private life out of the papers, he continually wrote the pain and fear of the "inside story" into his fiction. Should reviewers and publicity continue to confuse "Hemingway" and Hemingway, though, readers would assume that the story of Frederic Henry was but the story of the author.

The first draft of the manuscript was done. After visiting Owen Wister in Shell, Wyoming, the Hemingways drove to Piggott in the Ford model A coupé that Uncle Gus had given them. Back home the Pfeiffers had scooped up copies of the September *Vanity Fair*, for their son-in-law appeared in the monthly "Hall of Fame." Hemingway was chosen because, according to the caption beside the Breaker photograph, "in two years he has become one of the leading American novelists; because identifying his characters has become a national pastime; because he followed *The Sun Also Rises* with the equally successful *Men Without Women*, and finally because although he lives in France he writes about Americans." The other artists in the "Hall of Fame" wore coats and ties. Hemingway wore that sweater and open shirt, and the play of light and shade on his face sharpened his features, especially the penetrating eye beneath the flannel cap. He had looks, glamor, and allure. That the sheik could write was almost incidental.

In late September 1928 Hemingway let the story of Catherine and Frederic rest. He shadowboxed, took long afternoon runs, and invariably thought about the marketplace. He was loath to accept advances or even royalty checks, in part because money tended to slip through his fingers. Ideally, he told Perkins, Scribners would deposit all such earned dollars in Guaranty Trust, and he would spend only the interest they produced. He was not spendthrift but had expensive tastes in western ranches, sporting equipment, and travel. He had allowed Gus Pfeiffer to become his patron and benefactor, perhaps because he preferred avuncular money to royalty money, which was touched by the marketplace and could infect reputation or work in progress. Apropos the new novel, however, he wondered what he could expect from clothbound sales and the lagniappe of serialization.

In the nineteenth century, when it was de rigueur, Dickens and lesser Victorians had designed their work for installment publication. Hemingway had not, though as early as July 1928 he had asked Perkins about *Scribner's* rates for serialization, and in August 1928, in Wyoming, received a bouncy note from Pauline to continue working on the book for "Ray Long [the editor of *Cosmopolitan*] and the publisher."

"I think we have both learned it is better not to serialize," Alfred Harcourt had told Sinclair Lewis. Lewis was so popular and so productive that the ancillary money was incidental and the exposure potentially harmful; publisher and author alike feared that installment publication could siphon off dollars from clothbound sales. Perkins had not yet read the Hemingway manuscript but knew that, unlike Lewis, the author of *In Our Time* and *The Sun Also Rises* could benefit from the high visibility of serialization in one of the monthly magazines. The serialization—since Scribners had little contact with the motion picture studios—could introduce the movie companies to his novel. Moreover, the serialization would go not only into the offices of Broadway and Hollywood executives, to be scanned by story department readers, but into executives' homes, where the discussion of the first installment over cocktails could lead to studio offers the following morning.

Reciprocally, Hemingway was now attractive to magazine publishers. One year earlier, in summer 1927, *Cosmopolitan* had sent him a twenty-five-thousand-franc advance for serialization of his next novel, presumably *A New Slain Knight*. But he returned the check since, as he told the magazine's representative, he did not want the stress of installment publication to unconsciously affect the development of the novel. One year later, in summer 1928, *A Farewell to Arms* had superseded *A New Slain Knight*, yet the author felt a moral obligation to *Cosmopolitan*. Should he renegotiate with editor Ray Long?

When Curtis Publishing approached Sherwood Anderson in 1917 about an appearance in the *Ladies' Home Journal* or the *Saturday Evening Post*, Anderson "dismissed the idea," saying he could not "write to order," a stance that Hemingway had adopted before he sailed for Europe. "Women's magazines are no longer edited for clinging vines," the editor of the *Ladies' Home Journal* told prospective contributors, "for helpless, submerged, and inarticulate gentlewomen," and yet, as Pauline could have told her husband, the magazines were more retrograde than they appeared. Indeed, as one author found out, editors routinely cut the fiction in order to accommodate "the censorship in various states and possible prejudices of some of their readers." In one sense, though, *A Farewell to Arms* was made to order for the market, since Catherine blended the "New Woman" and the "Victorian Woman." Catherine favored sexual expression yet pursued romance: she had an androgynous appeal yet died like a sentimental bourgeois heroine too pure for the world. The serialization of the novel could bring as much as forty thousand dollars, Perkins said, more than the author could earn from royalties in one year, and would be likely to raise the price paid him in the future for short fiction. The "advertising" for the book on the cover of the magazine and the illustrations of the characters within would be another bonus.

For Hemingway, the question was not what the serialization would pay but what it would cost. Perkins was once more encouraging. "I believe, personally," he told Hemingway, "that you would do better to appear in Scribner's than the Cosmopolitan." But he had also said that Scribners *éminence* John Galsworthy had once serialized in *Cosmopolitan*, and that such magazines publish "better things" now than several years back.

Perkins was conflicted—and for good reason. " 'The Torrents' gets praise but not always comprehension," he had told Fitzgerald in June 1926. The manuscript of *The Sun Also Rises* "showed more 'genius' than I had inferred from 'The Torrents,' " he added, yet later he told Hadley that "many people supposedly intelligent, in fact the very great bulk of the reading public, of course, could make nothing of [*The Sun Also Rises*] at all." He hoped that the new manuscript would meet the reading public halfway, and understood that its appearance in a general interest magazine alongside horoscopes and recipes would take the author out of the salons and into the beauty parlors. In short, *Cosmopolitan* could suggest that Hemingway was accessible. It could even help make the new novel a best-seller.

Hemingway was unconvinced about *Cosmopolitan*, and anxious enough about installment publication generally to seek advice from acquaintances and friends. The expatriate American poet Evan Shipman told him that "serializing a book like yours hurts it for the reader. It is only by a real effort that you can get at all the unity that I know your Mss. has. It is an unnatural kind of publication for anyone with an idea of form." Archie MacLeish presumed that Hemingway needed the money but wanted him to refuse to serialize: "I hate to see your stuff go through the sausage mill with the other boys' stuff as though it were the same kind." Even Fitzgerald argued against serialization in *Cosmopolitan*, "absolute bitches who feed on contracts like vultures, if I may coin a neat simile."

Hemingway gracefully declined *Cosmopolitan* but sensed the loss. "I think it would be a good thing for me to serialize [somewhere] because it is not a good plan to wait *too* long between appearances," he wrote Perkins only weeks after he completed the first draft of the novel, "and as I will not have a book out this fall—nor until next fall—due to working so long on this one—it is good to keep something going." He thus wanted to serialize in *Scribner's*, where advertisements appeared in the endpapers, and where passages of serialized novels never bumped up against bottles of Listerine or Hardwick silver coffee sets. Perkins was content. While *Cosmopolitan* would no doubt have introduced Hemingway to general readers who occasionally bought books—its circulation was just under two million—*Scribner's Magazine* could introduce him to intelligent readers who frequently bought books, including those who had once thought he was "above" them or, based on the reception of *The Sun Also Rises* in certain corners, that he was a pornographer. Both author and magazine could gain in reputation and sales. *Scribner's* could use the novel as a circulation booster, and though Hemingway would earn less money and less publicity, he would be inoculated against charges that he had sold out to the slicks. As Galsworthy said in 1923, the "pleasure of being in *Scribner's* outweighed commercial lures."

Robert Bridges, the aging editor of *Scribner's*, could very well oppose the story of Frederic and Catherine as he probably had opposed the story of Brett and Jake. Owen Wister told Hemingway that Bridges had even been offered a selection of Theodore Roosevelt's letters, and he had refused the better ones. Bridges understood, though, that the promiscuous characters and original style of *The Sun Also Rises* (about which he had apparently had reservations) had represented the best and worst of the moderns, and that *Scribner's* had a responsibility to new American literature and serious American readers. He also understood that *Scribner's Magazine*—despite its face-lift in January 1928, despite its boasts in the trade press about new subscribers—was in ill financial health. The book branch of the company was carrying the magazine, whose earnings even for a literary monthly were poor. *Harper's* had a circulation of 120,000, *Atlantic Monthly* 130,000, *Scribner's* 70,000. Notwithstanding what he personally thought of Hemingway or *The Sun Also Rises*, Bridges was eager to see the new novel and told Perkins that he would agree to serialization—unless its character made it "unavailable."

In October 1928, as the first draft of the novel continued to cool, Ernest drove north to visit his parents in Oak Park. Doctor Hemingway was ill. Taciturn and depressed, he could not sleep nights. He worried about interest payments on land he owned in Florida, and he spent hours alone, locked in his office, doing, Grace told her daughter Marcelline, God knows what. He was close to Leicester, the youngest child, then thirteen years old, but he turned away from the others and was quick to take offense. Ernest thought his mother insensitive to his father's condition, more absorbed in her music and painting than in her husband.

Grace had long been the star of the family. In her youth in New York, she had studied with Madame Luisa Cappianni and performed one evening at Madison Square Garden (she told everyone) to discharge her one-thousand-dollar debt for vocal lessons. Since her weak eyes could not tolerate the glare of the footlights, though, her singing career ended before she was twenty. The details—nineteen years old, filling the Garden, earning one thousand dollars—do not bear close inspection, but by 1920 the conquest of the Garden had become part of Hemingway folklore. Ernest mocked her naked self-aggrandizement and, as the years passed, her need for more independence and more attention. And he disliked her for what she had done to his father, he would later say. He may also have disliked her for what he had to check in himself, the appetite for glory and fame.

In late October Pauline joined Ernest in Chicago. They visited the Art Institute, then Ada and Archie MacLeish in Massachusetts, then Max Perkins in New York. Though Perkins and Hemingway got on well, they had met only once before, briefly, and were still reluctant to call one another by their Christian names. They were an odd couple. Perkins was eccentric and prudish. He also loved routine. But he had catholic taste in fiction, and during the visit with Hemingway in November, they may have talked generally of *Scribner's* and the serialization of the new novel, which Perkins had still not read. They may not have talked, generally or otherwise, about money or "words."

Perkins had earlier told Hemingway that *Scribner's* would pay ten thousand dollars for the serial rights to the novel, yet behind the scenes pleaded with management for more. He was as wary as Bridges (or Hemingway) of precedent, for Galsworthy and others would take no pleasure in finding out that Hemingway earned more than they for a serial. But the magazine was in transition and the moment opportune; *Men Without Women* had shown that, no matter the content of the new Hemingway novel, the name "Hemingway" could attract the audience *Scribner's* needed. With Bridges posing no obstacle, Perkins told Hemingway in November that *Scribner's* could perhaps come closer than expected to the rates *Cosmopolitan* offered. Certainly they would "do everything they can to get [the novel], and if they do, will make more of it than they ever made of anything."

Hemingway was as vague about language as Perkins had been about money. The first draft of the manuscript had caught the vernacular of war. During the retreat, an officer segregates Frederic because he speaks Italian with an accent. " 'So do you, you *cocksucker*,' " Frederic responds. The manuscript also contained such words as "shit," "whorehound," and "son of a bitch," none of which Hemingway mentioned to Perkins, not only because Perkins (and in his presence Hemingway) might have winced but because, along with "fucking" and other words in the text, the language would have compromised utterly the chances of an appearance in *Scribner's* or any other magazine. Sensitive to market pressures, sincere about literary license, Hemingway invited Perkins to Florida the following spring. The revised manuscript would be finished, and under the spell of hard liquor and open seas they could no doubt reach an accord on "words."

On November 17 the Hemingways attended the Princeton-Yale football game with the Fitzgeralds. Speeding to the train, Fitzgerald was stopped by the police. My passenger's Ernest Hemingway, "a great writer," Fitzgerald explained. My driver's Scott Fitzgerald, "a great writer," Hemingway added. The "Cop was very nice," Hemingway later joked, "but he had never heard of either of us." As Fitzgerald told Perkins, Hemingway was "chiefly known" for short stories. *Men Without Women* had outsold *The Torrents of Spring* and almost outsold *The Sun Also Rises*. Since *The Torrents of Spring* had been a parody and *The Sun Also Rises* a coterie sensation, much rested on the manuscript in Arkansas, including the great name that so mattered to the author.

In late November Hemingway installed Pauline and Patrick in Key West, then returned to New York to meet Bumby. On December 6 Ernest and Bumby were en route to Florida for a six-month visit when the author received news about his father's suicide. Leicester had heard the shot. According to the cool prose of the medical report, "The bullet pierced the brain looping under the skin, after shattering the bone of the skull in the left temple 5 cm. above and 7 cm. posterior to the external auditory meatus. There were powder burns at the point of entrance of the bullet. Blood was oozing from the bullet wound."

Hemingway wired Perkins for one hundred dollars, sent four-year-old Bumby on to Pauline, and took the train to northern Illinois for the funeral. During the trial separation that Hadley had decreed, Ernest had "said perfectly calmly and not bluffingly and during one of the good times" that unless he could resolve the matter of Hadley and Pauline, he "would kill [him]self—because that would mean it wasn't going to clear up." Short fiction before and after the marriage to Hadley had explored death. The story of Frederic and Catherine would even open with a pointed metaphor of death in life: wearing capes that covered boxes of ammunition, the wet and muddy troops "marched as though they were six months gone with child." The knowledge that life was not always hell was a great prophylactic against suicide, Hemingway had once said. That was in October 1926, two years before the doctor pulled the trigger.

The suicide was reported in the *Chicago Tribune*, for Ernest—and Grace—were known locally as talents. The Chicago Society of Artists had voted Grace in, while collectors had paid as much as two hundred fifty dollars for her paintings. But she could not live on her art or the proceeds of her husband's modest estate. The twenty-five-thousand-dollar life insurance benefit would cover the mortgage and leave only ten thousand dollars to provide for widow and children yet at home. The financial needs of the family were obvious. The manuscript of Ernest's war novel was more important than ever.

Working over six hours daily throughout December and January, Hemingway was short-tempered. "My father shot himself in December," he wrote Sylvia Beach in early 1929, "so now—after having left my family when I was 14 and never taking anything from them—I now finally have the responsibility of them." For grief, Hemingway had substituted anger and hyperbole. The family had cared for him until he was eighteen years old, when family connections helped place him at the *Kansas City Star*. In addition, Grace had announced at Christmas 1928 that she would open her home to roomers and take on pupils in both painting and voice; Marcelline and Sterling Sanford, her daughter and son-in-law, could also help support her. Hemingway was edgy, for reasons less financial than literary.

In the final draft of the novel, the author had tested the bounds of what the conventionally minded would accept: he had treated an illicit relationship sympathetically, a war desertion objectively, and a death clinically. As compensation, however, he had used an ancient mode—tragedy—and once more calibrated the story to be "read by lowbrows" and "praised by highbrows." He had explored the love affair of two sensitive characters, Frederic and Catherine, in language pared down to convey emotion directly and economically. Occasionally he had addressed the audience he courted.

> I do not like to remember the trip back to Milan. [I]f you have never travelled in a hospital train there is no use making a picture of it. This is not a picture of war, nor really about war. It is only a story. That is why, sometimes, it may seem there are not enough people in it, nor enough noises, nor enough smells. There were always people and noises unless it was quiet and always smells but in trying to tell the story I cannot get them all in always but have a hard time keeping to the story alone and sometimes it seems as though it were all quiet[.] But it wasn't quiet[.] If you try and put in everything you would never get a single day done and then the one who reads it might not feel it so I will try to tell it straight along. . . .

That passage laid bare the process of narration; even more conspicuously, it asked for the tolerance, understanding, and acceptance of the audience, "the one who read it." Hemingway spoke directly to the reader—abjectly to the reader—when he was uncertain of the prose or its reception. In 1927 he had struggled with a satiric piece on Spain for *Vanity Fair*, the tone eluding him. "If the reader doesn't like me to write this way I can write a lot of other ways," he wrote, "but I have not seen a copy of Vanity Fair for a long time and I am just trying to write the way I remember it used to sound when I read it." Later he asked whether the reader liked the essay. "I'm afraid you don't. But, reader, be a sport. I don't like it either. I can't seem to get that real Spanish feeling into it." He never published the *Vanity Fair* essay, and cut Frederic's meditation on the trip back to Milan.

As scholar Michael Reynolds has shown, Hemingway also cut the passages that echoed even slightly the purple prose of other 1920s war novels.

> There was a whistling that changed to an inrushing scream of air and then a flash and crash outside in the brick yard. Then a bump and a sustained incoming shreak of air that exploded with a roar, the crash of high explosive tearing steel apart on contact and vomiting earth and brick.

"*Watch out for this*," Hemingway reminded himself. The revision showed what he meant:

> A big shell came in and burst outside in the brickyard. Another burst and in the noise you could hear the smaller noise of brick and dirt raining down.

The original was all pyrotechnics; the revision was more controlled. "I always try to write on the principle of the iceberg," Hemingway would later explain. "There is seven-eighths of it underwater for every part that shows. Anything you know you can eliminate and it only strengthens your iceberg. It is the part that doesn't show." Hemingway wanted to keep highbrows and lowbrows inside the story, to have them feel—not read—the emotion.

The concessions needed to make the manuscript "available" for *Scribner's* were another matter. Though magazine publishers could not afford to risk censorship or loss of audience, authors of war fiction could not avoid the gruesome, and in revising the manuscript Hemingway strove to elevate art and integrity over social and moral constraints. He retained the profanity and vulgarity, especially the stronger examples. He must have known that they would be cut, yet words like "fucking" not only accurately represented soldiers' speech but made expressions like "son of a bitch" more palatable by comparison. He also retained the accounts of medical procedures, including Catherine's labor and delivery. At Key West he even added details that *Scribner's* readers would not have encountered in that or most other magazines—the cutting, the stitches, and the wound, all of which made the operating theater resemble "a drawing of the Inquisition."

Founded on morbid recollections of Patrick Hemingway's birth, the account of the cesarean section was heavily revised. Hemingway not only added the word "forcep-spread" to the depiction of Catherine's "great long, thick-edged, wound" but also reduced her skin to shoe leather: "I watched the wound closed into a high welted ridge with quick skilful-looking stitches like a cobbler's, and was glad." The assault on human flesh was harsh. It was also anonymous. In revisions Hemingway stressed that the surgeon was masked and that another "doctor in a mask gave the anaesthetic. Two nurses in masks handed things." Veiled figures dominated the text. *They* sent nations to war, and *they* fixed the horse races the lovers attended. At Caporetto, Frederic renounced not war but *them*: "I was not against them. I was through. I wished them all the luck."

Hemingway understood *them*, the masked forms who, like the surgeons, were the "people with the knife out." Finishing the manuscript, he had racing thoughts. Should *they* remove passages or words from the story of Frederic and Catherine, *they* would affirm that, as Frederic said, "they killed you in the end. You could count on that. Stay around and they would kill you." Should *they* leave the manuscript intact, *they* would invite the bluenoses to damn the novel as succès de scandale. Should *they* decide that the book was only as good as *The Sun Also Rises* or *Men Without Women* . . . Hemingway could not postpone the inevitable, since "the only way you can keep a thing is to lose it." The exhausted author declared the manuscript done, and once more invited Perkins to Key West, "the sooner you come down the better."

Perkins hated travel, and hated vacations more than travel; he characterized one long summer holiday as "unavoidable." Heading south in 1929, he had left behind one thousand undigested pages of Thomas Wolfe's *O Lost*, eventually to become *Look Homeward, Angel*. His mind was elsewhere, and his body not fit for the arduous deep-sea fishing that Hemingway had planned. Though he had exercised at the gymnasium in New York, he had lost at handball to a teenaged boy and then an older man. On repeated tries he had also fumbled the medicine ball. "I thought I was above average," he wrote Hemingway only days before the departure for Key West. "I suppose all men in business lead a rotten life inevitably." What drove the editor to the gym and to Florida was not tarpon and barracuda but war and romance, the novel the author was now calling *A Farewell to Arms*.

Though Perkins had not gone south to assess Hemingway's character, the eight days they spent together not only enhanced his respect for the author but affected his, and later Charles Scribner II's, reaction to *A Farewell to Arms*. The author was ever the performer, the exuberant companion as older brother or teacher. He had insisted that Max (they finally used first names) land a tarpon during his stay. One day Hemingway hooked one and passed the editor the rod. A storm erupted. For fifty minutes rain and sea foam pounded the men who worked the fish, and Perkins saw again what he admired in Hemingway—the stamina, the courage, the generosity. The "masculine idea" was no mere gimmick. Hemingway was authentic, perhaps even noble.

Reading *A Farewell to Arms* was the occasion and real pleasure of the visit. What Perkins would do for Tom Wolfe he would not have to do for Hemingway: the novel was tight and could be published almost as the author had revised it. The narrative moved from the public realm of battlefield and hospital to the isolation of hotel room, operating theater, and what Frederic called the biological trap, the enclosure that *they* prepared for you. The style was also notable for its economy. The *poème en prose* that would open the novel was dominated by static constructions and verbs of being: "The plain was rich with crops; there were many orchards of fruit trees and beyond the plain the mountains were brown and bare. There was fighting in the mountains and at night we could see the flashes from the artillery. In the dark it was like summer lightning, but the nights were cool and there was not the feeling of a storm coming." The stillness and distance of the passage—typical Hemingway—served as an overture to the retreat. In the final chapters Perkins missed the attention to war that, early on, had made the love story so vivid. He understood the art of subtraction, though, and realized that the seclusion of Frederic and Catherine in Switzerland reflected the theme of the novel. And "in a deeper sense the reader does feel that War permeated the entire thing," he concluded. Saying that the war had produced Catherine's condition would only make the conclusion "*artificial*, or too *neat*."

Another concern was less easily dismissed. Hemingway lacked experience with "the 'genteel,' " Perkins told Owen Wister, thinking of the vulgarity and profanity in *A Farewell to Arms* and the author's language on the open seas. Packing for the return home, Perkins approached Hemingway gingerly. The "words" would probably make the manuscript "unavailable" for *Scribner's Magazine*, he told the author, and added sotto voce that "words" would also make it awkward for Scribners and the public. But he knew that Hemingway would put considerations of art over considerations of audience, and that no matter how much the author compromised, the language of the novel would be worrisome. As the publishing business headed into another of its periodic downturns, Perkins had to ready the drowsy house of Scribners for yet another awakening to contemporary literature. On February 6 he wired New York: "Book very fine but difficult in spots."

That "cocksucker" and "fucking" could make a 1929 novel "difficult" was an understatement. Just weeks before Perkins had boarded the train for Key West, Covici-Friede had published Radclyffe Hall's *The Well of Loneliness*, an inoffensive but notorious British novel about lesbianism. Vice society head John Sumner bought a copy, then had the stock confiscated and Friede arrested. Along Publishers Row, stories about Sumner were legion. He was stubborn and unpredictable, which made even respectable publishers like Scribners vulnerable to attack. Brewer & Warren learned that grim lesson when they published Nathan Asch's *Pay Day* and, almost within hours, Sumner and four plainclothesmen appeared with badges and official-looking documents. "I then asked for the search warrant," Edward Warren wrote his partner, "and they flashed on me a long, printed, legal form which, in the excitement of the moment I accepted as a warrant." Sumner then requested copies of the book. Waiting for them, he scoured the editors' offices, and collected other books and manuscripts. As the staff boxed up the confiscated *Pay Day*s, Sumner said "that [Warren] should be ashamed of publishing such a dirty book. Did [he] realize that the words 'God' and 'Jesus Christ' occurred a great many times? Then [Sumner] added, as an afterthought, that this was not exactly obscene." The prosecution that followed cost Brewer & Warren attorney fees and battered egos.

As Perkins had expected, Robert Bridges found *A Farewell to Arms* "unavailable" as written. Hemingway resented the broken promise of *Scribner's*, a *family* magazine, he jeered, yet Charles Scribner II may have shared Bridges's concerns. An advocate for *A Farewell to Arms*, Perkins tried to reassure Scribner about his young author. In Key West, Perkins had "formed a very high opinion of Hemingway's character. Nobody could be more altogether healthy and decent in every sense," he wrote to the publisher, "and no household could be more natural and simple than his, with his wife and sister and two children." Perkins granted, though, that *A Farewell to Arms* was "objectionable" in its detail and "violent" in its directness, particularly its presentation of Frederic's hospital care and Catherine's labor and childbirth. He furthermore ended that five-page letter to Scribner with a handwritten postscript, a tougher indictment than any Sumner could muster. "I was somewhat constrained in bringing out the difficult points in 'A Farewell' by dictating this to Miss Wykoff, but I thought your familiarity with Hemingway's way would sufficiently suppliment [sic] what I have said."

According to gossip, Perkins was more abashed by the language than Scribner was. "Perkins, do you think that Hemingway would respect you, if he knew that you were unable to say that word ["cocksucker"], but had to write it out?" the publisher asked when he and his editor met face to face. A "flustered" Perkins left the office, or so Edmund Wilson told Burton Rascoe. But the reference to Miss Wyckoff (whose name he misspelled) was nevertheless doubly telling. Perkins's secretary represented an important wedge of the novel's market, the audience the book needed in order to become breakthrough fiction—the middlebrow female reader. The generic middlebrow female reader may have existed only in the minds of editors, publishers, and sales representatives. Like John Sumner and the obscene, though, she was much discussed and, however inaccurately, much defined. According to one cultural historian, women dominated the middlebrow world on matters of taste. They selected the furniture, the wallpaper, the china, and the books; they belonged to the Book of the Month Club, and they read popular and literary books chosen by the BOMC judges. According to another historian, men gravitated toward newspapers, women toward magazines, which, more than newspapers, promoted books through serializations. Perkins's own doubts about *Look Homeward, Angel* had arisen not because it was too long but because it was "far more a man's book."

Hemingway had won the attention of female readers with *The Sun Also Rises* and (despite—or because of—the "little bull" and the title) *Men Without Women*. *A Farewell to Arms* would have stronger "woman interest" than anything the author had written—unless he was determined to make it "unavailable" for middlebrow female readers. Beyond the legal challenges, beyond the irreproachable reputation of the Scribner house, Perkins feared that "words" would scare away a portion of the novel's audience; they would suggest that it was indeed a "man's book." He knew what could and had been done throughout the industry, even by Liveright, who had used asterisks for four-letter words in Djuna Barnes's 1928 novel *Ryder*. As Perkins wrote on page one of that long letter to Scribner, "we can blank the words and the worst passages can be revised."

Perkins may have chosen the passive voice deliberately, for he could not say with assurance that Hemingway would revise the worst passages. He understood the author better in 1929 than he had in 1926, when *The Sun Also Rises* had appeared with "horns" for "balls." He may also have detected the conventional undercurrents that ran through the unconventional *The Sun Also Rises* and (at least in Frederic Henry) *A Farewell to Arms*. In Milan, Frederic urges Catherine to wed. They cannot because, she says, " 'they'd send me away.' " Frederic concedes the point, then adds: " 'I only wanted to for you.' " Her reassurances lead him to another question: " 'Couldn't we be married privately some way? Then if anything happened to me or if you had a child.' " In Switzerland, Frederic once again presses Catherine: " 'When will we be married?' " Quite pregnant, she once more puts him off.

A conventional undercurrent also ran through the author. Like Frederic Henry, Ernest Hemingway may not have been monogamous, yet he preferred the role of husband to lover or adulterer. Like Jake Barnes, he may have been smitten with the Brett Ashleys of the world, yet he would not have condoned their behavior (or called them "ladies") had they been under his protection. When Madelaine Hemingway went south to help type the manuscript of *A Farewell to Arms*, her brother reported to Grace that Sunny (her nickname) was interested only in chasing boys and petting. "Dirty slovenly sullen completely self-centered and without any manners," Ernest called her. In another letter home, he warned his sister Carol not to be "corrupted by the cheapness, flipness, petting instead of love, complete self-absorption and cheap, cheap, petting vacantness that has come to such a perfect flowering in Oak Park." And, finally, he sounded more like the priest than the protagonist of *A Farewell to Arms* when he told Hadley he wanted Bumby reared in the Church. Hadley would have the last word here. She would tell her former husband that her son would not "join any church until he's old enough to think or *feel* rationally for himself." Perkins could not be so direct, yet he could hope that the puritan in Ernest Hemingway would reconsider "words" like "cocksucker" and "fucking."

Hemingway had poured honesty and sweat into *A Farewell to Arms*, and would defend the story against charges of indecency or immorality. Moreover, sales of *The Sun Also Rises* and *Men Without Women* had earned the author leverage that he could use to protect the manuscript from editorial cleansing. But whether the age and the publisher were ready for the *appearance* of indecency or immorality was another question. As early as 1921, in the poem "Ultimately," Hemingway's persona tries "to spit out the truth" but succeeds only in having it "dribbling his chin." Paradoxically, by 1929 the patron of candor (if not truth) had an ally in the movies. Hemingway may rarely have gone to picture shows, but Pauline's mother did, and had observed and commented on the freedom of the screen. War pictures were especially bold. A lip-reader in the audience of *What Price Glory?* (1926) could "hear" what daily *Variety* called the "cuss words," and in *All Quiet on the Western Front*, in preproduction as a sound picture in 1929, Universal Studios planned to say those words. The industry's internal censors hoped that producer "Junior" Laemmle would use the English-language version of the novel, which had fewer vulgarities, but even the German version might pass muster; as the studio's censor, Jason Joy, noted, "the peculiar subject of the story and the tremendous hold which it is acquiring on all classes of the public makes me feel that the [state and local] censors would not object to a rather literal intepretation of the book."

Hollywood was not *Scribner's Magazine.* Nor was "goddamn" (mouthed) or "hell" (on a title card) tantamount to a printed "fucking," an obscenity that could cost a publisher its second-class mailing privileges. Hemingway understood all that. Perkins understood further that Hemingway was counting on the serialization money to help out his younger brother and sister in Oak Park, and that Hemingway had declined *Cosmopolitan* because he wanted to showcase the new novel in *Scribner's,* where he could reach a moderately large, yet fully respectable, audience. In February 1929, Perkins wired Hemingway the magazine's offer.

The sixteen thousand dollars was, according to one *Scribner's* associate, "way out of scale of our usual payments and the highest price we ever paid for a serial. We paid that because we were able to publish the whole novel." Hemingway confessed that he was "absolutely broke" (the ostensible reason he took any money for serialization), and then accepted the *Scribner's* offer that would more readily allow him to send his mother one hundred dollars a month for 1929 and 1930. Vowing again to be (he wrote) "not Unreasonable" about the language, he asked only that the magazine signify omissions with blanks rather than dots, which "writers employ when they wish to avoid biting on the nail and writing a hard part of a book to do." He even found he could rationalize certain cuts: readers would perhaps buy the clothbound novel just to see what had been dropped.

Perkins was elated, for he knew that writers could be adamant about tailoring a manuscript to fit the market. Faulkner wanted no changes in the work he finished in 1929. "I know you mean well," he told his editor, "but so do I." Cape and Smith published *The Sound and the Fury* as the author wrote it, then printed fewer than two thousand copies. Low sales followed. Hemingway's novel would have no confusing italics, no Proustian time scheme, and (in *Scribner's Magazine*) no "words." Perkins thought the cutting, like the serialization itself, would pay off. And so he told the author, though he refrained from specifics (the negotiations over each "word" would come later) and used a metaphor that touched more on reputation than money. The serialization would widen Hemingway's public; it would be instrumental in making him "understandable to a great many more people, and generally in helping [him] to gain complete recognition." It was as close as Perkins could come to telling him that many readers had been wholly confused by *The Sun Also Rises.*

Perhaps because Hemingway was so adept in the short form, *A Farewell to Arms* had evolved in blocks ideal for serialization: Frederic meets Catherine and later becomes a casualty; he recovers and falls in love in Milan; he returns to the front and, during the Caporetto retreat, deserts; he and Catherine reunite and sail to Switzerland, where she dies in childbirth. Unlike *The Sun Also Rises*, *A Farewell to Arms* had continuity and dramatic suspense: the love affair, the characters' separations and reunions, and the pregnancy that occurred at midpoint would have the power to hold readers from one *Scribner's* installment to the next. The near-equal size of the segments and the episodic and chronological structure of the novel would also make it easy for readers to recall the story from one month to the next. Roused, Max Perkins sent the manuscript to *Scribner's*, then turned to the book clubs.

Three years after *The Sun Also Rises*, many still viewed Hemingway as outside the mainstream, a radical writer unfit for middlebrow consumption. As Perkins told Wister, Hemingway was perceived "as *literary*,—as a writer for a special class, or group." *A Farewell to Arms* as the Book of the Month could change that perception overnight. Though both the Literary Guild and the BOMC paid publishers a meager 30 percent of list, they sold more than fifty thousand copies of the monthly selections, more than *In Our Time*, *The Sun Also Rises*, and *Men Without Women* had sold in toto to date. They attracted readers the bookstores missed, especially beyond urban areas, and they enhanced the status of popular writers. In addition, because they heavily advertised each book, they were great "property builders." Alfred Harcourt appreciated the value of an adoption: in 1927 he had moved the publication date of one Sinclair Lewis novel so that he could reap the promotional benefits of its book club selection.

Hemingway called the Book of the Month Club and the Literary Guild the "litero-menstrual clubs." They were the "extra dollar seeking organizations that have given a great blow to all good writing or anyway attempts at good writing." Despite the sniping, he knew that the clubs could help authors who had not yet broken through. Authors like Julian Green had become rich, Hemingway had crabbed to Perkins in 1928, while he, Ernest Hemingway, continued to earn less than the salary of a newspaper correspondent, considerably less when Scribners paid Hadley her share of the $8,942 in royalties he generated that year.

In February and March 1929, as the book clubs deliberated and Scribners planned the production of the novel, Hemingway was in Key West entertaining John Dos Passos and Waldo Peirce; he was also reading galley proof on the serialization of *A Farewell to Arms*.

Reading galley proof could unnerve the most assured author, but Hemingway voiced second thoughts only about the title of the novel that would debut in the May issue of *Scribner's Magazine*. He had doped out more than thirty possible titles, many of them variations of one another, most of them biblical or literary. He had considered *Patriots Progress*, an allusion to John Bunyan's *Pilgrim's Progress; Disorder and Early Sorrow*, stolen from the Thomas Mann short story; and *Education of the Flesh, The Carnal Education, The Sentimental Education of Frederick Henry*, and *The Sentimental Education*, all inspired by Gustav Flaubert's 1869 *L'Éducation sentimentale*. Most best-sellers had titles that were not self-consciously allusive: for instance, in 1928, Galsworthy's *Swan Song*, Booth Tarkington's *Claire Ambler*, and Louis Bromfield's *Strange Case of Miss Annie Spragg*. The best-seller of 1927 was called *Elmer Gantry* (née *The Rev. Dr. Mellish*) since, as Lewis told Harcourt, "having the name of the man in the title makes people remember it so much better—it identifies the man and the book." Hemingway would call none of his books by their characters' names. Finally, in the bedside *Oxford Book of English Verse*, he found George Peele and "A Farewell to Arms." The allusion would establish the novel as a serious work in a serious tradition. Once more Hemingway asked Perkins whether he liked "A Farewell to Arms." The editor found it a "bitter phrase," though as fine as the novel itself.

The first installment of the galleys contained the blanks and cuts the author had anticipated—until they suddenly accelerated. In what would become chapter 7, Frederic daydreams about a long romantic night with Catherine in a Milan hotel room. The bellboy would arrive with ice, Frederic says, which they would ask him to leave outside the door.

> Because we would not wear any clothes because it was so hot and the window open and the swallows flying over the roofs of the houses and when it was dark afterward and you went to the window very small bats hunting over the houses and close down over the trees and we would drink the capri and the door locked and it hot and only a sheet and the whole night and we would both love each other all night in the hot night in Milan.

Bridges cut that passage. The deletion undermined the poignance of the line, just over one hundred pages later, when Frederic takes Catherine to the recherché hotel room where she feels like a whore and he had not thought "it would be like this." But *Scribner's Magazine* was "collateral reading" in the schools, Bridges explained to Hemingway just as he had explained (almost verbatim) to Galsworthy the reason for cuts made in a 1915 serialization. Certain parts of *A Farewell to Arms* had no place in "mixed classes," perhaps even American parlors. Needless to say, Bridges also thought they would offend advertisers.

Perkins hastened to assure Hemingway that key passages cut from the magazine would be restored in the novel; he also sent the author an advance on the serialization. The six-thousand-dollar check seemed poor compensation for the cuts in the next installment of galleys. Bridges had trimmed the seduction scene and part of Rinaldi's advice to Frederic. " 'I tell you something about your good women. Your goddesses,' " Rinaldi says. Then Bridges cut what followed: " 'There is only one difference between taking a girl who has always been good and a woman. With a girl it is painful. That's all I know.' He slapped the bed with his glove. 'And you never know if the girl will really like it.' " Bridges also cut many "words," many more than Hemingway had expected. Gone were not only "balls," "shit," "cocksucker," and "fuck" but "whore," "whorehound," "Jesus Christ," and "son of a bitch."

Though Perkins once more assured Hemingway that the novel would restore much of the original language, he shared Bridges's worry and, in the margins of the galleys, debated Hemingway on taste and temerity, including such matters as the word "bed pan": "I should think this unpleasant implement might be omitted;—for the physiological function it relates to has no significance here anyhow." To which Hemingway replied:

> On the other hand this instrument dominates hospital life—I have only mentioned it once—I believe I mentioned it to give the natural and unembarrassed attitude of the nurse toward all the natural functions the first and biggest [words obscured] one who has never been in a hospital receives.

Perkins was content to keep "bed pan," and indeed even the movies of the late 1920s were frank about such matters. In one scene of the screenplay of *All Quiet on the Western Front*, Kat tells his untested young soldiers not to worry about the battle; afterwards, he says, "I'll get you all some nice clean underwear." For Perkins, though, "shit," "balls," "cocksucker," and "fuck" in *A Farewell to Arms* (or perhaps in *Scribners' Farewell to Arms*) crossed the line. Fitzgerald told Hemingway that if the book used such words it would be "suppressed + confiscated within two days of publication." Perkins had the more constructive opinion that "if we can keep people from being diverted from the qualities of the material itself, by words and passages which have on account of *conventions*, an astonishingly exaggerated importance to them, a great thing will have been done." He wrote "people" but probably meant "women." For the moment Hemingway was unmoved.

Perkins could have used the book clubs to convince Hemingway to remove the "words" from the manuscript, for bluster aside, the author was drawn to the clubs' access to the mass audience. When the English publisher of *A Farewell to Arms* turned down an offer from the Book Society (the British Book of the Month Club), Hemingway grieved to Perkins. Hemingway had endorsed the sale, no doubt because he was less well known in England than in America, but Jonathan Cape had refused to accommodate the Book Society's production schedule. The loss was appreciable, Hemingway said. Finally, though, Scribners had also ruled out the clubs. Charles Scribner II "didn't see why a book club should make a lot of money out of a book he had published," one associate later recalled. "Why couldn't *he* make that money out of it?" Perkins agreed. He had sensed the power of *A Farewell to Arms*, and gambled that the momentum of *The Sun Also Rises* and *Men Without Women* would sweep the new novel into the ranks of the best-sellers, and therefore that the BOMC or Literary Guild would erode earnings on the clothbound edition. Noting that the Book of the Month Club had "strongly recommended" changes on *All Quiet on the Western Front*, he told Hemingway that the clubs could do more harm than good.

Perkins nonetheless continued to recommend changes in *A Farewell to Arms*. He had snipped, among other things, the reference to "a fizzing and sulphuric fart" from *Look Homeward, Angel*, and wanted to serve *A Farewell to Arms* no less well. Hemingway could in theory accept certain deletions: no one should use words only to shock, including, for instance, the word "fart," which could work only in an "entirely rabelaisian" text. He could not accept emasculations, though, even if (as Perkins thought) the wide acceptance of *A Farewell to Arms* hinged on them. By April 1929 the Hemingways were in Paris, where readers could buy, uncut, *Ulysses*, *The Well of Loneliness*, and *All Quiet on the Western Front*. Perkins was unusually circumspect in approaching the author. Reducing the "medical details" and other "physical aspects" would cause no harm, he wrote, and would protect the novel from censorship. He meanwhile urged Owen Wister to talk with Hemingway. Though the author of *The Virginian* did not want to "perturb or disturb the lad," he had admired *The Sun Also Rises* and agreed that at the end of *A Farewell to Arms* "the reader suffers and shudders not because it is Catherine, but merely because of the horror of the thing itself." Once more the reader was the woman reader. On arrival in France, Wister would "try to impress our friend with the necessity of his modifying the frankness of his present manner."

The first installment of *A Farewell to Arms* appeared in *Scribner's* May 1929 issue with an exceptionally sober headnote. It had been written by Perkins (or less likely Bridges) and edited by Hemingway, who cut the word "sor-didness," which he said weakened the purpose. In tone the headnote echoed Perkins's statement that no one could be more healthy or decent than Hemingway.

> Proclaimed with enthusiasm by the critics of both England and America, his first novel was objected to by some on the curious theory that because he wrote of vice and dissipation he thereby registered approval. Others declared the book to be frivolous. In that respect 'A Farewell to Arms' will certainly satisfy them: no novel could have a more serious or significant motif than 'A Farewell,' nor a treatment more profoundly sincere.

The appeal to the *Scribner's* general reader was astonishing in its nakedness. It was also effective: the May issue appeared without incident.

The June issue was another story. Boston Superintendent of Police Michael H. Crowley found certain passages in *A Farewell to Arms* salacious and banned *Scribner's* from newsstands. Hemingway's supporters instantly rallied round. "To hell with the toughs of Boston," Fitzgerald said. Boston "meant nothing," both Perkins and Wister assured the author. Tongue in cheek, the *New York World* scolded "Naughty Ernest."

The action was more serious than anyone admitted. Once Crowley banned the June issue, the New England News Company, which distributed *Scribner's Magazine* along the upper East Coast, returned *all* its copies and forced the publisher to ship the magazine to individual dealers outside Boston. With Scribners' 1929 net earnings approaching only three hundred thousand dollars, the ban increased costs and narrowed profits. While the controversy sold copies elsewhere, Boston also affected both how and when readers encountered the novel. The ban focused debate on moral rather than artistic questions; it also prompted many curious readers to start the novel with the second installment, compounding the damage of serialization and inviting the vice society and even federal authorities to circle in red the publication date of the clothbound edition. As Perkins noted, touching on the legal and aesthetic questions the serialization had aroused, "only the very discerning could see from that [second installment] how fine a thing [the novel] was."

The ban earned Perkins leverage in addressing—one last time—the "words" of *A Farewell to Arms*. In chapter 22, when the head nurse charges that Frederic's jaundice is self-inflicted, the means of prolonging his stay in Milan, Frederic lashes out, and Perkins had cringed. " 'Miss Van Campen,' I said, 'did you ever know a man who tried to disable himself by kicking himself in the balls?' " Bridges had blanked the word "balls," and

Hemingway would eventually substitute the word "scrotum." Now Perkins wanted other concessions. He told Hemingway that legal challenges to the magazine could ripen into legal challenges to the novel, as indeed they could. If Boston booksellers had been reluctant to order (much less stock or sell) *An American Tragedy* and *Elmer Gantry*—though neither had been banned or contained the "words" that *A Farewell to Arms* did—how would they treat the work of an author less established than Dreiser and less certain of large sales than Lewis? Scribners could not with impunity print all that Hemingway had written. "I can't find *anyone* who thinks so," Perkins wrote, since, collectively, the "words" were a "supreme insult" that could "turn a judge right around against us" and "warrant (technically) action." In Paris, Owen Wister had found Hemingway "in a big gloom about Boston." It was the opportune moment for Perkins to oust not only "fuck" but "shit," "cocksucker," and even Hemingway's proposed "c—s—r."

Though Hemingway made what he later called "the polite Owen Wister compromise," the refined *Farewell to Arms* was otherwise hard and true. More important, its deliberate balance of preciseness and indirection—both in "words" and themes—made it ideally suited to the public the author yearned to reach. Hemingway may have thought he was "cooked," the euphemism he used repeatedly and ironically in a British major's speech in "Book Two" of the novel, but in the long run the blanks (as Perkins had predicted) would yield large dividends.

In late June, Hemingway corrected galleys for the last *Scribner's* installment and weighed its final paragraphs. The last sentences of the novel provided what Fitzgerald called an "old-fashioned Alger book summary" that told what became of Rinaldi and other characters, a summary that pulled the focus from Catherine, Frederic, and *them*. Though Hemingway had composed numerous variant endings, none was more understated than the one he chose for the serialization and the novel. Frederic wants to tell the dead Catherine farewell. "But after I had got [the nurses] out and shut the door and turned off the light it wasn't any good. It was like saying good-by to a statue. After a while I went out and left the hospital and walked back to the hotel in the rain." With those evocative sentences written in thick pencil strokes on the long galley sheet, Hemingway surrendered *A Farewell to Arms* to Perkins, Scribners, and ultimately the public.

In summer 1929 Scribners put *A Farewell to Arms* into production. It ordered the typesetting, the dust jacket, the trade announcements, the advertising copy. It also established the price and alerted the booksellers. Perkins was keen on the latter. "The book should be talked up ahead of its appearance to the trade," he told one author: "they should see sheets in advance,

etc. This is the plain truth of the matter." Two years before, in a *Publishers'*
Weekly advertisement for *The Sun Also Rises*, Perkins had reproduced an endorsement from a Charlottesville, Virginia, bookseller.

> The entire force (namely five of us) is reading 'The Sun Also Rises'
> and we are unanimous in a verdict of enthusiastic approval. It is
> annoying that we couldn't know the really fine books, such as the
> Hemingway has turned out to be, in those sultry summer days when
> publishers' representatives present the hopes and fears of the coming
> season.

Meanwhile, thanks to the installment publication of *A Farewell to Arms*,
Scribners' and the Hemingways' daily mail buzzed with comment.

From Elizabeth, New Jersey, one *Scribner's* reader wrote to cancel her
subscription to the magazine and report that she had burned "the offending number." From Mobile, Alabama, another reader blasted the serial as
"vulgar beyond expression" and reported that he had removed the magazine from the tables of the local Young Men's Christian Association. From
Arkansas, another reader penned an even more devastating comment.
"This week I have been reading the first installment of your story," Mary
Pfeiffer told her son-in-law, "and I like it. You have put us right back into
the war atmosphere. Everything reeks with it. If you had not told me that
it was not autobiographical I would think you were mistaken."

Hemingway had long opposed autobiographical readings of his fiction.
When "The Doctor and the Doctor's Wife" appeared in the *transatlantic
review* in December 1924, Ed Hemingway read the story (the article, he
called it), then opened the family albums to look at photographs of the
"characters." Ernest wrote home that he had used "real people" and "real
names" only because the Michigan natives would never read the *transatlantic review.* "I've written a number of stories about the Michigan country—
the country is always true—what happens in the stories is fiction." When
In Our Time appeared in 1925, the *Chicago Post* called it "obviously not
fiction" but "simply descriptive of passages" in the life of the Chicago author. Though Hemingway could not respond to the *Post* as he had to his
father, he was sensitive on the point. As he wrote Fitzgerald, "God what a
life I must have led."

In *The Torrents of Spring* Hemingway had laughed away the question of
autobiography.

> Please, reader, just get that idea out of your head. We have lived in
> Petoskey, Mich., it is true, and naturally many of the characters are
> drawn from life as we lived it then. But they are other people, not the
> author. The author only comes into the story in these little notes.

The author enters the text to announce that he does not enter the text—it was more amusing than persuasive. Like several longer short stories, including the celebrated "Fifty Grand," *The Sun Also Rises* was written in first person with the precision and spareness of front-page news. When that novel appeared, the *New York World* (and other papers) intimated that "it will become speedily patent that practically all of [the] characters are directly based on actual people." Readers could only conclude that—lacking the little notes of *The Torrents of Spring*—the afficionado and wounded war veteran Jake Barnes was Hemingway.

Hemingway appeared to record rather than create life: he was the youth up in Michigan, the mocker of Licherchure in Petoskey, the victim of *l'amour fou* in Paris and Pamplona. In addition, he continued to blur the line between fact and fiction. Not long after Scribners published *The Sun Also Rises*, he wrote an account of the motor trip that he and Guy Hickok took in spring 1927. The piece was more vignette than narrative, more "article" than story. In one memorable incident a waitress put her arm around the character named "Guy" while three other so-called waitresses in the café took turns standing in the doorway. When "Italy—1927" appeared in the *New Republic*, a magazine known for nonfiction, the pals of Guy Hickok needled him about the prostitutes (and authors) he consorted with. "I understand now," he wrote Hemingway, "why everybody you use in your stuff goes out and gets a gun. I feel like Duff. . . . Come in this week. I keep my gun here in my desk."

Hemingway may have wondered whether Mary Pfeiffer was right, whether parts of *A Farewell to Arms* were transparently autobiographical, and whether Frederic was (per Isidore Schneider) a goody picture of his creator. The author had sensed that the press's attention to the "autobiographical" could weaken his literary reputation and egg on the people with the knives out. The novel must convince everyone that the story of Frederic and Catherine was not à clef.

Hemingway's concern took a curious turn: he focused on the legal consequences of an "autobiography." Here at least he had history on his side. The British had been so nervous about litigation on *Men Without Women* that Jonathan Cape had held up publication for months while his attorneys combed through the manuscript, paying close attention to Jewish names. One woman had threatened legal action against Scribners because her name, Brett Ashley, had been used in *The Sun Also Rises*. "She might as well try and sue Robinson Crusoe," Hemingway told Perkins, but he was more worried than he appeared. Months later he was certain that the Italians would pursue him because of his presentation of the Caporetto retreat. He had read his contract, he told Perkins; he and not the publisher must answer libel suits. Since the Italians had barred the Caporetto retreat from their history books, it was possible that they would hunt down an American author who once more exposed their humiliation.

The novel needed a foreword, Hemingway decided. It was an exaggerated deterrent—but not a frivolous one. It would allow him not only to confront and squelch the Italian protests but to blunt the issue of autobiography. The chances for success were unlikely. For the May *Scribner's*, he had written a disclaimer that a member of his own family had barely believed. "The author [he wrote] wishes to state that this book is fiction; that although it is written in the first person it is not autobiographical and that it is no more intended as a picture or criticism of Italy or Italians than was 'Two Gentlemen of Verona.' " For the June *Scribner's* the publishers had abandoned the whimsy but again suggested that "autobiography" was very much the issue: "For those who missed the note on [Hemingway] last month, it may be stated again that although 'A Farewell to Arms' is told in the first person, it is not autobiographical." Perkins wanted neither of those statements in the novel, but Hemingway was resolute.

Throughout summer 1929, as the publication date approached, Hemingway was on the move—Pamplona and the fiesta, Montroig, Valencia. By early August, in Santiago de Compostela, he was "trying to write stories or a story rather and can't a damn bit." He was nervous about the reception of *A Farewell to Arms*, and had fallen heir to "that terrible mood of depression of whether it's any good or not." Such (he told Scott) was "The Artist's Reward." He was also nervous about those who would read the novel and sue. He was haunted by the threat of legal action, and something deeper. On reading *The Sun Also Rises* in 1926, Morley Callaghan had predicted that "Hemingway himself was going to be identified with his hero, Jake Barnes." On reading *A Farewell to Arms* in summer 1929, he predicted that the author would be identified with Frederic Henry, and that "his literary personality would grow apace. Was this what he wanted? Would there ever be a showdown between himself as he was and this growing literary personality? It bothered me."

Long before Callaghan, Fitzgerald had had like concerns about Hemingway and *A Farewell to Arms*.

> While in America don't cast any doubt on my statement that you held a bridgehead (or was it a hophead) at Caporetto for three days + utterly baffled the 2nd Austrian Army Corps. In 50 yrs all the people that could have denied it will be dead or busy holding their own bridgeheads—like Lawrence Stallings, who is slowly taking to himself the communal exploits of the 5th + 6th Marines. "Hebuterne—of course I know it—I took that village."

Beneath the froth was the acid that corroded the relationship. Hemingway had not been at Caporetto but had been at war, and like Frederic Henry, he had been wounded. The fact that Frederic had been eating cheese and Hemingway visiting an observation post made the shrapnel no less painful, the recovery no less prolonged. Fitzgerald knew enough of war and enough of Hemingway to caricature the way the personality threatened to tower over the author and the work. For a civilian, Scott was a first-class sharp-shooter.

In 1929, magazines and newspapers spoke of what one writer called "the *Hemingwayish* mode of existence." *A Farewell to Arms* would further the pub-lic reputation of Hemingway as the star of American fiction, and Scribners would help. Since 1926 Max Perkins had regularly asked Hemingway for photographs or portraits. Author and publisher had haphazardly pro-ceeded: Hemingway had stood before the camera when time or notion allowed; Scribners had reprinted whatever he sent. When *Men Without Women* was published in October 1927, the photograph in the 16 October *New York Times Book Review* showed the author in homburg hat, woolen suit coat, and tie, probably the picture that Man Ray had taken and that Ed and Grace Hemingway had so liked, perhaps because Ernest looked like an Oak Park alderman. The *Times* had called Hemingway the equal of Kipling, Maupassant, and Conrad. Hemingway, who quipped in "A Way You'll Never Be" that a homburg made a man "distinguished," told Perkins to withdraw the still—permanently.

The photographs of Hemingway that appeared in *Scribner's Magazine* concurrent with the serialization of *A Farewell to Arms* portrayed an author with the silver-screen allure of Gary Cooper. The appearance of the photo-graphs was itself remarkable, for *Scribner's* rarely published photographs of its fiction authors. For the May 1929 issue, Perkins chose the Helen Breaker portrait of Hemingway solemn in cap, dark sweater, and light shirt, the wide lapels falling gracefully across the collar of the sweater. For the June 1929 issue, he chose a snapshot. According to the caption, it showed how the author "spent much of the past winter when not working on his novel."

Hemingway had not yet mastered the visage he offered the lens or the canvas; he had nonetheless not been caught off guard by the camera. Whether portrait or snapshot, a picture represents a bargain struck by artist and subject. The artist knows how and where to position the subject, choos-ing the background, the props, the stance, and so on. But while the artist represents, the subject presents; that is, as Jackson Wilson notes, the "sub-ject proposes himself to the artist. In a word, he poses. And if he is skilled enough at looking his look, he may impose himself on the portrait." In the snapshot for the June 1929 *Scribner's*, Hemingway had just come ashore in Key West, and posed holding a fishing rod in one hand and an enormous tarpon in the other. He looked more like the soldier at ease than the fisherman proud of his catch, yet the photograph answered Perkins's needs. It replaced Hemingway the coterie author with Hemingway the robust American male. Enhancing the richness of the photograph, Hemingway squinted against the Florida sun and turned his head down and away. The dodge not only played against an excess of manliness but pulled the viewer into the photograph. The author had not asked if it pleased; he had done it all for himself inside.

"Sorry, I haven't got a picture," Faulkner told his agent several months after *The Sound and the Fury* was published in 1929. "I dont [*sic*] intend to have one that I know of, either." (And when his agent requested a short biography, Faulkner responded: "Dont tell the bastards anything.") Hemingway was not camera shy. Moreover, he closely read photographs or portraits of himself, especially those considered for publication. During the writing of *A Farewell to Arms*, Papa had grown a beard only (he said) to avoid the barber for a while. Like Frederic Henry, who had grown one only to indulge Catherine, he felt strange, then funny, but posed for Waldo Peirce, looking, he told Perkins, rather like Balzac. When Perkins saw the Balzac portrait, he wanted to use it in Scribners' promotion of *A Farewell to Arms*. Hemingway demurred, joking that beards ("or any hirsute irregularity") evoked suspicion, and could repel "my faithful public." Finally, however, he told Perkins that Scribners could use the portrait—but only "alongside of some tough snap shot to contrast two versions of [the] same pan." Though the portrait, along with stacks of the novel, would turn up alone in Scribners' display window on Fifth Avenue, Perkins must have been bewildered by the demand. For Hemingway the reason was plain. Concerned about how he should define himself for critics and readers, he had hedged bets: the portrait would add him to the pantheon of American literature; the photograph would ally him with the audience.

To announce to the trade the clothbound edition of *A Farewell to Arms*, Perkins wanted to use another of the Helen Breaker photographs, sans cap, sans bandage, so he ordered it retouched. "If we had retained [the gash on the forehead], we should have had to explain it," he wrote Hemingway, "and I know you do not like the exploitation of personalities." An unmarked face was also an exploitation of personality—in the right hands. That high-contrast portrait of the author accented the youth and Romanesque beauty that, according to Dorothy Parker, made young women quiver. As Parker later wrote, only half in jest, "the wide publication of that smiling photograph, the one with the slanted cap and the shirt flung open above the dark sweater, was perhaps a mistake." She may have confused two widely seen photographs, one with cap, one without. In the former, which appeared in *Vanity Fair* and *Scribner's Magazine*, the author wears the slanted cap but does not smile; in the latter, which appeared (retouched) in advertisements for *A Farewell to Arms* in the *New York Times Book Review* and elsewhere, he smiles but does not wear the cap. Any confusion notwithstanding, Parker had not misunderstood the photographs' impact on a flourishing celebrity culture.

In the August 10 *Publishers' Weekly*, Scribners ran a one-page trade notice for *A Farewell to Arms*. It featured Owen Wister, "author of 'The Virginian,'" and, retouched, Ernest Hemingway. Having seen William Lyon Phelps promoting Thornton Wilder's *The Bridge of San Luis Rey* (1927), that is, the older and much beloved writer leading the audience to the younger and more difficult one, Perkins had adopted the strategy for *A Farewell to Arms*. Wister looked like one of the Paramount extras in the recently released *The Virginian*; his hair was slicked down in nineteenth-century fashion, and he wore a detachable collar and narrow bow tie. Hemingway wore the dark sweater and open shirt, and smiled, as though he knew what Wister was saying in the advertisement. "This book is full of beauty and variety," Wister wrote. In Hemingway "lives a humble artisan who keeps him constantly true to his art." Hemingway should have resented the implication that there were *two* Ernests, one (the man of the public prints) hardly at all humble. He apparently resented only the association of Wister and *A Farewell to Arms*, though, and told Perkins so. Wister "knows he has compromised," Perkins responded. "His realization that you never do is one of the things he so much admires. Of course, having been a man who did temper himself to his times, and the conventions, he has naturally many prejudices. But who has not?" Would the endorsement adversely influence critics? Hemingway wondered. On the contrary, Perkins answered, it would assure conservative reviewers and booksellers that *A Farewell to Arms* was "beyond the reach of objection on grounds of conventional taboos; and this could only be done through the influence of someone, whatever his merits, who could speak with authority to them." Like the blanked words, the photographs and endorsement were roads to the popular audience that both editor and author wanted for the novel.

To design the *Farewell to Arms* dust jacket—yet another road—Scribners once more chose Cleonike Damianakes. The former University of California undergraduate found the publisher hard to please. Dominated by helmets and artillery, one design accented the war. When Perkins rejected the illustration, Cleon (Damianakes' nom de plume) returned to the drawing board. Perkins told the author that Scribners "were very nervous about the jacket because [they] did not want to bring out the book as a War book, that is as a combat book."

The literary periodicals were full of announcements and stories about the "Great German War Books" that season. William Scanlon's *God Have Mercy on Us!* and Mary Lee's *It's a Great War* had shared the Houghton Mifflin twenty-five-thousand-dollar War Novel Prize for 1929, and *God Have Mercy on Us!* would appear within weeks of *A Farewell to Arms*; according to the advance word, Scanlon would be "compared to Hemingway." Worse, *All Quiet on the Western Front* had been a German best-seller that, thanks in part to Book of the Month Club adoption, had already become an American best-seller and a screenplay for Universal on the West Coast. Hemingway loved competition, particularly against another author. But he was not one of the crowd, and neither was *A Farewell to Arms*. Perkins hoped the dust jacket could say precisely that.

Desperate, Scribners considered putting only the names of title and author on the dust jacket. Had Hemingway been better known (or "arms" been less identified with war), Scribners might have proceeded, but Perkins and others believed that the novel needed a stronger push on retailers' shelves. In late summer 1929 Damianakes submitted a third and final design for what Hemingway called his "long tale of transalpine fornication." An echo of what the artist had done for *The Sun Also Rises*, the illustration consisted of two figures of antiquity. The female reclined, her arms raised behind her head, her knees bent and touching; her breasts were globular. Except for the light-orange drape across her midsection, she was nude. The male figure to her left rested his head on his arm, and his arm on his raised knee; the other arm held a broken axle. Except for his light-green loincloth, he was also nude. Both figures sat on cobblestones, surrounded by a bower of foliage. Neither figure looked at the other. As the artist had done for *The Sun Also Rises*, Damianakes had made sex attractive and respectable. Above the illustration, in capital letters, appeared "A Farewell to Arms." Beneath the illustration, in smaller type, appeared the author's name. The only visual reference to war was two small boxed cannons pointed toward "A Farewell to Arms."

The false starts on the illustration for the dust jacket occasioned delays in production and, perhaps in turn, errors and oversights. On the front flap, "Caporetto" was spelled "Caparetto," and the name "Catherine Barkley" (whose variant spellings in the manuscript had been made consistent in the proof) was spelled "Katharine Barclay." Below "Ernest Hemingway" should have appeared "Author of *The Sun Also Rises* and *Men Without Women*," but the line was dropped. Perkins had not done to Hemingway what Liveright had done to S. J. Perelman, whose *Dawn Ginsbergh's Revenge* had appeared that season minus the author's name on the title page; the lapses on *A Farewell to Arms* were nevertheless embarrassing to the author and his venerable house.

Perhaps intentionally, perhaps not, Perkins had also dropped the foreword for the novel. "None of the characters in this book is a living person," it read, "nor are the units or military organizations mentioned actual units or organizations. E. H." The statement could suggest to women that the novel was more war story than love story, Perkins thought, yet he told the author it would only lead readers "to question whether [the book] was fiction;—that is, it would suggest the idea to them that it might not be, altogether so." And if, as Hemingway thought, it was also true that many reviewers read the blurb rather than the book, then Scribners had indeed helped lessen the musty odor of "autobiography" that the foreword secreted. In the event, the foreword would appear in the second edition.

On the back cover of the jacket, where Perkins further broke down book buyers' sales resistance, reviews of *The Sun Also Rises* and *Men Without Women* praised the original style of the author and the narrative skills that had made *The Sun Also Rises* "a truly gripping story." Clearly those who considered Hemingway a technician or pornographer would have to reconsider. On the front flap Perkins continued to pitch to the general reader and, perhaps, the Hollywood producer. Despite the powerful account of the Caporetto retreat, the story was "full of beauty," for *A Farewell to Arms* was a "novel of love in war." Readers would feel the pulse of war, certainly, but less on the battlefield than in the "overwhelming love" of Frederic and Catherine. Concerned once more about critics who read everything but the text of the books they reviewed, Hemingway (then as later) wanted to "keep a lot of horseshit about all the plums in the book off the jacket blurb." The last word belonged to Perkins, though, on the final line of the copy, which called the novel "a presentation of profound love."

Hemingway liked nothing about the dust jacket, least of all the design. Cleon was "the spirit of no sex appeal" whose illustration would probably undercut all that the deletion of "fuck" and "cocksucker" had done for *A Farewell to Arms*. As the author told Perkins,

> The Cleon drawing has a lousy and completely unattractive decadence i.e. large, misplaced breasts etc. about it which I think might be a challenge to anyone who was interested in suppressing the book. . . . I cannot admire the awful legs on that woman or the gigantic belly muscles [on the man]. I never liked the jacket on the Sun but side by side with this one The Sun jacket looks very fine now—So maybe this one is fine too—

More enticing than Hemingway allowed, the jackets lent *The Sun Also Rises* and *A Farewell to Arms* the aura of a racy, in-progress collected edition. But the author could not get past the misspellings of Caporetto and Nurse Barkley on the front flap. He had apparently changed the spelling from "Katharine" to "Catherine" because the former was too close to "Katharsis." Now Perkins had made the name "Katharine" obvious once more. Inside the book were more errors, enough to turn an inscription into an apology. "Excuse all the misspelled Italian words—they never sent me any page proofs," Hemingway wrote in the presentation copy he sent James Joyce. "Scribner's proofreading (in our time) has always been terrible," Edmund Wilson once wrote. "Max Perkins couldn't spell himself and couldn't be made to take proofreading seriously." Readers swept away by the presentation of profound love in *A Farewell to Arms* would probably never notice.

In fall 1929 Hemingway was a fixture at the racetracks and cafés of Paris. He also appeared in bars and corridas throughout Spain, where in Spanish he praised the Jewish-American bullfighter Sidney Franklin. Hemingway had heard of Franklin but not vice versa. "I saw no reason to tell him that I had written any books," Hemingway said, since authors, rather like all good professionals, toreros or whatever, worked for art and not for glory and recognition. Then too, Hemingway was not writing books. In July he had been fallow and written nothing. Or almost nothing. *The Forum* had asked Hemingway for some fiction, and he had doped out a close paraphrase of the form letter that bore the request. The parody that resulted sounded like self-reproach: "The editor writes that as the Forum reaches not only trained readers but the general public the story must contain narrative or at least plot. In other words it must not be merely a sketch. Two thousand words is the desired length. . . ."

Hemingway had composed *A Farewell to Arms* for the general public. Along with *The Sun Also Rises*, though, it had used up much of the personal experience that he counted on as the germ of his work. Now he understood Scripps O'Neil in *The Torrents of Spring*. Scripps was " 'hard up for plots' " and had listened with intent when Diana began to spin the marvelous tale of her visit to Paris. The author of *Torrents* was also hard up. Short of writing about "Hemingway," he was not sure what he could do about it.

"We came from Santiago to Orense and then down along the Portuguese Border," Hemingway wrote Dos Passos in September, "—Verin and a swell town Puebla de Sanabria—(where got drunk) on to Benavento—up to Leon—(a lousy hole) along to Palencia—worst road in Spain 120 Kil of potholes, dust, heat to crack your head open. Two *swell* bull fights in

Palencia—me in bed between fights with a busted gut—get up for the bull festival then back to bed—Then here by way of Valladolid and the Guadarramas—Damned nice—" Hemingway had been working at three "pieces." But why "pieces" and not stories? Perhaps it had been the constant travel, or the sun, or the confinement in bed. Writers could not work in summer, he told Fitzgerald. "You dont feel death coming on the way it does in the fall when the boys really put pen to paper."

Perhaps too it had been the prospect of real success. Corruption was rife—Don Stewart had sold out to Hollywood, John Peale Bishop had been "ruined by Mrs. Bishop's income." Hemingway called himself "Ernest the stinking serial king," and feared that the blanked words in *A Farewell to Arms* would prove that he valued sales more than honesty. Sales and honesty, commerce and art—the lines drawn so hard and fast in the 1920s look less so now, and were in truth less so then. Though a contemporaneous issue of the *Outlook and Independent* indicted the *Saturday Evening Post* for valuing the "popular mind" more than "literature," the *Saturday Review of Literature* later noted that only two sorts of writers shunned the *Post*: "those who have independent means or make satisfactory incomes from their other writing, and those who can't make the grade. Many of the former and practically all of the latter try to write for the Post." Royalty dollars could dull an author, and so in September, Ernest spent a hunk of the *Scribner's* money on three Goya lithographs for Hadley on her birthday; it was a gesture of affection, and a sacrifice to the art gods.

Should *A Farewell to Arms* take off, Hadley would have lithos to burn. Naturally Perkins had been apprehensive about the print run. Scribners was ever the conservative house, yet a sizable print run was itself a promotional strategy that, according to Alfred Harcourt, could "get the impression around generally" that a publisher had "a sure-fire big book." It could also affect the number of copies that major wholesalers like Baker & Taylor or American News bought. Wall Street told America in early fall 1929 that the economy was never better. Only months before, though, the book business had been flat. Market glut was one problem; from 1928 to 1929 alone the number of fiction titles published jumped by almost 20 percent to more than two thousand books. The rise of the book clubs was another problem. The Book of the Month Club served more than one hundred thousand subscribers in 1929, more than double the membership of three years before. The BOMC and the Literary Guild heaped so much publicity on twenty-four books annually that trade publishers were occasionally forced to shout about other books merely to be heard. Caught short on *A Farewell to Arms*, Scribners could hurt sales. Caught long, it could bloat inventory. The first run of *in our time* had been 170 copies, *The Torrents of Spring* 1,250, *The Sun Also Rises* 5,090, *Men Without Women* 7,650. Perkins read the momentum, and prodded Scribners to order 31,050 for *A Farewell to Arms*. The official publication date was 27 September 1929.

"Here Is Genius," the headline in the hometown *Chicago Tribune* read. Grace Hemingway clipped Fanny Butcher's adulatory notice, wrote " 'Yay' Fanne" across the top, and mailed it to her son in Paris. Though Hemingway sputtered over the references to Gertrude Stein's influence on the novel, Max Perkins could not have written a better review. The last sentences were an early Christmas present for Scribners' publicity department. Like another professional woman of her acquaintance, Butcher said, she found *A Farewell to Arms* coarse and beautiful and awesome, "all sorts of contradictory things." But both women, "after reading an absolutely brutal, cold blooded narrative, written in a manner which only the word vulgar describes when used in its original Latin meaning, when they came to the last page, were seized with absolutely uncontrollable sobs." "Naughty Ernest" not only promised tears and titillation; he had written a novel for women and for the *vulgus*, the common people.

Other reviewers hailed *A Farewell to Arms* as an advance over *The Sun Also Rises*. When they debated the nature of the book—war story or love story—they almost always decided on the latter. Agnes Smith and Mary Ross responded as Fanny Butcher had: in the *New Yorker* Smith called *A Farewell to Arms* a vibrant contemporary love story; in *Survey* Ross lauded the novel as "more of a romantic idyll than a 'war book.' " The *New York Sun* hailed the "tenderness and pity," while the *New York Times Book Review* found the "Romeo and Juliet" romance "poetic, idyllic, tragic." *A Farewell to Arms* was a "lovestory" (*New Masses*), "an erotic story" (*Saturday Review of Literature*), "a beautiful and moving love story" (*Springfield* [Illinois] *Republican*). "If love-stories mean nothing to you, gentle or hard-boiled reader," the *New Republic* advised, "this is not your book."

Opinions like those had wide circulation, for reviewers were both "writers" and "talkers," Perkins said. "Each one is the center of a little circle. Whatever they say about a book is to its advantage and that talk which they do after seeing and reading a book, among themselves, and with other people, counts for a great deal." Even sour notes could have worth. Frederic's desertion looked unethical, *Time* said, while the *Boston Transcript* condemned the "hard words" that lower the tone of literature. According to the *New York Sun*, "the army talk makes that in 'What Price Glory?' seem almost tame," a criticism that later appeared as a teaser in Scribners' advertisement for the novel in the *New York Times Book Review*. In "What Is Dirt?"

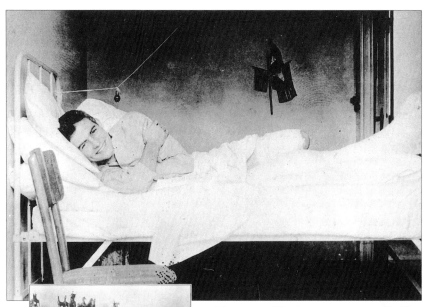

Lieutenant Hemingway was wounded by Austrian mortar fire in 1918; according to the Red Cross, which published the photograph left, he was "convalescing from 237 wounds." (both JFK Library; photograph above by Henry S. Villard, © Henry S. Villard)

In "A Very Short Story" Hemingway calls the romance of a nurse and her patient "only a boy and girl affair." Agnes Von Kurowsky was the model for the nurse. (JFK Library)

Hemingway and (on his right) his first wife, Hadley Richardson, along with his parents (Ed and Grace) and four of his five siblings. (Leicester, Sunny, Carol and Marcelline). (JFK Library)

The press reported in 1926 that Hemingway "has at one time and another fought bulls in Spain as a mode of making a livelihood." In 1927 he was a spectator, front row left center, with his eye on the camera. (JFK Library)

Foto BLANCO
6.099

THE SUN ALSO RISES

ERNEST HEMINGWAY
Author of
"IN OUR TIMES" and "THE TORRENTS OF SPRING"

The dust jacket of The Sun Also Rises—*the languor, the apple, the thigh—breathed sex yet also evoked classical Greece. Hemingway disliked the design, which was nonetheless a shrewd way for the publisher to market a sensational book.* (Princeton University Libraries)

Leslie Howard and Ann Harding (shown here in RKO's Animal Kingdom) *were cast as Jake Barnes and Brett Ashley in* The Sun Also Rises, *but the Hays Office censors, which called the novel "too salacious in essence" for the screen, blocked the production. Hays slowed—but could not stop—the production of Paramount's* A Farewell to Arms.
(Larry Edmonds Books)

By 1926, Hemingway was in love with Pauline Pfeiffer (shown in both photos). "She's an awfully nice girl," John Dos Passos told his anguished friend. "Why don't you get to be a Mormon." By April 1927, the divorce of Ernest and Hadley was final; Ernest and Pauline wed the following month. (JFK Library)

Scribners editor Max Perkins hated vacations, as his dress here may suggest. (Princeton University Libraries)

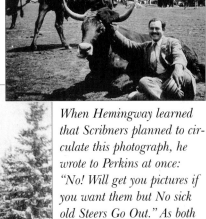

When Hemingway learned that Scribners planned to circulate this photograph, he wrote to Perkins at once: "No! Will get you pictures if you want them but No sick old Steers Go Out." As both men understood, photographs could play a vital role in making an author's public reputation. (JFK Library)

This photograph, taken in Gstaad, appeared in the October 1929 Scribner's, *the conservative monthly magazine that serialized the controversial* A Farewell to Arms. (JFK Library)

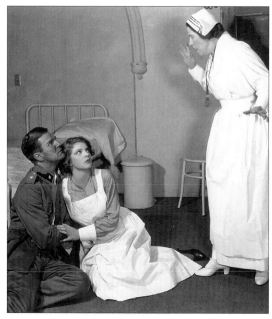

The 1930 stage production of A Farewell to Arms *riled the censors—and the critics. One newspaper called Glenn Anders (who played Lt. Henry to Elissa Landi's Catherine Barkley) "a fidgeting, gushing, blathering mummer."* (Billy Rose Theater Collection, New York Public Library for the Performing Arts, Astor, Lenox and Tilden Foundations)

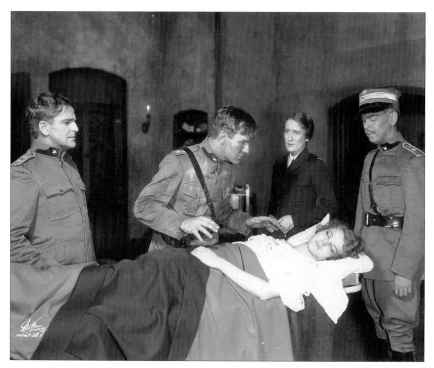

In spring 1928, soon after being injured by falling glass, Hemingway posed with Sylvia Beach before her Shakespeare and Company book shop. (Princeton University Libraries) *Joking that the wound made him resemble the agent of "Big Northern Bootleggers or Dope Peddlers," he took off the bandage when he sat for professional photographer Helen Breaker. Perkins retouched the gash since otherwise (he wrote the author) "we should have had to explain it, and I know you do not like the exploitation of personalities."* (Helen Breaker/JFK Library)

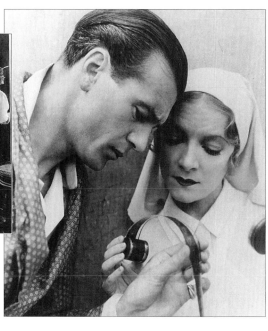

Gary Cooper and Helen Hayes starred in Paramount's 1932 A Farewell to Arms. (Museum of Modern Art/Eddie Brandt's Saturday Matinee)

The Hemingways' Key West home has lovely grounds and trees, Gus Pfeiffer wrote to his sister in 1933. "It is in the Spanish style, and is designed for comfort in hot weather, as the ceilings are high and the walls thick." House, car, safari—Uncle Gus was ever generous to his niece, Pauline, and her author-husband, whom he adored. (Linda Leavell)

Bookman critic Robert Herrick called Frederic and Catherine "but another couple on the loose in Europe during the War—there were so many of them!" The novel was "garbage," wrote Herrick, who also announced that he had stopped reading after the Milan episodes. Seconding the endorsement of Owen Wister, though, the *Atlantic Monthly* countered that *A Farewell to Arms* would earn favor among younger readers and broad-minded older ones. The contrary opinions of Herrick and the *Atlantic* and others opened debate on *A Farewell to Arms* as a social event. As the *Ponca City* (Oklahoma) *News* reported, the novel was being discussed "up and down the reading lanes." As *Town & Country* observed, it was "one of those things you simply have to read, because everybody else will be reading it."

The fame of the author was one reason for the large readership of *A Farewell to Arms*. According to Malcolm Cowley, writing in the books section of the *New York Herald Tribune*, the shining reputation of Ernest Hemingway

> may partly be attributed to his living away from New York and its literary jealousies, to his ability to surround himself with a legend, to the pride which has kept him from commercializing his work, and also in some degree to his use of rather sensational material; but nevertheless one is forced to conclude that the principal explanation lies in his having expressed, better than any other writer, the limited viewpoint of his contemporaries, of the generation which was formed by the war and which is still incompletely demobilized.

That critique would not hang in the bathroom. Cowley had fused the two pictures of Hemingway into one. There was the Waldo Peirce "Balzac" study, the classic author who rose above literary commerce to become legend. There was the tough snapshot, the modern author who used the sensational to tell the truth about the postwar human condition. By October 1929, per Cowley, *A Farewell to Arms* had guaranteed Hemingway "an extraordinary place in American letters." Even Boston had not banned the novel, Perkins later remarked, "presumably because it was thought by the authorities that they must be wrong in looking upon it as they did, in view of its overwhelming critical success."

As sales of the novel advanced, Pauline and Ernest were feted in Paris—a Saturday night at the Moulin with the expatriates Caresse and Harry Crosby, a spontaneous party hosted by James Joyce, meetings with Scott Fitzgerald and Allen Tate, who called *A Farewell to Arms* a masterpiece. But not unexpectedly, Hemingway was shaken by the reception of the novel. It had been one colossal disappointment, he told Perkins in October. He had serialized it to support the family in Oak Park but should never have consented to the blanks in the magazine or clothbound edition. He could have turned his discontent into annoyance had he known that the October 1929 issue of *Scribner's Magazine* had yoked him and one of the publisher's cash machines, the mystery writer S. S. Van Dine. The box that appeared below "The End" in the last installment of *A Farewell to Arms* read: "It is a pleasure to note that Mr. Hemingway's serial has achieved renown similar to the first two Van Dine stories serialized in *Scribner's*." Apparently heedless of the note, Hemingway turned his discontent into self-contempt. "I'm a Professional Writer now—Than which there isn't anything lower."

The Professional Writer had both ties and obligations to the public, and the blanks had implied them. Just before Caporetto, an Italian soldier offers a young woman a ride. When she hesitates, the soldier tells her not to worry. " 'No danger of —,' using the vulgar word. 'No place for —.' " Frederic "could see she understood the word." The dashes not only represented the soldiers' language and the censors' power; they challenged readers to games of "fill in the blanks" that added to the renown of the writer. One *Life* magazine cartoon showed a parent asking a teacher whether her first-grade classroom was up to date. " 'Indeed yes—we're asking Ernest Hemingway to write the primer!' " Posted on the wall was "Lesson Ten."

Did the d— bear eat the berries?
I should say the — – - — did eat the berries!

The evidence from *Life* and all over was incontrovertible: Hemingway and "Hemingway" were breaking through.

The conflict between the author and the Professional Writer was also heating up. The author told Oak Park not to peddle "Hemingway" to the press; he was not a commodity or a publicity monger. "I have told them just what you told me to say," Grace wrote her son. "That I had nothing to give out—so you need have no worry about that." Meanwhile, the Professional Writer not only asked whether Scribners needed more photographs to promote him and the novel but called on Perkins to reconsider their royalty arrangement; he wanted a graduated schedule that would increase his percentages as *A Farewell to Arms* sold 50,000, 75,000, and 100,000 copies. His demand was reasonable, for he had earned the financial rewards. But the Professional Writer also looked for ways to parade the fame that would further the sale of those copies. One evening he was pickpocketed on the streetcar in Madrid. When a reporter friend learned that passport, *carte d'identité*, and automobile papers had been stolen, he placed a notice in the local news "that [Hemingway] was an illustrious escritor and greatly handicapped by these documents being taken and the pickpocket turn[ed] them in." Scribners' publicity department could use the story, Hemingway told Perkins, though it should not tell the public that pickpockets "here always return papers."

By November 1929 *A Farewell to Arms* had sold thirty-three thousand copies. Shaken by the turmoil on Wall Street, the provident Scribners had ordered second and third printings of only ten thousand copies each, yet the demand for the novel had been steady and strong. While the author contended that the response of the public "only makes you embarrassed and uneasy and vaguely sick," the Professional Writer was concerned that the crash would arrest sales or impel Scribners to cut back on promotion. As most authors do, he believed that the publisher had not advertised his books widely or well. The *Saturday Evening Post* "now pay the old whore $4000. a screw," Fitzgerald had bragged that fall, and Hemingway had soon been convinced that at $2.50 per copy *A Farewell to Arms* could net tens of thousands. Scribners must concentrate on goals, Hemingway wrote Perkins. Had the Austrians targeted Milan rather than the Tagliamento, they would have gone beyond the Piave and won the war. The publisher must target the best-sellers list. And since most reviews had called the novel a love story, Scribners "should start hammering it as a love story—i.e. Farewell to Arms—A Gt. Modern Love Story." Scribners should also avoid fuzzy copy in the advertisements. Why say the novel was "The First Choice of Book Buyers" when it was "The Best Selling Book or AT The Head of Best Selling Lists"? Sinclair Lewis or S. S. Van Dine could not have said it better.

Despite Scribners' postcrash 10 percent pay cut for staff, the advertising continued, and the interest in *A Farewell to Arms* and Hemingway swelled. Merchandisers were especially drawn to the novel. In late 1929, Current News Features wanted to serialize it for readers of American newspapers. Though Current News would pay only a few hundred dollars—and cut the text to suit its subscribers—it would accord Hemingway and the story of *A Farewell to Arms* enormous exposure. For more money, Hemingway would have consented—another twist in the contest of author and Professional Writer. But Perkins recalled Fitzgerald among the daily papers' workaday features ("The Gumps" and "Doris Blake's Answers to Problems of Love") and scotched the offer: the "syndicating seems all just a part of the idea of killing a book off and getting it out of the way as soon as possible after publication." When the Broadway producer William Brady Jr. sent out feelers about a staged version of *A Farewell to Arms*, Hemingway referred him to agent Paul Reynolds, then dogged Scribners for sales figures on the novel. He wanted to gauge the reach of the depression and, more important, assess the negotiations for theatrical and moving picture adaptations.

By Thanksgiving, Scribners had printed seventy thousand copies of *A*

Farewell to Arms and reserved paper for twenty thousand more. The book market was torpid, Perkins wrote Hemingway, though "your book is the only one that does not seem to have been slowed up by it." Supported by advertisements in newspapers and magazines, the novel graced the weekly fall best-seller lists with *All Quiet on the Western Front* its only rival. But the author still grumbled to Perkins about "words." He had allowed *A Farewell to Arms* to be published with blanks to avoid its suppression, he wrote, and had "had no interest in it as a *book* since. It's something to sell."

Hemingway was nonetheless interested in *A Farewell to Arms* as a property, interested in the reviews, the sales, and the publicity, even the blarney that, according to one syndicated feature, he "wrote some 212 short stories before he sold one for $19." But he knew that the expansion of public reputation could backfire. John Dos Passos told *New Masses* readers it was "not surprising that *A Farewell to Arms*, that accidentally combines the selling points of having a lovestory and being about the war, should be going like hotcakes." Intended as applause, the pronouncement sounded like a raspberry. It was worse than the late November *New York Herald Tribune* story of how Hemingway had bullied Morley Callaghan and been decked by him. Hemingway insisted on a retraction that only added flesh to what Callaghan later called (and Malcolm Cowley had already more publicly called) the Hemingway legend. The *Herald Tribune* understood what others were also figuring out: the author had become "something to sell" apart from the books.

At Christmas 1926, Allen Tate had written that *The Sun Also Rises* "supports the recent prophecy that [Hemingway] will be the 'big man in American letters.'" By Christmas 1929, both the English and the American editions of *A Farewell to Arms* had appeared. "Personally I do not see that it is offensive at all," the *Listener* noted, and Jonathan Cape highlighted the quotation in advertisements so that the British could, like Charles Scribner, be reassured about Hemingway. German, Swedish, and Norwegian translations were also forthcoming. In America, Scribners pursued the widest possible audience for author and novel. "We are planning another advertisement which will have some such headline as 'English opinion on an American book,'" Perkins wrote Hemingway. The notice was intended to corral readers attracted to the author early on but alienated by the personal publicity about him or the popular success of his novel. "I admit with shame that it is partly intended to get the snob vote," Perkins added, "at least to tell the high-hats where they get off, if they have any doubts left." The centerpiece of another planned advertisement was a photograph of Hemingway on the ski slopes at Gstaad. In the snapshot he stood with arms on the poles, goggles above the bill of the cap, face to the camera, smiling, perhaps squinting from the sun; he wore several layers of clothing but no coat. The photograph, which had appeared in the October *Scribner's* along with the last installment of the novel, portrayed the author that Perkins had commended to Charles Scribner, pure as the snow that flocked the trees behind him. It was Hemingway for middlebrows, the author as selling point for occasional readers.

Further promotion of *A Farewell to Arms* would come from reissues of early Hemingway. Liveright announced its fourth printing of *In Our Time* in December 1929 and rejected Scribners' offer to buy the publishing rights. With more than twenty-five thousand copies of *The Sun Also Rises* sold, Scribners had announced its tenth printing of the fiesta novel in November 1929, and planned a third printing of *The Torrents of Spring* for March 1930. Grosset and Dunlap had finally put its nonexclusive edition of *The Sun Also Rises* into production, and the Modern Library was also actively interested in the novel.

Unlike Grosset books (even the Novels of Distinction), which had broad distribution, Modern Library editions were sold chiefly in bookshops. Donald Klopfer and Bennett Cerf had bought the imprint from Horace Liveright in 1925, and in less than four years changed its face. They dropped unpopular titles, added contemporary authors, and persuaded the retailer to stock the series near the entrance of the store. "You can't do that, not for our trade," Arthur Brentano said. Like others, though, he found that the Modern Library reprints of Joyce and Anderson and Balzac sold well across the economic spectrum. In 1929 Klopfer and Cerf proposed an open contract for *The Sun Also Rises*. They would pay three thousand dollars for the first fifty thousand copies sold and renegotiate the fee for the second fifty thousand. Perkins accepted, not only because the terms were favorable but because a ninety-five-cent Modern Library edition, along with an inexpensive Grosset edition, could lead readers to *A Farewell to Arms* and subsequent Hemingway works.

Was Hemingway of the bookstores also Hemingway of the public prints—Hemingway the expatriate, Hemingway the brawler, Hemingway the skirt chaser, and on and on? Hogwash, wrote Dorothy Parker in the 30 November 1929 *New Yorker*. "People so much wanted him to be a figure out of a saga that they went to the length of providing the saga themselves." According to Parker, the "real" Hemingway had left home to become a prizefighter, enlisted in the Italian army, and sustained seven major wounds. In fact, the real Hemingway had left home to become a reporter, volunteered for the Red Cross, and sustained only one major wound. No matter. Parker described an Ernest Hemingway "even better than those photographs," an Ernest Hemingway who lacked pretense and scoffed at authors who worked in luxe corners of the globe. " '——,' Ernest Hemingway said, mentioning a certain word by name, 'the only good place to work is in your head.' " The blanks were yet another advertisement for *A Farewell to Arms* and Hemingway the legend.

Hemingway "works like hell, and through it," Parker wrote. "Nothing comes easily to him; he struggles, sets down a word, scratches it out, and begins all over. He regards his art as hard and dirty work, with no hope of better conditions." Hemingway worked hard, that was true. As Parker noted, though, he was also aware of audience. When the reviewer for the *Middletown Observer-Companion* "does not find the new Hemingway book to her taste, that will be the one Our Hero will select to brood over." He nonetheless wrote the books for himself. "Ernest the serial king" was (for Parker) Hemingway the uncorrupted artist. He could not command "enormous prices for his short stories," *New Yorker* readers were assured, and he did not "make much money—not half as much as you do." Though an exaggeration (*Cosmopolitan* had offered him one thousand dollars per story two years before, and *Fortune* had just offered him no small fortune for an essay on bullfighting), the statement was good publicity, just the kind the author liked. So it should have been, for the author had "posed" for the interview no less than he had for the Helen Breaker portraits. "I had to write a piece about [Hemingway] for the New Yorker," Parker told her friend Robert Benchley just before the late November issue appeared. "All I couldn't say was anything about his father or his divorce or anything he ever did or said." Parker liked Hemingway, though, and she was "writer" and "talker" nonpareil; moreover, the power of her "little circle" was far reaching. Hemingway usually belittled articles about him, but not her profile. "So if it makes you vomit too much, please just return it to me by carrier pigeon," she wrote him, enclosing a copy, six weeks or so before publication. "But if you only vomit a little, please shoot it on to [editor Harold] Ross." Though Hemingway's response (if any) was not preserved, he found her work literally memorable. "I don't carry the piece with me unfortunately," he told Gilbert Seldes in late December 1929; he then quoted a passage from it verbatim.

Hearing the jingle of coins, Broadway and Hollywood once more thought of putting Hemingway in lights. William Brady had of course toyed with *The Sun Also Rises* in 1926, and several months later the colorful producer Jed Harris had asked Hemingway to write an original play for the 1927–1928 season. According to the *New York Sun*, "one wonders constantly, in reading his novels and short stories, why he has never tried his hand at playwriting."

Composed in 1926 and reprinted in *Men Without Women*, "Today Is Friday" was a "play" that ended on the word "CURTAIN" and told the Christ story in conversational dialogue.

2d Soldier. Why didn't he come down off the cross?

1st Soldier. He didn't want to come down off the cross. That's not his play.

2d Soldier. Show me a guy that doesn't want to come down off the cross.

1st Soldier. Aw, hell, you don't know anything about it. Ask George there. Did he want to come down off the cross, George?

Wine-seller. I'll tell you, gentlemen, I wasn't out there. It's a thing I haven't taken any interest in.

2d Soldier. Listen, I seen a lot of them—here and plenty of other places. Any time you show me one that doesn't want to get down off the cross when the time comes—when the time comes, I mean—I'll climb right up with him.

Though "Today Is Friday" may have suggested to Hemingway that he had no ear even for closet drama, he was attracted to playwriting if only as a precaution. An unproduced May 1929 adaptation of "The Killers" had been so bad that, according to Perkins, "I myself would almost rather that your name was not connected with the play, although the front page of [the] manuscript does bear the words, 'based on a story by Ernest Hemingway.' " The playwright had defiled "The Killers" and the name "Hemingway," an abuse that Hemingway as adaptor could end. Some months later, the Yale University Theater School wrote the author for permission to adapt *The Sun Also Rises* for the stage. Having once been stagestruck—he had not only been in *Beau Brummell* but memorized speeches from *Hamlet* and critiqued works by Hans Sachs and Bernard Shaw—Hemingway suspected that undergrads posing as Brett and Jake could poison whatever chances the novel had for professional production, especially since New Haven was so close to New York. "The trouble about the Sun is that I had and still have an idea of trying to make a play out of it myself," Hemingway told the students.

Hemingway lacked the stomach for the collaboration that theater involved, the endless conferences and compromises with producers and directors and actors before the opening-night curtain rose. He had an agent, whom Brady and others had already contacted. Better they haggle with the agent over novel and rights, Hemingway had told Perkins, and editor and author stay three thousand miles away and garner royalties. And thus the author curbed the Professional Writer.

Broadway dallied. "Christ knows I need money—not money advanced or loaned but money earned," the author told Perkins that winter, toting up the Goyas, the travel, the Paris and Key West houses, and the one-hundred-dollar monthly checks to Oak Park. Perhaps the agent should try Hollywood. Hemingway was unaware that the studios often wavered on novels, especially "literary" novels like *A Farewell to Arms*, until Broadway had mounted them. He was also unaware that Broadway success could boost the price Hollywood paid and that the price Hollywood paid was never quite as fabulous as it appeared. When the studios bought a stage adaptation rather than a novel, the agent took his fee, then divided the balance equally among the author, the dramatist, and the Broadway producer. Hemingway chose the movie route, though, and told Reynolds to put New York on hold and test the waters for *A Farewell to Arms* in Los Angeles.

In late 1929 Reynolds shopped *A Farewell to Arms* around the studios. Warner Bros., Metro-Goldwyn-Mayer, and Paramount were interested. "This is a magnificently written story and a great one," the Paramount reader reported to the front office, "but it is not a story for a picture." The movie censors were no more sanguine about the property. Like the Paramount reader, Lamar Trotti of the Motion Picture Association had been deeply moved by the novel but wondered how anyone could adapt it for the screen. "Much profanity—very much! Illicit love! Illegitimate birth! Desertion from the Army! Not very flattering picture of Italy in war days! A great book nevertheless."

Six studios read *A Farewell to Arms*, but only MGM chose to bid. "Reynolds balled up play and film negociations [*sic*] completely," Hemingway told Perkins. "He had an offer of $10,000 for movies and let it slide. . . ." Since Reynolds had recently fielded a one-thousand-dollar offer from *Collier's* just to read Hemingway's next novel, he may well have thought he could hold out for more. *The Middle Man* (authored by Reynolds's son) retraced the strategy. When Hemingway asked the Reynolds agency to "handle the motion picture rights to *A Farewell to Arms*," Reynolds "approached the six major motion picture companies, five of whom were uninterested. The sixth, MGM, offered $10,000. [Reynolds] thought this price was much too low and so informed Hemingway. What Hemingway thought was an enigma. He did not answer [Reynolds's] letter." As an irked Hemingway later told Perkins, "I kept insisting I wanted and preferred *cash* from movies," but Reynolds, who "morally disapproved" of *A Farewell to Arms*, "stalled until offers were withdrawn." Reynolds was an agent, however, not a seminarian. Moreover, uncertain about the magnitude of the depression, all the studios had turned almost as conservative as Scribners. In fall 1929 the Justice Department was pursuing Loew's (the parent corporation of

MGM studios) on antitrust violations, and the Hollywood production chiefs may have been content to forgo a story that would be costly to film. Whatever the case, Paul Reynolds, Jr., was soon handling *A Farewell to Arms*.

Confident that he could land Broadway and Hollywood, young Reynolds wanted Laurence Stallings to compose an adaptation to show around. Reynolds (a recent baccalaureate) had heard Stallings lecture at Williams College. Afterwards, "hobbling back and forth on his wooden leg, [the playwright] had talked into the wee hours of the morning," and as Reynolds later recalled, his "pacifist views fascinated me and the other undergraduates. I worshipped Stallings." Stallings was eager to take on *A Farewell to Arms*, and though wary, Hemingway acceded. Then (as he wrote Perkins) he heard from Fitzgerald that Stallings was "no good. Maxwell Anderson is the goods." Worse, Stallings had negotiated a fifty-fifty split with Hemingway for the theatrical and motion picture sale rights.

The percentages mirrored a standard adopted by the Broadway community less than eleven months before. In 1925 Fox had announced that it would produce plays as feeders for the screen. Unwilling to become "Caesar's kept woman," dramatists sued for what they called the Minimum Basic Agreement and in late 1928 won protection of both their artistic and their financial interests. As theater historian Alfred Bernheim says, the agreement afforded the author "not less than 50 per cent of the income accruing from the sale of motion picture and other rights. He had sometimes been forced to accept materially less as a result of commissions to agents actually in the employ of the producer, and of other subterfuges." The agreement did nothing for later relations between Hemingway and his agent. Hemingway wrote Perkins: "I'll be lucky to get $750 now minus [Reynolds's] 10%"

Despite what Hemingway and Fitzgerald thought of Stallings, Reynolds saw him as an alchemist who could turn *A Farewell to Arms* into Broadway *and* Hollywood gold. Stallings was well regarded on the West Coast. "It is marvelous the way Laurence Stallings has the Jews jumping," Sara Haardt (then in Hollywood) had told H. L. Mencken only two years before. "All of them hate him, but they are scared to death of him. He simply shouts them down." A veteran of the Great War, Stallings had coauthored the renowned *What Price Glory?* for stage (1924) and screen (1926). He had also written the story for *The Big Parade* (1925), not only the most honored of the silent war-films but among the top three box-office attractions of the 1920s. Moreover, since MGM had produced *The Big Parade*, the studio might see Stallings's name on a theatrical adaptation of *A Farewell to Arms*— the template for a motion picture script of *A Farewell to Arms*—and decide that the novel was worth considerably more than ten thousand dollars.

Stallings's three-act dramatization of *A Farewell to Arms* follows the chronology of Hemingway's novel and adopts much of its dialogue, including much of the frontline language that was not blanked out. The play opens on division headquarters for medical staff at the Italian front. Lieutenant Henry enters. He has been not to the Abruzzi but to an earthy spot that he describes for the priest. "I saw only the smoke of cafes and nights when the room whirled and you needed to look at the wall to make it stop," he says, "nights in bed, drunk, when you knew that that was all there was and the strange excitement of waking and not knowing who it was with you, and the world all unreal in the dark." Rinaldi is another hedonist, and Catherine Barkley appears to be yet another. When Frederic kisses her, she slaps him, then kisses him, open mouthed. Three days later, in scene 2, Frederic and Catherine have fallen hard for one another. The British are sending Catherine away, though, and when Frederic runs outside after her, he's hit by artillery. Rinaldi promises that Miss Barkley will nurse him back to health.

Act II develops the romance. At the end of scene 1, set in a room of the American hospital in Milan, Frederic pulls Catherine into bed with him. Five months later in scene 2, as the rain falls, Catherine tells Frederic she's pregnant. "You aren't angry?" she asks. "You don't feel—trapped?" Frederic responds: "You always feel trapped biologically." Scene 3 occurs in a hotel room near the depot. "Time's wingèd chariot" approaches as Frederic tells Catherine good-bye before returning to the front.

The compact and rushed final act opens on division headquarters, where Catherine has lost the baby. "If only she hadn't waited here for Henry," Nurse Ferguson tells the priest. "If only she had gone back when we first knew the Austrians had broken through. We could've given her the proper care and the boy would have lived and she wouldn't be facing death as she does now." The noise of the retreat (offstage) fills the proscenium. Sober at last, Frederic asks another officer to pray for Catherine. "I have grown old," the colonel responds. "I had hoped to become more devout, but somehow I haven't. I have outlived my religious feeling." So Frederic prays alone. Catherine hurts like hell, she says, and knows she will die, but rather than the priest, she wants only her lover, only Frederic. The rain continues to fall. The artillery screams down. And Catherine dies.

Though Stallings had not shown the war or the retreat, or fully translated the characters' laconic speech into stage dialogue, he had at least produced a serviceable play. Hemingway produced almost nothing that winter. Other than finishing the bullfight article for *Fortune*, he wrote only letters. He signed one of them "E. Cantwork Hemingstein."

As sales of *A Farewell to Arms* climbed toward eighty thousand in February

1930, the novel appeared on the *Bookman*'s "Monthly Score" of best-sellers, an unscientific (and unreliable) yardstick that publishers used as free advertising. *A Farewell to Arms* was at seventh place, and rising. Perhaps the reason was what one reporter called its "sex aberrations," or what Perkins regarded as its disdain for conventional taboos, or what one literary historian defined as its capacity to "domesticate alien, life-changing social ideas for the mass of the population." What was more certain was that along with the serialization, the photographs, the reviews, and the publicity, the sales had placed novel and author in the vanguard of American culture.

One day John Bishop and Allen Tate stopped by, and as they were leaving, Tate recalled, Ernest "called down the stairs and said, 'Wait a minute, I want to ask you something. The BBC has asked me to give a broadcast about *A Farewell to Arms*. Do you think it would violate the integrity of the writer to do that?' " Was the Professional Writer the camel with its nose under the tent, no longer pondering whether to enter, but when?

"It's hard enough to write," Hemingway told Perkins, "and writing prose is a full time job and all the best of it is done in your subconscious and when that is full of business, reviews, opinions etc. you don't get a damned thing." Putting business and reviews in the subconscious may have been a slip of the pen. It may also have been nearer the truth than the author knew.

Chapter Four

DEATH
IN THE
AFTERNOON

In January 1930, when Hemingway returned to America after more than ten months abroad, the burgeoning Hemingway legend had preceded him. Fitzgerald was telling "the god damndest stories about myself that I've ever heard," Hemingway wrote Perkins. He wanted the gossip stopped, and planned to settle up with Morley Callaghan and Robert McAlmon for rumors they had been spreading. He wrote Callaghan that on arrival in the States he would be "at your disposal any place where there is no publicity attached." The swagger (which others had also started to observe) may explain how the rumors had begun, and why they continued.

"Please don't tell *anybody* that we're coming," Hemingway had counseled Archie MacLeish. "Want to see you and Ada and a couple of fights maybe and not be a writer in N.Y." In Manhattan he probably saw Perkins, who had hoped for another manuscript—at least a collection of short stories—for the fall 1930 publishing season. He could not resist seeing old friends like Dorothy Parker, who promoted his work and his persona and who (in an occasional poem he wrote) functioned as his subject. He could likewise not resist trashing former old friends like Callaghan and Don Stewart, who had sold out. Though MacLeish was used to the bluster, he was on a short fuse that January. Ada had just had major surgery, and he was under the stress of a new job at *Fortune*, which had started "just at the time of the crash which was hard luck," Hemingway told Perkins. "But if ever a magazine sounded like useless balls this one does." MacLeish could have told Hemingway that *Fortune* served readers who bought and talked about contemporary literature, but MacLeish noticed that it was becoming hard to tell Hemingway anything, and the visit was strained.

Working with Paul Reynolds, Leland Hayward had meanwhile sold the *Farewell to Arms* playscript to theatrical producers William Brady and Al Woods in March 1930; the Reynolds and Hayward agencies split the commission. Reynolds's attorney also took a fractional percentage, and the Theatre Guild yet another. Perkins was hopeful. "I hear the play is going on this fall," he wrote Hemingway. "If only it makes a grand success, that would bring a big movie price. Then you might buy the Caroline and take us all on a trip." Hemingway was less sanguine: as he had foreseen months before, he had received a mere $750 advance, with which, as he later wrote Guy Hickok, "we bought our Beverly Hills Mansion."

Also that month *Fortune* published "Bullfighting: Sport and Industry," and the Modern Library issued *The Sun Also Rises* in maroon cloth and wrap. "What a shitty jacket! What a horrible looking broad!" Hemingway barked when he saw the Modern Library edition of the novel. The illustration featured Romero, Lady Ashley, and a bespectacled man wearing "goggles." That the jacket had an illustration at all was unusual. In 1930 the Modern Library used pictorial jackets only for its best-sellers, a prophecy usually fulfilled since, in the display racks of stores, the pictorial jackets stood out from the uniform ones. The Modern Library had decided that Hemingway would sell.

Had Hemingway looked beyond the jacket? Inside, Henry Seidel Canby had written an introduction whose first paragraph called the contents of *The Sun Also Rises* superior reportage. The author later called Canby a fool. "I'm a reporter *and an imaginative writer*," he told Perkins, "and I can still imagine plenty and there will be stories to write *as they happened* as long as I live." During the fishing party that he hosted in spring 1930, during the long days in the Dry Tortugas, Perkins gingerly lobbied for those stories. "Why don't you write about all this?" he asked the author. "I will in time, but I couldn't do it yet," Hemingway responded. According to Perkins, Hemingway meant that until the Gulf Stream penetrated his unconscious, it was useless to try to write about it. Another reason—not entirely unconscious—may also help explain his stalling.

"I am quite sure that I have no feeling for short stories," William Faulkner confessed, "yet for some strange reason I continue to [write them], and to try them on Scribners' with unflagging optimism." He also tried them on *College Humor* and *Liberty* and *Cosmopolitan*, and for reasons hardly strange to Hemingway. " 'I write stories,' " Scripps says in *The Torrents of Spring*. " 'I had a story in *The Post* and two in *The Dial*.' " The *Saturday Evening Post* was the patron whose bountiful rates allowed an author to write "seriously" for the *Dial,* or *Scribner's,* or book publishers. In the early 1930s, for instance, Faulkner could earn $750 for one *Post* story and only a $200 advance—and commensurate royalties—for one novel. Authors who wrote books like *The Sound and the Fury* (or like *A Farewell to Arms,* published ten days before *The Sound and the Fury*) could be destroyed (as was Fitzgerald) by writing for the *Post* or, say, *Woman's Home Companion,* where Faulkner published in April 1931, where Hemingway would have been embarrassed to publish. Hemingway had said as much to Philip Jordan, who wrote about his friend in the December 1929 *Everyman.*

> In America a well-known author can command such a fantastic price for a short story that he is often seduced from the path of novel writing, because a few short stories a year will keep him in comparative comfort in Europe. This lure, this stream of gold that pours out from the counting houses of magazines, Hemingway has so far resisted; and it looks as though he will go on resisting what to him cannot be so great a temptation as it is to less sincere writers.

Faulkner threaded through the slicks unmarred, but Hemingway feared that any work for the *Post* or *WHC,* or any work suited for publication there, could lay open his desire for fame and, worse, his having sold out to secure it.

What Hemingway produced in 1930 hints that he was caught in the middle. "The Sea Change" (about a young woman who leaves her young man because she has fallen for another woman) and "A Natural History of the Dead" (among other things, an attack on Robert Herrick, who penned the *Bookman*'s nasty review of *A Farewell to Arms*) could have been published in a literary magazine but not the *Saturday Evening Post.* "The Sea Change" was especially instructive since it addressed the struggle between the writer's need for privacy and the compulsion to use his inner life as the basis of authentic fiction. As Hemingway scholar Robert Fleming has shown, the story asks whether the male protagonist will "dehumanize himself if he encourages his lover in her sexual experiments so that he can write about her experiences." The nub of the question was as material to the character as to his creator.

By June 1930 Hemingway had finished a story for both "trained" and "general" readers, his first such story in more than a year. "Wine of Wyoming," really more long sketch than short story, portrays the Fontans, characters based on Signore and Signora Moncini of Sheridan, Wyoming. Monsieur and Madame Fontan are Prohibition Era bootleggers who run a distillery and roadhouse in country that, the narrator says, looks like Spain. The story is not much more than the Fontans' pointed and funny comments on European and American culture, but the last section alters the tone. The night before he leaves Wyoming for the season, the narrator chooses not to see the Fontans. " 'We ought to have gone last night,' " the narrator's companion says. She voices the unease that both couples sense. "Wine of Wyoming" was not vintage Hemingway. "I've never given you anything that wasn't good have I?" the author told Perkins in a defensive cover letter. "This is a 1st flight story I promise you." Apparently the story was written in 1929. The last section was added in 1930, and the seams showed. "There is quite a lot of French in the story," Perkins noted, alluding to questions of audience. There was also a lot of gamy language. But editor Robert Bridges was increasingly a figurehead on the magazine, and "goddam" and (repeatedly) "son of a bitch" were more proof that the author had not sold out. The story would appear in the August *Scribner's*.

"Wine of Wyoming" was the first and last publishable fiction Hemingway wrote in 1930. By summer he had turned to nonfiction, and by autumn he was well over 150 pages into a bullfight manuscript that would wed journalism and literature. The courage of his having chosen so doubtful (and doubtfully marketable) a subject should not be overlooked, for he could have knuckled under to the market and tried to produce the novel it wanted. Instead, he was pioneering a new genre. That said, though, he may also have been both exhausted and daunted by *A Farewell to Arms*, exhausted because he was best as a miniaturist and had been stretched by the story of Frederic and Catherine, daunted because the reception accorded that novel (which the American Library Association had honored as a "book of distinction" for 1929) pressured him to write another—as good or better—for trained and general readers. Rather than challenge the Hemingway of *A Farewell to Arms*, he may have sought breathing room in the nonfiction manuscript he had wanted to write for more than three years, the one that would allow "E. H." to speak directly to the highbrows who appreciated belles lettres and the middlebrows who could applaud a heroic narrator and guide.

In June Papa collected Bumby in New York. "Don't tell *anybody* I'm going to N.Y.," he had written Mike Strater, the painter who had done yet another portrait of the author in Key West that February and who, like MacLeish some months before, may have been expected to spread the word about the forthcoming trip to Gotham. Hemingway was indeed the public person. He was the author whose *Sun Also Rises* had absorbed Mrs. Gungen in the Dashiell Hammett short story "The Main Death." More than the author of à clef fiction, he was also, literally, a character. In the novel *Glass Mountain* (1930) he was the artist Max Harder, frank and "full of the zest for life," Joseph Warren Beach wrote, "though one soon tires of his type of conscious, flannel-shirted open-throated maleness." Though neither Hammett nor Beach knew Hemingway personally, they probably thought they did, thanks to the potency and lingering influence of the Breaker photographs.

In Wyoming that summer, Hemingway rode and fished and saw the bull-fight book grow. In Philadelphia meanwhile, the *Farewell to Arms* company was rehearsing for its pre-Broadway run. The large cast included Crane Wilbur as Rinaldi, Elissa Landi as Catherine, and Glenn Anders as Frederic. A young British actress, Landi brought an ethereal face and gentle manner to Nurse Barkley. Glenn Anders's body—the tensed muscles, the broad-bridged nose, the jutting jaw—projected a vitality that owed more to the roustabout Hemingway of the literary gossip columns than the more solemn Henry of *A Farewell to Arms*. But the script called for boldness. When Nurse Van Campen accuses Henry of having a self-inflicted wound, he asks whether she thinks a man would really try "to disable himself by kicking himself in the scrotum." In another scene Rinaldi explains the difference between sex with "a girl and a woman. With a girl it is painful. And you never know if the girl will really enjoy it!" The dialogue—franker when heard than read—was "about everything in general and biology in particular," one reporter noted; it offered up lessons in "masculine and feminine anatomy" and "much ado about the ladies of pleasure who have become 'war comrades.' "

A disciple of Stanislavsky, Rouben Mamoulian was the director of *A Farewell to Arms*. The thirty-one-year-old Russian émigré had been acclaimed for his lyrical direction of *Porgy* in 1926, and was expected to mount *A Farewell to Arms* with enough sensitivity and flair to compensate for its tough language and to ward off the censors. That Mamoulian had also directed a famed early sound picture, *Applause* (1929), could only augment the interest of Hollywood in the production.

The advertising for *A Farewell to Arms* in Philadelphia promoted the Grosset and Dunlap *Sun Also Rises*. Hemingway had seen an advance copy of the Grosset, and demanded that the publisher "at once remove that biographical *crap* [underlined twice] ie. *SHIT* about me on the back wrapper explaining to G. and D. what my position is about personal publicity." Scribners had apparently sent Grosset an old thumbnail biography, one that stopped short of saying that Hemingway had held a bridgehead at Caporetto. To soothe the author, Grosset destroyed the covers, and as Stallings's *Farewell to Arms* went into technical dress rehearsals in Philadelphia, *The Sun Also Rises* appeared in drugstores and depots.

"I do think it would be good for you to publish a number of stories now," Perkins told Hemingway. According to John Hall Wheelock, Scribners "went in more for the things that we knew would pay off," and the prospects for a book about the corrida, especially in the current business climate, were dour. The market wanted Hemingway fiction, not nonfiction; it wanted consolidation, not innovation, another *Farewell to Arms*, not an apologia for a sport foreign to American readers. Those were precisely the conventions and expectations that Hemingway the author so opposed, however, both in his writing and in his career. For the moment, Perkins would rely on the Grosset *Sun Also Rises* and the Broadway *Farewell to Arms* to keep the Professional Writer in the public eye.

Opening night, September 15, the Shubert Theater in Philadelphia was standing-room-only for what the press called a "play in three acts, arranged by Laurence Stallings." According to the "Program," though, Brady and Woods had billed Hemingway over both Stallings and the title, and the following day the critics hailed the author as the locomotive of the production. "For some years now," the review in the *Philadelphia Bulletin* noted, "Ernest Hemingway has held a rather enviable position in American literature. His style is unusual, his insight keen, his ability to draw a picture with a few strong dashes of literary color indisputable."

The *Bulletin*'s enthusiasm for the play itself was muted. "Without doubt, it contains great scenes. But these are great largely because in them one gets undiluted Hemingway." What the *Bulletin* missed were the memorable episodes: the retreat, the escape across the lake, the concentrated focus on Catherine's death. What it found too undiluted was Stallings's candor. Within forty-eight hours of the opening, producers Brady and Woods were meeting with the Philadelphia Board of Theatre Control. "It is necessary," Brady later told the press, "to observe the normal decencies." He would not detail the cuts or even admit that he had made them.

Like the publicity that Brady had wooed and won, sex and censorship were native to Broadway and Hollywood, especially Hollywood. The year Scribners published *A Farewell to Arms*, the studios had released a flood of "sex films" that trafficked in drinking, adultery, and fornication. In *Mad Hour*, a drunken couple awoke in a hotel double bed. "And if you don't hear those on the side lines at Burbank hollering, 'Make it hotter!' " daily *Variety* noted in its review, "then you have no imag." The month Stallings wrote *A Farewell to Arms* (another couple, another bed), the industry had surrendered to its critics and adopted a set of taboos on sex, language, costumes, and so on that warned producers away from content like that of *A Farewell to Arms*. Chafing under the Production Code that the Motion Picture Association had announced in March 1930, one filmmaker complained to *Variety* that two-thirds of the stories he now had under development "were based on 'Jack the Giant Killer' and the other third on 'Cinderella.' " Not surprisingly, then, the studios' commitment to the Production Code was not only hollow but short lived, and by September the movie companies had returned to the scripting of "sex films." Even less surprising, only hours after Brady and Woods opened *A Farewell to Arms*, the race for the screen rights to Hemingway's once-banned novel was on. Since the depression had not reached Hollywood, producers had deep pockets, especially for "hot" properties. Warner Bros. ended fiscal year 1930 with revenues of $130 million, while Loew's profits set a corporate record that would be unsurpassed for fifteen years. Radio-Keith-Orpheum and Universal had more modest balance sheets but considerable promise: RKO was associated with RCA, Universal with a newly launched program of big-budget films, including its 1929 adaptation of *All Quiet on the Western Front*. Paramount was the giant among the nascent Big Five. In 1930 it not only owned theaters across the country but had profits of $25 million and assets of more than $300 million. Paramount had once thought *A Farewell to Arms* not worth the $10,000 MGM had offered for it. Two days after the play opened, however, knowing that the price of the work could skyrocket with a long run, Paramount trumped the other studios with a bid of $80,000. Universal had paid only £40,000 for *All Quiet on the Western Front*, which by 1930 had sold well over three hundred thousand copies in the United States alone. Paramount had paid only $90,000 for the enormously successful and far more commercial dramatization of *The Virginian*, which by then was on movie screens everywhere. So the purchase price of *A Farewell to Arms* was extraordinary even by Hollywood standards. Ironically, though, only hours after Paramount bought the screen rights to the Hemingway work, Brady and Woods cut the two-week Philadelphia run of *A Farewell to Arms* in half. The box office showed that ticket sales would not support a second week.

On 22 September 1930, *A Farewell to Arms* opened at the National Theater in New York to "a thunderous reception." Once more, the press noted the candor of the play, which, "with no apologies to the censors in Flatbush, Jamaica and other hubs for Puritans, sticks as plainly as it can to Mr. Hemingway's own plain talk." And once more, the critics' enthusiasm for the drama was muted. According to the *New York Sun*, the uneven play "always shows plainly that it has once been a novel—a theatergoer who had never heard of the book, possibly because of a considerable period of detention on a desert island, could nevertheless hardly fail to suspect its existence." The reviewers generally liked Elissa Landi (who would soon go to Hollywood) but not Glenn Anders, whom the *Brooklyn Daily Eagle* called "a fidgeting, gushing, blathering mummer who has done very well in one or two parts before this but merely makes a monkey of Hemingway's plain and forthright hero." The *New York American* accused the entire play of grandstanding.

The finely casual ironical small-talk of the Italian officers becomes so much serio-comic wopologue now. Ideas which made permissible, in fact exquisite, musings in the book become heinously overblown speeches now. Little, unforgettable scenes like the lovers' parting in a tawdry Milan hotel room, so translucent to read, so sharp in print, are hurled fatally up to baby-grand opera emotionalism.

New York Evening Post critic John Mason Brown wrote that the play would confuse those who had not read the novel and in no way enrich those who had. "Be that as it may," he concluded, offering Scribners the best promotion it could hope for, " 'A Farewell to Arms' can be bought at the bookstore—as written by the author. So what does it all matter, anyway?" No succès d'estime, the dramatization nonetheless warned Hollywood screenwriters of pitfalls. It also added to the attention paid the author.

From Montana, where he was writing what he called the "bullfight book" as well as hunting mountain sheep and elk and supplying publishers with photographs of his exploits, Hemingway longed for news of Stallings's *Farewell to Arms*. "Write me what the damned play was like," he urged Perkins less than one week after the New York opening. Perkins wired back that the play was "not going well." Soon the novelist learned the unvarnished truth. "Honestly, Hemmie, it is an awful mess," wrote Milford Baker, a fellow veteran of the ambulance corps who had seen the play in Philadelphia, where he "sat in the tenth row with only three people back of me." Glenn Anders was "always disheveled, always drunk, always growling," and in general the adaptation was a hodge podge, "particularly the third act where the retreat and the hospital scenes are all jumbled in together." Unaware of the Paramount sale—which netted Hemingway twenty-four thousand dollars—Baker regretted that "they did not make a movie out of it which would have given them a wonderful opportunity to show the great scenes you give in the book—the retreat, the row down the lake and the wonderful scenes toward the close of the book in Switzerland."

Paramount may have seen what Baker saw—that Hollywood could accomplish what Broadway could not. The movies' internal regulators were less sure that Hollywood should try, and though Paramount (and other companies) tended to flaunt the Production Code, they could not quite ignore the office that enforced it. "A book describes; a film vividly presents," the Production Code stated. "The reaction of a reader to a book depends largely on the keenness of the reader's imagination; the reaction to a film depends on the vividness of presentation." About fornication—the glue of *A Farewell to Arms*—the code was blunt: "The sanctity of the institution of marriage and the home shall be upheld. Pictures shall not infer [*sic*] that low forms of sex relationship are the accepted or common thing."

Lamar Trotti of the Motion Picture Association had seen the play, and two days after the New York premiere had told West Coast Production Code Director Jason Joy that much of the action took place in beds, much of the diction was frank, and much of the labor scene with Catherine was repugnant. "In a word the play accentuates the objectionable features of the novel, and while I still think a treatment can be found in which delicacy and good taste will be exercised, the stage play certainly offers no hope in that direction." Bending the Production Code was de rigueur in Hollywood; Paramount and *A Farewell to Arms*, however, planned to break it.

The Production Code was not strong enough to stop the picture. Nor was the United States government. Well before the play opened in New York, the Italian ambassador to the United States had asked the Motion Picture Association to discourage a screen adaptation. The association's president, Will Hays, had warned Paramount that the "war business" in the novel could move Italy to ban not only *A Farewell to Arms* but all Paramount pictures, maybe even all American pictures. Hemingway, already careworn on this score, would have been concerned about the repercussions for his novel (or novels) abroad. But Paramount moguls were unmoved, and Hays could not have expected otherwise. In Hollywood, during the renaissance of "sex films," eighty-thousand-dollar investments outranked Production Code rules and diplomatic objections. The Paramount *Farewell to Arms* would thus go forward.

In October 1928 an adaptation of Floyd Dell's novel *An Unmarried Father* had opened successfully on Broadway and earned the author almost five hundred dollars per week; it was his "first serious money in years." Fitzgerald had of course earned even more on the stage production of *The Great Gatsby*. Hemingway was not so lucky. On 7 October 1930 Woods and Brady posted the closing notice for Stallings's version of *A Farewell to Arms*. The last performance was Saturday, October 11, precisely three weeks after the production opened on Broadway. The run might have been even shorter had Woods and Brady been assured of their slice of the Paramount pie. According to the Minimum Basic Agreement, the producer may "share with the author in all receipts from rights" only if the producer "has produced the play under his own direction in New York City for seventy-five performances, or, in the alternative, for three consecutive weeks."

"They took off the play last Saturday," Perkins wrote Hemingway, saying nothing about lost revenue but assuring him that the failure would not hurt his reputation. "In fact one reason [the play] did not succeed, I think was that all the reviewers began by praising the book, and explaining how hard it was to come up to such a book, and how it had not been possible for Stallings to do it in spite of some mighty clever work."

Though Broadway's *Farewell to Arms* had been admired, Perkins told Hemingway's English publisher that the depression had been too much for several plays that season to weather. Soon many actors would indeed be looking for work, and the banks, with their theater mortgages at risk, would begin producing shows themselves. But Stallings pooh-poohed such excuses. The play closed down the play, he told Perkins, not only apologizing but taking full responsibility for the short run. Months later Hemingway himself explained to MacLeish "the mystery of why there were fifteen curtain calls the night Farewell to Arms opened, and yet it only ran three weeks. They must have all been by people who wanted to sleep with either Mr. Anders or Miss Landi."

"Now we must get this straight," Hemingway told Perkins. He was concerned about the second edition of *In Our Time*, which Boni & Liveright had finally sold to Scribners in 1930. The book had been published when the author had been unknown and worth nothing. A reissue could invite libel suits or censorship. "Mr. and Mrs. Elliot," for instance, was a transparent and vicious attack on the poet Chard Powers Smith. Liveright had cut several passages to avoid charges of obscenity, but the Elliots were obviously the Smiths. For that reason alone, Hemingway ordered Perkins, Scribners must "put a iron clad protective notice in the front that there are no actual characters and that the names are not those of any living people." Perkins could "work out the wording and be responsible for it."

Perkins was so attuned to Hemingway's moods that he had reportedly forgone an opportunity to sign William Faulkner: he knew that Ernest would never have allowed the two authors under one roof. Again to reassure Hemingway, Perkins called in an attorney to concoct the "legal disclaimer" that would appear (hastily added, on a different paper stock) on page five of *In Our Time*. "In view of a recent tendency to identify characters in fiction with real people, it seems proper to state that there are no real people in this volume: both the characters and their names are fictitious. If the name of any living person has been used, the use was purely accidental."

Hemingway was anxious enough about audience and *In Our Time* to demand a foreword as well as a disclaimer. The former, he told Perkins, would guide inexperienced readers through the stories and lend the book a historical rather than commercial raison d'être. In the foreword, Edmund Wilson showered praise on Hemingway and his work. When he called *A Farewell to Arms* "a rather romanticized idyll," though, the author bristled. The phrase hinted that the novel was dishonest or catered to popular taste. If Hemingway disagreed with Wilson, whom he respected, it was not because he thought Wilson was "an ass." Instead, he said, it was "that possibly I've seen more people die than he has and that we differ in our attitude toward the pleasure of sexual intercourse." For better or worse, the authoritarian narrator of the bullfight manuscript talked just like that.

"Patrick says his father doesn't love him because he never comes to see him," Hemingway wrote MacLeish, yet the author was so focused on the bullfight book that he could not pause even to scan the proofs of Scribners' *In Our Time*. The second American edition would correct the "errors" of the first. A "woman having a kid" in Boni & Liveright would become a "woman having a baby" in Scribners. And a matador who "couldn't hardly get the sword in" in Boni & Liveright would become one who "could hardly get the sword in" in Scribners. Perkins's "straightlacedness" (according to one Hemingway scholar) caused the emendations in diction and grammar. Perkins also ordered the print run, a cautious 3,240 copies. At least a fraction of the tens of thousands who had read *A Farewell to Arms* wanted to see what they had missed when the author had been unknown, however, and a conservative second printing of 1,035 copies followed almost immediately on publication. Entering the stores just as Doubleday introduced a "dollar books" series, the reissued *In Our Time*—priced $2.50—had stiff competition yet sold exceptionally well. The collection showed what the author could do when he was in good form; the more he wrote on the bullfight manuscript, the more he felt that old confidence surge.

Then, just outside Billings, Montana, on November 1, Hemingway accidentally sent his car into a ditch and spent the following seven weeks in St. Vincent's Hospital. It was a dark winter. One brooding letter to Perkins was notable for the unusual lapses in spelling, punctuation, and gratitude.

> Don't let Reynolds tell you that I got two and a half times what the book would have brought for movies alone last fall a year ago. . . . $80,000 was paid for the picture rights, which was negotiated by Stallings, Woods and their attorneys, but Reynolds, by his own accounting received $8,000, that is a third as much as I got for writing the book or Stallings for making the play, or Woods for producing it. He manoeuvered it with the movie angle always in mind, so that he got the

maximum possible commission, and I got a flop on Broadway that didn't ever cover the advance.

On sleepless nights in the dark hospital room, Hemingway thought that even "Maxie has double-crossed me pretty badly" on theatrical deals. The more rational Hemingway could reflect on his manuscript in progress. In *The Sun Also Rises* and *A Farewell to Arms,* Jake Barnes and Frederic Henry had said much that Hemingway believed—and wanted said—about romance and courage and art. The authority on such matters was naturally the author, and in the bullfight book the author would be the narrator, at once the litterateur who had earned international acclaim, the patriarch who was expert on wine and toreros and boxing, the professor who had founded the so-called Hemingway school of writing, the glamor boy of the retouched photographs and *New Yorker* profiles, the black-bearded legend who, according to rumor around Billings, had cirrhosis of the liver. The narrator would be seasoned and informed, and the voice of the narrator would weave the reader into the pages of the text as though narrator and reader were one. Ernest Hemingway the public performer was now and ever "perfectly conscious of audience." The prophetic title of the book would be *Death in the Afternoon.*

On the shortest day of year, December 21, 1930, Hemingway was released from St. Vincent's Hospital. By Christmas Eve he was in Piggott, and by early January in Key West. Insulated from the depression, he soon learned that not all authors or publishers had been so fortunate. "Business seems to get worse and worse all the time," Perkins wrote. Charles Scribner had just found that an employee in the cashiers department had embezzled sixty-one thousand dollars, then squandered the entire sum on Wall Street. The double loss confirmed that the world was in trouble, that, as Perkins noted, people had become so desperate that they thought (or said) that capitalism was dissolving.

Publishers everywhere were at sixes and sevens. They granted booksellers generous terms, then looked for ways to undercut them, as at Putnam, where retailers could return one book for every two they promised to buy in the future. Pricing was also chaotic. Publishers brought out dozens of new fiction titles at one dollar, then wondered whether prices had any bearing on sales, especially after Dutton listed *The Story of San Michele* at $3.75 and sold over 170,000 copies. In general, publishers shaved expenses, products, and personnel. For an established company like Scribners the road was rough. As *Scribner's Magazine* editor Robert Bridges turned senile, he retired but would not leave. He was an old bachelor with no life apart from the firm, he said, and so Alfred Dashiell rose to editor and Bridges was moved to the sixth floor to vet manuscripts that house readers had already rejected.

Perkins also marked time. Hoping Wolfe and Fitzgerald could ride out the turbulence in their personal lives, he encouraged Tom to continue on *Of Time and the River* and Scott to return to work, even if, prophetically, all he could manufacture was an article about the end of the Jazz Age. Perkins took some risks, and lost; he published a book by Erskine Caldwell that went nowhere. He also declined risks. He turned down a Ford Madox Ford manuscript (*Where the Wicked Man*, later published by Viking) because of its latent anti-Semitism, and many other books because of their limited appeal. In 1923 Scribners had published Thomas Boyd's *Through the Wheat*, a successful novel that Hemingway had called "an awfully good book." Seven years later the house rejected two proposals from that author. Perkins wrote Boyd:

> The commercial requirements in publishing have become more exacting, and the considerations of intrinsic value—such as that which would come from the historical importance of what you plan—less effective. The market is so crowded with books, competition so acute, and people so much more inclined apparently, to travel in flocks even in their reading, that it is harder to get an adequate sale for books of the sort you speak of.

Perkins's assessment would have been equally germane for a book about the corrida.

According to *Death in the Afternoon*, "what you will want at a bullfight, good bulls and good matadors being given, is a good public." Hemingway also wanted a good public, and he had one for fiction. He had appeared in four anthologies in 1930, including the Modern Library *Great Modern Short Stories*; he would appear in four more in 1931, including *The Twenty-five Finest Short Stories*, which was promoted as both text and trade book. These collections would introduce him to general readers and college students who had missed him in *Scribner's Magazine* or hard cover, and would build his name. In 1931, though, they unnerved him. The anthologies had cannibalized *In Our Time* and *Men Without Women*, he told Perkins. They took the best of these collections for forty dollars per story and pocket change per year in royalties; worse, they made rinds of the original books, their cohesion gone, their capital disbursed. He was not worrying, he added, but he may have foreseen the consequences for *Death in the Afternoon*. The Hemingway audience craved new stories, new collections, and (especially) new novels—not new nonfiction, at least not in book form.

Hemingway sensed the pressure up close. *Cosmopolitan* had been pursuing him and his fiction since 1926, and in January 1931 editor Harry Burton appeared in Florida hat in hand. Though Hemingway had reneged on a *Cosmopolitan* contract in 1927, he now had an excuse for second thoughts: he wanted to go on safari. Burton told Hemingway that he would pay five thousand dollars a piece for stories, as much as he would have paid for five stories three years before, and (according to Paul Reynolds) double what *Collier's* would have paid for one story sixteen months before. Perkins hoped the author would accept; Hemingway had written virtually no fiction since January 1929, and the magazine contract could kindle the fire. Hemingway boasted that he would sooner chop the fingers off his hand than write for *Cosmopolitan* or the other monthlies. If he could write fiction on his own terms, however, he had no good reason to shun the slicks, and in January 1931 he had not ruled them out.

Like the anthologies and popular magazines, Broadway and Hollywood were also raising the demand for Hemingway fiction. In January, Perkins had read a revised dramatization of "The Killers." Though the play sentimentalized the story and once more cast away its undercurrent of terror, Perkins urged Hemingway to consider any reasonable offer for the theatrical rights. In February, confident that the sale of *A Farewell to Arms* to Paramount could prompt the sale of *The Sun Also Rises* to some other studio in Hollywood, agent Ann Watkins told Perkins that the fiesta novel could bring twenty-five thousand dollars, a fat price for the "literary" work of an author whose current best-seller had curdled when dramatized. Perkins was optimistic nonetheless. These "byproducts of your writing" could "make you freer to do just what you want with the writing itself," he told the author. "It is this side of the question that seems to me the important one." Whatever Perkins and Hemingway called them, however, adaptations were not by-products, not to the droves that attended the theaters or movie houses. They were *products* of an author of fiction, and rather than free him, they could further encourage the public to view any nonfiction he wrote as entr'acte, or by concentrating more publicity on his life than his work, persuade the public not to read him at all but to look on him as a literary character and celebrity.

Throughout late winter 1931 Ernest and Pauline entertained. Grace Hemingway visited for two days in late January, to meet her grandson Patrick and thank her son in person for the trust fund he had established in 1930. The trust fund for Grace was a blend of royalty money and Pfeiffer money that, like the money he had sent her in the months following the suicide, Hemingway used to reach—and shut out—his mother. "Poor Boy," Grace once wrote of her late husband to her son, "he worked so hard and got so little out of life. I could not wish him back for a minute. He earned his rest and peace and joy." Ernest was convinced that she had wished the doctor dead, and the wretchedness of that thought and the generosity of the trust fund connoted his unresolved feelings toward her.

By April 1931 Hemingway had resumed work on the bullfight manuscript but because of his broken arm could write only four hundred words or so per day. Pregnant again and looking for a home, Pauline settled on an old mansion with iron rails and balconies. Uncle Gus arrived to handle the purchase; he paid eight thousand dollars cash for the house, and repairs and improvements would soon add another four figures and more.

By summer Hemingway was at the bullfights in Spain, where one day he sat in the arena with Charlie Chaplin. They were "the focus of many admiring eyes and I felt very jealous of you," Caresse Crosby told Ernest. "It must be thrilling to be famous and I wondered how to set about it." Pauline was then closing the apartment in Paris. She had gotten a permanent wave, she wrote to her husband, and she thought he would like it. "Hurry up and grow yours and I will make braids or buckles in the back on rainy afternoons." Meanwhile Hemingway collected photographs for the book and finished the short essays that would become its glossary. When he and Pauline sailed for America in September, he had completed eighteen of twenty chapters.

The thick manuscript Hemingway carried on board the *Ile de France* was narrated by an *I* calculated to be the focus of many admiring eyes. Part encyclopedia, part vade mecum, and part belles lettres, it teemed with information, for the author had consulted more than two thousand books and attended hundreds of bullfights. He had conversed with matadors, dined and drunk with them, seen them gored and doctored, and watched them bleed and die. He had fought amateur bouts, and told readers he understood the valor and control of the bullfighter. He had followed the bull from breeding grounds to death in the arena, and told readers he understood his psyche. The most common mental stage of the bull and to Hemingway "the most interesting" was the development of the *querencia.* The *querencia* was the bull's "preferred locality" during the fight, his refuge and the place where he was most dangerous. In the *querencia* the bull was "altogether on the defensive." Occasionally he refused to move—and not because he was cowardly. When goaded he defended himself "seriously, desperately, wisely and ferociously."

The narrator of *Death in the Afternoon* was as testy as the bull in the querencia. On page 1 he acknowledged the cruelty of the bullfight but insisted on writing frankly about it. Some people with "fineness of feeling" will object, but "whoever reads this can only truly make such a judgment when he, or she, has seen the things that are spoken of and knows truly what their reactions to them would be." Seven pages later when he spoke of the *corrida de toros* as a Spanish institution, one that exists despite rather than because of foreigners and tourists, the narrator could have been speaking of the relationship of the manuscript to the general reader. The bullfight will never please the uninitiated, he said, and "any step to modify it to secure their approval" would destroy it. Like an honest matador, an author must perform "without tricks" and be content with only "a nucleus of spectators that he can play for." But the author may have been less the honest matador than the honest preacher who suspects he tends toward sin: the passage may have been a sermon by Hemingway, for "Hemingway."

The matador who loses his honor and lives "through his contracts, hating the public he fights before," was as despicable as the author who does not write truly, the narrator continued. Look at Faulkner. He had admitted writing *Sanctuary* (1931) in three weeks to make money, and according to the narrator of *Death in the Afternoon*, he was "prolific too. By the time you get them ordered there'll be new ones out." What did Hemingway resent more, the output or the publicity? Though the *Memphis Evening Appeal* had called *Sanctuary* a "devastating, inhuman monstrosity of a book that leaves one with the impression of having been vomited bodily from the sensual cruelty of its pages," the sensational novel, with its rape by corncob, had focused attention on the unknown author. Oh, Mr. Faulkner, one reader reportedly gushed on meeting him; authors always appear in their books, so which character were you? "Madam," he answered, "I was the corncob."

Hemingway needed no corncob. He had the *cojones* of the matadors of *Death in the Afternoon, cojones* enough not to cater to the public as Faulkner had. In one passage of the *Death in the Afternoon* manuscript, he said that he would tell stories. "I do not say they will equal those of Mr. Faulkner," he conceded, then scratched through the sentence. The irony was too heavy. The underlying point was nonetheless vital. Hemingway was no prostitute. He had dashed off *The Torrents of Spring* to cure Sherwood Anderson of an excess of style, and composed *The Sun Also Rises* and *A Farewell to Arms* all for himself inside. The public acceptance was secondary. Secondary, perhaps, but *there*. After words about love in one chapter of *Death in the Afternoon*, the narrator admitted that they had nothing to do with bullfighting, "nothing at all, it is only conversation to give you [readers] your money's worth." Though the irony was again too heavy, the passage remained in the text.

In chapter 7 of the manuscript Hemingway introduced the Old Lady. The simple woman was the proxy for readers who "want the old, the way it was that they remember it," readers who want "more dialogue" and more plot and more climax, readers who want value for money. When the narrator recounts a lovers quarrel between two homosexuals, the Old Lady frowns on the flat ending. "Ah, Madame, it is years since I added the wow to the end of a story," he protests. The more she listens to the narrator, the Old Lady says, the less she likes him. By chapter 16 she's gone. "What about the Old Lady?" the narrator asks in a rhetorical question. "We threw her out of the book, finally." Narrator and readers (we) had conspired to applaud "Hemingway." It was paradox par excellence. It was also impossible to tell whether the author loved or hated the audience.

The *Ile de France* docked on September 29, and the Hemingways spent the next week on the East Coast with the MacLeishes and Waldo Peirce. Three years before, young Mary MacLeish had been shocked to see Ernest with an open gash on his forehead. Her father rendered a snapshot of the moment in "White-Haired Girl."

> She ran to him,
> stopped, looked, screamed. It wasn't Ernest!
> wasn't Ernest! wasn't . . .
> She raced up the stair.

In 1931 it was MacLeish who thought it wasn't Ernest. Hemingway of *Death in the Afternoon* was the wow in the story. He was witty and caustic and overbearing, rather like an inflated version of his persona or press releases. He was once more the performer as reporter—of and at the event, the observer and the observed. There was an urgency and stridency not present earlier, though, a sense that he was manufacturing the personal publicity he once had scorned. He said he wanted to reach a nucleus of spectators, *only* a nucleus of spectators, and yet, in another paradox par excellence, he used the voice of the stentor as though he wanted to reach the mass audience. No bullfighter could work that close without feeling the brush of the horns.

In early October, Perkins talked with Hemingway about the manuscript of *Death in the Afternoon*. He probably also talked about the renewed interest in the screen rights to *The Sun Also Rises*. That past spring, having gotten no offers for the novel, Ann Watkins had passed it along to Leland Hayward, an even more powerful agent who thought he could sell it for $12,500; he too had gotten nowhere. As Watkins explained, "the difficulty at the bottom of the thing was that there was a story by a man named Saunders that had bull fighting in it and that this kept the other producers off the subject, and that they also feared the censorship on the bull fighting and on that other element in the story." Hemingway was galled. Hollywood no longer pursued *The Sun Also Rises,* he wrote Perkins, because scenarist John Monk Saunders had "swiped" its expatriate soldiers and postwar cynicism for the movie called *The Last Flight.* The guts of the novel "having now been stolen they dont want it anymore." Worse, Hemingway had been "royally buggared" of the money. Perkins advised him to be patient and not "give the impression that the rights [would] go cheap."

Cheap! The $30,000 "*as a minimum*" that Hemingway had once counted on for *The Sun Also Rises* had been marked down to $25,000, then $12,500, and even then would not sell. And though Perkins had reprinted *In Our Time* in late 1930 chiefly to promote the name of the author, Hollywood and the screen version of *The Sun Also Rises* or *A Farewell to Arms* (whose screenplay was slowly evolving) could have done the job far better.

Perkins was sanguine about neither *Death in the Afternoon* nor the career of the author. In the 1920s industry profits had been so hearty that Scribners had doubled Perkins's salary and increased his ownership of the house through stock shares, but in the 1930s the authors Perkins had wooed and won could no longer be depended on as assets. Ring Lardner was laid up with tuberculosis, worsened by alcohol and tobacco. Fitzgerald had written practically nothing since that article about the Jazz Age, and Wolfe, hating his "stinking remnant of a rotten fish" manuscript, told Perkins he was "out of the game—and it is a game, a racket. What I do now must be for myself. I don't care who 'gets ahead' of me—that game isn't worth a good goddamn." Hemingway at least was in the game, in the *querencia.* How readers would respond was another question.

At Charles Scribner's Sons net earnings had fallen 40 percent in two years, and the 1932 forecasts were even more grim. In better times the sales force would have seized on anything by Hemingway, even a bullfight book; the popular reputation of the author and *A Farewell to Arms* would insure decent sales, and the publicity fanned by the new book would generate backlist orders. The new book sounded like an appendix to the 1926 fiesta novel, though, one that could generate orders for the Grosset or Modern Library reprints of *The Sun Also Rises.* Booksellers were not likely to reorder *A Farewell to Arms* from Scribners either, since Scribners was already negotiating with Grosset and Modern Library to give them reprint rights. In bad times the sales force needed continuity of product. "It takes a year or eighteen months for a book to get known outside of the centres," Perkins told Hemingway, "and often its biggest sale in the old days came after a year or eighteen months." Whether retailers would allow a book called *Death in the Afternoon* to linger unsold on shelves well into 1933 was yet another question.

By late November, Ernest and Pauline were parents of a second son, Gregory Hancock Hemingway, "Gregory" for several popes and "Hancock" for Caroline Hancock Hall, his maternal great-grandmother, another sign that Ernest may have wanted to honor his mother even though he disliked her. He had meanwhile revised and cut the first eighteen chapters of *Death in the Afternoon*. And once in Key West, in the mansion on Whitehead Street, he worked to finish the book. "I hate like hell to end it—could write on for another year easily enough," he told Perkins the day after Christmas.

Happily for Scribners, chatter about Laurence Stallings's stage adaptation and the forthcoming Hollywood film based on *A Farewell to Arms* had kept Hemingway in the news throughout 1930 and 1931. Paul Pfeiffer had told his daughter Pauline and her husband that according to the March 1930 *Photoplay*, " 'Farewell to Arms' will be filmed with John Gilbert as the leading star. We think he will make a fine lieutenant. Mother and I are both anxious to see this new talking movie. How soon may we look for it?" The costar then attached to *A Farewell to Arms* was Ernest Hemingway. According to the *New Republic*, his "open-throated pictures are now well known, and [his] abstention from any upkeep of his celebrity by a circulation around New York has added to the somewhat romantic impression of him that has got about." Lacking usable new photographs of the author, and laying the groundwork for *Death in the Afternoon*, Scribners printed up copies of a snapshot taken four years before in Pamplona. Hemingway was seated on the ground beside a steer, both facing the camera, with the author resting one hand on one of the horns. When he spotted the photo in print, Hemingway ordered it withdrawn. The docile animal looked like a house pet. It wasn't Ernest! wasn't Ernest! wasn't . . .

He was no less concerned about words. When he spotted errors about "Hemingway" in the 1931 *Living Authors*, he ordered the entry withdrawn. Less than one week later he recanted. As he probably understood, his absence from an edition that included William Faulkner, Sinclair Lewis, and others could damage his reputation. Tell the "Living Author pimps" (he wrote Perkins) that he would "cut the worst crap" from the sketch and allow its publication. *Living Authors* could underscore the fact that the "Hemingway" franchise belonged only to Ernest Hemingway, that he had earned his personal reputation, and that he, and he alone, not poachers like scenarist John Monk Saunders, could trade on it.

The Hemingway persona almost made one forget the Hemingway legacy. His fiction of the 1920s had been subtle, evocative, sensual, and translucent. Like Cézanne, he had portrayed sensation—condensed and concentrated, clean and delicate. Much happened between the lines.

Much even happened between the words, as when Frederic and Catherine sleep together. In a hotel room opposite the train station, the waiter "came and took away the things. After a while we were very still and we could hear the rain." Attentive readers understood what happened during "a while."

Hemingway's prose was rather like the world of Jake Barnes, "very clear and bright, and inclined to blur at the edges." In "Indian Camp," for instance, Nick Adams's father performs a cesarean on a scared Indian woman. The action of the scene is clear and bright, the depiction of feeling blurred.

> Inside on a wooden bunk lay a young Indian woman. She had been trying to have her baby for two days. All the old women in the camp had been helping her. The men had moved off up the road to sit in the dark and smoke out of range of the noise she made. She screamed just as Nick and the two Indians followed his father and Uncle George into the shanty. She lay in the lower bunk, very big under a quilt. Her head was turned to one side. In the upper bunk was her husband. He had cut his foot very badly with an ax three days before. He was smoking a pipe. The room smelled very bad.

Less stoic in tone than *In Our Time* (from which the example above is taken), *The Sun Also Rises* and *A Farewell to Arms* retain the focus on death and fear. They also retain the vivid diction. Hemingway had reinvented the language of the novel. He had moved more toward poetry, here Pound, there Whitman. His accretion of detail was especially powerful in *The Sun Also Rises*. Early on, Jake watches Brett enter a café with a group of young men whose manicured appearance riles Jake and amuses a policeman who looks at Jake and smiles. As the group entered, Jake says, "I saw white hands, wavy hair, white faces, grimacing, gesturing, talking. With them was Brett. She looked very lovely and she was very much with them." The refrain "with them" conveys Jake's sadness, as Linda Wagner has pointed out. And the passage conveys the richness of the whole work, at once a novel of manners, a social history, and (the hands and the smile) a representation of codes. The century that was new when Hemingway wrote his best work would end with few other writers leaving so indelible a mark on American literature and American readers.

Five o'clock weekday afternoons Max Perkins left Scribners for "tea" at the Ritz Bar, then boarded the 6:02 for New Canaan. One evening he met a young woman on the train. Conversing as they sped along, he learned that she was an avid reader and an admirer of *The Sun Also Rises* and *A Farewell to Arms*. She was also a domestic servant. So you see, Perkins wrote

Hemingway, "you are getting far beyond [the] intelligensia [*sic*]." Having that large audience was the goal of the author, and the fear of the author, as his fiction once more hinted.

Composed of fragments written throughout 1930 and 1931, "A Natural History of the Dead" was for the elite. If the study of all branches of natural history proves the existence of God, the narrator says, then so should the study of the dead. What followed—part expository prose, part satire—described the victims of the Austrian offensive of June 1918.

If left long enough in the heat the flesh comes to resemble coal-tar, especially where it has been broken or torn, and it has quite a visible tarlike iridescence. The dead grow larger each day until sometimes they become quite too big for their uniforms, filling these until they seem blown tight enough to burst. The individual members may increase in girth to an unbelievable extent and faces fill as taut and globular as balloons.

The story detoured into an attack on "Humanists" who had skewered Hemingway in the book review pages, then closed with a dialogue between a lieutenant of artillery and a doctor who refuses to kill a gravely wounded soldier. "Fuck yourself," the lieutenant tells the doctor. "Fuck yourself. Fuck your mother. Fuck your sister. . . ." And fuck *Cosmopolitan* and its general reader, Hemingway silently added.

On several occasions Caresse Crosby (who would publish the French edition of *In Our Time*) had entreated Hemingway to send her fiction for her Black Sun Press. He offered her "A Natural History" in early fall 1931, and she later "very reluctantly" returned the manuscript. "A Natural History" was *expérimental* with a vengeance. It juggled the expository and the dramatic, and the macabre, the parodic, and the violent. It might have cohered as a story—except for its condescending attack on the "Humanists." The narrator asked how the "Humanists" could espouse decorum when the future of the race hinged on the indecorous act of procreation. He jeered at these "children of decorous cohabitation" and longed for the moment that "worms will try that long preserved sterility; with their quaint pamphlets gone to bust and into foot-notes all their lust."

Hemingway had chosen a 30.06 Mauser to shoot skeet. He had trivialized the war dead, using them not to denounce romantic idealism but to harass the critics, including the "Humanist" Robert Herrick, who wrote "What Is Dirt?" "A Natural History" was sardonic, and not always intentionally. After making some minor revisions, Hemingway wove "A Natural History" into *Death in the Afternoon*. Since the two narrators shared one brazen voice, the patchwork hardly showed.

"After the Storm" was fiction for Perkins's young woman on the train. In the story a fisherman near Sou'west Key finds a wrecked ocean liner that "must have had five million dollars worth in her." Through one porthole he sees a woman "with her hair floating all out" and rings on one hand. He dives again and again but cannot smash the glass. Days later, once "the Greeks" have blasted the liner and harvested the wealth, the fisherman wonders about the night the ship went down. Apparently, however, he feels nothing for the victims. "First there was the birds," he says as the story ends, "then me, then the Greeks, and even the birds got more out of her than I did."

Captain Eddie "Bra" Saunders had told Hemingway the story, which was supposedly based on fact. In an early manuscript, Hemingway had conspicuously framed the tale with both a narrator and an audience of hangers-on. "Waldo" and "Dos" asked questions, spurred digressions, and fed on accounts of the bad luck of the liner passengers and the narrator; they were the last to "get more out of her." In the final manuscript, though, Hemingway cut them. Perhaps he disliked the resemblance to Conrad and *Heart of Darkness*, where Marlow tells the mariners of the horror he found. Perhaps as well, he thought the frame knotted the story. "Waldo" and "Dos" made "After the Storm" less a sea yarn (the tale of the one that got away) than a complex study of bottomless greed; they allowed Hemingway to place another layer of irony in the space between author and characters. For readers more interested in plot than theme, "Waldo" and "Dos" were expendable. Hemingway thinned the narration, and sold the story to *Cosmopolitan*. Paid a dollar a word, the author was the very last to get more out of her.

Hemingway was no Grub Street hack. When the prose of *Death in the Afternoon* was good, it caught the sensuousness of *The Sun Also Rises* and *A Farewell to Arms*: "On hot nights [in Madrid] you can go to the Bombilla to sit and drink cider and dance and it is always cool when you stop dancing there in the leafyness of the long plantings of trees where the mist rises from the small river. On cold nights you can drink sherry brandy and go to bed." When the prose foundered, however, it laid bare the harshness in the narration. In January 1932, proofreading the 320 typescript pages of the book, Hemingway had spotted the flaws. Though he would assure readers that *Death in the Afternoon* contained no "horseshit," he called the text an "abortion," and told Dos Passos that if "it were all as bad as some of it it would be pretty bloody awful but if it were all as ok as some of it [it] would be pretty good. Am trying to excise the larger gobs of shyte."

Hemingway understood that the literary market would not support a "punk" book. Between 1931, when the editor of "that stink *Cosmopolitan*" visited Florida, and 1932, when the magazine accepted "After the Storm," rates had dropped 50 percent. Though Hemingway routinely sold by the piece rather than the word, he had accepted $2,642 for "After the Storm" since, as he told Guy Hickok, "this depression is hell." He also understood that he needed some new fiction in print and, moreover, that he needed money. He could hardly count on RKO (notwithstanding rumors of interest) to do more than natter about options and screen rights on *The Sun Also Rises*. In early 1932, however, MGM offered short-term contracts to Faulkner and Hemingway. The author of *Sanctuary* accepted, and in six weeks earned three thousand dollars, just short of what he had earned on his writing in ten years. Hemingway declined. MGM had wanted him to script a bullfight picture, which would have doubled his selling out, once by going to Hollywood, then by trading on "the masculine idea." Key West expenses meanwhile included not only renovation of the house and up-keep on the car but salaries of the nursemaid, the gardener, and the maid. Literature was "a very tough business," he told Mary Pfeiffer, and should *Death in the Afternoon* fail he would have no alibis. What he called his revived interest in the short story that February 1932 may have been the obverse of his worry that *Death in the Afternoon* would not succeed, that the shouts he had used to rally the mass audience would fall on deaf ears.

"The book piles upon you wonderfully," Perkins wrote Hemingway, "and becomes to one reading it—who at first thinks bullfighting only a small matter—immensely important." As Perkins read through the type-script of *Death in the Afternoon* in February 1932, the book market was continuing to head down. The Hemingway market, though, was heading up. Grosset and Dunlap had contracted to reprint seventy-five thousand copies of *A Farewell to Arms* and ordered a first printing of twenty-five thousand. The author feigned indifference. He had no royalty arrangement, he told Perkins, and in addition he preferred the Modern Library to the mass-distribution Grosset and Dunlap, which wanted *A Farewell to Arms* only because it was destined for Paramount and the "moom pictures," a phrase coined by Walter Winchell, whom Hemingway admired, one man having reinvigorated slang, the other prose fiction. The Modern Library was no less high on Hemingway; it had contracted for twenty-five thousand copies of *A Farewell to Arms* and printed seven thousand. That revived interest in the short story had occurred none too soon, for reprints of *A Farewell to Arms* would buoy the demand for Hemingway fiction, if not (as Perkins soon would see) *Death in the Afternoon*.

Perkins declined the annual invitation to Key West that spring because of his daughter's illness and his own "bad luck in bunches." Another reason may have been his reticence to discuss *Death in the Afternoon* with the author face to face. He thought he could persuade Hemingway to tone down the attacks on living writers like Waldo Frank, whose *Virgin Spring* (1926) had also been about Spain but was, according to Hemingway, shallow and uninformed; he also knew that the author would defer to the obscenity laws on "words." But who could tell Hemingway that the manuscript was overlong? the bloodshed of soldiers and matadors and bulls overdone? the *macho* philosophizing and posturing overweening? In chapter 15 the Old Lady tired of talk of dying and death. "Ah, Madame, the dead are tired too," the narrator responded. "No tireder than I am of hearing of them and I can speak my wishes." The comic moment was too little too late.

Perkins's headaches were legion. Hemingway wanted *Death in the Afternoon* to include one hundred photographs, drawings, and paintings. Though they could enrich the value of the book, they would also boost its printing bill and selling price. Even in prosperous times, books that sold for more than five dollars—a conservative figure should *Death* contain the one hundred illustrations—were hard to market; an era of dollar books and price wars made them exceptional risks. Illustrations or not, Perkins could rely on the publicity department to advertise *Death* and the sales department to flog it, but he would have to order the first printing. The number was never easy to calculate, especially during a depression that would punish the company that printed too few or too many.

Perkins's uncertainty about *Death in the Afternoon* also touched the debate over installment publication. That any popular magazine would serialize the entire book was doubtful since, unlike *A Farewell to Arms*, *Death in the Afternoon* had no narrative line that could propel readers from one monthly issue to the next. It would be possible to serialize parts of the book, however, either condensed or excerpted; some parts, for example "A Natural History of the Dead," could even be published as short stories, assuming the author would launder them. *Cosmopolitan* wanted Hemingway badly enough to offer a contract for nonexclusive serialization of *Death in the Afternoon*. Perkins was pleased. Though he conceded that publication in *Cosmopolitan* or even *Saturday Evening Post* could harm sales of the clothbound edition, he added that *Cosmopolitan* would "undoubtedly arouse interest and expectation." Hemingway had apparently written *Death in the Afternoon* for the cognoscenti, though, and the appropriate venue for serialization was not *Cosmopolitan* but *Scribner's Magazine*.

Robert Bridges's *Scribner's* had been less than hospitable to Hemingway, and Fritz Dashiell's promised no better treatment. Dashiell found *Death in the Afternoon* too long and too technical. He understood that the Hemingway name could translate into newsstand sales, though, and in early 1932 he offered the author $500 each for several "articles" from the book. Five hundred dollars may have been double *Scribner's* usual rate for nonfiction, but it was $100 less than the magazine had paid for "Wine of Wyoming" almost two years before, and considerably less than the $16,000 it had paid for serialization of *A Farewell to Arms*. Hemingway acknowledged that the depression had affected prices, and that the magazine served writers extremely well. After all, he had chosen *Scribner's* over other magazines because of its prestige. But business was business. As he told Perkins, he was selling his capital and two solid years' work.

Opening an old wound, Hemingway told Dashiell that *Scribner's* had once offered a meager $250 for a shortened version of "Fifty Grand," then paid another author $5,000 for the story that won its fiction contest. Now the magazine planned to mince *Death in the Afternoon* into " 'articles' " and, worse, pay less than their market value. Dashiell regretted what had happened with "Fifty Grand." "But really, Ernest, the choice did not rest with me, and the incident happened five years ago." The reason he could publish no more than "articles" from *Death in the Afternoon* was even more barbed and could hardly have been what the author of a forthcoming nonfiction book wanted to hear: "from the purely practical standpoint, fiction has the greatest drawing power." The battle over articles and money ended with *Death in the Afternoon* serialized—and thus publicized—nowhere.

Several weeks after Hemingway returned from the annual spring trip to the Dry Tortugas, with the hold full of muttonfish, he received the first galleys for *Death in the Afternoon*. They were slugged "Hemingway's Death," and the superstitious author called it "a hell of a damn dirty business to stare at that a thousand times." Other bad omens followed.

Perkins talked not only of cutting back the illustrations from one hundred to thirty-two pages but of approaching the Book of the Month Club about *Death in the Afternoon*. Though many subscribers had fallen away during the depression, the club retained its substantial publicity value, and "in these times we ought to think about the possibility even if we would not in other times." Scribners' pursuit of the club resulted from the disarray of the industry and the need to lower costs, and Hemingway accurately read Perkins's scheme as lack of faith in *Death in the Afternoon*.

Hemingway again protested. Rather than push *Death in the Afternoon* in magazines and bookstores, where sales would reward both publisher and author, Scribners was intent on "selling it down the river to the Book of the Month Club to get some one a sure seven thousand dollars to cover margins with." Hemingway had cooled on the book clubs after hearing about Lardner's *Round Up*. Scribners had sworn to the journalist that the

Literary Guild would advance his sales and reputation. But once readers saw that they could order the book through the club, retail sales halted. The Literary Guild sold seventy thousand copies, the booksellers fifteen thousand. Had the figures been reversed, the impecunious Lardner would have been, for the moment, less poor.

Lincoln Steffens's *Autobiography* was another story. Published in 1931 at $7.50, the book was a "flat flop." Within months, though, the Literary Guild made the book so famous that in late 1931 Harcourt issued a second edition for $3.75 that was "a great success." Hemingway was still attracted to the money and the publicity—but not the aura of mass merchandise the clubs generated. Only on two conditions, he told Perkins, would he allow the sale of *Death in the Afternoon* to the BOMC. The first was monetary: Scribners must pay the author his agreed-on advance of sixty-five hundred dollars as well as the club advance of seven thousand dollars. The second was punitive. Though the club could censor the manuscript ("they cannot insist in ramming the good word shit or the sound old word fuck down the throats of a lot of clubwomen"), Scribners would have to publish the trade edition uncut to compensate the author for loss of integrity.

The club may not have wanted *Death in the Afternoon,* cut or uncut. "I do not like the man," panelist Heywood Broun said of Hemingway, "yet I must admit that I know no other phony in the whole course of English letters who could write so well about things of which he had not the slightest comprehension." Conservative panelists like Dorothy Canfield Fisher would have forecast objections to the language and content of the book. Hemingway's having demanded identical trade and club editions mooted the question since the sale would apparently not have been cost effective unless Scribners and the club could share plates. Perkins sensed the author's outrage. In the wake of the tirade he agreed to double the number of pages of illustrations (to sixty-four) and hold the price at $3.50.

In late spring 1932, as Hemingway read and cut galleys, the check from *Cosmopolitan* for "After the Storm" was another reminder of the drawing power of fiction. And so, finally, was the imminent sale of *The Sun Also Rises* to Hollywood. Despite net losses of almost six million dollars in 1931 (and double that in 1932), David Sarnoff had continued to expand RKO. On 6 May 1932, for eighteen hundred dollars, with vague assurances of an eventual fifteen-thousand-dollar sale, the studio optioned *The Sun Also Rises* for sixty days.

As Hemingway reminded his attorney, Maurice Speiser, Hadley would get the RKO money from *The Sun Also Rises*, but Ernest would control the negotiations. Perkins was characteristically cautious. "I hope a sale is made even though the price does not seem very large," he wrote the author. As he understood, the exposure was worth considerably more than the cash for a writer who had published virtually no new work for almost two years.

Will Hays had urged Sarnoff not to buy or option *The Sun Also Rises*. Sarnoff had proceeded, though, and that spring, in Hollywood, other studios wondered whether RKO could "lick" the story and thus make a picture that local and state censors could pass. RKO had rehearsed the question with Production Code representatives Lamar Trotti and Jason Joy. As Trotti wrote,

> This story by Ernest Hemingway was discussed with [RKO producers James] McGuinness and [Horace] Jackson. It is our understanding that it has not yet been purchased, but that they intend to make a treatment which they hope will be satisfactory. The two important factors, of course, are the impotency of the man as a result of a wound in the war, and the promiscuity of the girl whom he cannot marry as a result. Mr. McGuinnes [*sic*] said that their idea is to make this a tragic story, and to develop the thought that the couple have found something more valuable than sex, to wit: companionship, friendship, etc. Colonel Joy suggested that they undertake the treatment with the full realization that they had a problem on their hands.

Chastened by the meeting, RKO wavered, and the clock on the option slowly ticked on.

Across the continent, even as he corrected galleys on *Death in the Afternoon*, Hemingway was turning out stories. That was good news for his publisher, which since Charles Scribner's death in 1930, had been concerned with Hemingway's productivity. By late June the author had contracted a respiratory ailment. By early July, having convalesced in Florida for several days, he was on the road to Piggott in a new Ford V8. In small towns he would send his sister Carol into roadside diners for food because, she recalled, "he didn't want to be recognized." Had the open-throated pictures really reached Huntsville (Alabama) or Cleveland (Tennessee)? If not, the Hollywood version of *The Sun Also Rises* would speed them along: on July 5, only hours before the option expired, only days before Paramount at last started principal photography on *A Farewell to Arms*, RKO purchased the screen rights to the fiesta novel for fifteen thousand dollars.

By July 1932 Ernest and Pauline had arrived at the Nordquist ranch near the Wyoming and Montana border. They would remain there for several months, the African trip once more postponed, the juice flowing. The stories Hemingway wrote were funny, obscure, philosophical, ironic, provocative, and, in quality, mixed. And the more he produced, the more possible became the book Scribners had wanted since 1930. It was not the novel that Perkins would have preferred. Nonetheless, it would do.

"A Way You'll Never Be" was another Nick Adams story, begun in the 1920s, probably before *A Farewell to Arms,* and completed in 1932. It opens on a scarred plain littered with war dead. A second lieutenant with blood-shot eyes escorts Nick to the company commander, who orders him to move around to show the uniform. Nick tells his friend Paravicini that if the Italian soldiers " 'see one American uniform that is supposed to make them believe others are coming.' " Nick Adams exists in shade, the hollow man, bone and flesh for the uniform. He has suffered a head wound, and Paravicini has him lie down. Roused from anxious dreams, Nick rants on about war and valor and the American locust. " 'Gentlemen,' " he announces to the band of awed soldiers around him, " 'either you must govern—or you must be governed.' " He lies down again but cannot rest. He leaves for Fornaci, alone and confused.

The second lieutenant with the "stubble of beard and red-rimmed, very blood-shot eyes" echoes Charon in *The Inferno.* Unwilling to escort the living Dante "across" to the realm of the dead, Charon suffers from an anxiety of performance that also plagues the Hemingway hero. Nick Adams calls the battle "the show," and the "actors" include even the Austrian soldier-rapist who posed for propaganda postcards issued before the offensive. As frozen in time as the soldier-rapist, Nick dons the costume and collects the props of the American he plays, but he cannot keep the drama straight; he fuses dreams of moving "up that slope" during battle with dreams of walking "up the hill" in Montmartre to catch the act of the Parisian feather dancer Gaby Delys. Naturally, thoughts of performance lead to thoughts of reception. " 'What's the matter?' " Nick asks Paravicini. " 'I don't seem crazy to you, do I?' " For someone with a head wound, the answer is ambiguous: "You seem in top-hole shape."

"A Way You'll Never Be" was not only about performance, it *was* a performance: Ernest Hemingway as author of fiction. He had not found the performance easy, and the story had undercurrents of hostility toward audience. In his dissertation on the American locust, as full of authority and arrogance (and also prescience) as any story the narrator of *Death in the Afternoon* tells, Nick mocks not only the soldiers who swallow the fiction of the American uniform but, perhaps, the imperial narration of *Death in the Afternoon.* Finally, though, that whisper of friction between Hemingway and the audience made the story a strong blend of the conventional and the *expérimental.*

"Give Us a Prescription, Doctor" was a more accessible work full of performers and performances—from the street band and the football match to the radio that plays throughout the night. The main character is Mr. Frazer, a writer ("Phraser") who has been hospitalized just as Hemingway had been following his automobile accident in November 1930. Frazer connects with none of the activity about him. He occupies a single room, and receives no mail of consequence. He listens to the radio without thinking. " 'You wouldn't like the way I write,' " he tells the nun on duty; his isolation suggests that no one would. Another hollow man, Frazer has neither faith nor audience. The story—part humorous and part tragic—ends with a meditation on opiates of the people. Whether the author renounces or advocates nihilism or revolution seems unclear and unimportant; he invites dialogue on political disillusionment. For the politically minded Fritz Dashiell, who accepted the story for *Scribner's Magazine*, that was probably enough.

"Homage to Switzerland" was an exercise in theme and variation, and a homage to Joyce and (*Death in the Afternoon* notwithstanding) Faulkner. It concerned, serially, three male characters awaiting three trains in three Swiss depot cafés. Like "A Way You'll Never Be," it dealt with arrested time but was richer in biographical than literary significance. "Homage to Switzerland" not only evoked the uneasiness of the separation from Hadley but sparked questions about whether, because of a young woman (Jane Mason) with whom he had become involved, the author foresaw a separation from Pauline. Hemingway sent the story to *Cosmopolitan* with a queer cover letter. "This is a damned good story—3 stories in one," he told editor Will Lengel, but it was as though the author was putting Christmas wrap round a busted toy. Perkins understood why *Cosmopolitan* rejected "Homage." It was the "sort of story which many people do not seem to understand," he told Hemingway, "at least the sort who read magazines."

Other stories belonged to no reader Perkins or Lengel could fathom. The six-hundred-word "One Reader Writes" consisted of one poor woman seeking medical advice on "sifilus" from a doctor-columnist. The Kansas City physician Logan Clendening had sent Hemingway the letter, and the author added a two-hundred-word frame to complete the story. Hemingway was drawn to the vignette and what the dadaists called the objet trouvée, like the form letter he had adapted from *The Forum* in July 1929. As fiction, "One Reader" appeared slight and exploitative. In "The Mother of a Queen" a matador buries his mother in the public bone-heap; the narrator (his manager) asks: "What kind of blood is it that makes a man like that?" The two characters' quarrels over money hinted at the author's anger toward Grace Hemingway, while the narrator's ill-expressed homosexual desires lent the story tension. "The Light of the World" focused on a gathering of whores at a northern Michigan depot. It was another "literary" story, the title probably borrowed from the Holman Hunt picture *I Am the Light of the World*, a folksy portrait of Jesus widely reproduced in the early 1900s. Less rounded and less rewarding than the fiction of *Men Without Women*, these stories proceeded from an author whose passion for literature was fully engaged if not (or not then) especially fecund. These were stories "done for a book," Hemingway said, as though the stories were an assignment, as though the teacher were the marketplace whose yearning for fiction was apparently insatiable.

Scribners had ordered 10,300 copies for the first printing of *Death in the Afternoon*, an enormous number for a bullfight book, an "ultra-conservative" number for an author whose last novel had sold almost 100,000 copies. Scribners planned to advertise *Death in the Afternoon* as a miscellany, promising readers the stuff of fiction—story and action and dialogue. Hemingway found the ploy a misrepresentation of the book, and a miscalculation. "You sell the intelligent ones first," he contended. "Then you have to hammer hammer hammer on some simple thing to sell the rest." In other words, the general reader would purchase a book endorsed by the literati, but not vice versa. Scribners should tout *Death in the Afternoon* for what it was, Hemingway told Perkins, "a great classic goddamned book on bull fighting."

"*What did you do to the words?*" Hemingway asked Perkins in late July 1932. He was writing from the Nordquist ranch, and wanted to know as well when he would get the page proofs, the jacket, and the frontispiece—"you haven't even asked what title goes on Frontispiece." Apropos "words" in the text, Scribners' lawyer had recommended substituting "damn" for "fuck," but added that context now mattered more than "words." Perkins was less concerned about the courts than about the vice society that could seize *Death in the Afternoon*, suspend distribution for months, and boost Scribners' taxes on inventory. In July 1932 John Sumner had raided Manhattan's Gotham Book Mart and had the owner arrested for selling allegedly pornographic literature. Neither the magistrate's court nor the grand jury was interested in the case, but the tabloids were. Granted, the publicity of a vice raid could have had unusual value for *Death in the Afternoon*. Should reporters conclude that the book was more instructive than sensational, though, they could destroy it before readers or even reviewers had discovered it. Hemingway feared litigation sufficiently to let Perkins make the call and keep them both out of jail. He was nonetheless frustrated and skeptical. "F-ck the whole business—that looks all right. It's legal isn't it." It was—but the first edition would carry the word as "f——ing." For Hemingway, who wished he "was with some firm [he] hated so [he] could put the screws on and rachet them from the other side," the blanks would only add to the feeling that Scribners had abandoned the book.

The cursory editing of *Death in the Afternoon* tended to support that feeling. The manuscript assumed that lay readers would be interested in the bloodlines of bulls, the education of matadors, and the inadequacies of authors like Waldo Frank. That they would be interested in tales of a matador with "wound full of pus, delirious and dying," of a disemboweled horse "emptied of its visceral content," and of two gypsies who ate the testicles of the bull that killed their brother. And interested in the voice of a narrator with the lusty manner of Ignacio Sanchez Mejias, the banderillero whose bravery "was as though he were constantly showing you the quantity of hair on his chest or the way in which he was built in his more private parts." According to the narrator, "The dignity of movement of an ice-berg is due to only one-eighth of it being above water." Parts of the manuscript, though, were (as Pauline once quipped) about "twelve tenths out of the water." If *Look Homeward, Angel* affirmed the beauty of editorial compression, *Death in the Afternoon* exposed the hazard of editorial forbearance.

Perkins must have known that parts of *Death in the Afternoon* lacked the clean prose of *The Sun Also Rises* and *A Farewell to Arms.* "Let those who want to save the world if you can get to see it clear and as a whole," Hemingway wrote only four sentences from the end of the book. Art was a higher calling than politics, the author appeared to say, but the syntax tortured the idea. Other passages lacked much-needed punctuation: "Used for this purpose the worst horses possible, that is those past any other usefulness, but which are solid on their feet and moderately manageable, are the best." Still other passages were gnarled and oversubordinated: "Every novel which is truly written contributes to the total of knowledge which is there at the disposal of the next writer who comes, but the next writer must pay, always, a certain nominal percentage in experience to be able to understand and assimilate what is available as his birthright and what he must, in turn, take his departure from." Still other passages, reeling like drunken matadors, illustrated what Jimmy Crane had said about his father's incessant opinions in *A New Slain Knight*: "Greco liked to paint religious pictures because he was very evidently religious and because his incomparable art was not then limited to accurate reproducing of the faces of the noblemen who were his sitters for portraits and he could go as far into his other world as he wanted and, consciously or unconsciously, paint saints, apostles, Christs and Virgins with the androgynous faces and forms that filled his imagination."

Perkins may have thought that the Hemingway persona and "the masculine idea" would be enough to sell *Death in the Afternoon*. He could also plead extenuating circumstances. That summer he began regular treatment at Johns Hopkins for a malady of the ear, and worried constantly about a daughter whose seizures the neurologists could not diagnose. "At other times a number of things have always been going wrong but you could always look upon *something* that was going right," he wrote one friend in June 1932, the same month he corresponded with Hemingway about references to Waldo Frank. "But lately, everywhere I have looked, ruin threatened." On July 3, Arthur Scribner, then only twenty-six months into his tenure as head of the firm, died suddenly of a heart attack. Succeeding his Uncle Arthur, Charles Scribner III was responsible for conserving the capital surplus that had seen the firm through the depression. It was an exacting task, and one that he shared fully with his new vice-president and editor-in-chief. Perkins was grateful for the promotion yet "practically sleepwalked through his work that year." Disinclined to edit Hemingway as he edited Wolfe, he may also have lacked the energy. "*What did you do to the words?*" Hemingway had asked. Regrettably, almost nothing.

The Nordquist ranch offered Hemingway distractions from the fate of *Death in the Afternoon*. Some days he hunted or fished; other days he worked at a writing table in a small cabin beside the river. The work went almost well enough to keep his mind off *Death in the Afternoon*. He hated "that little shit Dashiell" for having devalued the manuscript of the book; as he told Perkins, he would rather use his short-story manuscripts for bathroom tissue than "engage in polemics with that twirp." In August he added another name to the blacklist. Chicago bookseller Paul Romaine had warned the author that he would soon be forgotten if he continued to write about "[l]ost generations and bulls." A touchy Hemingway responded that the bullfight was his "recreation and amusement," and that he could earn a living "in at least three other ways than by selling what I write."

Hemingway wanted and deserved the income (if not the questionable fame) of the Professional Writer. *Death in the Afternoon* represented two years' labor: good notices could elevate the author in the pantheon of American letters, while good sales could fund an African safari without assistance from Uncle Gus. The notices and the sales could also help ensure an audience for an evolving short-story collection that would challenge readers of *A Farewell to Arms*. Recent fiction like "A Way You'll Never Be" and "One Reader Writes" was for educated general readers. More complex than "The Killers" or "Fifty Grand" (the best of *Men Without Women*), other recent fiction leaned toward the *expérimental*, and only theoretically could be "praised by highbrows" and "read by lowbrows."

Hemingway wrote the latter stories as an assault on tradition; as he had done in the 1930s, he hoped to revitalize the rhetoric of fiction. But his defense of the collection well before its completion hints at his own doubts about its quality. He had already warned Perkins that the new work would be less "popular" than that of *Men Without Women*. Readers "always want a story like the last one," he wrote his editor in November 1932, but the "one thing that I will not do is repeat myself on anything." He knew that the manuscript, however uneven its quality, would prove that he was an advocate of what he later called "the art of the short story"; indeed the recondite stories in the collection have their adherents today because they show an artist struggling to develop. He could nonetheless not have been content. "I am a careerist, as you can read in the papers, and my idea of a career is never to write a phony line," he would soon tell Perkins. "But that isn't enough. If you want to make a living out of it you have to, in addition every so often, without faking, cheating or deviating from the above to give them something they understand and that has a story—not a plot—just a story that they can follow instead of simply feel, the way most of the stories are." He would be held in that vise for another thirty years.

Published on 23 September 1932, *Death in the Afternoon* earned reviews of text and author. The book contained "remarkable illustrations" of matadors and "harrowing episodes" of death, the *New York Sun* noted; it was full of "strength and gusto and honesty." The review appeared on the publication date, written by Laurence Stallings; he was not only atoning for the poor performance of his adaptation of *A Farewell to Arms* but supplying the apologia he thought the new Hemingway book would need. The scholarly and the effeminate should keep away from *Death in the Afternoon*, he wrote, for "some of its jests are too deeply barbed to be merciful to the thin hides of the fashionably perverted." The cautionary note could have been prompted by, among others, the book's Johnsonian definition of *maricón*:

> a sodomite, nance, queen, fairy, fag, etc. They have these in Spain too, but I only know of two of them among the forty-some matadors de toros. This is no guaranty that those interested parties who are continually proving that Leonardo da Vinci, Shakespeare, etc., were fags would not be able to find more. Of the two, one is almost pathologically miserly, is lacking in valor but is very skillful and delicate with the cape, a sort of exterior decorator of bullfighting, and the other has a reputation for great valor and awkwardness and has been unable to save a peseta. In bullfighting circles the word is used as a term of opprobrium or ridicule or as an insult. There are many very, very funny Spanish fairy stories.

Stallings ended the puff with an invocation: *Death in the Afternoon* "will be chopped to pieces in many a literary dissecting before the winter is over. God bless old Dr. Hemingstein!"

The magazine more than one million people read for the certitude of its opinions called its long review of *Death in the Afternoon* "Olé! Olé!" *Time* illustrated the review with Spanish painter Luis Quintanilla's portrait of the author. Hemingway was seated with papers, drinking glass, and small book. The suit that outlined his broad shoulders and barrel chest almost made the head seem too small for the body, and he wore a severe expression, partly the result of the cut of his mustache, which drooped below the lip line. Shadows falling across his brow heightened the scar from the horse-shoe gash. He was Lord Byron as Latin boulevardier. The prose that surrounded the portrait also romanticized the author—but not at the expense of his masculinity. Short on evaluation and long on summary, the review applauded Hemingway as a literary phenomenon whose *Farewell to Arms* had earned "Hollywood and high-brow huzzas." In the section called "The Author," *Time* played kingmaker:

> A leading light of U. S. letters, his influence is far out of proportion to the amount of his published work. A rabid sportsman and anti-"literary" writer, he eschews Manhattan and its cliques, would rather fish than drink tea. At 34 he has become a U. S. legend.

One critic called *Death in the Afternoon* "an interlude of reporting and miscellaneous comment in a career chiefly devoted to fiction." As *Time* noted, though, "New books are news," and the *Nation* (among others) encouraged the perception that Hemingway had "triumphed more as hero than as artist."

Death in the Afternoon was "a Baedeker of bulls," nonfiction for "Hemingway addicts," wrote the *New Republic* and the *New York Times Book Review.* Far more harsh, other notices suggested that the book raised the legend of Hemingway to the level of hubris. *Death in the Afternoon* bore the reader malice, the *New Yorker* charged; it was enough to turn a popular writer unpopular. The opinion magazines picked up the scent. Hemingway was at his "most objectionable" when he pretended to confide in the reader, Granville Hicks wrote in the *Nation.* The *Bookman* found the "extreme coarseness of language" in the American edition "an amazing sidelight on publishing conditions today," while, swinging an ax in the *American Mercury*, Mencken noted that Hemingway had fashioned the reader as an Oak Park matron; the "way to shock this innocent grandam, obviously, is to have at her with the ancient four-letter words. Mr. Hemingway does so with moral industry; he even drags her into the story as a character, to gloat over her horror."

Death in the Afternoon was not about matadors and bulls but (as reviewers sensed) about author and audience. Hemingway had had as his goal "the holding of his purity of line through the maximum of exposure" and the desire "never to write a phony line." The tone and content of the "bull-fight book," though, along with the publicity it occasioned and the culture of celebrity that *Time* and others reinforced, had now fully drawn the Hemingway persona.

Unaware of the reviews or the implications, Hemingway left the Nordquist ranch in October. He and Key West pal, Charles Thompson encountered blizzards in Wyoming and Nebraska but found bargains there in food and gasoline. Late that month, back in Florida, he wrote Guy Hickok that *Death in the Afternoon* was "*selling*—What do you think of that? I thought of it as a book to end publishers." Scribners had already advertised a third printing, and early sales were so good, the author added, that Hickok, should he choose, could find work as an expert on the big man in American letters. More specifically, he could "go out to Hollywood when they start making bull pictures and say, 'No good. You gotta get more bull in it. Like Hemingway.' " The quip was prophetic.

By early November Pauline had gone to Arkansas, and Ernest was supervising the last improvements on the Key West house. "Have been working like hell writing," he told Perkins. "No obligation to take them but they are very good stories." Joking about Scribners "asking waivers on me or losing all confidence in me," he suspected that the ten new stories could not redeem the promise of *A Farewell to Arms* or even *Men Without Women*. He finally understood that—whether or not *Death in the Afternoon* continued to sell—the market would need a fast dose of Hemingway fiction. "Next fall might be a good time. Have been working until my eyes haywire every day. Gone back to the old system of starting in bed when I wake and working through until toward noon." He enclosed some photographs with the letter. "If you want to use any of these pictures it is O.K." The only pictures that counted now, though, were in southern California.

Chapter Five

WINNER
TAKE
NOTHING

FOR MONTHS ON END *NEW MOVIE* PUBLISHED PHOTOGRAPHS OF THE HOLLY-
wood stars' pink and gold boudoirs. One month the editors honored a
"special request" and featured "a real he-man's boudoir, graced by stuffed
eagles, Indian bonnets, real Navajo rugs, skins, and pictures with the spirit
of the outdoors." The oxymoron "he-man's boudoir" was the bright idea
of the *New Movie* reporter, inspired by the bright idea of the studio decora-
tor who had created the room, inspired by the actor who supposedly inhab-
ited it, the actor who sat at the writing table beneath the trophies. Though
tanned and lined from the Montana sun, the actor sported the barbered
hair and tailored clothes of Sunset Boulevard. The natural and the artistic,
the masculine and the domestic, the spirit of the outdoors . . . indoors.

Gary Cooper, the he-man of *The Virginian* (1929) and *Morocco* (1930),
was a notorious man-about-town who had been involved with actresses
Clara Bow, Evelyn Brent, and, as screenwriters worked on *A Farewell to Arms*,
Lupe Velez. He was nonetheless surprisingly anxious about his masculinity.
In appearance the willowy actor resembled the "Christs and Virgins with
the androgynous faces." He was the "tough fellow" and the "sensitive
type," and had the virility and beauty that could be found in the Helen
Breaker photographs of another young American performer. In November
1931, when Cooper embarked on safari with a caravan of five light trucks
and two passenger cars, he told the press: "Don't get the idea this was dude
hunting. It's just sensible. Real safari only came into its own with the motor
car. There are no horses down there because they can't stand up under the

heat, and a hunter is lost without a car for any lengthy jaunt. You drive where you can, then when the end of the car's possibilities is reached, you get out and walk." The actor understood the *querencia*. He would be ideal as the Hemingway lieutenant.

The screenplay of *A Farewell to Arms* had evolved over 1931 and 1932, when John Gilbert, then Fredric March, then Cooper had been cast as Frederic Henry. Though the script followed the outline of the play and the book, including a vivid account of the Italian retreat, it altered the structure of act 3. Rinaldi was the heavy; he intercepted Catherine's letters to Frederic, and the letters' return to her—unopened—hastened her labor. The screenwriters Oliver Garrett and Benjamin Glazer intercut her confinement in hospital with Henry's rowing up the lake to meet her in Switzerland. Later, Paramount rationalized the departure from the novel: "We could not have brought them together—the officer and the girl—as Hemingway did, in the Swiss resort, without killing our suspense. . . . We would have had no climax."

Responding to the same political concerns that Hemingway had once had, Paramount boss Ben Schulberg had told both Washington diplomats and Motion Picture Association head Will Hays that the picture would not tarnish the reputation of Italy. *A Farewell to Arms* focused not on the Caporetto retreat but on seduction, love, and loss. Besides, he added, Paramount liked Italians, especially Italian moviegoers. The studio had been equally candid about the sexuality of the film. On July 14, 1932, the day shooting started, the studio announced that "they intend[ed] to live or die by this picture and that they [were] going to be as daring as possible."

As story and cast showed, Paramount had constructed *A Farewell to Arms* to appeal to lowbrows and highbrows. Gary Cooper would deliver his lines mechanically, rather like Frederic Henry, who talked " 'like a time-table.' " Cooper had the "presence" and "absence" fundamental to stardom, however, and would lasso the audience and help recoup the expense of production. As Catherine Barkley, Helen Hayes would lend the picture enough integrity to persuade the censors and the public that, though provocative, the story also had class. Hollywood called Norma Shearer the First Lady of the Screen, Jean Harlow the Blonde Bombshell, and Helen Hayes the Great Actress. For fifty-two thousand dollars—twice what Cooper earned—she came to *A Farewell to Arms* from two years on Broadway.

The first morning I reported at Paramount I was rushed into makeup and my face was hastily applied. That's funny, I thought, but maybe that's the way they do things at Paramount. Then I was rushed into wardrobe where I was hastily pinned into a nurse's uniform. Then they rushed me into the studio. 'Miss Hayes,' someone said, 'this is Gary Cooper. Now, can you get into bed together?' It was all set up for the stills photographers so that they might have a photograph in the newspapers that evening!

It was odd and wonderful casting, the Montana cowboy and the *jeune fille* with stage training. Production photographs of the screen lovers—as lovers—were fine publicity for the picture and for *Death in the Afternoon*. According to the *New York Times Book Review*, *Death in the Afternoon* was full of "good Anglo-Saxon, with anything but a shrinking from calling a spade a spade." *Town and Country* (like the *Bookman* and other reviewers) found only "smut . . . lugged in by the ears." The daring of Paramount and the daring of Hemingway would reinforce and promote one another.

The veteran director Frank Borzage shot *A Farewell to Arms* in sequence at the studio and on location at the Paramount Ranch and Devil's Gate Dam near Pasadena. When the average Paramount production cost $306,000, *A Farewell to Arms* was budgeted at $550,000 and, moreover, went two weeks over schedule and $250,000 over budget. In the argot of Hollywood, the dollars were on the screen. The cast featured Adolph Menjou as Rinaldi and Jack LaRue (scripted to use the corncob in a 1933 adaptation of *Sanctuary*) as the priest. The performers were good, especially Menjou. Technically the picture was excellent. Despite the marked difference in height between Cooper and Hayes (whom Hemingway called "the peanut"), the boom operator and sound recorder achieved clarity, even when the lovers whispered. According to cameraman Charles Lang, Borzage "was always saying 'Let's go for it, let's go for it!' " He tinted one of the battle sequences red, and shot Henry's entrance to the hospital from Henry's point of view—flat on his back. *Variety* called it "a new and artistic note."

Pace Frederic Henry, Frank Borzage found nothing obscene about "words such as glory, honor, courage, or hallow." He liked abstractions—the transcendence of love, the horror of war—and italicized them in the film. Though the scenes in Milan had the flavor of cotton candy, the somber Caporetto retreat was full of iconography and symbol. In Switzerland, Catherine dies as bells sound the armistice: her love has transfigured the world and cured war. It was less an interpretation of *A Farewell to Arms* than a grand tapestry of its characters and themes. It was Ernest Hemingway illustrated by Rockwell Kent. Then again, the movies enlarged all that they touched, including authors. The studios that produced *Ben Hur* and *Rebecca of Sunnybrook Farm* had made the writers Lew Wallace and Kate Wiggin better known as authorial properties; having invested eight hundred thousand dollars in *A Farewell to Arms,* Paramount would likewise shine klieg lights on "Ernest Hemingway" as durable goods.

Should Paramount's *Farewell to Arms* succeed at Christmas 1932, *The Sun Also Rises* could become a top attraction for Christmas 1933. And suddenly, for RKO, the fifteen-thousand-dollar purchase price was an even better bargain than it had appeared.

David Selznick was RKO's production head. Next to MGM's Irving Thalberg, he was also the most "literary" producer in Hollywood. In 1930 he had even considered leaving movies for books. He had met with " [Harold] Guinzburg of The Viking Press, to whom Oliver Garrett has kindly sent me, to discuss publishing," he wrote to his wife from New York. "Later with [Ben] Hecht to [Pascal] Covici." Fortunately for Hollywood, and probably the publishing business, he returned to Los Angeles.

Though Selznick preferred Robert Louis Stevenson to Henry James, and Ben Hecht to Scott Fitzgerald, he had long been interested in Hemingway. He had wanted to buy *A Farewell to Arms* in October 1929, when he worked for Paramount. The studio had turned down the novel (not then a Broadway play) because of the "tragic unhappy ending," and furthermore berated Selznick for the "so-called 'tragic ending' " he had allowed on *Street of Chance* (1930). One year later he had gone to RKO, where he planned, personally, to produce *The Sun Also Rises.* "Mr. Selznick is anxious to have you read the attached script and treatment on 'The Sun Also Rises,' " an RKO staff assistant wrote to Production Code representatives only two months after securing the option, "and give him your opinion of same at the earliest possible moment."

Production Code head Jason Joy was more tolerant than his superior, Will Hays, of projects like *The Sun Also Rises.* He nonetheless noted the references to "Drinking," "Venereal disease," "Harlot's talk," "Fairie," "Brett's sleeping around," "Bull fights," and (mainly) Jake's "wounds," and when he conferred with Selznick, he predicted that state censors would never approve the picture. Selznick argued that the war wound was an essential plot point, and Joy agreed to see how the New York censors—the bellwether for other boards—would respond to it. The précis in his letter to New York shows why Joy, who had approved *Cock of the Air, She Done Him Wrong, The Blue Angel,* and other controversial pictures of the early 1930s—including the screenplay of *A Farewell to Arms,* then in postproduction—was timorous about *The Sun Also Rises.*

A young man has been wounded in such manner as to make it impossible for him ever to marry or to have children. He is, and has been, very much in love with an English woman who is in full possession of all her sense and who is unable to forget her love for him. The story, thus, is one of great frustration, as it is obviously impossible for the couple to do anything to remedy the unfortunate situation.

Joy dressed up the problem as love and marriage when it was fundamentally the wound, and what it connoted, the loss of masculinity. The irresistible screen heroes of the early 1930s were the gangsters, pathological killers like Rico Bandello in *Little Caesar* and Tony Camonte in *Scarface*. They were flawed, certainly, but sexually functional and sexually precocious, their manly vigor the locus of their broad appeal. Colonel Joy, who was leaving the Production Code office to take a post at Fox, could see that Jake Barnes went against the grain. For Selznick, though, Jake was potentially a new and contrarian screen hero.

In early October 1932, as Paramount produced a rough cut of *A Farewell to Arms*—and turned the Caporetto scene into a clash of soldiers unidentified by nationality—the New York censors received the précis of *The Sun Also Rises*. James Wingate, director of the New York censors, director designate of the Production Code office, was cornered. Blocking the production of *The Sun Also Rises* would alienate the Hollywood studios even before he arrived on site, while endorsing it would invite headaches in the future. Using notes prepared by "Miss Farrell" (an office staffer in New York), he wrote to Joy that the promiscuity and "impotency" could be overcome with, respectively, proper punishment and "good taste and delicacy." The conciliatory tone indicated to Miss Farrell and Irwin Esmond, the director designate of the New York censors, that Wingate had gone over to the other side. Miss Farrell stated:

> I do not see how the character of Jacob Barnes can be portrayed on the screen without the actual knowlege of his incapacity being described to the audience. There is no other apparent way to narrate the story—unless he is shown crippled or shell-shocked from the war. It seems to me that this is one subject that the motion picture industry should avoid in all common decency. I presume that with the detailed accounts of Paul Bern's life and recent death in the newspapers, and the recent disclosures in the Smith-Reynolds' case, they feel that the public is alive to this situation in mankind and that it is not taboo.

MGM executive Paul Bern, wed to actress Jean Harlow, had killed himself in July 1932; despite the efforts of studio heads to squash the rumors, the press implied that impotence had caused the suicide. Smith Reynolds had been found dead of gunshot wounds that same summer. The boyish tobacco heir, wed to torch singer Libby Holman, had often threatened suicide. "We used to discuss those moods when he would come out of them," Holman recalled at the inquest, "and he would say, 'I know it. I make you unhappy. I can't help it.' " The tabloids hinted at not only foul play but sexual dysfunction. Though Selznick would later make a picture based loosely on Reynolds and Holman, called *Reckless* (MGM, 1935), he and other producers shunned the Bern story lest it foul the Hollywood nest. Like the censors, though, he knew that both Bern and Reynolds had helped expand the audience for *The Sun Also Rises*.

Less than one week before Wingate left for the West Coast, Irwin Esmond rethought *The Sun Also Rises* and announced that the story was "not good picture material." Selznick was irate. He may also have suspected that Wingate was using Esmond as stalking-horse: the new head of the Production Code office was letting the New York censors do his dirty work. Joy, mediating during his last days as director, told Selznick that Esmond's was "apparently a more mature conclusion." And thus the case of the fiesta novel was closed.

Sanctuary reopened the case. *Sanctuary* was "probably the most sickening novel ever written in this country," Lamar Trotti told Hays; it was "utterly unthinkable as a motion picture." On arrival in Hollywood, Wingate suggested as much to Paramount, but in its "live or die" mood the studio had acquired the property. The censorship issue was the rape by corncob. Wingate wanted the scene deleted, and scanned the Production Code for a "definite decision upon the Phallic symbol" or a "declaration of principle, namely, that the Phallic symbol has no place in pictures produced for public entertainment." The search was in vain; moreover, when Paramount sent the William Faulkner story into production, RKO moved forward on the Ernest Hemingway.

Selznick had initially cast Leslie Howard as Jake and Constance Bennett as Brett. Selznick found Howard "the most charming [man] in the American theater" and "an unusually intelligent actor," and though Bennett could have used her husky voice and offhand manner to good effect as Lady Ashley, the producer of *The Sun Also Rises*, as happened so often, had soon had second thoughts. The trade press reported the story.

There's a situation over at Radio [RKO] between Ann Harding and Connie Bennett that calls to mind the famous [Gloria] Swanson-[Pola] Negri feud. Seems Ann pleaded with studio execs to let her do "Sun Also Rises," feeling that the Hemingway novel would offer the kind of acting part she needs and hasn't had. She put her case so eloquently that the powers that be said yes, although picture was scheduled for Connie Bennett and Leslie Howard. Then Connie heard about it and hit the ceiling. Studio wishes at the moment it had never heard of Hemingway.

Usually cast as the noble woman or loyal wife, Harding got the part only to lose it when interest in the project once more cooled. The studio had apparently purchased the Hemingway novel for Selznick, the wunderkind producer who, by December 1932, as Paramount fine-tuned *A Farewell to Arms*, was again squabbling with his employers. He saw RKO as an atelier, not a factory, and the weaker-than-expected box-office showings of his two holiday pictures, *Rockabye* and *The Conquerors*, had increased friction between him and the company. In the event, preproduction on *The Sun Also Rises* stalled.

Books and movies were synergistic: *Death in the Afternoon* had revived press interest in Hemingway the literary character and celebrity, and RKO's *The Sun Also Rises*—a far more palatable dose of bullfighting than *Death in the Afternoon*, especially once the public saw the names Ann Harding and Leslie Howard on the marquee—could have heaped still more publicity on the author-aficionado. But RKO had no firm plans for *The Sun Also Rises*. Hemingway likewise had none for a short-story collection or novel.

In early November, Paramount screened the rough cut of *A Farewell to Arms* for the one audience that mattered to the industry, the American woman. The cheering from one hundred in-house stenographers encouraged the studio to preview the film in Santa Barbara, then Long Beach. *A Farewell to Arms* played as a romance, as the producers had intended. "War? Yes, but it was nothing to the tempest of love that burned in the hearts of this boy and girl," read the caption of one production-still of Hayes and Cooper. According to a reporter in Long Beach, though, *A Farewell to Arms* was "not a great picture, due largely to the fact that it follows Hemingway's novel rather closely." The question was, must Catherine die?

As early as September the Associated Press had reported that Paramount would produce one version of *A Farewell to Arms* for urban theaters, another for small towns; the versions would differ only in the final shots. The plan was not unprecedented. MGM had just shot two endings for *Hell Divers*: "Taps" for Wallace Beery in urban theaters, more cheerful music in others. *A Farewell to Arms* was no *Hell Divers*, and Paramount had budgeted only one version—until the preview cards apparently told the producers that *A Farewell to Arms* was too sad. Two months after principal photography had closed, Borzage had arrived on the hospital set to reshoot the fade-out. From her bed Catherine notices that the rain has stopped. "Then I'm not afraid any more," she tells Frederic. "Open the window." He does, then looks at her. The light fills her smiling face, Frederic goes to her, and the picture ends.

Countering the jeers of the Hollywood press corps, Paramount announced that Hemingway had once considered a happy ending for the novel. Asserting even closer ties to the author, the studio also released a flood of stories on the background of *A Farewell to Arms*. One blurb compared the "story-book hero" Frederic Henry to the author Ernest Hemingway. Both were "seriously injured in action," and Hemingway "still carries a silver plate in place of a bit of bone in one shoulder as a result of these injuries." Another blurb showed that the author was not one to nurse old wounds. "At a middleweight boxing championship bout in Paris," the studio told the press, the author "became incensed when the champion struck one foul after another at his opponent. Abandoning his ringside seat, Hemingway climbed into the ring, took a single sock at the champion, and knocked him out cold."

The stories had been in circulation for more than three years. But even when they ran in syndicated columns around the country, they lacked the prominence and authority that Paramount could give them. American motion picture companies had invested heavily in their promotions departments, for unlike their peers, American publishers, they not only believed in saturation advertising but could unload tons of free "news" on the national press. Motion pictures may have been a ribbon of dreams; thanks to studio flacks, however, millions believed that movie publicity was not fancy or hyperbole but truth.

Hemingway heard about the Paramount stories in Arkansas, where he and Bumby had gone for Thanksgiving. He had written dozens of possible endings for *A Farewell to Arms*. He had even written one in which Frederic and Catherine's baby survived. He had chosen the most tragic one, though, and he wired Gus Pfeiffer and also reported to the movie company that he had not contemplated any other ending of the novel. The *Arkansas Democrat* duly reported that according to the author, the studio had bought *A Farewell to Arms* but not the author's sanction of the Hollywood adaptation.

Wisdom suggested that Hemingway ignore the Paramount nonsense about the silver plate and the boxing match, however specious, however embarrassing. Emotion suggested otherwise. By early December he had scrawled a correction for Max Perkins to "spread around." Winking at the reader, as he had done in *The Torrents of Spring*, and saying that he was no "glamorous personality" like Floyd Gibbons or Tom Mix's horse, the statement contained more wit than conviction. It appeared to invite everyone except Paramount to notice Ernest Hemingway (who referred to himself therein as "a writer of fiction"). It even appeared to stir up what Hollywood was famous for—the mock quarrel. "Hemingway Battles Paramount" was another twist on "Swanson Battles Negri." The studio happily picked up the cue.

"Fame Follows Adventurous Career—Yet He Shuns Limelight" was the headline on one Paramount story about Hemingway in December 1932. "Fisherman, Bullfighter, Boxer—He's 'The Author', Modest Ernest Hemingway" was another.

The Hemingway who in 1929 had become the "Professional Writer . . . than which there isn't anything lower" had not reckoned on the rise of the Author. According to Paramount, the Author "volunteered for an American ambulance unit serving in France, and saw several months' service there." So far so good, since Hemingway had at least been in Paris in 1918 en route to Schio. "Then he enlisted in an Italian unit, and saw service along the Italian front," where he was "seriously injured in action." The movie wanted it both ways. "I was blown up eating cheese," the laconic Gary Cooper tells the doctor. The shrapnel and pain were real, though, and audiences would assume that anyone so badly wounded "along the Italian front" was wounded "in action." They would also assume that Modest Gary Cooper was Modest Ernest Hemingway.

"Author Lived Story Showing on Screen Here" was the headline on one story about Hemingway in the *Los Angeles Times*. The paper based the account on one of hundreds of studio press releases that had poured forth, and that showed up, frequently verbatim, in newspapers and magazines throughout the country. Occasionally the whole truth was reported. Marcella Burke told her readers that the accuracy of *A Farewell to Arms* had been assured by "technical men on the set who had driven ambulances with Ernest Hemingway in the Big War." Usually the half-truth was fostered. The *New York Mirror* stated that "much of Hemingway's material [was] autobiographical," and the *Los Angeles Illustrated Daily News* said that the author "lived the story of which he wrote." The story was *A Farewell to Arms*; the story was Ernest Hemingway.

Having restored the death of Catherine, Paramount shipped *A Farewell to Arms* to New York for the forthcoming world premiere, then previewed the film one last time at a neighborhood theater in Los Angeles. In her widely syndicated column Mollie Merrick reported that "the very sight of the title brought forth such a storm of applause from the audience that any sort of a performance at all would have been hailed with delight." With talk of prostitutes and brothels, the picture was daring, so daring that it turned the Hollywood censors—whom Paramount had defied—into ostriches. As one member of the East Coast Production Code staff told another: "I have not seen [the picture] and have purposely not asked any questions in any way shape or form of Paramount, and won't let any one in this office ask any question. When it is shown in a theatre here I will pay to see it. I hope they get away with it, but I am not going to put myself in the position again of being told to mind my own business."

On December 8 *A Farewell to Arms* opened at the Criterion Theatre in New York, two shows daily, $1.65 per ticket. The credits announced that the production was "Based on the Novel by Ernest Hemingway." Enhancing the capital letters, the souvenir program treated the author as the Master. The program contained portraits of Helen Hayes, Gary Cooper, Frank Borzage, and Hemingway, who looked more like a brahmin of Boston than a writer once banned there. The fact that he was the only one represented by a drawing rather than a photograph lent him the "artistic treatment" the studio hoped would transfer to the film. In late 1932 Paramount was on the edge of receivership, and studio president Adolph Zukor and new production chief Emmanuel Cohen used Hemingway (as they had used Helen Hayes) as window dressing for their product. Though the author could not necessarily change red ink to black, he could lend the company the *je ne sais quoi* that occasionally dazzled Wall Street bankers and investors.

The capacity crowd at the opening included Edward G. Robinson, Fannie Hurst, and Louise and Gus Pfeiffer. Uncle Gus understood that his nephew—appearances to the contrary—was keen on news of the premiere. That evening he wired Arkansas that "closing not happy instead sad and impressive like book. Audience interest held all through picture and deeply impressed with ending." He added that Paramount was eager to have the author see the film and suggest changes. Hemingway refused. He saw Cohen and the movie producers as the West Coast version of the "well-fed, skull and bones-ed, porcellian-ed, beach-tanned, flannelled, Panama-hatted, sport-shod" pretenders who, per *Death in the Afternoon,* turned out for bullfights in Spain. Moreover, as he wired Gus Pfeiffer, "submitting to publicity schemes gives you temporary notoriety but makes public sick of you quickly."

Early trade reviews of *A Farewell to Arms* were mixed. *Daily Variety* called the outlook on the picture unfavorable. *A Farewell to Arms* "aims at people who occasionally do their own thinking and while it may draw emotionally-attuned women of all classes in addition, this is mainly a class-patronage film." Weekly *Variety* was the money review, though, the one read by distributors and exhibitors. It told readers that *A Farewell to Arms* was "a corking flicker" that could "be labeled the femmes' 'All Quiet'—the romantic side of the great holocaust."

Newspaper and magazine reviews were generally positive. *Photoplay* informed movie fans that *A Farewell to Arms* was a "picture you should see." "And please, Mr. Hemingway," scolded Regina Crewe of the *New York American*, "don't make yourself ridiculous by finding the slightest of faults with Paramount's production of your tale, for in Frank Borzage's picturization there lies a thousand times more than you, or any of you, will ever put in the sterile, colorless black and white of type and paper."

Parmount kept the pot boiling by offering to ship two prints of *A Farewell to Arms* south to Arkansas so that the author and his family could see the picture. Though the younger Pfeiffer women would have adored the absurdity of a World Premiere of *A Farewell to Arms* in Piggott, the pious Mary Pfeiffer (Jinny and Pauline's mother) found the movies "too wild and sexy for any self-respecting woman to attend." But *A Farewell to Arms* was not as wanton as she feared, or as bad as Hemingway thought, as the *Saturday Review of Literature* had bluntly told him. The magazine had hailed the disclaimer that Scribners had "spread around" but also noted that the author "seemed—we say 'seemed,' for we know only what we read in the newspapers,—to be under the erroneous impression that they had tacked a happy ending on the screen version of 'A Farewell to Arms.' Apparently this is not so." Hemingway was nonetheless adamant.

Use your imagination as to where Paramount can put two prints unexpectedly available of Borsage version a Farewell to Arms [he wired the studio] but do not send them here. If book lasts and motion pictures also endure a real film will eventually be made of that novel. Meanwhile although Paramount bought picture rights and the chance to make a great picture they did not buy the right to make me look at a silly one.

Paramount alone had not made Hemingway angry. In December, Pauline and the boys contracted influenza. Worse, the barn the author used as a studio caught fire. And worse, he heard from Scribners about *Death in the Afternoon*.

Confusing orders with sales, Hemingway had believed that *Death in the Afternoon* sold out on its publication date. The book had "started off very well indeed," Perkins wrote the author, glossing over complications; the reviews were "good from the publisher's standpoint," and there was "much good in them from the author's standpoint." For once, however, the conservative print runs had been warranted. Scribners had grasped at straws. When the editor of *Polo: The Magazine for Horsemen* wrote Charles Scribner III to praise the book, the publisher answered immediately that *Death in the Afternoon* was a tough sell. "If you could find a way of mentioning it, even on the basis of the cruelty of the horse side, I would certainly appreciate it." Perkins had advertised *Death in the Afternoon* in the *New York Times Book Review* and elsewhere, and assured Hemingway that despite scant sales between election day and Thanksgiving ("a very bad time" for nonfiction), the book would pick up before Christmas. But *Death in the Afternoon* was hard to market, not really a gift book (though it contained photographs), not really a sports book (though it discussed contests), not really literary criticism (though it analyzed writing). The owner of the Channel Book Store in Manhattan had "a decided aversion to the idea of bull fighting" yet told *Publishers' Weekly* that "there would always be some customers who would want the Hemingway book, even though it was about bull fighting, and even though it was not a novel." But not enough had wanted the book. The volunteers of the Piggott fire department had hauled from the barn what they should have let burn—the sales reports and especially the notices on *Death in the Afternoon*. Though the book was promoted as a best-seller, the sales were a grave disappointment, and the reviews the worst of the author's career. Hemingway needed Perkins to assure him, in person, that Scribners was not losing all confidence.

That December Perkins spent "some of the coldest hours of [his] life" shooting duck with Hemingway on the White River in northeast Arkansas. The men rose before dawn, long before the author had said they would and even before they could see, but Perkins "never said anything more about it to Hem, because he is not the man to argue such matters with." Certainly not that winter. In the blind, Perkins could have added to the litany of excuses for the relatively poor performance of *Death in the Afternoon*—booksellers were broke, reprints were popular, competition was ruthless. The author would have known better. "Dont try to sell [the book] down the river to the Grossett and Dunlop boys," he had warned Perkins in October, aware that Scribners would want to cut its losses. "It's not that kind of a book." Matters were worse than Hemingway presumed: Grosset and Dunlap wanted *Death in the Afternoon* no more than the public did.

A short-story collection would "come at a good moment after 'Death in the Afternoon,' " Perkins had told the author that fall, hinting broadly that it would assert Hemingway's preeminence as fiction writer, a point that several reviewers had underscored even as they denounced *Death in the Afternoon*. Two months later Perkins had again asked for a short-story collection; rather than interfere with *Death in the Afternoon*, "it would keep the whole matter to the front and be helped by it, and help it." In Arkansas

Perkins encouraged Hemingway to write a novel on fishing and Key West, "full of incidents about people and about weather and the way things looked and all that." In response the editor probably heard talk of a short-story collection and even a novel but finally departed for New York with nothing for spring publication. Hemingway was philosophical about it all. As he wrote to one new acquaintance, Arnold Gingrich, at *Apparel Arts* magazine: "Am getting pretty well rid of a good lot of unsought popularity with this last book." Or so he thought until Hollywood sent *A Farewell to Arms* into general release.

The display advertisement for the Paramount *Farewell to Arms* in the *Tulsa Tribune* contained not only an illustration of the book and the name of the author but the usual Hollywood purple prose: "The mad mating of two souls lost for love's sake to the thunder of a world gone mad." The public was roused. A PTA committeewoman in Denver (where a preview audience filled out comment cards) called *A Farewell to Arms* a "lovely picture and story of real life." A waitress thought it "was going to be a war picture but it's the best love picture I ever saw." The Italian consul found it an "elemental tragedy, where realism and idealism are blended in forms of beauty seldom achieved on the screen." And a transient wrote that it was "pretty touchy stuff but I guess nobody will get sore at it. I never heard of the book but I guess it must be pretty hot stuff."

The trade papers had warned theater owners about the frankness of the picture. "The obstetrics of human motherhood are shocking enough," wrote Rob Wagner of *Script*, "but the physical background of a Caesarean operation with its mechanical paraphernalia robs the miracle of childbirth of much of its sentiment." As the movies' Production Code staff had expected, the studio had been forced to haggle with the New York, Massachusetts, Chicago, Maryland, Pennsylvania, and Ohio censors over retention of the childbirth and other scenes. Several boards had ordered cuts, two pages' worth in Pennsylvania and Ohio, including the following:

> After scenes of head nurse and girls exiting from concert, eliminate all views of Catherine and Frederic lying on ground.
>
> Eliminate following conversation between them:
>
> *Frederic.* Why didn't you tell me?
>
> *Catherine.* It doesn't matter. If it had to happen, I'd rather it were like this—
>
> *Frederic.* I couldn't know.
>
> *Catherine.* —in a churchyard under the stars.

Banned in Egypt, British Columbia, Italy, and (in deference to the Italians) Brazil but shown elsewhere throughout the world, *A Farewell to Arms* was that happy cross between "sex picture" and "class-patronage film." In January and February 1933, as the depression finally pinched the studios' box-office revenue and theater attendance, audiences thronged to the story of Frederic and Catherine. The picture was held over in New York for four weeks, Chicago for three, and Philadelphia, Detroit, and Los Angeles for two. At theaters in Montreal, Kansas City, and San Francisco the picture did above average business. At the Metropolitan in Boston, it grossed thirty-nine thousand dollars on tickets that cost between thirty-five and sixty-five cents, and as it had in Cleveland and Minneapolis theaters, challenged the house record.

"Sadie Glutz and her low brow swain will be apt to snicker," one Los Angeles reviewer wrote of *A Farewell to Arms*, yet the picture also earned money in rural America, perhaps because Frederic Henry was another "forgotten man." The Italy on screen and the America beyond the lobby were disintegrating societies whose leadership appeared oblivious to human suffering. *A Farewell to Arms* mirrored the concern, and prospered. "[Business p]icked up on Monday," the manager of the Illinois Theater in Macomb, Illinois, reported in a column for theater owners in *Motion Picture Herald*, where opinion on *A Farewell to Arms* was generally favorable. He added: "Push this one, you won't be disappointed." The manager of the Niles in Anamosa, Iowa, concurred. "Great advertising possibilities. Get behind it." The manager of the Palace and Princess in Cedartown, Georgia, agreed that *A Farewell to Arms* had "tremendous drawing power and should do a good business in all localities." He was right: by March 1933 the picture had appeared on the *Motion Picture Herald* roster of "Box Office Champions."

Scribners welcomed the exposure. In September 1932, when Scribners published *Death in the Afternoon*, *Publishers' Weekly* had offered its readers an index of consumers' interests. Eight hundred and six books had been published that month; "Games and Sports" had accounted for 18, and "Fiction" for 225, considerably more than any other category. *Death in the Afternoon* belonged in the former category, and the content of the book may have suggested that the author had abandoned the thousands who had read (or because of Paramount were now reading) *A Farewell to Arms*. According to the *Kansas City Star*, the picture version of *A Farewell to Arms* was for everyone, "whether you be lowbrow or highbrow, man or woman." Hemingway was accessible, the reception of the picture said to people in Macomb or Anamosa who had never heard of the author or his work. For the studios, Hemingway was proving a Kate Wiggin or Lew Wallace with the added bonus of an exploitable personality.

One movie company offered Hemingway "plenty of money" for the title—solely the title—of *Death in the Afternoon*. Another wanted "to secure Hemingway at his price for bull fight picture to be written here in Hollywood." Another wanted to purchase *The Sun Also Rises* from RKO. The studio refused: once more, on the heels of the success of *A Farewell to Arms*, *The Sun Also Rises* was on the production schedule.

Death in the Afternoon aside, the trade also loved Hemingway. The Modern Library *A Farewell to Arms* sold well in bookshops, while the Grosset and Dunlap seventy-five-cent "photoplay edition" sold well in depots and drugstores. The red dust jacket of the second Grosset printing of *A Farewell to Arms* sported a photograph of Helen Hayes and Gary Cooper. "A GREAT BOOK A GREATER PICTURE!" roared the copy for one Paramount advertising poster. Though the poster reproduced a page from chapter 5 of the Grosset edition, another photograph of Hayes and Cooper obscured the text: "I looked in her eyes and pu . . . had before and kissed her . . . her tight and tried to open . . . tight." The tease was in the elision.

Who kissed her? Frederic Henry, who narrated the story? Gary Cooper, who made love to Clara Bow and Lupe Velez? Or Ernest Hemingway, who based Lieutenant Henry on personal experience? Frederic Henry *was* Gary Cooper *was* Ernest Hemingway. Paramount had brought the glamorous Helen Breaker photographs vividly to life. Though Hemingway could continue to pretend to be "perfectly unconscious of audience," the media culture and the population it served were no longer unconscious of him.

Had Scribners aggressively promoted *Death in the Afternoon* in winter 1933, the hoopla over the Paramount *Farewell to Arms* might—but only might—have spurred yet other printings. Perkins thought that advertising could not save the book, though, and allowed it to die. That March the printer billed Hemingway for expenses incurred on the illustrations for *Death*. When Houghton Mifflin billed Willa Cather $244 for corrections on *My Antonia*, the author was so angered that eventually she left Houghton for Knopf. Hemingway was surprisingly rational about his refusal to pay, and Perkins assured him that Scribners was ready to move on to the next book. "Havent written because started a novel," Hemingway had told one correspondent in February 1933. "—have $3^1/_2$ chapters done and 2 stories finished. Going well."

Hemingway would not abandon *Death in the Afternoon*, though, and resorted to movies to revive it. Sidney Franklin wanted to produce a motion picture based on *Death in the Afternoon* and the romantic Spanish novel *Currito de la Cruz*. Hemingway found the latter a readable account of Seville and the bullfight milieu, and was willing to assist Franklin with the translation and to collaborate on the screen story. Since an American edition of

Currito would broaden the appeal of the package for potential investors, Hemingway asked Scribners to option the translation. Perkins understood that talk of motion picture adaptations was hot air, and that to Hemingway, *Currito* and the movie were probably salvage operations for *Death in the Afternoon*. Should the motion picture be produced, however, Scribners could promote not only an English-language *Currito* but the reprint rights of *Death in the Afternoon*. For a nominal one hundred dollars, Perkins signed author Alejandro Pérez Lugín and translator Sidney Franklin for an American *Currito*. Now perhaps Hemingway could lay the ghost of *Death in the Afternoon* and finish another short story collection or the novel in progress.

"I don't think anybody did like [*Death in the Afternoon*] very much," Hemingway told Janet Flanner. It had sold, yes, but not as *A Farewell to Arms* had sold, and as the months passed, the author's resentment swelled. The critics were "swine" not "worth writing for." The public was merely ignorant. "Most people will not even read the Torrents," he told another correspondent in spring 1933, "but [James] Joyce and Ezra [Pound] like it and so does everybody that knows a damned thing about what I'm trying to do." The new story collection would have its fair share of the oblique and the *expérimental*—"The Light of the World," "A Way You'll Never Be," "The Mother of a Queen." But Hemingway could not decide whether to be defensive or proud. The stories were "mostly about things and people that people won't care about—or will actively dislike. All right," he told Mary Pfeiffer. "Sooner or later as the wheel keeps turning I will have ones that they *will* like." He had shaped "After the Storm" and "The Gambler, the Nun, and the Radio" (formerly called "Give Us a Prescription, Doctor") more for the general than the trained reader. He had also based the lead character in the novel on a rumrunner he knew and whose adventures would take place around Key West and Cuba. He sensed the chapters he had finished were "very good," no doubt because they had the robust action that would recapture the *Farewell to Arms* audience.

"Fisherman, Bullfighter, Boxer—He's 'The Author.' " The capital letters had been much in evidence during a trip to Manhattan early in 1933, when Perkins introduced Hemingway to Thomas Wolfe. Wolfe later called the performance grand but unaffecting. In Key West the capital letters spoke again. "I'm going to pay your expenses from N.Y. to N.Y. everything," he told MacLeish in spring 1933. He was planning to suspend work and host another rod and reel adventure. Mike Strater had already bailed out, "to snoot me," Hemingway griped, and MacLeish would also decline. The men liked Hemingway; in the confined space of a small boat on the open seas, however, he was too intense and too *macho*, which the glossary of *Death in the Afternoon* had defined as "male, masculine, abundantly endowed with male reproductive organs."

"Fame Follows Adventurous Career—Yet He Shuns Limelight." Rather than ditch the narrative voice that had undermined *Death in the Afternoon* and daunted friends, Hemingway turned up fresh occasions to deploy it. In March he promised an essay for the first issue of Arnold Gingrich's new quarterly magazine, *Esquire*; he would not contract for more unless he needed money. One month later, the potential rewards obvious, he agreed to write three additional "letters" for the magazine.

The rarefied market for *Death in the Afternoon* and the success of the Paramount *Farewell to Arms* had not made Hemingway easy to live with, yet the reputation of the Author had expanded even as that of the author had flagged. The local gazettes of small towns, as well as the *Saturday Review of Literature* and the urban press, now covered Hemingway as news. *Time* and *Vogue* covered him as luminary. In May 1933 *Vogue* celebrated five "bright people, gay people" (among them Katherine Cornell, Cyrus McCormick, and Ernest Hemingway) whose "diet of city life and organized resort life" could prove fatal to "their wit, their health, their backchat." Hemingway escaped "the steady grind" by living in Key West, where he could eat and drink inexpensively, and swim and fish twelve months a year. The note was more of the "unsought popularity" that—as the *Esquire* commitment would soon show—he could no longer do without.

In spring 1933 Scribners needed Hemingway more than ever. Though the house had sold Marjorie Rawlings's *South Moon Under* to the Book of the Month Club, the publication date collided with the March 1933 national bank holiday, and sales that should have totaled one hundred thousand stalled at ten thousand. Scott Fitzgerald had dozens of promotional schemes for the novel that would become *Tender Is the Night* but could not complete the manuscript. Also running in place, Thomas Wolfe had written more than three hundred thousand words of an unfinished manuscript (*Of Time and the River*) that had neither shape nor structure. "We did so well with *Look Homeward, Angel*," British publishing executive A. S. Frere-Reeves had told Perkins in February 1933, "but marching time draws on, and the public memory is painfully short." Booksellers meanwhile shipped unsold copies of *Death in the Afternoon* back to the publisher. For Scribners and Perkins the depression was suddenly personal.

Scribners was no longer what it once had been, or so it must have seemed to Perkins. Now Knopf was associated with Willa Cather (*Shadows on the Rock*); Covici-Friede with John Steinbeck (*Tortilla Flat*); and other publishers with William Faulkner and Ellen Glasgow, James T. Farrell and

John O'Hara, Robert Frost and Archibald MacLeish. Still other publishers would acquire the best-sellers of the 1930s, Hervey Allen's *Anthony Adverse* (Farrar & Rinehart, 1933) and Margaret Mitchell's *Gone with the Wind* (Macmillan, 1936). Treating the question of momentum as lightly as he could, Perkins once more urged Hemingway to complete the short story collection and rumrunner novel he had started. The author needed no reminders. "But always at your back you hear [Scribners advertising chief] Sir Whitney Darrow hurrying near," Ernest wrote Max, the *you* not only second but first person, "while before you lie deserts of lost publicity."

Hollywood and *The Sun Also Rises* could fill the vacuum. In February 1933 David Sarnoff had appointed Merian C. Cooper head of the studio; ordered to prune costs, Cooper trimmed the payroll and cut picture expenses by as much as 75 percent. On February 20, he had had an associate telephone James Wingate at the Production Code office. The studio has fifteen thousand dollars "sunk" in *The Sun Also Rises*, Wingate duly reported to Hays, and "is very anxious to make a treatment that will be satisfactory." Hays only confirmed Cooper's own "misgivings" about the property and "its suitability as screen entertainment," especially in early 1933, when state censors had increased their vigilance and activity. In spring 1933, though, aware of the ink that the press accorded Hemingway, the studio again passed the treatment by the Production Code office, and Wingate again reported to Hays. Leslie Howard and Ann Harding, said Wingate, paraphrasing Cooper, "would give a dignity to the portrayal of the two leads which might possibly overcome the difficulties." Wingate then passed the project to an assistant, Joseph I. Breen.

A staunch Irish Catholic, as bombastic as any studio head, Joe Breen understood that "racy" pictures produced revenue and misfortune—in equal measure—for the industry. He also understood that Wingate (and Hays) lacked spine. In March, under threat of burgeoning state censorship, Hays induced the moguls to renew support for the Production Code. So they should, thought Breen, who minced no words on the *The Sun Also Rises* screenplay he read in May 1933.

[I]t is the story of a nymphomaniac in love with a drunken newspaper man who persists in referring to "the mean trick" the war played upon him. There is no indication in the script as to what is meant by this "mean trick"—all of which contributes to the confusion in reading it. The story, as I read it, is the story of the various affairs which this nymphomaniac has with a number of men, all of them cursed with an overfondness for strong drink. Because of the brazenness with which this lady carries on her sexual indulgences, it is my judgment that the [screen]play which I read is quite definitely in violation of the Code and, of course, this is highly censorable. It is the kind of material which ought not to be used for screen dramatization.

Once more, production halted.

Whether the Author still needed the publicity of an RKO *Sun Also Rises* was questionable, for publicity there was—in abundance. In *The Autobiography of Alice B. Toklas* (1933) Gertrude Stein wrote that Hemingway had earned his literary baccalaureate in 1924 by proofing the serialization of her *Making of Americans*. She also wrote that she and Sherwood Anderson had created Hemingway, and were both proud and ashamed of their work. "But what a book, they both agreed, would be the real story of Hemingway, not those he writes but the confessions of the real Ernest Hemingway. It would be for another audience than the audience Hemingway now has but it would be very wonderful." That Stein should attack Hemingway for currying public favor was ironic since, à la *Death in the Afternoon*, the *Autobiography* had cast Stein herself as the Author and Alice B. Toklas as her Old Lady. That Stein should attack Hemingway for refusing to tell the story of "the real Hemingway" was laughable. The *Autobiography* was the story of Gertrude Stein the Professional Writer and Publicity Genius. The book was much talked about, and its notes on Hemingway—cycled through the *Atlantic Monthly* serialization in spring 1933, the hardcover publication in summer, and the reviews and literary gossip columns well into fall—only authenticated his fame.

In June 1933 Max Eastman's incendiary review of *Death in the Afternoon* appeared in the *New Republic*. *Death in the Afternoon* should have been called *Killing in the Afternoon*, Eastman wrote, for the author loves slaughter, not death. Called an arena for honor and glory, the *plaza de toros* was in fact an abattoir. Then again, everyone knew that the adolescent swagger and manly dress of the author were the cover for doubts about manhood. Hemingway was the champion of "a literary style, you might say, of wearing false hair on the chest." As Eastman concluded, it was tragic that someone as intelligent and sensitive as Hemingway should not only equate killing with religious ecstasy but fail to understand the larger implications of his work.

Hemingway heard about the Eastman review only days after he had chosen the title for his forthcoming short story collection, *Winner Take Nothing*. Only a fraction of the millions who had read about the sanctification of an "American legend" in *Time* would read of his crucifixion in the *New Republic*, in the review called "Bull in the Afternoon." They were nonetheless a strategic fraction. They wrote reviews, edited anthologies, traded opinions, and taught high school and college literature students. As Hemingway understood, they shaped literary reputations.

Hemingway was enraged. Not only was Gertrude Stein spreading rumors that he was "very queer indeed" but Eastman was corroborating them in print. He wanted to ghost a letter that MacLeish would send to the *New Republic*. But what would he say? That his and Hadley's fathers had committed suicide and thus prompted his interest in death? That he had never been attracted to men and had never doubted his sexual prowess with women? That he had more hairs on his chest than he could count and that "my cock measures $7^{1}/_{2}$ inches in action and retires comfortably in repose to a small space"? He had been shot through the scrotum at Fossalta, he told MacLeish, and spent weeks with his testicles on a pillow. The war wound (inches lower than Hemingway averred) had inspired *The Sun Also Rises* but had not turned the author into Jake Barnes, as subsequent "testimonials from satisfied customers" could prove. Could he say that? Could he say anything?

Hemingway crowbarred an apology from Eastman, who denied that he had ever heard "the breath of a rumor that you were sexually or any other way impotent." The author of *Death in the Afternoon* then flung that hairy chest into the public eye. According to "Prowess in Action" in the July 24 *Time*, Hemingway had recently landed a twelve-foot-plus marlin weighing 468 pounds. The author had been hardened by the "usual wicker demijohn of wine," and "had fought the bucking sea bronco alone and *without harness*." The catch was a "convincing . . . rebuttal to the Eastman attack," the editors noted, granting the weight of the review even as they purported to contain it. Though in *Time* Hemingway was the champion he had longed to become, the magazine tended to validate Eastman. The accompanying photograph of the huge marlin and proud fisherman, like the location of the article, which appeared in "Sports" rather than "Books," suggested that the debate over Hemingway could not be confined to his work alone. As one early biographer wrote, "far from presenting the literal record of a life which might counteract the legend, until the last years the photogenic Hemingway vastly confused the record by glamorizing it further."

Authors could stray from "Books" to "National Affairs" or other sections of the news, and even when photographed not only retain but enhance their reputations. But Ernest Hemingway was not Upton Sinclair or John Dos Passos; he was not fashionably political, and knew—even as he was drawn to pose for them—that photographs of Fisherman, Bullfighter, Boxer could mar the literary persona he wanted to project. "There is no quieter and less eventful life than that of a writer when he is working hard," he would tell *Esquire* readers, as he continued fishing for marlin and posing for the camera; "if he is working as hard as he should everything goes into the writing." Another Ernest Hemingway had appeared in *Vanity Fair,* though, as a cartoon character with a rose clutched in his hairy tattooed fist. Would readers construe *Winner Take Nothing* as the work of the author or the Author?

"You know us word merchants," Hemingway wrote Fitzgerald, "always ready to give comforting advice to others while pewking with the other hand about our own troubles." Concentrating on fiction, he might have moved beyond the celebrity of the Paramount publicity and *New Republic* panning. Though his best writing still equaled his best of three years before, much of what he wrote now was no longer his best. In addition, he liked to settle scores. For instance, even as he completed the short story collection for Scribners, he plotted to sic attorney Maurice Speiser on Eastman and to write "damned good memoirs" that would set the record straight on Stein and, for good measure, the adoption of her book by the Literary Guild. Autobiography was of course a one-way avenue to the audience, the audience that, increasingly, could never be large enough.

Hemingway had accepted a six-thousand-dollar advance on *Winner Take Nothing,* and within months the collection was finished. In addition to "After the Storm," "Wine of Wyoming," and "The Gambler, the Nun, and the Radio," it would contain two of his most compelling stories, "A Clean, Well-Lighted Place" and (finished in apparent haste in July 1933) "Fathers and Sons." "A Clean, Well-Lighted Place" focused on two waiters and the deaf old man they served. A failed suicide, the last customer of a long night, the old man has only the café and the brandy. The younger waiter wants to go home, but the older waiter knows what his customer knows and what his coworker must learn: "It was all a nothing and a man was nothing too. It was only that and light was all it needed and a certain cleanness and order." It was about the thin wall that separates life from nothingness, a wall as thin as the taut dialogue, the short sentences, and the spare action, in other words a wall as thin as a short story. Rich in philosophical and religious implications, the story had the cool sense of dread that pervaded "The Killers" and "Soldier's Home."

In "Fathers and Sons" Nick Adams drives along as his son sleeps beside him. Nick recalls his father's eyes, the eyes of an eagle or bighorn ram, eyes that saw "literally." Myopic about sex, his father warned that buggery was a heinous crime, masturbation produced blindness, and prostitutes caused venereal diseases. He also warned against "mashing," which his son imagined involved a woman, a man, and a kitchen tool. Nick "resolved, with considerable horror, that when he was old enough he would try mashing at least once." Nick turns from thoughts of the apparently violent death of his father toward more pleasant recollections of Billy and Trudy, Ojibway brother and sister. In the "virgin forest where the trees grew high" Trudy initiated him sexually, while Billy skulked about waiting for them. The recollection winds back to the father, though after adolescence Nick "shared nothing with him." Nick's son awakens. " 'What was it like, Papa, when you were a little boy and used to hunt with the Indians?' " And Nick's reverie ends.

The relationship of Nick and Trudy alluded to miscegenation, while Billy's restlessness as Trudy "was exploring with her hand in Nick's pocket" touched on homosexuality and incest. " 'I get tired this,' " Billy grunts. " 'What we come? Hunt or what?' " Billy was not the only primitive. Nick "liked the smell" of one of his sisters, and could, when whipped for trashing a pair of long johns he shared with his father, unleash strong oedipal urges. He also liked riffing about Trudy and her "plump brown legs, flat belly, hard little breasts, well holding arms, [and] quick searching tongue" or the way she made love, "tightly, sweetly, moistly, lovely, tightly, achingly, fully, finally, unendingly, never-endingly, never-to-endingly, suddenly ended, the great bird flown like an owl in the twilight." In *Death in the Afternoon* Hemingway had mocked stories that contained "popular appeal" and a "touch of sex," that pandered to what Faulkner called "the Kotex Age." But if the sensuality of the stories in *Winner Take Nothing* was commercial, it was also "true." The collection could by and large show that the author was doing it for himself inside. All he had to do was silence the Author.

As Max Perkins arranged the contents in *Winner Take Nothing*, Arnold Gingrich lined up the inaugural issue of *Esquire*. Hemingway needed the $250 per article he had settled for. Royalties from *Death in the Afternoon* would cover a fraction of the costs of two months' fishing near Havana, and in search of cash Hemingway had even conferred with director Lewis Milestone on a moving picture about Spain. Aside from the practical, the *Esquire* money could help paper over the adverse reception of *Death in the Afternoon* and assure the author that his nonfiction had value. *Esquire* would also offer a seductive forum for Ernest Hemingway the one-man show.

Though the lead article in the autumn *Esquire* ("Marlin off the Morro") was purportedly about fishing near Havana, the voice was avuncular, authoritative, and above all personal. Sport fishing required enormous strength, Hemingway said, and he offered in evidence his recent one-hour battle against a black marlin. The sixteen photographs that Gingrich reproduced were further evidence of the attractive power of the author. In 1921

Helen Breaker had seen how the camera loved the musk of Hemingway; the snapshots in *Esquire* caught it and spread it around.

During the editing of *Winner Take Nothing*, which contained the strange "Mother of a Queen" and "One Reader Writes," Perkins had made some token remarks about the relative value of stories in the collection. Hemingway simmered, then boiled over. Because of what Gertrude Stein and Max Eastman had written, he thought that he could count on Scribners' loyalty. He could of course return the puny advance and look for another publisher, he told Perkins, but Scribners would be the loser since, despite the storm that raged about *Death in the Afternoon*, Hemingway was not "washed up." Quite the reverse: the rumrunner novel was already "100 leagues" better than what Scribners' "poor twirps" could produce.

No less than Hemingway, Perkins wanted the audience back, the audience that had embraced *A Farewell to Arms* and resisted *Death in the Afternoon*, the audience that had discovered Hemingway via Hollywood. The campaign would start with *Winner Take Nothing*. Though the author chose to open the collection with "The Light of the World," Perkins argued that it was "the one to which people will most object." Hemingway understood that the "words" and content of the story, especially as the lead story, could prejudice certain reviewers and readers against the entire book. He would not graciously surrender to the genteel, but he had taken Scribners' money—so he said—and agreed to honor Perkins's wishes. *Winner Take Nothing* would open with "After the Storm" and close with "Fathers and Sons." He and Perkins must have known that "After the Storm" and "Fathers and Sons" were the more accessible stories in the collection and that, along with their shrewd mix of literary and popular conventions, their positions in the volume would shore up the lesser or more problematic material in between.

In August *Esquire* appeared on the stands. The blurb on the author in "Backstage with *Esquire*" puffed *Winner Take Nothing* and underscored the physical prowess of Ernest Hemingway: for readers with waistlines, "we wish that Mr. Hemingway had included, in his account of marlin fishing, the fact that he lost 26 pounds during the three months he spent fishing the Cuban Coast." The text and photographs of "Marlin off the Morro" not only accented the muscle of the author but introduced him to a public located somewhere between Scribners and Paramount, and attracted to male pin-ups and derring-do. The 105,000 copies of the autumn number sold out at once. *Esquire* would henceforth be published monthly, and future Hemingway "Letters" would further lash the personal to the literary.

By October Hemingway had read galley proof on *Winner Take Nothing* and rewritten parts of *Shadows of the Sun*, Sidney Franklin's translation of the bullfight novel *Currito de la Cruz*, which Scribners would publish in 1934. (The motion picture based on *Death in the Afternoon* and *Currito* would go unproduced.) He had also completed the draft of "One Trip Across." Without blinking he sent the tough action story to *Cosmopolitan*, which paid him $5,500, a record amount. "You can't dodge the big magazines much longer," a representative from the Curtis Brown agency wrote Hemingway. Since Paramount had boosted the allure of the author, *Cosmopolitan* was "not the only one who [was] ready to pay money." Hemingway was known—and wanted others to know it. In the "Spanish Letter" he had just finished for *Esquire*, he reported on a recent story in the Madrid Sunday paper, a story called "Mister Hemingway, Friend of Spain." Hemingway insinuated that he had not "sucked after" anyone for the honor but earned it as the conscience and soul of the nation. He then assessed contemporary matadors and bullfighting. "And what else do you want to know?" the author asked readers near the end of the essay.

Hemingway the actor was now frequently on stage, even in personal correspondence. He had lived through inflation in three countries over ten years, he told Mary Pfeiffer in October 1933, "and I know exactly how it works, what the various steps are and what it leads to. So far I have made money on it and anyone having followed my advice would have made a great deal of money." The boast about money was in character. Hemingway had long equated money and masculinity, perhaps since Grace Hemingway had warned her adolescent son that "lazy loafing and pleasure seeking" led away from "manhood" and toward "bankruptcy." He had indeed prospered while traveling through Germany in 1922, but only passively, through the luck of the inflationary spiral. No matter. What counted was the performance, or so he tried to convince himself. What others had begun to sense was the pathology.

Scribners published *Winner Take Nothing* on 27 October 1933. The first printing was 20,300—double the number ordered for the nonfiction *Death in the Afternoon*. Fiction was the thing, particularly when its author was a Paramount star. The price was two dollars, and the back cover of the red, white, and black dust jacket featured a portion of Laurence Stallings's review of *Death in the Afternoon*.

In the *Chicago Tribune* Fanny Butcher praised *Winner Take Nothing*, especially "A Natural History of the Dead," whose accounts of war could "tear at a woman's heart as cruelly as ever they would at a man's." *Time* also endorsed the book as one that would please critics, disciples, and ordinary readers, men and women. And though Perkins called many of the negative reviews "absolutely enraging," he knew that *Winner Take Nothing* had had more press attention—including photographs of the author—than previous Hemingway books, and that the fanfare from *Esquire* and Paramount would help neutralize the bad reviews. "Hemingway's fame began as a writer of short stories," one trade advertisement of *Winner Take Nothing* read. "Your records will show that 'Men Without Women' was the best-selling volume of its kind published in recent years. This new book has an even wider appeal, as the Hemingway audience has grown tremendously in the last four years." Orders and sales quickly reached eleven thousand copies. Then, the pace slowed.

No doubt Christmas shoppers found *Winner Take Nothing* a dubious gift prospect: the title was at odds with tinsel and ribbon, and the content (short stories) belonged in magazines rather than books. The key to the market was still the novel. Perhaps more important, as John Raeburn has shown in *Fame Became of Him*, the "Hemingway audience" that had "grown tremendously" was more interested *in* Hemingway than in books *by* Hemingway. Unless prodded by laudatory reviews or Hollywood publicity, the audience was content merely to read about the author. For *Winner Take Nothing* Perkins ordered no second edition.

Hemingway was bitter about the bad notices. But he had no illusions about *Winner Take Nothing*. In separate letters months before publication he had told Janet Flanner and John Dos Passos that the book contained "some good ones" and, by tacit admission, that others were less than good. He also told Perkins that "it doesn't do anyone any particular harm to publish literature once in a while. Especially as I have always paid my way."

According to Horace Gregory in the *New York Herald Tribune*, the literature of Ernest Hemingway was the life of Ernest Hemingway. Hemingway countered that he had invented all but three or four incidents in *A Farewell to Arms* and that "95 per cent of The Sun Also was pure imagination." Among the general public, though, wholly ignorant of Horace Gregory, Paramount had merged Ernest Hemingway and Frederic Henry, and the nonfiction *Death in the Afternoon* and *Esquire* letters only reinforced the "single protagonist" theory. In fiction, Hemingway had not always given the public what it wanted. In life, he would henceforth give the public nothing less.

AFTERWORD

On board the *Ile de France*, Cherbourg to New York, April 1934, were Marlene Dietrich and Katharine Hepburn. As the cabaret singer in *Morocco*, dressed in white tie and tails, Dietrich had shown one facet of her elusive screen persona; she had taken the gardenia from the hair of a woman patron, kissed the patron square on the lips, and tossed the flower to costar Gary Cooper. One evening on the *France* she entered the dining salon to find that hers was the thirteenth seat at table. Superstitious, she asked to be excused, but a large passenger blocked her way and offered to become the fourteenth. "The man was Hemingway," she said. The dinner partners were well matched since both advocated an iceberg theory of art: danger beneath the waterline, sharp edges above. Hemingway liked Dietrich, whom he nicknamed "the Kraut."

Like Dietrich, Hepburn had a confrontational sexuality. She wore slacks when dresses were the norm, and challenged Hollywood about her roles and her contracts. In New York harbor the press thronged her suite, where she was interviewed with her new pal. " 'Gentlemen, meet Mr. Hemingway,' " she told the crowd. He was "a tall, broad-shouldered man, with a healthy sun tan and wearing a dark mustache and eye-glasses," one reporter wrote. " 'Gentlemen,' " he said, " 'Miss Hepburn.' " Will the men drink? Miss Hepburn asked bashfully. " 'Sure, they'll drink,' said Hemingway, not bashful at all." She took orders for Perrier and whiskeys. " 'Why did you change your mind so suddenly and stay abroad only five days?' " another reporter asked. And Miss Hepburn responded: " 'Ernest, what can

I say that's really witty? I guess I'm supposed to say something witty.' " And Mr. Hemingway responded: " 'I don't know anything witty.' " The Gallagher and Sheen of the *France* buttressed one another's celebrity, and days later, convinced that Hepburn would look smart among the marlin, kudu, and other conquests of the last twelve months, Hemingway asked Paramount—the company he had once battled over *A Farewell to Arms*—to obtain prints of news photos of the couple taken during the interview.

In 1934, as the author headed for Key West, another movie star renewed her interest in his work. Ann Harding was determined to portray Lady Ashley. Recently divorced, she had been dogged by press reports that she had "slipped professionally" since starring in *The Animal Kingdom* (1932) with Leslie Howard. "Few stars have started out with greater possibilities and faltered so sadly in their screen careers," one paper reported. Just as Dietrich's and Hepburn's association with the "literary" Hemingway had added a soupçon of gravity to their renown, Harding's association with the "scandalous" *The Sun Also Rises* could have changed her persona and reestablished her as an important actress. By October 1933, when Scribners published *Winner Take Nothing*, she and Edward H. Griffith (the director of *The Animal Kingdom*) had formed a company and optioned *The Sun Also Rises.*

RKO was asking twenty-five thousand dollars for the property, the studio's investment to date, or so the accountants claimed; more likely, Hemingway's marquee value had appreciated since RKO purchased the work. Harding and Griffith first sought financing outside Hollywood, hoping to elude the chill of the Production Code, but when they were turned down by Joseph P. Kennedy and others—who, sub rosa, had telephoned the Production Code office for advice—they returned to the studio system and the self-censorship it entailed. James Wingate was being eased out of the office, and Jason Joy, on loan from Fox during the transition, told the would-be producers that *The Sun Also Rises* could be approved as long as it underplayed "the nymphomaniacal tendencies of the heroine" and "the impotency of the hero." Based on that curious opinion, Fox and Ann Harding bought *The Sun Also Rises*. According to one studio associate, the negotiations had been "very confidential," perhaps to keep Hemingway (who had sold all film rights to the novel) from learning that he had been "royally buggared."

Joe Breen, now de facto the director of the Production Code agency, had decided that no studio would produce and release *The Sun Also Rises*. Angered by RKO's sale, he telephoned Fox's head of production. Winfield Sheehan "stated that he knew nothing about it, that he did not favor the material, and that he would talk to Mr. Kent." But Fox President Sidney

Kent was a plain dealer. He wrote Breen that according to Will Hays, "the story was not banned entirely" and that he (Kent) would personally supervise its production as an "outside picture." Having been in the distribution wing of Paramount before leaving for Fox in 1932, Kent understood merchandising and sales. He thus saw that Hemingway was exploitable and that the press on *Death in the Afternoon* and the author's regular appearances in *Esquire* were good "advance" for a Hollywood *Sun Also Rises*. As the Catholic Legion of Decency noisily planned boycotts, however, Hays and Breen forced Kent, reluctantly, to halt production even before it began.

In July 1934 Hays formed the Production Code Administration and named Breen director; he would hold the post for twenty years. Ann Harding had ten thousand dollars in *The Sun Also Rises* and, still hoping to make the picture herself, purchased Fox's fifteen-thousand-dollar interest. Then, as agent Ann Watkins had done more than three years before, the actress shopped the story around Hollywood. In late 1934 Irving Thalberg was interested in *The Sun Also Rises*, for MGM and Greta Garbo. Harding apparently considered selling, conditional on her portrayal as Lady Ashley, but the Production Code Administration intervened. "We have urged Mr. Thalberg to dismiss this story entirely from any thought he may have had for its adaptation for screen purpose," Breen told Louis Mayer. Breen then lobbied Hays to have adaptations of the book suppressed—forever. Eventually the Motion Picture Association passed a unanimous resolution that the novel was "so salacious in essence" that a motion picture based on it "should not be made at all." And until Joe Breen retired and Twentieth Century-Fox (Fox's successor company) made the film with producer Charles Feldman, who had bought the rights from Harding's ex-husband, *The Sun Also Rises* lay dormant in Hollywood.

In 1934 the Author who had "lived" the war in *A Farewell to Arms* hardly needed to become the Author who had "lived" the libertine adventures of Jake Barnes and the other expatriates. The author was already the victim of too much publicity. In Key West, he said, he planned "to write a novel with lion and buffalo hunting as the framework," but what started as fiction soon shaded into nonfiction. One passage in *Green Hills of Africa* was a threnody on the destruction of authors.

We destroy them in many ways. First, economically. They make money. It is only by hazard that a writer makes money although good books always make money eventually. Then our writers when they have made some money increase their standard of living and they are caught. They have to write to keep up their establishments, their wives, and so on, and they write slop. It is slop not on purpose but because it is hurried. Because they write when there is nothing to say or no water in the well. Because they are ambitious. Then, once they have betrayed themselves, they justify it and you get more slop. Or else they read the critics. If they believe the critics when they say they are great then they must believe them when they say they are rotten and they lose confidence.

In retrospect Hemingway would refer to "my sonofabitching epoch of 1934," the year of the twenty-five-thousand-dollar safari and the million-dollar movie stars, the year of damaged friendships and nasty cracks about Fitzgerald and MacLeish, the year of the *Vanity Fair* Hemingway "paper dolls," including "Ernie, the Neanderthal Man" (in loincloth and with club and rabbit in hand), "Ernie as the Lost Generation" (seated at a café table surrounded by bottles), "Ernie as Don Jose, the Toreador" (standing over a dead bull), and "Ernie the Unknown Soldier" (the bowed survivor of war).

Apologizing later to MacLeish for remarks made on the *Pilar,* Hemingway appeared to have understood the consequences of his behavior. Or had he? "You see what they [the critics] can't get over is (1) that I *am* a man (2) that I can beat the shit out of any of them (3) that I can write. The last hurts them the worst. But they don't like any of it. But Papa will make them like it." The rank order was telling. Papa will make them like it (1) because of who he is, (2) because of who he is, (3) because of what he can do. Sucked in by fame, Hemingway was now in third place behind "Hemingway," and the ground lost was lost forever.

"I want, like hell, to get published," Hemingway had said in 1923. Three years later he was the author who "has only to publish to be read by a certain circle of the intelligentsia, and not even to publish to be discussed." Six years later, he was the Author. He was aped, optioned, caricatured, adapted, praised, roasted, celebrated, mocked, filmed, honored, scorned, and quoted. In short, he was famous.

The fiction and nonfiction of Ernest Hemingway appeared to support a theory that reached a crescendo in the modern age, the theory that we were less than what moved about and through us. Copernicus, Darwin, and Freud, and then the Great War and the Great Depression, turned theory to fact: they appeared to prove that we had lost control over ourselves. Hemingway wrote about how *they* had conquered *us,* how *they* had daunted Nick Adams, wounded Jake Barnes, and killed Catherine Barkley. But his work, and even the conduct of his vigorous life, was a continuous—if doomed—protest against forces greater than himself, and that assertion of *I* against *them* had enormous appeal to *us*.

Anyone popular in the early twentieth century could hardly have chosen to be otherwise. In *Personality: How to Build It* (1915) Henri Laurent enshrined "the quality of being Somebody," of standing out from the crowd. In another of the many books that touched on the subject, *The Promise of American Life* (1909), Herbert Croly noted that success was contingent on "some sort of personal impression" and "a numerous and faithful body of admirers." The Hemingway perpendicular pronoun (as he called the *I*) was the exhibition of *Somebody* before the *you* of the crowd, a word that recurred in self-help books and *Death in the Afternoon* and other works. George F. Babbitt understood the need for personality and an audience. So did Ernest M. Hemingway.

Hemingway would not have read Laurent or others. He would nonetheless have absorbed their theorems in Oak Park, where Grace Hall Hemingway exuded "the quality of being Somebody." Without changes in the American literary marketplace, though, the Somebody would only have been somebody. In the 1920s mass readership, mass advertising, and mass curiosity about postwar mores and behavior raised book sales and made books news. The *New York Evening Post* occasionally ran book reviews on the front page, and other papers ran stories on books and authors in the book and other sections. Rich in revenue, the slick magazines paid top dollar to attract the authors that the newpapers and the public consecrated. Finally, for the right authors, Hollywood could attach the capital *S* to somebody.

Hemingway genuinely tried to forestall publicity. He often wrote to Perkins about personal incidents or the writing process but asked the editor to keep his letters private: he wrote when he was tired (or tight), and what he wrote about life or art could sound pretentious in the hands of publicity agents. In July and August 1929 letters, for instance, he pondered the roots of imagination and again begged Perkins not to share the musings with the advertising department. In a June 1932 letter, he not only wondered why the ballyhoo he had cut from a press release on *Death in the Afternoon* had somehow been restored but told Perkins to quit sending out the Helen Breaker photographs, the "open mouth open collar wonders." The hoopla and photos were inescapable, though, as Edward Bernays, the founder of modern public relations, noted in his memoirs. Bernays, who worked for Horace Liveright in the early 1920s, asked his boss early on "for his comments on each author, for I thought his appraisal might help me decide which books to promote heavily." The congruence of the period and his personality decreed that Hemingway would be Somebody in the twentieth century.

"Fisherman, Bullfighter, Boxer—He's 'The Author.' " In 1935 Scribners informed the trade that the safari book *Green Hills of Africa* was for "the *whole* Hemingway audience—'Death in the Afternoon' enthusiasts and 'A Farewell to Arms' readers alike." The whole audience, though, was less interested in safari books or even great fiction (like "The Short Happy Life of Francis Macomber" and "The Snows of Kilimanjaro," published in 1936) than in the fisticuffs that broke out between the author and Max Eastman in Perkins's office in 1937. The tabloids carried the story, and then, two months later, ostensibly for other reasons, *Time* put Hemingway on its cover. "He is living at the present in a world so entirely his own that it is impossible to help him," Scott told Max, "even if I felt close to him at the moment, which I don't."

Hemingway used his personality, what his sister called (referring to their mother) press agenting, to move his books. *For Whom the Bell Tolls* (1940) was another story of love and war, set against the Spanish Civil War; it was told with sweep and assurance, and laced with allusions to death and self-destruction, physical and (perhaps) literary. Scott told Zelda that the novel "would please the average type of reader, the mind who used to enjoy Sinclair Lewis." Perkins was also wistful about the amity of author and market. The novel "has been taken by the Book of the Month Club," he wrote Fitzgerald, the "stamp of bourgeois approval. [Hemingway] would hate to think of it that way, and yet it is a good thing, practically speaking." Indeed, after 1940 he "was a household name for BOMC members. His books were never ignored and they all received major attention." His books were likewise adapted for film; three short stories alone—"The Killers," "The Short Happy Life of Francis Macomber," and "The Snows of Kilimanjaro"—netted him just over one hundred thousand dollars.

Between 1940 and 1946, Hemingway wrote nothing substantial. He conducted submarine patrols near Cuba, and divorced two wives, Pauline in 1940 and the journalist Martha Gellhorn in late 1945. Viking issued *The Portable Hemingway* in 1944; though it reintroduced the public to the author, it had, like *The Fifth Column and the First Forty-Nine Stories* (1938), a retrospective cast. In early 1946 he wed the journalist Mary Welsh. The Hemingway women were an audience close at hand. They served a man who rarely liked to be by himself: from 1921 until his death he was unmarried for less than twenty weeks total. The press zealously covered the adventures, divorces, accidents, and illnesses, among them the extraordinary string of concussions and motor crack-ups in May and August 1944, June 1945, and July 1950. Above all, the press photographed Hemingway—in Mexico City, Sun Valley, New Orleans, Hong Kong, and Paris. And his name and his photograph on reprints, magazine stories, and book club advertisements were enough to spark sales and make publisher and author wealthy.

"The only thing that has ever worried me is the long interval between your books of fiction," Perkins had once told Hemingway. That is "the way publishers look at things, being conscious of the trade." Sadly, the energy that drove *The Sun Also Rises* and *A Farewell to Arms*—absent in minor or second-rate fiction like *To Have and Have Not* (1937) and *Across the River and Into the Trees* (1950)—was present only in nonfiction like the *Esquire* letters, whose content and form (Perkins thought) had "not been much." The last novel Scribners published before his death was *The Old Man and the Sea* (1952), the story of a fisherman and the giant marlin he snags. It was an affirmation of the human spirit and a huge popular success. By then, though, Hemingway the writer mattered less to the public than Hemingway the icon. In the famous portrait by Yousuf Karsh, Papa looked every inch the lion. Inside, he felt too often like Ad Francis, the former champion of "The Battler" who, his friend says, " 'took too many beatings, for one thing.' " Inside he felt like a hunted lion, and a physical coward.

Hemingway had won the Pulitzer (1953) and the Nobel (1954) when he started "The Dangerous Summer." He accepted one hundred thousand dollars from *Life* for the manuscript, the story of the battle of two matadors and the consequences of fame, but was "ashamed and sick" to have written it. He needed the exposure, though. He needed the audience. "Publicity, admiration, adulation, or simply being fashionable are all worthless and are extremely harmful if one is susceptible to them," he once wrote Bernard Berenson. He had written as much to others, and to readers of *Death in the Afternoon*. Then as now, it was no defense against the cancer of celebrity that devoured the private person within.

Hemingway recalled the 1920s in *A Moveable Feast*, the bittersweet memoir about the writer who lived on leeks and drank water and wrote great books. Long before the last years of his life, he had understood that he could no longer supply the vast audience of the twentieth century with work that was quick, honest, and controlled, work as powerful or as enduring as *In Our Time*, *The Sun Also Rises*, and *A Farewell to Arms*. He could supply the audience only with himself, Ernest Hemingway the Professonal Writer, Ernest Hemingway the husk. He had often thought of the way out, and on the second day of July 1961 he loaded his shotgun. The Author put the muzzle in his mouth. The author pulled the trigger.

NOTES

LIST OF ABBREVIATIONS

AFTA	Ernest Hemingway. *A Farewell to Arms.*
AH	Michael Reynolds. *Hemingway: The American Homecoming.*
AMPAS	Paramount Pictures Collection. Margaret Herrick Library, Academy of Motion Picture Arts and Sciences, Beverly Hills, Calif.
Baker	Carlos Baker. *Ernest Hemingway: A Life Story.*
Bruccoli	Matthew J. Bruccoli. *Fitzgerald and Hemingway: A Dangerous Friendship.*
BS/AMPAS	Frank Borzage Scrapbook. Margaret Herrick Library, Academy of Motion Picture Arts and Sciences, Beverly Hills, Calif.
CF/LCLPA	*SAFTA* Clippings File. LCLPA.
CS/JFK	Hemingway Clippings Scrapbook. JFK.
COHC	Columbia Univ. Oral History Collection. Butler Library, Columbia Univ., New York.
CR	Robert O. Stephens, ed. *Ernest Hemingway: The Critical Reception.*
DIA	Ernest Hemingway. *Death in the Afternoon.*
DS	John Kuehl and Jackson R. Bryer, eds. *Dear Scott / Dear Max: The Fitzgerald-Perkins Correspondence.*
EH	Ernest Hemingway.
FCLD	Fox Collection (Legal Department). Theatre Collection. University Research Library, Univ. of California at Los Angeles.

FMS	Harrison Smith, ed. *From Main Street to Stockholm: Letters of Sinclair Lewis, 1919–1930.*
FSF	F. Scott Fitzgerald.
HFW	Michael Reynolds. *Hemingway's First War: The Making of* A Farewell to Arms.
IOT	Ernest Hemingway. *In Our Time.*
JFK	Hemingway Collection. John F. Kennedy Library, Boston.
LCLPA	Lincoln Center Library for the Performing Arts, New York.
MP	Max Perkins.
MPAA	Motion Picture Association of America (formerly Motion Picture Producers and Distributors of America). Margaret Herrick Library, Academy of Motion Picture Arts and Sciences, Beverly Hills, Calif.
MWW	Ernest Hemingway. *Men Without Women.*
OT	Matthew J. Bruccoli, ed. *The Only Thing That Counts: The Ernest Hemingway / Maxwell Perkins Correspondence, 1925–1947.*
PUL	Charles Scribner's Sons Archives. Manuscripts Division, Department of Rare Books and Special Collections. Princeton Univ. Libraries, Princeton, N.J.
PW	*Publishers' Weekly.*
PY	Michael Reynolds. *Hemingway: The Paris Years.*
SAFTA	Laurence Stallings. *A Farewell to Arms* [play]. 1930. TS. LCLPA.
SL	Carlos Baker. *Ernest Hemingway: Selected Letters, 1917–1961.*
TSAR	Ernest Hemingway. *The Sun Also Rises.*
TTOS	Ernest Hemingway. *The Torrents of Spring.*
WTN	Ernest Hemingway. *Winner Take Nothing.*
YH	Michael Reynolds. *The Young Hemingway.*

PREFACE

xi *"Not long before"* Advertisement, c. 1 July 1929, JFK. Citations of clippings contain as much information—author, title, source, date, page number—as available in the archive of origin.

xi *"good books"* EH to MP, 3 Oct. 1929, JFK.

xi *The first matador* Unless otherwise indicated, citations of Hemingway's writing—including the passage from chapter ix of *IOT* cited here—have been drawn from published versions (see Works Cited) rather than manuscripts. No "definitive, complete edition of Hemingway's short fiction" now exists (Susan F. Beegel, ed., *Hem-*

ingway's Neglected Short Fiction: New Perspectives [Ann Arbor: UMI Research, 1989], 6); absent one, *Complete Short Stories of Ernest Hemingway*, Finca Vigía edition (New York: Scribners, 1987), stands as the most readily accessible such text. On the composition of the vignettes that appeared originally in the *Little Review* 9 (Spring 1923): 3–5, see *PY*, 114–15, 369 n. 49.

xii *"for the relief"* R. Jackson Wilson, *Figures of Speech: American Writers and the Literary Marketplace, from Benjamin Franklin to Emily Dickinson* (New York: Knopf, 1989), 227; MP to FSF, 3 Feb. 1926, *DS*, 132.

xii *The nonfiction sales* John Tebbel, *The Golden Age between Two Wars, 1920–1940*, vol. 3 of *A History of Book Publishing in the United States* (New York: Bowker, 1978), 88–89.

xii *"Did you see"* MP to FSF, 18 June 1926, *DS*, 143; Roger Burlingame, *Of Making Many Books: A Hundred Years of Reading, Writing and Publishing* (New York: Scribners, 1946), 15–16. According to James Hinkle, in "Scribner, Scribners, Scribner's," "the man is *Scribner*, the adjective is *Scribner*, the noun and short firm name is *Scribners*, the official firm name is *Charles Scribner's Sons*, and *Scribner's* is almost never right" except for the magazine (*Hemingway Review* 6, no. 1 [Fall 1986]: 42). In "Scribner, Scribners, Scribner's Revisited," Robert W. Lewis argues that the "most acceptable shortened form" for the publishing house is *Scribner* (*Hemingway Review* 6, no.2 [Spring 1987]: 54–55), and indeed books recently published by the house (now a division of Simon & Schuster) bear the "Scribner" imprint. Such persuasive evidence notwithstanding, *Hemingway and His Conspirators* follows Hinkle throughout in order to prevent confusion between the man and the short firm name; unless otherwise indicated, "the man" is Charles Scribner II.

xiii *"Get acquainted"* Clarence Hemingway to EH, 4 Feb. 1920, JFK; Ralph Waldo Emerson, "Character," in *Essays: Second Series*, vol. 3 of *The Collected Works of Ralph Waldo Emerson* (Cambridge: Harvard Univ. Press, 1983), 56.

xiii *"announces, proclaims"* Leopold Wagner, *How to Publish a Book or Article* (London: George Redway, 1898), 60, qtd. in N. N. Feltes, *Literary Capital and the Late Victorian Novel* (Madison: Univ. of Wisconsin Press, 1993), 12; Tebbel, *Golden Age*, 91. On character, charisma, and celebrity, see (in addition to Works Cited) Daniel J. Boorstin, *The Image: A Guide to Pseudo-Events in America* (New York: Harper, 1961); Leo Braudy, *The Frenzy of Renown: Fame and Its History* (New York: Oxford Univ. Press, 1986); Jib Fowles, *Celebrity Performers and the American Public* (Washington: Smithsonian, 1992); Robert E. Kapsis, *Hitchcock: The Making of a Reputation* (Chicago: Univ. of Chicago Press, 1992); Leo Lowenthal, *Literature, Popular Culture, and Society* (Englewood Cliffs, N. J.: Prentice-Hall, 1961); Charles J. Maland, *Chaplin and American Culture: The Evolution of a Star Image* (Princeton: Princeton Univ. Press, 1989); Richard Schickel, *His Picture in the Papers: A Speculation on Celebrity in America, Based on the Life of Douglas Fairbanks, Sr.* (New York: Charterhouse, 1973); Warren Susman, *Culture as History* (New York: Pantheon, 1984), 273–77.

xiv *"publicity hypnosis"* Tebbel, *Golden Age*, 324–27, 319; Alfred Harcourt to Sinclair Lewis, 11 Apr. 1928, *FMS*, 266.

xiv *Max Perkins could appear* A. Scott Berg, *Max Perkins: Editor of Genius* (New York: Dutton, 1978), 27, passim.

xiv *"He calls"* James L. W. West III, *American Authors and the Literary Marketplace since 1900* (Philadelphia: Univ. of Pennsylvania Press, 1988), 140.

xv *Accepting* This Side MP to FSF, 16 Sept. 1919; FSF to MP, 18 Sept. 1919; MP to FSF, 6 Jan. 1920, *DS*, 21, 22, 24.

xv *"to be endorsed"* FSF to MP, c. 10 Dec. 1921, *DS*, 47.

xvi *"I want, like"* EH to Edward O'Brien, 21 May 1923, *SL*, 82.

xvi *"to put [Hemingway]"* Scott Donaldson, "The Wooing of Ernest Hemingway," *American Literature* 53 (1982): 699; Feltes, *Literary Capital*, 18–19; Charles Scribner to EH, 5 July 1927, JFK.

xvii *"worthwhile to get"* EH to MP, 15 Apr. 1925, *SL*, 156.

xvii *"glamorous personality"* On the eve of the premiere of the motion picture version of *AFTA*, Hemingway mocked Paramount Pictures's having fabricated a "glamorous personality" for the author of the novel (EH to MP, 7 Dec. 1932, *SL*, 379). On Hemingway and the movies, see (in addition to Works Cited) Charles M. Oliver, ed., *A Moving Picture Feast: A Filmgoer's Hemingway* (New York: Praeger, 1989), and Gene D. Phillips, *Hemingway and Film* (New York: Ungar, 1980).

CHAPTER ONE: THE BATTLER

1 *"without stopping"* Grace Hemingway Memory Book 2: 24, 25, 49, JFK.

1 *No longer content* Griffin, 22, 26, 29, passim.

2 *At Oak Park High* Baker, 23. Denis Brian says that Hemingstein "was a nickname [Ernest] adopted in adolescence when he and his friends were pretending to be Jewish pawnbrokers. He also called himself Ernie Hemorrhoid, which I presume didn't show his respect for piles" (*The True Gen: An Intimate Portrait of Hemingway by Those Who Knew Him* [New York: Delta, 1988], 110).

2 *"the romance"* YH, 14; Baker, 33; *PY*, 25.

2 *He later recalled* Baker, 38.

2 *"was always"* HFW, 193, 195; EH to William Smith, Jr., 13 Dec. 1918, *SL*, 20. See also Henry Villard and James Nagel, eds., *Hemingway in Love and War: The Lost Diary of Agnes von Kurowsky* (Boston: Northeastern Univ. Press, 1989).

2 *"Gee, Family"* EH to his family, 18 Aug. 1918, *SL*, 13.

3 *"If you do"* Clarence Hemingway to EH, 11 Aug. 1918, JFK; Joshua Gamson, *Claims to Fame: Celebrity in Contemporary America* (Berkeley: Univ. of California Press, 1994), 23; Marcelline Hemingway to EH, 24 Oct. 1918, JFK.

3 Red Book *and* Woman's Maureen Honey, ed., *Breaking the Ties That Bind: Popular Stories of the New Woman, 1915–1930* (Norman: Univ. of Oklahoma Press, 1992), 6;

Richard Fine, *Hollywood and the Profession of Authorship, 1928–1940* (Ann Arbor: UMI Research, 1985), 43, 47; *YH*, 13; William Lord Wright, "For Photoplay Authors, Real and Near," *New York Dramatic Mirror*, 3 Feb. 1915, 30; "Film Rights, and What They Are Worth," *New York Times*, 27 June 1920, VI:1.

4 *"I've written"* EH to James Gamble, 3 Mar. 1919, *SL*, 22. This and subsequent citations have been reproduced as Hemingway wrote them; "[*sic*]" has been added only when an error confuses the sense of the quotation. Also, unless otherwise indicated, all italics appearing in quotations in this book are the original writer's.

4 *"I set out"* EH to Howell Jenkins, 16 June 1919, *SL*, 25.

4 *"down Traverse"* Max Westbrook, "Grace Under Pressure: Hemingway and the Summer of 1920," in James Nagel, ed., *Ernest Hemingway: The Writer in Context* (Madison: Univ. of Wisconsin Press, 1984), 77, 86. See also *YH*, 70.

4 *"I doubt"* Paul Smith, *A Reader's Guide to the Short Stories of Ernest Hemingway* (Boston: G. K. Hall, 1989), xxvi–xxvii; *YH*, 137.

5 *" 'had been badly' "* *PY*, 50.

5 *Hadley Richardson* Gioia Diliberto, *Hadley* (New York: Ticknor & Fields, 1992), x, 48, 40.

6 *"No, really"* EH to Grace Quinlan, 19 Aug. 1921, *SL*, 54.

6 *Anderson had met YH*, 185, 252. See also Sherwood Anderson to Lewis Galantière, 28 Nov. 1921, in Howard Mumford Jones and Walter B. Rideout, eds., *Letters of Sherwood Anderson* (Boston: Little, Brown, 1953), 83.

6 *He lacked "seeds"* EH to Grace Hemingway, 10 Jan. 1921, *SL*, 44; Fine, *Hollywood and the Profession*, 49; Baker, 33; A. Scott Berg, *Goldwyn: A Biography* (New York: Knopf, 1989), 101–2.

7 *Ernest was* Anderson to Galantière, 82–83; EH to Sherwood and Tennessee Anderson, c. 23 Dec. 1921, *SL*, 59.

7 *" 'It was an event' "* Brian, *True Gen*, 54; Bernice Kert, *The Hemingway Women* (New York: Norton, 1983), 133; EH to Howell Jenkins, 20 Mar. 1922, *SL*, 64.

8 *"You can write"* *PY*, 78.

9 *Hearst's corporations* Honey, *New Woman*, 5; Peter Baxter, *Just Watch! Sternberg, Paramount, and America* (London: British Film Institute, 1993), 19; Fine, *Hollywood and the Profession*, 33. "Reading anything as a serial is awfully hard on it," Hemingway wrote Sherwood Anderson (23 May 1925, *SL*, 161–62).

9 *Ezra Pound was PY*, 23; EH to Anderson, 9 Mar. 1922, *SL*, 62.

9 *In February 1922* James R. Mellow, *Hemingway: A Life Without Consequences* (New York: Houghton, 1992), 148–53; EH to Anderson, 9 Mar. 1922, *SL*, 62.

9 *The manuscript opens* Paul Smith, "Three Versions of 'Up in Michigan': 1921–1930," *Resources for American Literary Study* 15 (1985): 168, 170; E. W. Howe, "The Anthology of Another Town," *Saturday Evening Post*, 20 Mar. 1920, 14. See also *YH*, 96–97.

11 *"a very good story"* EH to Ivan Kashkin, 12 Jan. 1936, *SL*, 431.

11 *"proper construction"* Smith, *Reader's Guide*, xv; EH to Edward O'Brien, c. 20 Nov. 1923, *SL*, 104; *YH*, 240.

11 *The hotel gave PY*, 93.

12 *"Nonsense"* Baker, 126; EH to Pound, c. 2 May, 19 July 1924, *SL*, 116, 119; Diliberto, *Hadley*, 169, 177.

13 *"very silly"* EH to Edmund Wilson, 18 Oct. 1924, *SL*, 128.

13 *"epic talents"* Diliberto, *Hadley*, 182.

13 *Boni & Liveright* Louis Kronenberger, "Gambler in Publishing: Horace Liveright," *Atlantic Monthly*, January 1965, 97; "Accuses Boni & Liveright," *New York Times*, 19 Feb. 1925, 6. See also Tom Dardis, *Firebrand: The Life of Horace Liveright* (New York: Random, 1995).

14 *"Double god damned"* PY, 242; Kert, *Hemingway Women*, 153; Diliberto, *Hadley*, 112.

14 *"I'm sending you"* EH to Ernest Walsh and Ethel Moorhead, c. 12 Jan. 1925, *SL*, 144; EH, *A Moveable Feast*, 76.

14 *In* Winesburg Sherwood Anderson, *Sherwood Anderson's Memoirs: A Critical Edition*, ed. Ray Lewis White (Chapel Hill: Univ. of North Carolina Press, 1969), 349; Tebbel, *Golden Age*, 116.

15 *By September 1919* Berg, *Perkins*, 15; FSF to MP, 1 June 1925, *DS*, 108. Princeton graduate Charles Scribner, who founded Baker & Scribner in 1846, died in 1871. Princeton graduate Charles Scribner II ("old CS") ran Charles Scribner's Sons until his death in 1930; he was succeeded for two years by his brother Arthur, then by Charles Scribner III. By 1946, Charles Scribner IV had joined the firm; he died in 1995. See "Obituary: Charles Scribner," *New York Times*, 28 Aug. 1971, 4; and *Hemingway Newsletter* 31 (1996): 4.

16 *He had sent PY*, 271; EH to George Lorimer, 21 Jan. 1925, *SL*, 148; Smith, *Reader's Guide*, 103; EH to FSF, c. 24 Dec. 1925, *SL*, 180.

16 *"all for keeping"* EH to William Smith, Jr., 6 Dec. 1924, *SL*, 137; EH to Smith, 26 Feb. 1925, "Hemingway Accessions," JFK; Dardis, *Liveright*, 254; Kronenberger, "Gambler," 97.

17 *According to* EH, *A Moveable Feast*, 15; EH to Smith, 26 Feb. 1925; Marcelline Hemingway Sanford, *At the Hemingways* (Boston: Little, Brown, 1962), 219. See also *PY*, 80, 278.

17 *In "The Cat"* Honey reprints "The Cat and the King" in her *New Woman*, 125–42; EH to Horace Liveright, 31 Mar. 1925, *SL*, 155.

18 *She was very* Hadley Richardson Mowrer, Interview by Carlos Baker, n.d., Question 30, JFK; Baker, 142.

18 *"Didn't miss one"* Mellow, *Without Consequences*, 290, 299.

18 *"personality of you"* FSF to MP, 1 June 1925, *DS*, 108; Berg, *Perkins*, 418; MP to

Charles Scribner, 27 May 1926, *OT*, 39; Charles Scribner to W. Baker, 2 Sept. 1930, Charles Scribner's Sons Archives, Business Records ("B General"), Box 1/3, PUL. This and all subsequent citations from the Scribner's Archives at PUL have been published with permission of the Princeton Univ. Libraries.

19 *Hadley need not* Diliberto, *Hadley*, 45, 95, 66; *YH*, 206–7; *PY*, 34.

19 *In February 1925* MP to EH, 21 Feb. 1925, Charles Scribner's Sons Archives, Hemingway Series, Box 1/3, PUL; Alfred Harcourt to Sinclair Lewis, 29 May 1925, *FMS*, 185. Unless otherwise indicated, subsequent citations from the Scribner's Archives at PUL will be from the Hemingway Series.

20 *"I was very"* EH to MP, 15 Apr. 1925, *SL*, 156; Nelson Lichtenstein, "Authorial Professionalism and the Literary Marketplace, 1885–1900," *American Studies* 19 (1978): 45; [Charles Scribner] to EH, 17 Oct. 1927, Box 1/4, PUL; EH to Horace Liveright, 15 May 1925, *SL*, 160.

20 *"bring out"* EH to Edward O'Brien, 2 May 1924; EH to MP, 15 Apr. 1925, *SL*, 117, 156.

21 *"The title"* Mellow, *Without Consequences*, 291; *PY*, 290.

21 *"Seems he"* Herbert Cranston, "When Hemingway Earned Half a Cent a Word on 'The Toronto Star,' " *New York Herald Tribune Book Review*, 13 Jan. 1952, 6; Mellow, *Without Consequences*, 299; Baker, 151.

21 *"The story"* Mellow, *Without Consequences*, 302–3.

22 *"sort of brave"* Audre Hanneman, *Ernest Hemingway: A Comprehensive Bibliography: Supplement* (Princeton: Princeton Univ. Press, 1975), 212.

22 *"I'm sure"* Dardis, *Liveright*, 255, 115; (Hartford, Conn.) *Times*, 26 Dec. 1925, CS/JFK; FSF to MP, c. 19 Jan. 1926, *DS*, 131; "Michael Curtiz Force of Arms" file, Warner Bros. Archive, PUL.

23 *"not the thing"* EH to FSF, c. 24 Dec. 1925, *SL*, 180.

23 *"We've been"* *PY*, 332, 330, 183–84.

24 *The press hailed* Revs. of *IOT*: "American Author," (St. Louis) *Globe Democrat*, CS/JFK; *Daily Oklahoman*, 13 Dec. 1925, CS/JFK; Paul Rosenfeld, *New Republic*, 24 Nov. 1925, 22–23; Louis Kronenberger, *Saturday Review of Literature*, 13 Feb. 1926, 555, rpt. *CR*, 15; Robert Wolf, *New York Herald Tribune Books*, 14 Feb. 1926, 3, rpt. *CR*, 16.

25 *It was "enough"* EH to Isabel Godolphin, 3 Dec. 1925, *SL*, 171.

26 *Liveright had promised* Walker Gilmer, *Horace Liveright: Publisher of the Twenties* (New York: Lewis, 1970), 112, 123; Dardis, *Liveright*, 256–61; EH to FSF, 31 Dec. 1925–1 Jan. 1926, *SL*, 185. Anderson later had another view of the relationship with his publisher: "If I had ever been a special pet of the Liveright firm I wish someone had let me know of it. I might have got more money from them" (*Sherwood Anderson's Memoirs*, 463).

26 *"Pauline Pfeiffer gets"* EH to FSF, c. 24 Dec. 1925, *SL*, 182.

26 *"That you"* Gilmer, *Liveright*, 124.

27 *Liveright rejected* Baker, 159; Pauline Pfeiffer to "Mes jolis enfants," 16 Jan. 1926, JFK.

27 *"had broken up"* FSF to MP, c. 19 Jan. 1926, *DS*, 131; EH to FSF, 31 Dec. 1925–1 Jan. 1926, *SL*, 184; Alfred Harcourt to Sinclair Lewis, 18 Feb. 1926, *FMS*, 196.

27 *"Perhaps if"* PY, 348.

28 *"Ernest said"* PY, 351.

28 *"business trip"* Baker, 163; Ben Hecht, *A Child of the Century* (New York: Simon & Schuster, 1954), 372.

28 *"who leased"* Ann Watkins, "Literature for Sale," *Bowker Lectures on Book Publishing* (New York: Bowker, 1957), 97; Tino Balio, ed., *The American Film Industry* (Madison: Univ. of Wisconsin Press, 1976), 116, 147.

29 *In the early 1920s* James Woodress, *Willa Cather: A Literary Life* (Lincoln: Univ. of Nebraska Press, 1987), 352; R. W. B. Lewis, *Edith Wharton: A Biography* (New York: Harper, 1975), 423, 429, 444.

29 *" 'a coupla thousand' "* Watkins, "Literature for Sale," 100, 108–9.

29 *The success* Lewis, *Wharton*, 444; James L. Baughman, *Henry R. Luce and the Rise of the American News Media* (Boston: Twayne, 1987), 45; rev. of *Black Oxen*, by Gertrude Atherton, *Time*, 3 Mar. 1924, 12.

30 *"He appears"* Rev. of *IOT*, in *Time*, 18 Jan. 1926, 39; Richard Schickel, *Intimate Strangers: The Culture of Celebrity* (Garden City, N.Y.: Doubleday, 1985), 63; Richard Lingeman, *Theodore Dreiser: An American Journey, 1908–1945* (New York: Putnam, 1990), 207.

30 *In Oak Park* PY, 178; EH to Horace Liveright, 19 Jan. 1926, *SL*, 191; EH to FSF, 31 Dec. 1925–1 Jan. 1926, *SL*, 185.

31 *Scribners was* Lingeman, *Theodore Dreiser*, 209; Edith M. Stern, "A Man Who Was Unafraid," *Saturday Review of Literature*, 28 June 1941, 10.

31 *Another of* Bennett Cerf, *At Random: The Reminiscences of Bennett Cerf* (New York: Random, 1977), 41; FSF to EH, c. 30 Dec. 1925, *DS*, 128.

31 *The third floor* Berg, *Perkins*, 10; Malcolm Cowley, "Profiles: Unshaken Friend," part 2, *New Yorker*, 8 Apr. 1944, 30; James Hinkle, " 'Dear Mr. Scribner': About the Published Text of *The Sun Also Rises*," *Hemingway Review* 6, no. 1 (Fall 1986): 54.

32 *Unlike Liveright* John Hall Wheelock, COHC (1967), 1: 232–34; Berg, *Perkins*, 56, 70; Millicent Bell, *Marquand: An American Life* (Boston: Little, Brown, 1979), 152.

33 *"just concluded"* AH, 13.

33 *In early April* EH to MP, 31 Aug. 1927, *SL*, 256; L. E. Pollinger to EH, n.d., JFK.

34 *hadn't "had them"* EH to MP, 5 June 1926, *SL*, 209; FSF to MP, c. 1 Mar. 1926, *DS*, 135; AH, 57.

34 *"no finer" Scribner's Magazine*, May 1929, inside front cover; Burlingame, *Of Making Many Books*, 219, 220; Lawrence W. Levine, *Highbrow/Lowbrow: The Emergence of*

Cultural Hierarchy in America (Cambridge: Harvard Univ. Press, 1988), 218; MP to FSF, 21 May 1931, *DS*, 171.

35 *"American in scene"* Burlingame, *Of Making Many Books*, 211; Madison, *Book Publishing in America* (New York: McGraw-Hill, 1966), 200; MP to EH, 14 June 1926, Box 1/3, PUL; EH to Ernest Walsh and Ethel Moorhead, c. 12 Jan. 1925, *SL*, 145.

CHAPTER TWO: THE SUN ALSO RISES

37 *"You've got"* Berg, *Perkins*, 95.

38 *In 1925* Ernest W. Mandeville, "Gutter Literature," *New Republic*, 17 Feb. 1926, 350–51.

38 *Alfred Knopf had* Woodress, *Willa Cather*, 312–13.

39 *"almost unpublishable"* MP to FSF, 29 May 1926, JFK.

39 *Three advertisements* John J. Fenstermaker, "The Search for an American Audience: Marketing Ernest Hemingway, 1925–1930," in *Hemingway: The Oak Park Legacy*, ed. James Nagel (Tuscaloosa: Univ. of Alabama Press, 1996), 183–84.

39 *"The publishers"* Rev. of *TTOS*, in *Outlook and Independent*, 15 Sept. 1926, 91, rpt. *CR*, 29.

39 *According to* Margery Latimer, rev. of *TTOS*, in *New York Herald Tribune Books*, 18 July 1926, 16, rpt. *CR*, 25; Harry Hansen, rev. of *TTOS*, in *New York World*, 30 May 1926, 4M, rpt. Jeffrey Meyers, ed., *Hemingway: The Critical Heritage* (Boston: Routledge, 1982), 77; Allen Tate, rev. of *TTOS*, in *Nation*, 28 July 1926, 89; rev. of *TTOS*, in *Kansas City Star*, CS/JFK; rev. of *TTOS*, in *Time*, 28 June 1926, 31; Westbrook, "Grace Under Pressure," 82.

40 *In 1919 PW*, 22 Mar. 1919, 858.

40 *The* Authors' League Tebbel, *Golden Age*, 20.

41 *Loosely written* Bruccoli, 64; *AH*, 41.

41 *Fitzgerald had noted AH*, 41, 23; EH to MP, c. 4 or 11 Feb. 1940, *SL*, 501; Berg, *Perkins*, 97; EH to MP, 16 Nov. 1926, *SL*, 223–24; Kenneth McCormick, COHC (1975), 45.

42 *"simply an historical"* EH to MP, 5 June 1926, *SL*, 209.

42 *"moronic yappers"* MP to EH, 20 July 1926, *OT*, 42; Tebbel, *Golden Age*, 400.

43 *The stink* Garth Jowett, *Film: The Democratic Art* (Boston: Little, Brown, 1976), 466. The industry trade group popularly known as the Hays office was originally called the Motion Picture Producers and Distributors of America; it later changed its name to the Motion Picture Association of America, shortened in the present text to the Motion Picture Association.

43 *What Liveright* Lingeman, *Theodore Dreiser,* 267–71; EH to MP, 24 July, 26, 21 Aug. 1926, *SL,* 211, 215, 213.

43 *Gossip about* Tebbel, *Golden Age,* 328; *Book Review Digest* (1925): 19; James David Hart, *The Popular Book: A History of America's Literary Taste* (New York: Oxford Univ. Press, 1950), 233–34; *YH,* 120–21, 184–85.

44 *"will be praised"* EH to Horace Liveright, 31 Mar. 1925; EH to Gertrude Stein and Alice B. Toklas, 20 Jan. 1925; EH to Harold Loeb, 5 Jan. 1925, *SL,* 155, 147, 143.

45 *"with an eye"* MP to EH, 14 Oct. 1927, *OT,* 66.

45 *"They really"* Harry Scherman, COHC (1954–55), 116–17; Tebbel, *Golden Age,* 290; *The Book of the Month: Sixty Years of Books in American Life,* ed. Al Silverman (Boston: Little, Brown, 1986), 3. In 1993 the Book of the Month Club featured a two-column by seventeen-centimeter portrait of Hemingway in its full-page ads. The cutline read: "Ernest Hemingway, *The Sun Also Rises,* Book-of-the-Month Club Selection, December, 1926." See, for example, the back cover of the *New York Times Book Review,* 7 Mar. 1993. The novel had been *a* but not *the* selection that month, and both it and Hemingway were as obscure in the 1926 advertisements as they were prominent in the 1993 ones.

45 *"I've tried"* EH to MP, 21 Aug. 1926, *SL,* 213–14.

46 *Just before Scribners* EH to Sherwood Anderson, 21 May 1926, *SL,* 205–6.

46 *"In those days"* Hinkle, " 'Dear Mr. Scribner,' " 54; Tebbel, *Golden Age,* 52.

46 *"the most peurile"* EH to FSF, c. 7 Sept. 1926, *SL,* 216; EH to MP, 15 Dec. 1926, Box 1/3, PUL; EH to MP, 21 Dec. 1926, *SL,* 239.

49 *"Christ's own"* EH to Anderson, c. 7 Sept. 1926; EH to FSF, c. 7 Sept. 1926; EH to MP, 19 Nov. 1926; *SL,* 218, 217, 229–30; Kenneth Lynn, *Hemingway* (New York: Simon & Schuster, 1987), 167; rev. of *IOT,* in *New York Times Book Review,* 18 Oct. 1925, 8.

49 *"I hardly think"* MP to FSF, 13 Jan. 1926, *DS,* 129; EH to FSF, c. 7 Sept. 1926, *SL,* 217–18.

49 *"I hope they"* Sinclair Lewis to Alfred Harcourt, 4 Apr. 1926, 12 July 1921, *FMS,* 203, 77.

50 *"the joy of reading"* Tebbel, *Golden Age,* 332, 334; Woodress, *Willa Cather,* 307; MP to EH, 8 Sept. 1926, Box 1/3, PUL; advertisement for *TSAR,* in *New Yorker,* 23 Oct. 1926, 82.

50 *The misspelling* Baker, 178; Louis Feipel, "The Present State of Book Editing," *PW,* 9 June 1923, 1760–61; Donaldson, "Wooing," 709; Hinkle, " 'Dear Mr. Scribner,' " 50–51; Lewis, *Wharton,* 311; West, *American Authors,* 57.

51 *"a writer who"* EH to MP, 16 Nov. 1926, *SL,* 223; MP to EH, 26 Nov. 1926, Box 1/3, PUL.

51 *"the feminine readers"* Jack Stillinger, *Multiple Authorship and the Myth of Solitary Genius* (New York: Oxford Univ. Press, 1991), 157; Edward de Grazia and Roger K.

Newman, *Banned Films: Movies, Censors, and the First Amendment* (New York: Bowker, 1982), 29; *OT*, 118n.

51 *"This novel"* Revs. of *TSAR: New York Times Book Review*, 31 Oct. 1926, 27; *Cincinnati Enquirer*, 30 Oct. 1926, 5; *Springfield Republican*, 28 Nov. 1926, 7F, rpt. *CR*, 31, 40.

51 *"What have"* EH to Isabel Godolphin, 3 Dec. 1925; EH to Grace Hemingway, 5 Feb. 1927, *SL*, 172, 243; Kert, *Hemingway Women*, 197.

52 *"The heroine"* Rev. of *TSAR*, in *Chicago Tribune*, 27 Nov. 1926, 13, rpt. *CR*, 39; EH to MP, 16 Nov. 1926, *SL*, 224; Carl Van Vechten to Hugh Walpole, 29 Apr. 1925, in Bruce Kellner, ed., *Letters of Carl Van Vechten* (New Haven: Yale Univ. Press, 1987), 75–76; EH to MP, 7 Dec. 1926, *SL*, 238; MP to EH, 26 Nov. 1926, JFK. In *A Moveable Feast* (which blends fact and fiction) Hemingway reports that Fitzgerald told him to read and learn from Arlen. "I said I could not read the books. He said I did not have to. He would tell me the plots and describe the characters." In summer 1926 Fitzgerald had written Hemingway that the opening section of *TSAR* "hasn't even your rhythm. It's bad Arlen and the fact that ~~it's true~~ it may be 'true' is utterly immaterial" (*AH*, 41).

52 *"for the sake"* William Faulkner, *Essays, Speeches, & Public Letters*, ed. James B. Meriwether (New York: Random, 1965), 180; "S. E. F.," rev. of *TSAR*, in *Miami News*, CS/JFK.

52 *"coarse and"* M. J. Levey to Scribners, 28 Apr. 1927, Box 1/4, PUL; Edward Smith to Scribners, 24 Mar. 1928, Box 1/5, PUL; MP to EH, 11 June 1932, *OT*, 170; Hart, *Popular Book*, 237.

53 *"It is rumored"* Revs. of *TSAR*: Conrad Aiken, *New York Herald Tribune Books*, 31 Oct. 1926, VII-4, rpt. *CR*, 32; "Sad Young Men," *Time*, 1 Nov. 1926, 48.

53 *"every conceivable"* Oliver Wendell Holmes, "The Stereoscope and the Stereograph," *Atlantic Monthly*, 3 June 1859, 747; MP to EH, 2 Mar. 1927, Box 1/4, PUL; revs. of *TSAR*, CS/JFK: *Dayton News*, 18 July 1926; *Johnstown* (Pennsylvania) *Democrat*, 12 July 1926; *Haverhill* (Massachusetts) *Gazette*, n.d.; *Toledo Times*, 25 July 1926; *Helena Independent*, 21 July 1926; *San Francisco Argonaut*, 24 July 1926; Hansen (syndicated), *St. Paul Dispatch*, 5 Nov. 1926.

54 *"the wrong psychology"* FSF to MP, 27 Oct. 1924, *DS*, 80; EH to MP, 19 Feb. 1927, *SL*, 247–48.

54 *"Robust, hulking"* Crystal Ross, "Ernest Hemingway, Expatriate," *Dallas News*, 16 Jan. 1927, CS/JFK; *AH*, 98.

54 *In England* C. S. Evans to EH, 1 Dec. 1926, JFK; *PY*, 330; West, *American Authors*, 29; idem, "Did F. Scott Fitzgerald Have the Right Publisher?" *Sewanee Review* 100 (1992): 648; Tebbel, *Golden Age*, 329.

55 *"sucked in"* EH to FSF, c. 24 Nov. 1926, *SL*, 232; *AH*, 69; Thornton Wilder to EH, 15 Feb. 1927, JFK; Herschell Brickell, "Books on Our Table," *New York Evening Post*, CS/JFK.

57 *"for next fall"* Alfred Harcourt to Sinclair Lewis, 7 Nov. 1927, *FMS*, 257; MP to EH, 23 Dec. 1926, JFK.

58 *"In Our Time came"* EH to MP, 6 Dec. 1926, *SL*, 236–37.

58 *"sat at his"* Brian, *True Gen*, 19; EH to MP, c. 20 Aug. 1928, JFK; EH to MP, 15 Jan. 1928, *SL*, 270; MP to EH, 23 Aug. 1926, JFK.

58 *"The [Saturday"* FSF to EH, Oct. 1927, Bruccoli, 90; Robert Bridges to EH, 15 Sept. 1926, Box 1/3, PUL; EH to MP, 21 Dec. 1926, 31 Aug. 1927, *SL*, 240, 256.

59 *"Gahd though"* William Smith, Jr., to EH, Dec. 1926, JFK.

59 *"It will be"* EH to Smith, c. 21 Jan. 1927; EH to Grace Hemingway, 5 Feb. 1927, *SL*, 242, 244.

59 *"utter trivialities"* Rev. of *TSAR*, in *Chicago Tribune*, 27 Nov. 1926, 13, rpt. *CR*, 39; EH to MP, 7 Dec. 1926, *SL*, 238.

60 *"actually as dull"* Isidore Schneider to EH, 10 June, c. Nov. 1926, JFK; EH to MP, 21 Dec. 1926, *SL*, 240.

61 *Hemingway saw Frank* EH to Grace Hemingway, 14 Dec. 1925, *SL*, 175.

61 *"by those"* MP to EH, 23 Aug. 1926, JFK.

61 *"help to break"* Waldo Frank to MP, 28 Oct. 1933; Dorothy Canfield Fisher to MP, 5 Sept. 1934; Frank to MP, 23 Sept. 1934, Scribners Author Files, Box 55/1, PUL.

62 *"discreet but"* MP to FSF, 13 June 1921; FSF to MP, 31 Jan. 1922, *DS*, 38, 52.

62 *In 1923* James L. W. West III, "The Second Serials of *This Side of Paradise* and *The Beautiful and Damned*," *Papers of the Bibliographical Society of America* 73 (1979): 70, 65, 74.

62 *"personal reputation"* MP to Ring Lardner, 1 June 1925, in Clifford M. Caruthers, ed., *Ring Around Max: The Correspondence of Ring Lardner & Max Perkins* (DeKalb: Northern Illinois Univ. Press, 1973), 68.

62 *"real places"* EH to MP, 19 Sept. 1927, Box 1/4, PUL.

63 *"I don't mind"* Pauline Pfeiffer to EH, 6 Dec. 1926; Thornton Wilder to EH, 15 Feb. 1927, JFK; Baker, 180; *AH*, 137.

63 *"As for movie"* EH to MP, 7 Dec. 1926, *SL*, 236.

63 *In 1919 Broadway* Burns Mantle, *The Best Plays of 1919–20 to 1929–30*, 11 vols. (New York: Dodd, 1920–30); FSF to Harold Ober, c. 3 June 1926, in Andrew Turnbull, ed., *The Letters of F. Scott Fitzgerald* (New York: Scribners, 1963), 392; George Ade to Jesse Lasky, 8 Mar. 1922, in George Ade, *Letters of George Ade* (West Lafayette, Ind.: Purdue Univ. Studies, 1973), 80.

64 *"There were certainly"* MP to EH, 22 Nov. 1926, JFK.

64 *"the line"* Walter Prichard Eaton, "Class-Consciousness and the 'Movies,'" *Atlantic Monthly*, Jan. 1915, 53; EH to MP, 15 Dec. 1926, JFK.

64 *"If one"* Rev. of *TSAR*, Aiken, *New York Herald Tribune Books*, rpt. *CR*, 34; Berg, *Goldwyn*, 151.

64 *"These people"* MP to EH, 3 Dec. 1926, JFK; Eugene O'Neill to Agnes Boulton, [29?] Sept., [2?] Dec. 1927, in Travis Bogard and Jackson R. Bryer, eds., *Selected Letters of Eugene O'Neill* (New Haven: Yale Univ. Press, 1988), 262, 268; EH to MP, 14 Oct. 1931, JFK; FSF to EH, mailed 23 Dec. 1926, Bruccoli, 79.

65 *In early 1927* Burton Rascoe, "Sketches of 'Little Old New York,' " 14 Feb. 1927, CS/JFK; EH to MP, 29 Feb. 1927, *SL*, 247; EH, "My Own Life," *New Yorker*, 12 Feb. 1927, 24; FSF to EH, 18 Mar. 1927, Bruccoli, 82; EH to MP, 19 Feb. 1927, *SL*, 247; MP to EH, 25 Jan. 1927, JFK; MP to EH, 28 Jan. 1927, Box 1/4, PUL.

66 *He spent much* Donaldson, "Wooing," 699; EH to MP, 14 Feb. 1927, *SL*, 246.

67 *"I want"* EH to MP, 4 May, 19 Feb. 1927; EH to FSF, c. 15 Sept. 1927, *SL*, 251, 246, 260.

67 *"a man's book"* FSF to MP, c. 20 Dec. 1924, *DS*, 90; Donaldson, "Wooing," 700; EH to MP, c. 11 Apr. 1932, Box 2/10, PUL; EH to MP, 4 May 1927, *SL*, 251.

67 *"that while such"* FSF to MP, c. 12 May 1927, *DS*, 148.

68 *The dust jacket* EH to MP, 10 June 1927; MP to EH, 8 Sept. 1927, Box 1/4, PUL.

68 *"We get small"* MP to EH, 29 Apr. 1927, JFK; EH to MP, 19 Nov. 1926, *SL*, 229.

69 *"I guess"* EH to FSF, c. 15 Dec. 1927, *SL*, 268.

69 *"I think it"* Barklie Henry to EH, 29 June 1927, JFK; Woodress, *Willa Cather*, 316; EH to FSF, 31 Mar. 1927, *SL*, 248–49; Baker, 182.

70 *"Now I Lay Me"* Smith, *Reader's Guide*, 173; EH to Clarence Hemingway, 14 Sept. 1927, *SL*, 258–60.

70 *"We are going"* EH to Clarence Hemingway, 14 Sept. 1927, *SL*, 259; *AH*, 140.

70 *"I have looked"* Alfred Harcourt to Sinclair Lewis, 10 Apr. 1925, *FMS*, 184. "It was probably Harcourt who pulled the wires that got Red the Nobel Prize, though when he hinted as much to Red, Red was indignant, and insisted he had been nominated by a Swede" (H. L. Mencken, *My Life as Author and Editor* [New York: Knopf, 1993], 338).

71 *"going to write"* EH to FSF, c. 15 Sept. 1927; EH to Archibald MacLeish, 8 Oct. 1927, *SL*, 261, 262; Baker, 166; *AH*, 151, 154.

72 *"Everybody is"* MP to EH, 22 July 1927, Box 1/4, PUL.

72 *"one form"* EH to Wyndham Lewis, 24 Oct. 1927, *SL*, 264.

72 *"Figured I"* EH to MP, 15 Jan. 1928, *SL*, 270.

73 *Hemingway scoffed* "Isn't it fine about Mencken," Hemingway wrote to Fitzgerald. "Well well well pitcher that. That last is the Sinclair Lewis influence. That's the way his characters talk" (31 Mar. 1927, *SL*, 249). The manuscript of "Hills Like White Elephants," probably composed in spring 1927, bears the following pencil inscription on its final page: "Mss for Pauline—well, well, well" (Smith, *Reader's Guide*, 206).

73 *"I should have"* EH to MP, 24 Nov. 1927, Box 1/4, PUL; EH to MP, 17 Mar. 1928, *SL*, 274; Dorothy Parker, rev. of *MWW*, in *New Yorker*, 29 Oct. 1927, 94.

73 Men Without Women *was published* See EH to MP, 4 May 1927, *SL*, 250.

73 *Pauline's uncle* Gus Pfeiffer to EH, 18 Oct. 1927, JFK; Virginia Woolf, rev. of *MWW*, in *New York Herald Tribune Books*, 9 Oct. 1927, 1, 8, rpt. *CR*, 54.

74 *"on a hook"* Wallace Meyer to MP, 27 Nov. 1927, Box 1/4, PUL; EH, "Valentine," *Little Review* 12 (May 1929): 42; Meyer to MP, 27 Nov. 1927, Box 1/4, PUL.

74 *"the curious"* MP to EH, 30 Nov. 1927, JFK; advertisement for *MWW*, in *New York Times Book Review*, 27 Nov. 1927, 26.

75 *'has to be"* EH to MP, 7 Mar. 1928, *SL*, 274; EH to Archibald MacLeish, 20 Dec. 1925, *SL*, 179; MP to Marjorie Rawlings, 27 Oct. 1933, in John Hall Wheelock, ed., *Editor to Author: The Letters of Maxwell E. Perkins* (New York: Scribners, 1950), 84.

75 *"Author Hemingway"* Rev. of *MWW*, in *Time*, 14 Oct. 1927, 38; John Riddell, "A Parody Interview with Mr. Hemingway," *Vanity Fair*, Jan. 1928, 78; Grace Hemingway to EH, 14 Oct. 1927, JFK; EH to FSF, c. 15 Dec. 1927, *SL*, 267. Grace Hemingway was mother of six, with Ursula born in 1902, Madelaine in 1904, Carol in 1911, and Leicester in 1915, when Grace was forty-two years old and Ernest fifteen.

76 *"Your name"* MP to EH, 18 Jan. 1928, Box 1/4, PUL; *AH*, 182; EH to MP, 16 Nov. 1926, *SL*, 225; EH to MP, 15 Sept. 1927, Box 1/4, PUL; EH to MP, 19 Oct. 1927, Box 1/4, PUL.

76 *"would give"* MP to EH, 14 June 1927, JFK; EH to MP, 19 Feb. 1927, *SL*, 246.

77 *"I mean, good Lord"* Wheelock, COHC (1967), 1: 118.

77 *"the best agent"* MP to EH, 9 May 1927, Box 1/4, PUL; EH to MP, 19 Nov. 1926, *SL*, 229; Woodress, *Willa Cather*, 363; FSF to EH, Oct. 1927, Bruccoli, 90.

77 *"Max Ravage"* Guy Hickok to EH, 25 Jan. 1928, JFK.

77 *In short* West, "Did F. Scott," 644–56; Scherman, COHC (1954–55), 116–17; Ellen Glasgow to Irita Van Doren, 17 Aug. 1934, Glasgow, *Letters* (New York: Harcourt, 1958), 164; [Charles Scribner] to EH, 17 Oct. 1927, Box 1/4, PUL; EH to MP, c. 14 Jan. 1940, *OT*, 278; Marshall Best, COHC (1976), 25.

78 *When stores* Fenstermaker, "Marketing EH," 184–89; MP to EH, 10 Dec. 1926; Gus Pfeiffer to EH, 22 Jan. 1928, JFK; EH to MP, 15 Sept. 1927, Box 1/4, PUL.

79 *"Wrote a story"* EH to MP, 12 Feb. 1928, *SL*, 271.

79 *As adolescents* HFW, 38–39; EH to MP, 17 Mar., 31 May 1928, *SL*, 273, 279.

80 *"I work all"* EH to MP, 17 Mar. 1928, *SL*, 273; Wallace Meyer to MP, 27 Nov. 1927, Box 1/4, PUL; EH to MP, c. 1 Nov. 1927, *SL*, 265.

80 *"Haow the"* Baker, 190.

80 *"Pictures we do"* MP to EH, 10 Nov. 1927, Box 1/4, PUL.

80 *"You are magnificent"* Diliberto, *Hadley*, 77.

81 *"I think she"* EH to MP, 17 Mar. 1928, *SL*, 273; Kert, *Hemingway Women*, 201.

81 *"goes on"* EH to MP, 17 Mar. 1928, *SL*, 273.

CHAPTER THREE: A FAREWELL TO ARMS

83 *"We are five"* EH to Pauline Hemingway, c. 28 Mar. 1928, *SL*, 275.

83 *"going finely"* *HFW*, 26; EH to MP, 21 Apr. 1928, *SL*, 276.

83 *The novel that* On the provenance of the novel, see *HFW* and Paul Smith, "Hemingway's Apprentice Fiction: 1919–1921," *American Literature* 58 (1986): 574–88.

84 *In November 1926* Bernard Oldsey, *Hemingway's Hidden Craft* (University Park: Pennsylvania State Univ. Press, 1979), 96.

84 *"the only decent"* EH to MP, 21 Apr. 1928, *SL*, 276–77.

85 *"one of the"* *AH*, 182; EH to MP, 21 Apr. 1928, *SL*, 277. "Would appreciate your asking them to send and charge to me 3 Sun Alsos and 3 Men Without Women (as soon as possible). Nobody believes me when I say I'm a writer" (EH to MP, 21 Apr. 1928, *SL*, 277).

85 *"a christ offal"* EH to MP, 31 May 1928, *SL*, 278; *HFW*, 24; EH to Guy Hickok, c. 27 July 1928, *SL*, 280.

85 *"I think I"* EH to MP, 31 May 1928, *SL*, 278.

85 *"The photograph"* MP to EH, 18 June 1928, Box 1/5, PUL; EH to MP, 21 Apr. 1928, *SL*, 277.

86 *"This Breaker"* Hickok to EH, c. spring 1928, JFK; Miles Orvell, *The Real Thing: Imitation and Authenticity in American Culture, 1880–1940* (Chapel Hill: Univ. of North Carolina Press, 1989), 12–13.

86 *"The fate"* EH to MP, c. June 1928; MP to EH, 24 Oct. 1928, Box 1/5, PUL.

86 *"in all sorts"* MP to EH, 24 Oct. 1928, Box 1/5, PUL; William Faulkner to Mr. Chase, recd. 13 Apr. 1929, in Joseph Blotner, ed., *Selected Letters of William Faulkner* (New York: Random, 1977), 43; Sinclair Lewis to Alfred Harcourt, 16 July 1929, *FMS*, 276; MP to EH, 23 Jan. 1929, Box 1/6, PUL.

87 *had a scar* *AH*, 196; EH to Hickok, c. 27 July 1928; EH to Waldo Peirce, 9 Aug. 1928, *SL*, 281, 283.

87 *"mentally pooped"* EH to FSF, c. 9 Oct. 1928; EH to Archibald MacLeish, 18 July 1929; EH to Isabel Godolphin, c. 12 Aug. 1928, *SL*, 287, 300, 283.

88 *"Wait until"* EH to Hickok, 18 Aug. 1928, *SL*, 284.

88 *"in two years"* "We Nominate for the Hall of Fame," *Vanity Fair*, Sept. 1928, 79.

88 *Ideally* EH to MP, 28 Sept. 1928, *SL*, 285–86.

89 *"Ray Long"* Pauline Hemingway to EH, 14 Aug. 1928, JFK.

89 *"I think"* Harcourt to Lewis, 14 Oct. 1927, *FMS*, 253; West, *American Authors*, 133.

89 *But he returned* EH to Mildred Temple, 24 June 1927, Box 1/4, PUL.

89 *Anderson "dismissed"* Sherwood Anderson to Waldo Frank, c. 7 Nov. 1917, in Jones and Rideout, *Letters of Sherwood Anderson*, 22; Honey, *New Woman*, 9; Theodore Dreiser to Grant Knight, 13 May 1929, in Lingeman, *Theodore Dreiser*, 323.

90 *"I believe"* MP to EH, 2 Oct., 26 June 1928, Box 1/5, PUL.

90 " *'The Torrents'* " MP to FSF, 18 June 1926, *DS*, 142; MP to Hadley Hemingway, 30 Aug. 1928, Box 1/5, PUL.

90 *"serializing a book"* Evan Shipman to EH, 20 June 1929, JFK; MacLeish to EH, 4 Feb. 1929, in R. H. Winnick, ed., *Letters of Archibald MacLeish, 1907–1982* (Boston: Houghton, 1983), 224; FSF to EH, Dec. 1927, Bruccoli, 93.

90 *"I think it would"* EH to MP, 28 Sept. 1928, *SL*, 286; Madison, *Book Publishing*, 201.

91 *Owen Wister told* EH to MP, c. June 1928, Box 1/5, PUL; Frank Luther Mott, *A History of American Magazines* (Cambridge: Harvard Univ. Press, 1957), 4: 729; MP to EH, 8 Aug. 1928, Box 1/5, PUL; Fenstermaker, "Marketing EH," 189.

92 *Grace had long* Kert, *Hemingway Women*, 213, 24–25. See also photograph of "Madison Square Gardens [*sic*]" inside Grace Hemingway, Memory Book, vol. 2, JFK.

92 *"do everything"* MP to EH, 17 Sept. 1928, JFK.

92 " *'So do you'* " *HFW*, 63.

93 *On November 17* EH to FSF and Zelda Fitzgerald, c. 18 Nov. 1928, *SL*, 290; FSF to MP, Feb. 1929, in Matthew J. Bruccoli and Margaret M. Duggan, eds., with Susan Walker, *The Correspondence of F. Scott Fitzgerald* (New York: Random, 1980), 224.

93 *"The bullet"* Mellow, *Without Consequences*, 368.

93 *"said perfectly"* EH to Pauline Pfeiffer, 12 Nov. 1926, *SL*, 222; Scott Donaldson, *By Force of Will: The Life and Art of Ernest Hemingway* (New York: Viking, 1977), 289. In a letter written 9 March 1934, Madelaine told Ernest that their mother was so selfish and so demanding that she (Madelaine) not only understood the reason for their father's suicide but was tempted to follow his lead and take her own life (9 Mar. 1934, JFK). In 1966 and 1982, respectively, Ernest's sister Ursula and his brother, Leicester, would in fact commit suicide.

94 *The suicide was* Kert, *Hemingway Women*, 202.

94 *"My father"* EH to Sylvia Beach, 2 Dec. 1929, Beach Collection, Box 201/5, PUL.

94 *I do not like* HFW, 32–33; *AH*, 118–19. Michael Reynolds (*HFW*, 32–33) cites the long, indented passage and includes what Hemingway struck out as well as what let stand, at least for that moment; Paul Smith pointed out to me the resonance of "the one who reads it."

95 *As scholar HFW*, 59; EH, "Ernest Hemingway: An Interview," by George Plimpton, *Paris Review* 18 (Spring 1958): 84.

96 *Founded on HFW*, 45.

96 *"people with"* EH to MP, 6 Dec. 1926, *SL*, 237; *HFW*, 40; EH to MP, 22 Jan. 1929, *SL*, 294.

96 *"unavoidable"* MP to Ring Lardner, 1 Aug. 1928, in Caruthers, *Ring Around Max*, 123; Berg, *Perkins*, 133; MP to EH, 29 Jan. 1929, JFK.

97 *"in a deeper"* MP to EH, 24 May 1929, Box 1/6, PUL.

97 *"the 'genteel'"* MP to Owen Wister, 16 Apr. 1929, Box 1/6, PUL; Berg, *Perkins*, 141.

98 *"I then"* Edward Warren to Joseph Brewer, 23 Apr. 1930, Morris Ernst Collection, Humanities Research Center, Univ. of Texas at Austin; Tebbel, *Golden Age*, 637. On Sumner and the vice society, see also Dardis, *Liveright*, 153–75.

98 *Hemingway resented* EH to Beach, 12 Feb. 1929, Beach Collection, Box 201/5, PUL; MP to Charles Scribner, 14 Feb. 1929, Scribners Author Files, Box 134/14, PUL.

99 *A "flustered"* Edmund Wilson to Burton Rascoe, 6 Sept. 1929, in Elena Wilson, ed., *Letters* [of Edmund Wilson] *on Literature and Politics, 1912–1972* (New York: Farrar, 1977), 168; Russell Lynes, *The Tastemakers* (New York: Harper, 1954), 331; Nelson Lichtenstein, "Authorial Professionalism," 38; Berg, *Perkins*, 180.

99 *He knew what* Dardis, *Liveright*, 234; MP to Charles Scribner, 14 Feb. 1929, Scribners Author Files, Box 134/14, PUL.

100 *"Dirty slovenly"* EH to Grace Hemingway, c. late May 1929, JFK; EH to Carol Hemingway, c. 5 Oct. 1929, *SL*, 308; Kert, *Hemingway Women*, 228.

100 *A lipreader* Rev. of *What Price Glory?*, dir. Raoul Walsh, *Variety*, 1 Dec. 1926, rpt. vol. 3 of *Variety Film Reviews* (New York: Garland, 1983), n. p.; Jason Joy to "Junior" Laemmle, 21 Aug. 1929, *All Quiet on the Western Front* file, MPAA.

101 *"way out"* Alfred Dashiell to EH, 15 Feb. 1932, Box 2/10, PUL; EH to John Dos Passos, 9 Feb. 1929, *SL*, 295; EH to MP, 16 Feb. 1929, *OT*, 91.

101 *Faulkner wanted* Frederick R. Karl, *William Faulkner: American Writer: A Biography* (New York: Weidenfeld, 1989), 358, 381; MP to EH, 19 Feb. 1929, Box 1/6, PUL.

102 *Perhaps because* West, *American Authors*, 108. See also *HFW*.

102 *"as literary"* MP to Owen Wister, 1 May 1929, Box 1/6, PUL; Alfred Harcourt to Sinclair Lewis, 22 Dec. 1927, *FMS*, 262.

102 *"litero-menstrual"* EH to MP, 15 Sept. 1927, 26 July 1929, *OT*, 64, 111; EH to MP, 31 May 1928, *SL*, 278; MP to EH, 12 June 1929, Box 1/6, PUL; *HFW*, 70. "I trust yr contract dont include turning over proceeds of ALL best sellers to your late consort," Ezra Pound wrote Hemingway in late January 1927 (*AH*, 100). Perkins explained that Green owed his financial success solely to the Book of the Month Club. As Perkins concluded, no author could afford to overlook "the importance of this other possibility" (MP to EH, 4 June 1928, Box 1/5, PUL).

103 *He had considered* Oldsey, *Hidden Craft*, 16, 18; Lewis to Harcourt, 9 June 1926,

FMS, 219; *HFW*, 64–66, 295–97; MP to Charles Scribner, 14 Feb. 1929, Scribners Author Files, Box 134/14, PUL. The Hemingway manuscripts contain inconsistent spellings of the two major characters' first names, thus *The Sentimental Education of Frederick* [*sic*] *Henry*.

103 *The first installment HFW*, 69; Burlingame, *Of Making Many Books*, 82; Robert Bridges to EH, 19 Feb. 1929, Box 1/6, PUL.

104 *Though Perkins* Galleys for *AFTA*, *Scribner's Magazine*, Box 6/72–2, JFK; John V. Wilson to Jason Joy, 31 Dec. 1929, *All Quiet* file, MPAA; FSF to EH, June 1929, in Bruccoli and Duggan, *Correspondence of Fitzgerald*, 227; MP to EH, 19 Feb. 1929, Box 1/6, PUL.

105 *When the English* EH to MP, 20 Oct. 1929, Box 1/7, PUL; Wheelock, COHC (1967), 1: 173. See also EH to MP, 24 June 1929, *SL*, 298; MP to EH, 12 Nov. 1929, Box 1/7, PUL.

105 *He had snipped* Francis E. Skipp, "The Editing of *Look Homeward, Angel*," *Papers of the Bibliographical Society of America* 57, no. 1 (1963): 10; EH to MP, 16 Feb. 1929, Box 1/6, PUL; EH to MP, 7 June 1929, *SL*, 297; MP to Owen Wister, 1 May 1929; MP to EH, 24 May 1929; Wister to MP, 30 Apr., 4 June 1929, Box 1/6, PUL. See also Alan Price, " 'I'm Not an Old Fogey and You're Not a Young Ass': Owen Wister and Ernest Hemingway," *Hemingway Review* 9, no. 1 (Fall 1989): 82–90.

106 *"sordidness"* Foreword to "A Farewell to Arms," *Scribner's Magazine*, May 1929, 43.

106 *"To hell"* FSF to MP, c. June 1929, in Turnbull, *Letters of Fitzgerald*, 215; MP to EH, 8 June 1927, Box 1/4, PUL; EH to MP, 24 June 1929, *SL*, 299; EH to MP, 31 July 1929, Box 1/7, PUL.

106 *With Scribners'* Berg, *Perkins*, 207; MP to Wister, 8 Oct. 1929, Box 1/7, PUL.

107 *If Boston* Donald Brace to Sinclair Lewis, 22 Apr. 1927, *FMS*, 239; MP to EH, 27 June 1929, Box 1/6, PUL; Wister to MP, 7 Oct. 1929, Box 1/7, PUL. See also Scott Donaldson, "Censorship and *A Farewell to Arms*," *Studies in American Fiction* 19 (1991): 85–93.

107 *Though Hemingway made* EH to MP, 3 Oct. 1929, JFK.

107 *The last sentences* Oldsey, *Hidden Craft*, 75, 79.

107 *"The book"* MP to FSF, 28 July 1919, *DS*, 18; advertisement for *TSAR*, in *PW*, 25 Dec. 1926, 2307.

108 *"the offending"* HFW, 82–83; Mary Pfeiffer to EH, 4 May 1929, JFK.

108 *When "The Doctor"* Lynn, *Hemingway*, 256; EH to Clarence Hemingway, 20 Mar. 1925, *SL*, 153; EH to FSF, c. 24 Dec. 1925, *SL*, 182.

109 *"It will become"* Herbert S. Gorman, rev. of *TSAR*, in *New York World*, 14 Nov. 1926, 10M, rpt. *CR*, 38.

109 *"I understand now"* Baker, 595.

110 *The novel needed* EH to MP, 31 May 1928, *SL*, 278; EH to MP, 4 Oct. 1929, Box

1/7, PUL; *Scribner's Magazine*, May 1929, 43; June 1929, 42. See also EH to Jonathan Cape, c. Feb. 1928, JFK.

110 *"trying to write"* EH to Wister, c. 25 July 1929; EH to FSF, 13 Sept. 1929, *SL*, 301, 306; EH to MP, 26 July 1929, Box 1/7, PUL; Morley Callaghan, *That Summer in Paris: Memories of Tangled Friendships with Hemingway, Fitzgerald, and Some Others* (New York: Coward-McCann, 1963), 107.

110 *While in America* "FSF to EH, c. July 1928, Bruccoli, 97–98.

111 *"the* Hemingwayish*"* "New York Life," CS/JFK; EH to his family, 1 Dec. 1926, *SL*, 233; MP to EH, 17 Oct. 1927, Box 1/4, PUL.

111 *"subject proposes"* Wilson, *Figures*, 67.

112 *"Sorry, I"* William Faulkner to Ben Wasson, c. spring 1930, in Blotner, *Selected Letters*, 48; EH to MP, c. 29 Apr. 1929, Box 1/6, PUL.

112 *"If we had"* MP to EH, 25 May 1928, Box 1/5, PUL; Dorothy Parker, "Profiles: The Artist's Reward," *New Yorker*, 30 Nov. 1929, 28.

113 *"author of"* Advertisement for *AFTA*, in *PW*, 10 Aug. 1929, 526; MP to EH, 31 May 1929, Box 1/6, PUL.

113 *"were very nervous"* MP to EH, 15 Oct. 1929, Box 1/7, PUL.

114 *The literary periodicals* EH to FSF, 13 Sept. 1929, *SL*, 307; advertisement for *AFTA*, in *New York Times Book Review*, 24 Nov. 1929, 20; Tebbel, *Golden Age*, 308–9.

114 *"long tale"* Anthony Burgess, *Ernest Hemingway and His World* (New York: Scribners, 1978), 50.

114 *Perkins had not done* Dorothy Herrmann, *S.J. Perelman: A Life* (New York: Putnam, 1986), 60.

115 *"to question"* MP to EH, 23 Sept. 1929, Box 1/7, PUL; EH to MP, 23 Feb. 1929, Box 1/6, PUL.

115 *"keep a lot"* EH to MP, 15 July 1932, Box 2/11, PUL.

115 *"the spirit of"* EH to MP, 3 Oct. 1929, *OT*, 118; EH to MP, 4 Oct. 1929, Box 1/7, PUL; Hinkle, " 'Dear Mr. Scribner,' " 56; Edmund Wilson to Malcolm Cowley, c. 1951, in Wilson, *Letters*, 253–54. In *A Moveable Feast*, Hemingway recalled that *The Great Gatsby* "had a garish dust jacket and I remember being embarrassed by the violence, bad taste and slippery look of it. It looked [like] the book jacket for a book of bad science fiction. Scott told me not to be put off by it, that it had to do with a billboard along a highway in Long Island that was important in the story. He said he had liked the jacket and now he didn't like it. I took it off to read the book."

116 *"I saw no"* Baker, 203; Smith, *Reader's Guide*, 223.

116 *"We came"* EH to John Dos Passos, 4 Sept. 1929; EH to MP, 28 Aug. 1929; EH to FSF, 13 Sept. 1929, *SL*, 303, 302, 306.

117 *"ruined by"* EH to Dos Passos, 4 Sept. 1929; EH to FSF, 13 Sept. 1929, *SL*, 303, 306; Benjamin Stolberg, "Merchant in Letters," *Outlook and Independent*, 21 May

1930, 85; Bernard de Voto, "Writing for Money," *Saturday Review of Literature*, 9 Oct. 1937, 3.

117 *"get the impression"* Alfred Harcourt to Sinclair Lewis, 14 Mar. 1929, *FMS*, 270; Tebbel, *Golden Age*, 683; Scherman, COHC (1954–55), 202–3.

118 *"Here Is"* Fanny Butcher, "Here Is Genius," rev. of *AFTA*, in *Chicago Tribune*, 28 Sept. 1929, 11, CS/JFK.

118 *Agnes Smith* Revs. of *AFTA*: [Agnes Smith], *New Yorker*, 12 Oct. 1929, 120; Mary Ross, *Survey*, 1 Nov. 1929, 166, rpt. *CR*, 90; Henry Hazlitt, *New York Sun*, 28 Sept. 1929, 38, rpt. *CR*, 69; Percy Hutchison, *New York Times Book Review*, 29 Sept. 1929, 5; John Dos Passos, *New Masses*, 1 Dec. 1929, 16, rpt. *CR*, 96; Henry Seidel Canby, *Saturday Review of Literature*, 12 Oct. 1929, 231; *Springfield* (Illinois) *Republican*, 10 Nov. 1929, 4E, rpt. *CR*, 94; T. S. Matthews, *New Republic*, 9 Oct. 1929, 208–10, rpt. *CR*, 77.

118 *"writers" and "talkers"* MP to FSF, 1 Feb. 1922, *DS*, 271; revs. of *AFTA*: *Time*, 14 Oct. 1929, 80; "A. C.," *Boston Transcript*, 19 Oct. 1929, Book Section 2, rpt. *CR*, 82; Henry Hazlitt, *New York Sun*, 28 Sept. 1929, 38, rpt. *CR*, 70 (qtd. in advertisement for *AFTA*, in *New York Times Book Review*, 10 Nov. 1929, 19); Robert Herrick, *Bookman*, Nov. 1929, 261; Mary Ross, *Atlantic Monthly*, Nov. 1929, 20; *Ponca City* (Oklahoma) *News*, 13 Oct. 1929, CS/JFK; William Curtis, *Town & Country*, 1 Nov. 1929, 86, 146, rpt. *CR*, 92.

119 *may partly* Malcolm Cowley, rev. of *AFTA*, in *New York Herald Tribune Books*, 6 Oct. 1929, 1, 6, rpt. *CR*, 74; MP to Ann Barnes, 25 Dec. 1934, Box 3/14, PUL.

120 *"It is a pleasure"* *Scribner's Magazine*, October 1929, 472; EH to MP, 3 Oct. 1929, *OT*, 119.

120 *"Lesson Ten"* Paul Reilly, cartoon ("Is your school up to date?"), *Life*, 15 Nov. 1929, 9.

120 *"I have told"* Grace Hemingway to EH, 11 Nov. 1929, JFK; EH to MP, 9 Sept. 1929, Box 1/7, PUL.

121 *By November 1929* MP to EH, 15 Oct. 1929, JFK; EH to MP, 15 Dec. 1929, *SL*, 316; FSF to EH, 9 Sept. 1929, Bruccoli, 134; EH to MP, 19 Nov. 1929, *OT*, 126.

121 *the "syndicating"* MP to EH, 18 Sept. 1929; EH to MP, 4 Oct., 19 Nov. 1929, Box 1/7, PUL.

122 *"your book is"* MP to EH, 12, 21 Nov. 1929, Box 1/7, PUL; EH to MP, 20 Nov. 1929, *OT*, 128.

122 *"wrote some 212"* Burlington (Vermont) *Free Press*, 4 Jan. 1930, CS/JFK; John Dos Passos, rev. of *AFTA*, in *New Masses*, rpt. *CR*, 96; Lynn, *Hemingway*, 393; Callaghan, *Summer in Paris*, 241.

122 *"supports the"* Allen Tate, rev. of *TSAR*, in *Nation*, 15 Dec. 1926, 642; advertisement for *AFTA*, in *Everyman*, 12 Dec. 1929, 549; MP to EH, 25 Nov. 1929, Box 1/7, PUL.

123 *Further promotion* MP to EH, 8 Oct. 1929, JFK.

123 *"You can't do"* Arthur Brentano, qtd. in Joseph A. Margolies, COHC (1971), 10; MP to EH, 22, 25 Oct. 1929, Box 1/7, PUL.

123 *"People so much"* Parker, "Profiles," 28–30; Ray Long to EH, 22 June 1927, Box 1/4, PUL; Dorothy Parker to Robert Benchley, 7 Nov. 1929, in Linda Patterson Miller, ed., *Letters from the Lost Generation: Gerald and Sara Murphy and Friends* (New Brunswick: Rutgers Univ. Press, 1991), 53; Parker to EH, c. Sept. 1929, JFK; EH to Gilbert Seldes, 30 Dec. 1929, *SL*, 318.

124 *"one wonders"* Hazlitt, rev. of *AFTA*, in *CR*, 70.

125 *"I myself"* MP to EH, 31 May 1929, Box 1/6, PUL; EH to B. C. Schoenfeld, 5 Nov. 1929, *SL*, 312.

125 *Better they haggle* EH to MP, 24 Nov. 1927, Box 1/4, PUL.

126 *"Christ knows"* EH to MP, 10 Nov. [1929], *OT*, 121.

126 *"This is a"* Report, Paramount Story Department, 26 Sept. 1929; Lamar Trotti to Jason Joy, 11 Oct. 1929, *AFTA* file, MPAA.

126 *Six studios read* Paul Reynolds to MP, 30 Aug. 1929, JFK; EH to MP, 4 Jan. 1930, Box 2/8, PUL; Paul Reynolds, *The Middle Man: The Adventures of a Literary Agent* (New York: Morrow, 1972), 36; Pamela King Hanson, ed., *American Film Institute Catalog: Feature Films, 1931–1940* (Berkeley: Univ. of California Press, 1993), 613.

127 *"hobbling back"* Reynolds, *Middle Man*, 36; EH to MP, 10 Nov. [1929], *OT*, 121.

127 *The percentages* Alfred L. Bernheim, *The Business of the Theatre: An Economic History of the American Theatre, 1750–1932* (New York: Blom, 1964), 90; EH to MP, 4 Jan. 1930, Box 2/8, PUL.

127 *"It is marvelous"* Sara Haardt to H. L. Mencken, 19 Oct. 1927, in Marion Elizabeth Rodgers, ed., *Mencken and Sara: A Life in Letters: The Private Correspondence of H.L. Mencken and Sara Haardt* (New York: McGraw-Hill, 1987), 303; "All-Time Best-Sellers," in *International Motion Picture Almanac*, ed. Terry Ramsaye (New York: Quigley Publishing Co., 1941–42), 984.

128 *The play opens* Quoted matter from Laurence Stallings's dramatization of *AFTA* has been taken from S*AFTA*.

128 *"E. Cantwork"* Baker, 202.

128 *As sales of* EH to MP, 31 July 1929, Box 1/7, PUL; John Sutherland, *Bestsellers: Popular Fiction of the 1970s* (London: Routledge, 1981), 246.

129 *"called down"* Allen Tate, "Interview with Allen Tate," by Matthew J. Bruccoli, *Fitzgerald/Hemingway Annual, 1974* (1975): 101–2.

129 *"It's hard"* EH to MP, 15 Dec. 1929, *SL*, 316–17.

CHAPTER FOUR: DEATH IN THE AFTERNOON

131 *"the god damndest"* EH to MP, 15 Dec. 1929; EH to Morley Callaghan, 4 Jan. 1930, *SL*, 315, 319.

131 *"Please don't"* Scott Donaldson, *Archibald MacLeish: An American Life* (Boston: Houghton, 1992), 199; EH to MP, 15 Dec. 1929, *SL*, 317.

132 *Working with* Paul Reynolds, *Middle Man*, 36–37; MP to EH, 3 June 1930, JFK; EH to Guy Hickok, 5 Dec. 1930, *SL*, 333.

132 *"What a shitty"* EH to Sylvia Beach, n.d., Beach Collection, Box 201/6, PUL; Gordon B. Neavill, "The Modern Library Series: Format and Design, 1917–1977," *Printing History* 1 (1979): 33.

132 *"I'm a reporter"* EH to MP, 16 Nov. 1933, *SL*, 400; MP to John Mulliken, 17 May 1945, in Wheelock, *Letters of Perkins*, 266.

132 *"I am quite"* Karl, *Faulkner*, 350, 375, 401, 409; Philip Jordan, "Ernest Hemingway: A Personal Study," *Everyman*, 12 Dec. 1929, 541.

133 *"dehumanize himself"* Robert E. Fleming, *The Face in the Mirror: Hemingway's Writers* (Tuscaloosa: Univ. of Alabama Press, 1994), 10.

133 *By June 1930* Susan F. Beegel, *Hemingway's Craft of Omission: Four Manuscript Examples* (Ann Arbor: UMI Research, 1988), 35–36; Baker, 210.

134 *"I've never"* EH to MP, 31 May 1930, *SL*, 323; MP to EH, 3 June 1930, Box 2/8, PUL.

134 *"book of distinction"* MP to EH, 30 Apr. 1930, Box 2/8, PUL.

134 *"Don't tell"* EH to Henry Strater, c. 20 June 1930, *SL*, 324; William F. Nolan, "The Man Behind the Masks: Hemingway as a Fictional Character," *Fitzgerald/Hemingway Annual, 1974* (1975): 207.

135 *In Philadelphia* Pictorial documentation of the 1930 dramatization of *AFTA* may be found in thirty-six black-and-white production photographs, Keybooks Collection, White Studios, Inc., MWEZ + n. c. 16563, pp. 10–11, LCLPA; Edwin C. Stein, rev. of S*AFTA*, as perf. at the National Theater, New York, *Brooklyn Standard Union*, 23 Sept. 1930, CF/LCLPA.

135 *A disciple* On Mamoulian's career, see Tom Milne, *Rouben Mamoulian* (Bloomington: Indiana Univ. Press, 1970); Mark Spergel, *Reinventing Reality: The Art and Life of Rouben Mamoulian* (Metuchen, N.J.: Scarecrow, 1993).

135 *"at once remove"* EH to MP, 31 July 1930; MP to EH, 6 Aug. 1930, Box 2/8, PUL.

135 *"I do think"* MP to EH, 28 May 1930, Box 2/8, PUL; Wheelock, COHC (1967), 1: 160.

136 *"For some years"* John Mason Brown, rev. of S*AFTA*, as perf. at the National Theater, New York, *New York Evening Post*, 23 Sept. 1930, CF/LCLPA; rev of S*AFTA*, as perf. at the Shubert Theater, Philadelphia, *Philadelphia Bulletin*, 16 Sept. 1930, CF/LCLPA.

136 *"Without doubt"* *Philadelphia Bulletin*, 16 Sept. 1930, CF/LCLPA; "Satisfy Theatre Censors," *New York Times*, 17 Sept. 1930, 30.

136 *In* Mad Hour Rev. of *Mad Hour*, director Jos. C. Boyle, *Variety*, 18 Apr. 1928,

Variety Film Reviews, n. p.; Ted Taylor, "1930 in the Land of Nod," *Variety*, 31 Dec. 1930, 20.

137 *Warner Bros. ended* Douglas Gomery, *The Hollywood Studio System* (New York: St. Martin's, 1986); "Budgets," n.d., file #901, AMPAS; Jerold Simmons, "Film and International Politics: The Banning of *All Quiet on the Western Front* in Germany and Austria, 1930–1931," *Historian: A Journal of History* 52, no. 1 (1989): 41; Tebbel, *Golden Age*, 309; Richard Koszarski, *An Evening's Entertainment*, vol. 3 of *History of the American Cinema* (New York: Scribner, 1990), 108.

137 *"a thunderous"* Revs. of S*AFTA*, as perf. at the National Theater, New York: [reviewer's name effaced], *New York American*, 23 Sept. 1930; Richard Lockridge, *New York Sun*, 23 Sept. 1930; [name effaced], *Brooklyn Daily Eagle*, 23 Sept. 1930; John Mason Brown, *New York Evening Post*, 23 Sept. 1930, CF/LCLPA.

138 *"Write me"* EH to MP, 28 Sept. 1930; MP to EH, 30 Sept. 1930, JFK; Milford Baker to EH, 24 Sept. 1930, Baker/Hemingway Correspondence, PUL.

138 *"A book describes"* "Adopted Code to Govern the Production of Motion Pictures [1930]," Production Code Administration File, David O. Selznick Collection, Hoblitzelle Theatre Arts Library, Humanities Research Center, Univ. of Texas at Austin, n. p.

139 *"In a word"* Lamar Trotti to Jason Joy, 25 Sept. 1930, *AFTA* file, MPAA.

139 *The Paramount AFTA* was one of several flash points in the long battle over film regulation. On the Production Code Administration and the Catholic Legion of Decency, see Gregory Black, *Hollywood Censored: Morality Codes, Catholics, and the Movies* (Cambridge: Cambridge Univ. Press, 1994); Leonard J. Leff and Jerold Simmons, *The Dame in the Kimono: Hollywood, Censorship, and the Production Code from the 1920s to the 1960s* (New York: Grove Weidenfeld, 1990); Frank Walsh, *Sin and Censorship: The Catholic Church and the Motion Picture Industry* (New Haven: Yale Univ. Press, 1996).

139 *"first serious"* Douglas Clayton, *Floyd Dell: The Life and Times of an American Rebel* (Chicago: Dee, 1994), 248; Bernheim, *Business of the Theatre*, 116.

140 *"They took"* MP to EH, 15 Oct. 1930, Box 2/8, PUL.

140 *The play closed* Perkins to Jonathan Cape, 1 Nov., 5 Dec. 1930, Box 2/8, PUL; EH to Archibald MacLeish, 22 Nov. 1930, *SL*, 331.

140 *"Now we"* EH to MP, 3 Sept. 1930, *OT*, 147.

140 *Perkins was so* Berg, *Perkins*, 181.

141 *In the foreword* Baker, 219; EH to MP, 1 Dec. 1930, *OT*, 151.

141 *"Patrick says"* EH to MacLeish, 22 Nov. 1930, *SL*, 331; Berg, *Perkins*, 159; E. R. Hagemann, "A Collation, with Commentary, of the Five Texts of the Chapters in Hemingway's *In Our Time*, 1923–38," in Michael Reynolds, ed., *Critical Essays on Ernest Hemingway's* In Our Time (Boston: G. K. Hall, 1983), 45.

141 *Don't let* EH to MP, c. Nov. 1930, Box 2/8, PUL; EH to Henry Strater, c. 15 Dec. 1930, *SL*, 336.

142 *"Business seems"* MP to EH, 5 Dec. 1930, Box 2/8, PUL.

142 *Publishers everywhere* Tebbel, *Golden Age*, 429–30, 433–34; Wheelock, COHC (1967), 1: 171–72; 2: 250.

143 *Hoping Wolfe* Berg, *Perkins*, 168–78; EH to MP, 24 Apr. 1926, *SL*, 202; MP to Thomas Boyd, 14 Jan. 1931, Scribners Author Files, Box 19/4, PUL. Scribners published *Of Time and the River* in 1935; *Scribner's Magazine* published Fitzgerald's "Echoes of the Jazz Age" in November 1931.

143 *The anthologies* EH to MP, 27 Apr. 1931, Box 2/9, PUL. In 1992 the editors of an anthology for college literature classes paid $5,100 for one Hemingway story, almost twice what they paid for one Fitzgerald story (Charles R. Larson, "Book Buying: A Luxury for the Rich?" *Chronicle of Higher Education*, 11 Mar. 1992, A44).

144 *Cosmopolitan had* EH to Buzz Henry, 29 Jan. 1931, JFK; Paul Reynolds to EH, 30 Aug. 1929, JFK; EH to MP, 21 Jan. 1932, Box 2/10, PUL.

144 *In January* MP to EH, 9 Jan. 1931, Box 2/9, PUL.

144 *"Poor Boy"* Lynn, *Hemingway*, 394–95.

145 *"the focus"* Caresse Crosby to EH, Dec. 1931, Hagemann Collection, HN-74, JFK; Kert, *Hemingway Women*, 233.

146 *Though the* Memphis Joseph Blotner, *Faulkner: A Biography* (New York: Random, 1974), I: 686, 777.

146 *"I do not say"* Robert W. Lewis, "The Making of *Death in the Afternoon*," in Nagel, *Context*, 44.

147 *Three years before* Donaldson, *Archibald MacLeish*, 186.

147 *That past* MP to EH, 16 Oct. 1931; EH to MP, between 12 and 25 Nov. 1931; EH to MP, c. 20 Oct. 1931, Box 2/9, PUL.

148 *In the 1920s* Berg, *Perkins*, 122, 183–86.

148 *"It takes"* MP to EH, 11 June 1931, Box 2/9, PUL.

149 *"I hate like"* EH to MP, 26 Dec. 1931, *SL*, 346.

149 *" 'Farewell to Arms' will"* Paul Pfeiffer to EH, 20 Mar. 1930, JFK; Stark Young, rev. of S*AFTA*, as perf. at the National Theater, New York, *New Republic*, 8 Oct. 1930, 208.

149 *"Living Authors"* EH to MP, 14 Oct., c. 20 Oct. 1931, Box 2/9, PUL.

149 *Like Cézanne* Arnold Gingrich, Hemingway's editor at *Esquire*, claimed to have originated the now familiar pairing of Hemingway and Cézanne. " 'You're asking for changes in the copy of a man who *has* been likened to Cézanne, for bringing "a new way of seeing" into American literature,' " Hemingway reportedly told Gingrich. "This outsized ham was quoting *me* to my face, and without giving me any credit," Gingrich later recalled. " 'For chris'sake,' " Gingrich told Hemingway, " 'that was *me*, that Cézanne stuff.' [Hemingway] looked honestly surprised, then sheepish" ("Scott, Ernest, and Whoever," *Esquire*, October 1973, 376).

150 *The refrain* Linda W. Wagner, "*The Sun Also Rises*: One Debt to Imagism," in

Harold Bloom, ed. *Ernest Hemingway's* The Sun Also Rises, (New York: Chelsea House, 1987), 107.

151 *"you are getting"* MP to EH, 23 Apr. 1931, Box 2/9, PUL.

152 *Captain Eddie* See Beegel, *Hemingway's Craft.*

152 *"horseshit"* Lynn, *Hemingway*, 397.

152 *a "punk"* EH to Mary Pfeiffer, 5 Jan. 1932, *SL*, 350; EH to Will Lengel, 1 Mar. 1932, JFK; EH to Waldo Peirce, 15 Apr. 1932, *SL*, 358; Baker, 603; Karl, *Faulkner*, 405; EH to Guy Hickok, 14 Oct. 1932; EH to MP, 5–6 Jan. 1932, *SL*, 373, 351.

153 *"The book piles"* Berg, *Perkins*, 194; EH to MP, 27 Apr. 1931, Box 2/9, PUL; Neal Gabler, *Winchell: Gossip, Power and the Culture of Celebrity* (New York: Knopf, 1994), xii.

153 *"bad luck"* Berg, *Perkins*, 195.

154 Cosmopolitan *wanted* EH to MP, 21 Jan. 1932, 2/10, PUL; MP to EH, 30 Nov. 1931, Box 2/9, PUL.

154 *Dashiell found* Alfred Dashiell to EH, 5 Feb. 1932; EH to MP, 7 Feb. 1932, Box 2/10, PUL.

155 *Opening an old* EH to Dashiell, 7 Feb. 1932; Dashiell to EH, 15 Feb. 1932, Box 2/10, PUL.

155 *"a hell of"* EH to MP, 28 June 1932, *SL*, 361.

155 *"in these times"* MP to EH, 2 Apr. 1932, Box 2/10, PUL.

155 *"selling it"* EH to MP, 4 Apr. 1932, *OT*, 161; MP to Ring Lardner, 27 Dec. 1928, 13 Mar. 1930, in Caruthers, *Ring Around Max*, 130–31, 149, 159.

156 *"flat flop"* MP to EH, 7 Apr. 1932; EH to MP, 4 Apr. 1932, Box 2/10, PUL.

156 *"I do not"* John Raeburn, *Fame Became of Him: Hemingway as Public Writer* (Bloomington: Indiana Univ. Press, 1984), 65; EH to MP, 4 Apr. 1932; MP to EH, 8 Apr. 1932, Box 2/10, PUL.

156 *As Hemingway reminded* Roy Obringer, Memo of Record, 11 Feb. 1946, Warner Bros. Collection, Univ. of Southern California, Los Angeles, Box 2776; EH to Speiser, c. Apr. 1932; MP to EH, 7 Apr. 1932, JFK.

157 *This story* Lamar Trotti, Memo of Record, 1 Apr. 1932, *TSAR* file, MPAA.

157 *In small towns* Jeffrey Meyers, *Hemingway: A Biography* (New York: Harper, 1985), 235. On the purchase price, see MP to EH, 7 July 1932 ("The check for $13,200 came yesterday in purchase of the picture rights to 'The Sun Also Rises' "), JFK; Copy of Contract between Ernest Hemingway and RKO, 5 July 1932 (with note that screen rights were sold through Ann Watkins), Box FX-LR-826, FCLD.

159 *"This is"* EH to Will Lengel, c. 15 Aug. 1932, *SL*, 367; MP to EH, 26 Aug. 1932, Box 2/11, PUL.

159 *The Kansas City* Baker, 606; Smith, *Reader's Guide*, 265.

160 *"You sell"* EH to MP, 17 Nov. [1929], *OT*, 124; EH to MP, 28 June 1932, *SL*, 362.

160 "What did" EH to MP, 27 July 1932, *SL*, 364; Tebbell, *Golden Age*, 642; EH to MP, 28 June 1932, *SL*, 362; EH to MP, 2 June 1932; MP to EH, 11 June 1932, Box 2/10, PUL; EH to MP, 3 Oct. 1929, JFK. One year after publication of *DIA*, Perkins suspected that he had been more conservative than necessary yet noted that "several self-righteous 'gentlemen' probably in the Union Club, or the University, wrote [in fall 1932] that they were bringing 'Death in the Afternoon' to the attention of [vice society head] William Sumner, for instance, and would never buy another Scribner book." In England Jonathan Cape went further than Perkins, and had no regrets. Where he found it, he changed "fuck" to "damn" or "blast" or "go and hang yourselves." Occasionally the text lost its moorings. The narrator says, "Madame . . . it may well be that we are talking nonsense." The Old Lady responds: "That is an odd term and one I did not encounter in my youth." In the original, the narrator had used "horseshit" instead of "nonsense." The change made hash of the text (Robert W. Lewis, "Making of *Death in the Afternoon*," in Nagel, *Context*, 48).

161 "*twelve tenths*" Michael Reynolds points out that Pauline's (in 1926) may be the earliest written allusion to her husband's theory of the iceberg (*AH*, 82).

162 *That summer* Berg, *Perkins*, 191, 197.

162 "*that little*" EH to MP, 9 Aug. 1932, *OT*, 177; EH to Paul Romaine, 9 Aug. 1932, *SL*, 366.

163 "*always want*" EH to MP, 15 Nov. 1932, *SL*, 377; EH to MP, 30 Apr. 1934, *OT*, 208.

163 "*remarkable*" Laurence Stallings, rev. of *DIA*, in *New York Sun*, 23 Sept. 1932, 34, rpt. *CR*, 108–9.

164 "*Olé! Olé!*" Rev. of *DIA*, *Time*, 26 Sept. 1932, 47. Though Hemingway was only thirty-three years old when *Time* published the review, the magazine was usually more interested in legend than facts when it wrote about the author.

164 "*an interlude*" Revs. of *DIA*: Seward Collins, *Bookman*, Oct. 1932, 624; Clifton Fadiman, *Nation*, 18 Jan. 1933, 63.

164 "*a Baedeker*" Revs. of *DIA*: Malcolm Cowley, *New Republic*, 30 Nov. 1932, 76; R. L. Duffus, *New York Times Book Review*, 25 Sept. 1932, 17; Robert M. Coates, *New Yorker*, 1 Oct. 1932, 63; Granville Hicks, *Nation*, 9 Nov. 1932, 461; Collins, *Bookman*, Oct. 1932, 624; H. L. Mencken, *American Mercury*, Dec. 1932, 506.

165 "selling—*What*" EH to Guy Hickok, 29 Oct. 1932, *SL*, 376; advertisement for *DIA*, in *PW*, 8 Oct. 1932, 1399.

165 "*Have been*" EH to MP, 15 Nov. 1932, *SL*, 376–77.

CHAPTER FIVE: WINNER TAKE NOTHING

167 "*special request*" Gary Cooper file, AMPAS.

167 *Gary Cooper, the he-man* Lynn, *Hemingway*, 162; Larry Swindell, *The Last Hero: A*

Biography of Gary Cooper (Garden City, N.Y.: Doubleday, 1980), 137–38. "Hemingway was a great pal of Joyce's, and Joyce remarked to me one day that he thought it was a mistake, Hemingway's thinking himself such a tough fellow and McAlmon trying to pass himself off as the sensitive type. It was the other way round, he thought. So Joyce found you out, Hemingway!" (Sylvia Beach, *Shakespeare and Company* [New York: Harcourt, 1959], 78).

168 *"We could not"* Clipping, BS/AMPAS.

168 *"they intend[ed]"* Lamar Trotti, Memo of Record, 19 July 1932, *AFTA* file, MPAA. Throughout 1930 and 1931 and continuing into 1932, Italian diplomats in Washington and Los Angeles had pressured Will Hays and (through Hays) Paramount not to produce *AFTA*. See, for instance, John Wilson to Lamar Trotti, 30 Oct. 1930; Trotti to Wilson, 5 Nov. 1930; Jason Joy to Hays, 25 July 1932; Wilson for the Files, 25 Nov. 1932, *AFTA* file, MPAA.

168 *Hollywood called* Clipping, 11 Oct. 1932, Helen Hayes file, AMPAS; Kenneth Barrow, *Helen Hayes: First Lady of the American Theatre* (Garden City, N.Y.: Doubleday, 1985), 108–9; revs. of *DIA*: R. L. Duffus, *New York Times Book Review*, 25 Sept. 1932, 5; Curtis Patterson, *Town & Country*, 15 Oct. 1932, 50, rpt. *CR*, 118.

169 *When the average* Henry Herzbrun to Adolph Zukor, 5 Mar. 1935, Zukor Collection, AMPAS; *AFTA*, Paramount Pictures Files, #901, AMPAS; Clippings, BS/AMPAS; Frank M. Laurence, *Hemingway and the Movies* (Jackson: Univ. Press of Mississippi, 1981), 237; Kevin Thomas, "An Unsung Starmaker of Cinematography," *Los Angeles Times*, n.d., Charles Lang file, AMPAS.

169 *The studios that* Tebbel, *Golden Age*, 20.

170 *"[Harold] Guinzburg"* David Selznick to Irene Selznick, 30 Jan. 1930, in Rudy Behlmer, ed., *Memo from David O. Selznick* (New York: Viking, 1972), 26.

170 *He had wanted* Selznick to EH [not sent], 14 Aug. 1957, in Behlmer, *Memo*, 460; Behlmer, *Memo*, 43; David Thomson, *Showman: The Life of David O. Selznick* (New York: Knopf, 1992), 98; M. Bell to Jason Joy, 19 Sept. 1932, *TSAR* file, MPAA.

170 *"Drinking"* Handwritten note, 20 Sept. 1932; Joy to James Wingate, "Personal and Confidential," 28 Sept. 1932; *TSAR* file, MPAA.

171 *Using notes* Wingate to Joy, 7 Oct. 1932; Farrell, note, n.d., *TSAR* file, MPAA; Jon Bradshaw, *Dreams That Money Can Buy: The Tragic Life of Libby Holman* (New York: Morrow, 1985), 146.

172 *"not good picture"* Irwin Esmond, qtd. in Wingate to Joy, 14 Oct. 1932, *TSAR* file, MPAA; Joy to (Selznick associate) Kenneth McGowan, 14 Oct. 1932, *TSAR* file, MPAA.

172 *"probably the"* Lamar Trotti to (Hays associate) Carl Milliken, 6 June 1930; Wingate to Hays, 8 May 1933, *The Story of Temple Drake* file, MPAA.

172 *Selznick found Howard* Selznick to Louis Brock and Mark Sandrich, 13 Jan. 1933; Selznick to Daniel O'Shea, 20 Oct. 1938, in Behlmer, *Memo*, 53, 172; Clipping, 4 Oct. 1932, Ann Harding file, AMPAS.

173 *In early November* Clippings, BS/AMPAS; *AFTA* Press Book, Paramount, AMPAS.

173 *As early as* Clippings, BS/AMPAS.

174 *"story-book"* Laurence, *Hemingway and the Movies*, 260, 259.

174 *He had chosen* EH to Gus Pfeiffer, c. 9 Dec. 1932, JFK; Oldsey, *Hidden Craft*, 72.

174 *"spread around"* Hemingway drafted two versions of the statement. See EH to MP, c. 15 Nov. 1932, JFK; EH to MP, 7 Dec. 1932, *SL*, 379.

175 *"volunteered for"* AFTA Press Book, Paramount, AMPAS.

175 *"Author Lived"* AFTA Press Book, Paramount, AMPAS; Clippings, BS/AMPAS.

175 *"the very sight"* Clipping, BS/AMPAS; Fred Beetson to John Wilson, 5 Dec. 1932, *AFTA* file, MPAA.

176 *Enhancing* Program, Paramount Pictures' *AFTA*, BS/AMPAS.

176 *"closing not"* Gus Pfeiffer to EH, 8 Dec. 1932, JFK; EH to Pfeiffer, c. 9 Dec. 1932, JFK.

176 *"aims at"* Clippings, BS/AMPAS.

177 *"picture you"* Rev. of *AFTA*, *Photoplay*, Feb. 1933, 57; Clipping, BS/AMPAS.

177 *"too wild"* Mary Pfeiffer to Pauline Hemingway, 31 Oct. 1931; EH to Ralph Stitt, n.d., JFK; "The Phoenix Nest," *Saturday Review of Literature*, 24 Dec. 1932, 348.

177 *Confusing orders* EH to Guy Hickok, 14 Oct. 1932, *SL*, 372; Baker, 233; Charles Scribner to Peter Vischer, 19 Sept. 1932; MP to EH, 12 Nov. 1932, Box 2/11, PUL; *PW*, 8 Oct. 1932, 1433. See also *PW*, 15 Oct. 1932, 1514; 12 Nov. 1932, 1868; 17 Dec. 1932, 2246.

178 *"some of the"* MP to Marjorie Rawlings, 5 Jan. 1940, in Wheelock, *Letters of Perkins*, 151; EH to MP, 14 Oct. 1932, Box 2/11, PUL.

178 *"come at a"* MP to EH, 19 Sept., 18 Nov. 1932, Box 2/11, PUL; Berg, *Perkins*, 214; EH to Arnold Gingrich, 4 Dec. 1932, *SL*, 378.

179 *"The mad"* Clipping, BS/AMPAS.

179 *"The obstetrics"* Wagner, *Rob Wagner's Script*, 31 Dec. 1932, 8; *AFTA* file, MPAA. Though Paramount was still at war with the Hays office when *AFTA* reached theaters in December 1932, the issue by then was chiefly the "illicit love" that had worried Trotti since 1930. The motion picture version of *AFTA* seen today on television and video cassette is not the one released in 1932 but the one recut by the Production Code censors in 1938. See Leonard J. Leff, "A Farewell to Arms," *Film Comment*, Jan.–Feb. 1995, 71, 73.

180 *The picture was* Motion Picture Herald, 7, 14, and 21 Jan. 1933. Hemingway's novel (*AFTA*) had reportedly been banned in Australia, where the motion picture was also banned—until Paramount removed the screen credit "From the Novel by Ernest Hemingway" (*AFTA* file, MPAA).

180 *"Sadie Glutz"* Clippings, BS/AMPAS; "What the Picture Did for Me," *Motion Picture Herald*, 4, 11, 25 Feb. 1933; "January Box Office Champions," *Motion Picture Herald*, 11 Mar. 1933, 4.

180 *In September 1932 PW,* 1 Oct. 1932, 1360; Clipping, BS/AMPAS.

180 *"plenty of"* EH to Gingrich, 3 Apr. 1933, *SL,* 385; MP to EH, 5 Jan. 1933, JFK; James Wingate to Will Hays, 26 May 1933, *TSAR* file, MPAA.

181 *The Modern* Tebbel, *Golden Age,* 500; *AFTA* Press Book, Paramount, AMPAS.

181 *That March* EH to MP, 31 Mar. 1933, Box 2/12, PUL; Woodress, *Willa Cather,* 306; EH to Archibald MacLeish, 27 Feb. 1933, *SL,* 381.

181 *Hemingway would not* EH to MP, 8 Apr. 1933, Box 2/12, PUL.

182 *"I don't"* EH to Janet Flanner, 8 Apr. 1933; EH to MP, 13 June 1933; EH to Gingrich, 3 Apr. 1933; EH to Mary Pfeiffer, 16 Oct. 1933; EH to MacLeish, 27 Feb. 1933, *SL,* 387, 394, 385, 397, 382.

182 *The capital* Berg, *Perkins,* 215–16; EH to MacLeish, 27 Feb. 1933, *SL,* 382.

183 *"Fame Follows"* AFTA Press Book, Paramount, AMPAS; EH to Gingrich, 13 Mar., 3 Apr. 1933, *SL,* 383, 385.

183 *"bright people"* Raeburn, *Fame Became of Him,* 48–49.

183 *In spring* Berg, *Perkins,* 229, 221.

183 *Now Knopf* Tebbel, *Golden Age,* 553, 564; EH to MP, 8 Apr. 1933, *OT,* 189.

184 *In February 1933* James Wingate, Memo of Record, 20 Feb. 1933; Merian Cooper, qtd. in Wingate to Will Hays, 5 June 1933; Wingate to Hays, 26 May 1933, *TSAR* file, MPAA.

184 *[I]t is the* Joseph Breen to Hays, 24 May 1933, *TSAR* file, MPAA.

185 *Whether the* Baker, 239–40; Gertrude Stein, *The Autobiography of Alice B. Toklas* (New York: Vintage, 1960), 265.

185 *In June 1933* Max Eastman, "Bull in the Afternoon," *New Republic,* 7 June 1933, 96.

186 *"very queer"* EH to Flanner, 8 Apr. 1933, *SL,* 387; EH to MacLeish, 7 June 1933, JFK.

186 *"the breath"* Max Eastman to EH, 15 June 1933, JFK; "Prowess in Action," *Time,* 24 July 1933, 24; Philip Young, *Ernest Hemingway: A Reconsideration* (University Park: Pennsylvania State Univ. Press, 1966), 148–49.

186 *"There is"* EH, "Letter," *Esquire,* May 1934, 25, 156; Raeburn, *Fame Became of Him,* 50, 59.

187 *"You know"* EH to FSF, 12 Apr. 1931; EH to MP, 13 June, 26 July 1933, *SL,* 339–40, 394, 396; Raeburn, *Fame Became of Him,* 62–63.

188 *"the Kotex"* William Faulkner to Morton Goldman, c. June 1936, in Blotner, *Selected Letters,* 96.

188 *As Max* Baker, 239; Raeburn, *Fame Became of Him,* 45.

189 *During the editing* Berg, *Perkins,* 218.

189 *"the one to"* MP to EH, 2 Aug. 1933; EH to MP, 31 Aug. 1933, Box 3/13, PUL.

189 *By October* Baker, 607–8; Helen Goetzman Everitt to EH, 16 May 1933, JFK.

190 *"and I know"* EH to Mary Pfeiffer, 16 Oct. 1933, *SL*, 398; Donaldson, *By Force*, 15, 11.

190 *"tear at a"* Fanny Butcher, rev. of *WTN*, in *Chicago Tribune*, 28 Oct. 1933, 16, rpt. *CR*, 135; Baker, 246; rev. of *WTN*, in *Time*, 6 Nov. 1933, 59–60; advertisement for *WTN*, in *PW*, 20 May 1933, 1587.

191 *"some good ones"* EH to Janet Flanner, 8 Apr. 1933; EH to John Dos Passos, c. 15 May 1933; EH to MP, 16 Nov. 1933, *SL*, 387, 390, 399.

191 *According to* Horace Gregory, rev. of *WTN*, in *New York Herald Tribune Books*, 29 Oct. 1933, VII-5, rpt. *CR*, 139; EH to MP, 16 Nov. 1933, *SL*, 400.

AFTERWORD

193 *"The man"* Lynn, *Hemingway*, 417; *SL*, 581.

193 *"Gentlemen"* Willard L. Wiener, "Hepburn Back from Paris, 'Homesick'; Star of Films Will Play Joan of Arc, Ernest Hemingway Reveals," *New York Evening Journal*, 4 Apr. 1934, CS/JFK; EH to Richard Halliday, 25 Apr. 1934, JFK.

194 *"slipped"* *Denver Post*, 15 Jan. 1933; Clipping, 24 Feb. 1933, Ann Harding file, AMPAS.

194 *RKO was asking* Alfred Wright to George Wasson, 27 Dec. 1933, FCLD; Maurice McKenzie, Memo of Record, 13 Sept. 1933; Jason Joy to E. H. Griffith, 13 Sept. 1933, *TSAR* file, MPAA; Wasson to E. P. Kilroe, 10 Feb. 1934, FCLD.

194 *"stated that"* McKenzie to "COAST" (Will Hays), 4 Jan. 1934; Sidney Kent to Joseph Breen, 11 Jan. 1934, *TSAR* file, MPAA.

195 *Ann Harding had* Alfred Wright to Jack Gain, 18 July 1934, FCLD; Breen to Louis Mayer, 8 Feb. 1935; Hays Memo of Record, 25 Mar. 1935, *TSAR* file, MPAA. The resolution notwithstanding, a treatment of the novel was forwarded to the Production Code office in December 1935, when, as John Raeburn notes in *Fame Became of Him*, Hemingway had become better known to the general public as sportsman and bon vivant than as author. The "essence" of the treatment may be gauged by notes that Karl Lischka prepared for his boss, Joseph Breen. The theme of the story was "Love Handicapped by Sexual Impotence." The snags (in part) follow:

> 2. Brett, the heroine, marries Hugh, a man she does not love, then suddenly and simply leaves him to steep herself in riotous living. That's the last we hear of the marriage. This looks like a major objection. . . .
>
> 4. The several love scenes between Jake and Brett, pointing up the futility of any attempt at physical "love," are extremely dangerous.
>
> 5. There is, of course, a sickening superabundance of drinking.
>
> 6. The business of Brett being taken in by the nuns strikes me as a deliberate and obvious phoney.

Breen telephoned RKO to chastise the studio for even sending the treatment. He learned that the query was only provisional, "at the request of Miss Harding and as a courtesy to her" concurrent with her return to the studio fold (Lischka, Memo of Record, 12 Dec. 1935; B. B. Kahane to Breen, 16 Dec. 1935, *TSAR* file, MPAA). See also Edwin Schallert, " 'Sun Also Rises' Filmed After 30-Year Wait," *Los Angeles Times*, 2 June 1957. After World War II, according to producer Charles Feldman, qtd. in Schallert, Jake Barnes's impotence posed fewer problems than the "danger of the character of Robert Cohn giving offense because by implication it was derogatory to a Jewish type" (*TSAR* file, AMPAS).

195 *"to write a"* "Hemingway Here, Avid for Lion Hunt," *New York Times*, 4 Apr. 1934, 18; Baker, 260; Meyers, *Hemingway: A Biography*, 282; Raeburn, *Fame Became of Him*, 59.

196 *"You see"* EH to MP, 13 June 1933, *SL*, 395.

196 *"I want"* EH to Edward O'Brien, 21 May 1923, *SL*, 82; "Dounce," rev. of *TSAR*, in *New Yorker*, 20 Nov. 1926, 90.

197 *Anyone popular* Susman, "Twentieth Century Culture," 218, 221; Donaldson, *By Force*, 199.

197 *He often wrote* EH to MP, 26 July 1929, Aug. 1929, c. June 1932, JFK; Edward L. Bernays, *Biography of an Idea: Memoirs of Public Relations Counsel Edward L. Bernays* (New York: Simon & Schuster, 1965), 279.

198 *"the* whole*"* Advertisement for *Green Hills of Africa*, in *PW*, 8 June 1935, 2200; FSF to MP, 3 Sept. 1937, *DS*, 241.

198 *Hemingway used* Ursula Jepson to EH, 15 Mar. 1928, JFK; FSF to Zelda Fitzgerald, 26 Oct. 1940, Bruccoli, 202; MP to FSF, 19 Sept. 1940, *DS*, 266; Laurence, *Hemingway and the Movies*, 15; Joan Shelley Rubin, letter to author, 1 June 1992. See also Joan Shelley Rubin, "Self, Culture, and Self-Culture in Modern America: The Early History of the Book-of-the-Month Club," *Journal of American History* 71 (1985): 772–806.

198 *The press zealously* In appendix 1 of *Hemingway: A Biography* (573–75), Jeffrey Meyers lists "Accidents and Injuries."

199 *"The only"* MP to EH, 21 July 1936, Box 3/16, PUL; MP to Owen Wister, 21 Nov. 1934, Box 3/14, PUL.

199 *He accepted* Baker, 554; EH to Bernard Berenson, 24 Sept. 1954, *SL*, 837.

WORKS CITED

Ade, George. *Letters of George Ade.* West Lafayette, Ind.: Purdue Univ. Studies, 1973.

"All-Time Best-Sellers." In *International Motion Picture Almanac,* ed. Terry Ramsaye. New York: Quigley, 1941–42.

Anderson, Sherwood. *Letters of Sherwood Anderson.* Ed. Howard Mumford Jones and Walter B. Rideout. Boston: Little, Brown, 1953.

———. *Sherwood Anderson's Memoirs: A Critical Edition.* Ed. Ray Lewis White. Chapel Hill: Univ. of North Carolina Press, 1969.

Baker, Carlos. *Ernest Hemingway: A Life Story.* New York: Scribners, 1969.

Balio, Tino, ed. *The American Film Industry.* Madison: Univ. of Wisconsin Press, 1976.

Barrow, Kenneth. *Helen Hayes: First Lady of the American Theatre.* Garden City, N.Y.: Doubleday, 1985.

Baughman, James L. *Henry R. Luce and the Rise of the American News Media.* Boston: Twayne, 1987.

Baxter, Peter. *Just Watch! Sternberg, Paramount, and America.* London: British Film Institute, 1993.

Beach, Sylvia. *Shakespeare and Company.* New York: Harcourt, 1959.

Beegel, Susan F. *Hemingway's Craft of Omission: Four Manuscript Examples.* Ann Arbor: UMI Research, 1988.

Bell, Millicent. *Marquand: An American Life.* Boston: Little, Brown, 1979.

Berg, A. Scott. *Goldwyn: A Biography.* New York: Knopf, 1989.

———. *Max Perkins: Editor of Genius.* New York: Dutton, 1978.

Bernays, Edward L. *Biography of an Idea: Memoirs of Public Relations Counsel Edward L. Bernays.* New York: Simon & Schuster, 1965.

Bernheim, Alfred L. *The Business of the Theatre: An Economic History of the American Theatre, 1750–1932.* 1932. New York: Blom, 1964.

Best, Marshall. Columbia Univ. Oral History Collection. Butler Library. 1976.

Blotner, Joseph. *Faulkner: A Biography.* 2 vols. New York: Random, 1974.

Brian, Denis. *The True Gen: An Intimate Portrait of Hemingway by Those Who Knew Him.* New York: Delta, 1988.

Bruccoli, Matthew J. *Fitzgerald and Hemingway: A Dangerous Friendship.* New York: Carroll & Graf, 1994.

Burlingame, Roger. *Of Making Many Books: A Hundred Years of Reading, Writing, and Publishing.* New York: Scribners, 1946.

Callaghan, Morley. *That Summer in Paris: Memories of Tangled Friendships with Hemingway, Fitzgerald, and Some Others.* New York: Coward-McCann, 1963.

Cerf, Bennett. *At Random: The Reminiscences of Bennett Cerf.* New York: Random, 1977.

Clayton, Douglas. *Floyd Dell: The Life and Times of an American Rebel.* Chicago: Dee, 1994.

Cowley, Malcolm. "Profiles: Unshaken Friend." Part 2. *New Yorker,* 8 April 1944, 30–43.

Dardis, Tom. *Firebrand: The Life of Horace Liveright.* New York: Random, 1995.

de Grazia, Edward, and Roger K. Newman. *Banned Films: Movies, Censors, and the First Amendment.* New York: Bowker, 1982.

Diliberto, Gioia. *Hadley.* New York: Ticknor & Fields, 1992.

Donaldson, Scott. *Archibald MacLeish: An American Life.* Boston: Houghton, 1992.

———. *By Force of Will: The Life and Art of Ernest Hemingway.* New York: Viking, 1977.

———. "The Wooing of Ernest Hemingway." *American Literature* 53 (1982): 691–710.

Faulkner, William. *Essays, Speeches, and Public Letters.* Ed. James B. Meriwether. New York: Random, 1965.

———. *Selected Letters of William Faulkner.* Ed. Joseph Blotner. New York: Random, 1977.

Feltes, N. N. *Literary Capital and the Late Victorian Novel.* Madison: Univ. of Wisconsin Press, 1993.

Fenstermaker, John J. "The Search for an American Audience: Marketing Ernest Hemingway, 1925–1930." In *Hemingway: The Oak Park Legacy,* ed. James Nagel, 179–98. Tuscaloosa: Univ. of Alabama Press, 1996.

Fine, Richard. *Hollywood and the Profession of Authorship, 1928–1940.* Ann Arbor: UMI Research, 1985.

Fitzgerald, F. Scott. *The Correspondence of F. Scott Fitzgerald.* Ed. Matthew J. Bruccoli and Margaret M. Duggan, with Susan Walker. New York: Random, 1980.

———. *The Letters of F. Scott Fitzgerald.* Ed. Andrew Turnbull. New York: Scribners, 1963.

Fitzgerald, F. Scott, and Maxwell Perkins. *Dear Scott / Dear Max: The Fitzgerald-Perkins Correspondence.* Ed. John Kuehl and Jackson R. Bryer. New York: Scribners, 1971.

Fleming, Robert E. *The Face in the Mirror: Hemingway's Writers.* Tuscaloosa: Univ. of Alabama Press, 1994.

Gabler, Neal. *Winchell: Gossip, Power, and the Culture of Celebrity.* New York: Knopf, 1994.

Gamson, Joshua. *Claims to Fame: Celebrity in Contemporary America.* Berkeley: Univ. of California Press, 1994.

Gilmer, Walker. *Horace Liveright: Publisher of the Twenties.* New York: Lewis, 1970.

Glasgow, Ellen. *Letters.* New York: Harcourt, 1958.

Gomery, Douglas. *The Hollywood Studio System.* New York: St. Martin's, 1986.

Griffin, Peter. *Along With Youth: Hemingway: The Early Years.* New York: Oxford Univ. Press, 1985.

Hanneman, Audre. *Ernest Hemingway: A Comprehensive Bibliography.* Princeton: Princeton Univ. Press, 1967.

———. *Ernest Hemingway: A Comprehensive Bibliography: Supplement.* Princeton: Princeton Univ. Press, 1975.

Hanson, Pamela King, ed. *American Film Institute Catalog: Feature Films, 1931–1940.* Berkeley: Univ. of California Press, 1993.

Hart, James David. *The Popular Book: A History of America's Literary Taste.* New York: Oxford Univ. Press, 1950.

Hecht, Ben. *A Child of the Century.* New York: Simon & Schuster, 1954.

Hemingway, Ernest. *Across the River and Into the Trees.* New York: Scribners, 1950.

———. *The Complete Short Stories of Ernest Hemingway.* The Finca Vigía Edition. New York: Scribners, 1987.

———. *Death in the Afternoon.* New York: Scribners, 1932.

———. "Ernest Hemingway: An Interview." By George Plimpton. *Paris Review* 18 (Spring 1958): 61–89.

———. *Ernest Hemingway: Selected Letters, 1917–1961.* Ed. Carlos Baker. New York: Scribners, 1981.

———. *A Farewell to Arms.* New York: Scribners, 1929.

———. *The Garden of Eden.* New York: Scribners, 1986.

———. *Green Hills of Africa.* New York: Scribners, 1935.

————. *A Moveable Feast.* New York: Scribners, 1964.

————. "My Own Life." *New Yorker,* 12 February 1927, 23–24.

————. *The Sun Also Rises.* New York: Scribners, 1926.

————. *To Have and Have Not.* New York: Scribners, 1937.

————. *The Torrents of Spring.* New York: Scribners, 1926.

Hemingway, Ernest, and Maxwell Perkins. *The Only Thing That Counts: The Ernest Hemingway / Maxwell Perkins Correspondence, 1925–1947.* Ed. Matthew J. Bruccoli. New York: Scribners, 1996.

Hinkle, James. " 'Dear Mr. Scribner': About the Published Text of *The Sun Also Rises.*" *Hemingway Review* 6, no. 1 (Fall 1986): 43–64.

Honey, Maureen, ed. *Breaking the Ties That Bind: Popular Stories of the New Woman, 1915–1930.* Norman: Univ. of Oklahoma Press, 1992.

Jowett, Garth. *Film: The Democratic Art.* Boston: Little, Brown, 1976.

Karl, Frederick R. *William Faulkner: American Writer: A Biography.* New York: Weidenfeld & Nicolson, 1989.

Kert, Bernice. *The Hemingway Women.* New York: Norton, 1983.

Kronenberger, Louis. "Gambler in Publishing: Horace Liveright." *Atlantic Monthly,* January 1965, 94–104.

Lardner, Ring, and Maxwell Perkins. *Ring Around Max: The Correspondence of Ring Lardner and Max Perkins.* Ed. Clifford M. Caruthers. DeKalb: Northern Illinois Univ. Press, 1973.

Laurence, Frank M. *Hemingway and the Movies.* Jackson: Univ. Press of Mississippi, 1981.

Levine, Lawrence W. *Highbrow/Lowbrow: The Emergence of Cultural Hierarchy in America.* Cambridge: Harvard Univ. Press, 1988.

Lewis, R. W. B. *Edith Wharton: A Biography.* New York: Harper, 1975.

Lewis, Sinclair. *From Main Street to Stockholm: Letters of Sinclair Lewis, 1919–1930.* Ed. Harrison Smith. New York: Harcourt, 1952.

Lichtenstein, Nelson. "Authorial Professionalism and the Literary Marketplace, 1885–1900." *American Studies* 19 (1978): 35–53.

Lingeman, Richard. *Theodore Dreiser: An American Journey, 1908–1945.* New York: Putnam, 1990.

Lynes, Russell. *The Tastemakers.* New York: Harper, 1954.

Lynn, Kenneth S. *Hemingway.* New York: Simon & Schuster, 1987.

MacLeish, Archibald. *Letters of Archibald MacLeish, 1907–1982.* Ed. R. H. Winnick. Boston: Houghton, 1983.

Madison, Charles. *Book Publishing in America.* New York: McGraw-Hill, 1966.

Mantle, Burns. *The Best Plays of 1919–20 to 1929–30.* 11 vols. New York: Dodd, 1920–30.

Margolies, Joseph A. Columbia Univ. Oral History Collection. Butler Library. 1971.

McCormick, Kenneth. Columbia Univ. Oral History Collection. Butler Library. 1975.

Mellow, James R. *Hemingway: A Life without Consequences.* New York: Houghton, 1992.

Mencken, H. L., and Sara Haardt. *Mencken and Sara: A Life in Letters: The Private Correspondence of H. L. Mencken and Sara Haardt.* Ed. Marion Elizabeth Rodgers. New York: McGraw-Hill, 1987.

Meyers, Jeffrey. *Hemingway: A Biography.* New York: Harper, 1985.

Meyers, Jeffrey, ed. *Hemingway: The Critical Heritage.* Boston: Routledge, 1982.

Motion Picture Association. "Adopted Code to Govern the Production of Motion Pictures [1930]." Production Code Administration File. David O. Selznick Collection. Hoblitzelle Theatre Arts Library, Humanities Research Center, Univ. of Texas, Austin.

Mott, Frank Luther. *A History of American Magazines.* Vol. 4. Cambridge: Harvard Univ. Press, 1957.

Murphy, Gerald, and Sara Murphy. *Letters from the Lost Generation: Gerald and Sara Murphy and Friends.* Ed. Linda Patterson Miller. New Brunswick: Rutgers Univ. Press, 1991.

Nagel, James, ed. *Ernest Hemingway: The Writer in Context.* Madison: Univ. of Wisconsin Press, 1984.

Neavill, Gordon B. "The Modern Library Series: Format and Design, 1917–1977." *Printing History* 1 (1979): 26–37.

Nolan, William F. "The Man behind the Masks: Hemingway as a Fictional Character." *Fitzgerald/Hemingway Annual, 1974* (1975): 207–13.

Oldsey, Bernard. *Hemingway's Hidden Craft.* University Park: Pennsylvania State Univ. Press, 1979.

O'Neill, Eugene. *Selected Letters of Eugene O'Neill.* Ed. Travis Bogard and Jackson R. Bryer. New Haven: Yale Univ. Press, 1988.

Orvell, Miles. *The Real Thing: Imitation and Authenticity in American Culture, 1880–1940.* Chapel Hill: Univ. of North Carolina Press, 1989.

Parker, Dorothy. "Profiles: The Artist's Reward." *New Yorker,* 30 November 1929, 28 + .

Perkins, Maxwell. *Editor to Author: The Letters of Maxwell E. Perkins.* Ed. John Hall Wheelock. New York: Scribners, 1950.

"Program," *A Farewell to Arms* (Paramount, 1930). N.p., n.d. Lincoln Center Library for the Performing Arts, New York.

Raeburn, John. *Fame Became of Him: Hemingway as Public Writer.* Bloomington: Indiana Univ. Press, 1984.

Reynolds, Michael. *Hemingway: The American Homecoming.* New York: Blackwell, 1992.

———. *Hemingway: The Paris Years.* New York: Blackwell, 1989.

———. *Hemingway's First War: The Making of A Farewell to Arms.* Princeton: Princeton Univ. Press, 1976.

———. *The Young Hemingway.* New York: Blackwell, 1986.

Reynolds, Michael, ed. *Critical Essays on Ernest Hemingway's In Our Time.* Boston: G. K. Hall, 1983.

Reynolds, Paul R. *The Middle Man: The Adventures of a Literary Agent.* New York: Morrow, 1972.

Sanford, Marcelline Hemingway. *At the Hemingways.* Boston: Little, Brown, 1962.

Scherman, Harry. Columbia Univ. Oral History Collection. Butler Library. 1954–55.

Schickel, Richard. *Intimate Strangers: The Culture of Celebrity.* Garden City, N.Y.: Doubleday, 1985.

Selznick, David O. *Memo from David O. Selznick.* Ed. Rudy Behlmer. New York: Viking, 1972.

Silverman, Al, ed. *The Book of the Month: Sixty Years of Books in American Life.* Boston: Little, Brown, 1986.

Simmons, Jerold. "Film and International Politics: The Banning of *All Quiet on the Western Front* in Germany and Austria, 1930–1931." *Historian: A Journal of History* 52, no. 1 (1989): 40–60.

Skipp, Francis E. "The Editing of *Look Homeward, Angel.*" *Papers of the Bibliographical Society of America* 57, no. 1 (1963): 1–13.

Smith, Paul. "Hemingway's Apprentice Fiction: 1919–1921." *American Literature* 58 (1986): 574–88.

———. *A Reader's Guide to the Short Stories of Ernest Hemingway.* Boston: G. K. Hall, 1989.

———. "Three Versions of 'Up in Michigan': 1921–1930." *Resources for American Literary Study* 15 (1985): 163–77.

Stallings, Laurence. *A Farewell to Arms* [play]. 1930. TS. Lincoln Center Library for the Performing Arts, New York.

Stein, Gertrude. *The Autobiography of Alice B. Toklas.* New York: Vintage, 1960.

Stephens, Robert O., ed. *Ernest Hemingway: The Critical Reception.* N.p.: Burt Franklin, 1977.

Stern, Edith M. "A Man Who Was Unafraid." *Saturday Review of Literature,* 28 June 1941, 10, 14.

Stillinger, Jack. *Multiple Authorship and the Myth of Solitary Genius.* New York: Oxford Univ. Press, 1991.

Susman, Warren I. " 'Personality' and the Making of Twentieth Century Culture." In *New Directions in American Intellectual History*, ed. John Higham and Paul K. Conkin, 212–34. Baltimore: Johns Hopkins Univ. Press, 1979.

Sutherland, John. *Bestsellers: Popular Fiction of the 1970s*. London: Routledge, 1981.

Swindell, Larry. *The Last Hero: A Biography of Gary Cooper*. Garden City, N.Y.: Doubleday, 1980.

Tate, Allen. "Interview with Allen Tate." By Matthew J. Bruccoli. *Fitzgerald/Hemingway Annual, 1974* (1975): 101–13.

Tebbel, John. *The Golden Age between Two Wars, 1920–1940*. Vol. 3 of *A History of Book Publishing in the United States*. New York: Bowker, 1978.

Thomson, David. *Showman: The Life of David O. Selznick*. New York: Knopf, 1992.

Van Vechten, Carl. *Letters of Carl Van Vechten*. Ed. Bruce Kellner. New Haven: Yale Univ. Press, 1987.

Wagner, Linda W. "*The Sun Also Rises*: One Debt to Imagism." In *Ernest Hemingway's* The Sun Also Rises, ed. Harold Bloom, 103–15. New York: Chelsea, 1987.

Watkins, Ann. "Literature for Sale." In *Bowker Lectures on Book Publishing*, 95–113. New York: Bowker, 1957.

West, James L. W., III. *American Authors and the Literary Marketplace since 1900*. Philadelphia: Univ. of Pennsylvania Press, 1988.

———. "Did F. Scott Fitzgerald Have the Right Publisher?" *Sewanee Review* 100 (1992): 644–56.

———. "The Second Serials of *This Side of Paradise* and *The Beautiful and Damned*." *Papers of the Bibliographical Society of America* 73 (1979): 63–74.

Wheelock, John Hall. Columbia Univ. Oral History Collection. Butler Library. 2 vols. 1967.

Wilson, Edmund. *Letters on Literature and Politics, 1912–1972*. Ed. Elena Wilson. New York: Farrar, 1977.

Wilson, R. Jackson. *Figures of Speech: American Writers and the Literary Marketplace, from Benjamin Franklin to Emily Dickinson*. New York: Knopf, 1989.

Woodress, James. *Willa Cather: A Literary Life*. Lincoln: Univ. of Nebraska Press, 1987.

Young, Philip. *Ernest Hemingway: A Reconsideration*. University Park: Pennsylvania State Univ. Press, 1966.

ACKNOWLEDGMENTS

DEAN BIRKENKAMP GUIDED *HEMINGWAY AND HIS CONSPIRATORS* THROUGH the publishing process; I thank him for his strong support of the manuscript—and I thank Gladys Topkis of Yale University Press for bringing us together. From production through promotion, the entire staff of Rowman & Littlefield has been knowledgeable and enthusiastic about this book.

Numerous persons at libraries and archives generously offered assistance during the research and writing phases: the Humanities and Social Sciences Divisions, the Interlibrary Services area, and the staff of the Low Library, Oklahoma State University; Jean Preston, Margaret Sherry, and the staff of the Princeton University Libraries; Samuel Gill, Howard Prouty, and the staff of the Margaret Herrick Library, Academy of Motion Picture Arts and Sciences (which houses the Paramount and the Motion Picture Association Collections); and Megan Floyd Desnoyers, Lisa Middents, and—especially—Stephen Plotkin of the John F. Kennedy Library (which houses the Hemingway Collection).

Excerpts from unpublished Hemingway correspondence have been reprinted with permission of The Ernest Hemingway Foundation; certain excerpts from published Hemingway correspondence have been reprinted with permission of Scribner, a Division of Simon and Schuster, from *Ernest Hemingway: Selected Letters, 1917–1961*, edited by Carlos Baker, copyright © 1981 The Ernest Hemingway Foundation, Inc.; excerpts from Hemingway short stories have been reprinted with permission of Scribner, a Division of

Simon and Schuster, from *The Complete Short Stories of Ernest Hemingway*, The Finca Vigía Edition, Copyright © 1987 Charles Scribner's Sons. In altered form, portions of chapters 4 and 5 first appeared in the *Arizona Quarterly* (winter 1995) and the *Hemingway Review* (spring 1996). As the present manuscript evolved, Allen Josephs (president of The Ernest Hemingway Foundation) and Susan Beegel (editor of the *Hemingway Review*) were especially helpful.

Regarding photographs, Alan Goodrich and Rachel Murray of the John F. Kennedy Library, Jennifer Bowden of the Princeton University Libraries, Ann Wilkins of the Wisconsin Center for Film and Theater Research, and Robert Taylor and Kevin Winkler of the New York Public Library for the Performing Arts offered their expertise and cooperation. Author and publisher have endeavored to identify the owners of all copyrighted photographs and—when required—to secure the owners' permission; any oversights reported to the publisher will be corrected in subsequent printings.

Jerold Simmons, Edward Walkiewicz, and Paul Smith read early drafts of the manuscript, which, from first draft to last, owed much to extant Hemingway scholarship, especially that of Smith (the founding president of the Hemingway Society), Carlos Baker, and Michael Reynolds. My thanks to them all. Hemingway scholar Frank Laurence and literary agent Nat Sobel lent support. So did research grants from the John F. Kennedy Foundation, the Oklahoma Foundation for the Humanities, and Southwestern Bell; at Oklahoma State University, Smith L. Holt (dean of the College of Arts and Sciences) as well as English department heads Guy Bailey and Jeffrey Walker were instrumental in securing such funding. Michael Day helped early on with research. Robert Brown, Linda Leavell, and Jonathan Leff helped sharpen the preface. Linda Leff helped see manuscript—and author—through to the end.

INDEX

About the Author

Leonard J. Leff teaches film and literature in the English department at Oklahoma State University. His books include *Hitchcock and Selznick: The Rich and Strange Collaboration of Alfred Hitchcock and David O. Selznick in Hollywood* (1987), which won the British Film Institute Book Award, and *The Dame in the Kimono: Hollywood, Censorship, and the Production Code from the 1920s to the 1960s* (coauthor Jerold Simmons, 1990). His work has also appeared in *PMLA*, the *Georgia Review*, and *Premiere*.